PHIL RICKMAN

The Smile of a Ghost

CORVUS

First published in Great Britain in 2005 by Macmillan.

This paperback edition first published in the UK in 2012 by Corvus, an imprint of Atlantic Books Ltd.

9 8 7 6 5 4

A CIP catalogue record for this book is available from the British Library.

ISBN: 978-0-85789-015-3 (paperback)
ISBN: 978-0-85789-022-1 (eBook)

Printed by CPI Group (UK) Ltd, Croydon, CR0 4YY

Corvus
An imprint of Grove Atlantic Ltd
Ormond House
26-27 Boswell Street
London WC1N 3JZ

www.corvus-books.co.uk

The Smile of a Ghost

Mumford

ALL THE PEOPLE who'd told Mumford, It's a new beginning.

All the beaming faces blurred by pint glasses frosted with froth, all the damp handshakes. Mumford mumbling, Ah, thanks… thank you… very nice… 'course I will… No, I won't be going nowhere… yes… no… thank you.

Andy Mumford, who didn't see the point of new beginnings – complete waste of half a lifetime's experience. Andy Mumford who had just wanted to carry on.

The way this town had carried on: the oldest town he knew – or at least the one that looked oldest. Bent and sagging, and people loved it for that, and nobody looked up at the crooked gables and the worm-riddled beams and said, What this old place needs is A New Beginning.

Mumford felt a gassy fury inside, like in one of the first-ever pictures he could remember – in a children's encyclopaedia, it was, and it showed the inside of a volcano close to eruption. How many years ago was that now – forty-four, forty-five? God almighty.

Not that anybody would ever know about the volcano in Mumford. Not showing it was the one thing he was real good at. Not showing his excitement when the suspect in the interview room said the wrong thing at the right time, springing the trap. Not showing what he really wanted to do to the rat-eyed rapist with a cellar full of porno videos. Never showing his feelings because he was a professional and because he was…

… imperturbable.

1

Clumsy old word, bit of a mouthful, but probably the nicest thing anybody ever said about him in all those years in the Job. And that was all right. Imperturbable implied solid, reliable... professional.

Only, what bloody use was being totally professional when you didn't have a profession any more? What use was imperturbable ever going to be to him again?

Mumford walked up Broad Street, Ludlow, which some folk maintained was the most beautiful street in the most beautiful medieval market town in the country, and it might as well have been a semi-derelict industrial estate for all he noticed.

Warmish evening now, Easter just gone and the town coming alive for the tourists, everybody's world opening up, Mumford's closing down. What would he do, day to day, through the summer? And then the autumn and the winter and then another year. Another thirty years, if he was spared. The length of his career all over again. Thirty years of what's the point?

He reached the top of the wide street, across from the Buttercross, the old market building with its fancy little clock, behind it the tower of St Laurence's soaring over a tight mesh of streets and alleys. The whole scene warm and golden. Andy Mumford feeling as warm and golden, frankly, as shit.

Ludlow wasn't his town, mind. Mumford came from Leominster, back in Herefordshire, a dozen or so miles down the A49. It was just that his Mam and Dad had moved here to take over a little shop after the old man retired from the Force ('Why don't you get yourself a little shop, Andy?' some bastard had said in the pub; Andy could've nutted him) and now Gail was working part-time as an auxiliary nurse at Ludlow Community Hospital.

Because Gail was still a professional.

For probably the first time ever, Mumford had brought his wife to work this morning and he'd come back now – after what had to have been the longest day of his entire life – to pick her up. Tonight they were going to have a meal at one of the fancy new restaurants that had opened up here.

A celebration meal. A couple of extra glasses of wine for him because Gail would be driving them home. A toast to a new beginning. A meal they wouldn't normally think of affording in the town that, with all these new eateries, had become the Food Capital of the Welsh Marches – Mumford conceding that, for the town, this probably did, in fact, qualify as a new beginning. Always been prosperous, but it had real wealth now, all these poncy-voiced bastards moving up from London with their silver knives and forks.

Mumford glared, with this new resentment, at the little shops with their blinds down and the dark windows of the Buttercross where the town councillors met and patted each other on the back and swapped the odd Masonic handshake.

He was in his best suit, the suit he'd last worn to collect his commendation from the Chief Constable, and Gail had brought to work some nice clothes to change into at his Mam and Dad's house down the bottom of town, behind the new Tesco's.

Which was why Mumford was walking uptown... trying to get himself into the right mood to face his Mam and his bloody Dad for the first time since the Home Office had officially repossessed his warrant card. Needing to sound a bit jovial from now on, on account of *imperturbable* was no longer enough to see him through. He was expected to become a member of the human race. To become Andy.

Andy, the dumpy, middle-aged, genial, smiling, bastard civilian.

We'll likely be seeing a bit more of you at last, then, Andy, Mam had said the other night on the phone. *You can do a bit of decorating for us, if you want to. And Robbie, he wants to show you all his favourite places in the town, don't you, Robbie? He's nodding, see. He's always saying when's Uncle Andy coming?*

Robbie, his young nephew, his sister's boy from Hereford, who preferred to spend the school holidays with his grandparents in Ludlow, even though his grandad despised him.

3

I'll be getting some kind of job, Mumford had snapped back. *En't that old yet.*

Guessing that when he got there tonight she'd have forgotten he was even retired. In any other job he wouldn't have been. If he'd just been a bit more ambitious in the early years, if he'd pushed a bit more, he could've made Inspector and stayed on till he was sixty. But he was a plodder, and the plodders didn't get promoted and so they were forced into retirement at fifty. And everybody thought that, being plodders, they were looking forward to it: crown-green bowls, growing sprouts, bloody line-dancing.

Surprisingly, the only bit of understanding had come from Francis Bliss, his last boss, who was fifteen years younger and, as a senior officer, still had another twenty-odd years to serve if he wanted it.

CID room, Mumford's last morning, Bliss frowning.

This is all to cock, this system, Andy. We just throw away our best natural resources, like pressing the fuckin' delete button on thirty years of database.

He'd respected Bliss for that. Realized how much he'd come to respect Bliss as a detective, too, despite him being a smart-mouth from Merseyside. Knew that when the time came, unless the world was a very different place by then, Bliss – never a man you'd call imperturbable – would go out cursing.

Cursing.

Mumford looked up at the hard, shiny evening sky, ready to curse God.

But God got in first.

God pulled the rug from under the slippers that Mumford was never going to wear.

He was turning the corner to walk up to Castle Square when he heard it coming up behind him, a sound that used to make his blood race but now seemed more like a taunt, and he wanted to shut it out. The way this morning he'd punched in the button on his alarm clock – which he'd routinely set without a thought last night – and then lain there staring into the white-skied emptiness of a new day.

4

Ambulance. He stood on the corner under the dull maroon façade of McCartney's estate agents, and watched it barrelling through the narrows, a couple of tourists glancing up in annoyance like it ought to be horse-drawn in Ludlow.

He didn't really mean to follow the thing. It wasn't even instinct, just that it was heading the same way as he was. In fact, he nearly turned back when he saw the patrol car on the square under the Cheddar-cheese-coloured perimeter wall of Ludlow Castle.

He did, in fact, turn away when the first copper came out of the gateway, near the old cannon from Sevastopol, and he saw it was Steve Britton, station sergeant at Ludlow – no hair left but still a few years yet to serve, and even then they'd probably keep him on as a civilian.

But Steve had seen him.

'Andy?'

Mumford kept on walking, figuring Steve would think it was a case of mistaken identity or that Mumford hadn't heard him. But then he heard footsteps – not merely footsteps, police boots – clattering across the empty square, and Steve Britton was shouting now.

'Andy!'

So he had to stop and stand there, waiting wearily, in front of Woolworths, staring down at the pavement, steeling himself for what was coming: Andy, mate, I've only just heard. Free at last then, eh? Look, I get off in an hour, we'll have a couple of jars.

But when Steve Britton drew level with him it was different.

Steve's long melon face was damp with sweat and his eyes had a look that Mumford recognized straight off. A look he'd probably had on a few dozen times himself over the years, carrying out just about the worst chore you ever got saddled with as a copper.

Confusing, though, on account of he'd never faced it before.

Never actually been on the receiving end, feeling that sharp, flat punch of dread – a punch deep to the gut, right where, a few minutes ago, the volcano had been simmering.

Andy couldn't say anything. He just stared at Steve, and at his uniform. Wobbling slightly, experiencing, for the first time ever, what the sight of that uniform on your doorstep meant to the average person with no drugs in the house.

'Andy...' Steve getting his breath back. 'You been down to your mother's tonight?'

'Not yet.' His mother? Andy felt his own breath catch. 'Something happened? Something happened, Steve?'

Far from bloody imperturbable, the way that came out. Realizing how scared he was now, how exposed, the streets spinning.

'Yes,' Steve said. 'Something's happened.'

Walking with Steve Britton back to the castle.

The castle, of all places. Christ.

The castle was ruined but pretty big, a lot of it left. You couldn't see much from here, the town side, but from down below, across the river, it was still massive and imposing and had been dominating Ludlow for most of the last millennium.

Mumford had probably been in there just twice in the whole of his life, and never in the last twenty years.

But Robbie practically lived here when he was staying with his grandparents, which was every school holiday since his mother moved in with the toe-rag. Robbie, the history buff. Quiet, likeable boy, covering up for his gran, day after day.

Please God, not Robbie. This'll destroy her.

Couldn't be, anyway. No logic to it.

'How'd this boy gain access, Steve?'

'We figure he stayed in. Hid somewhere after they closed the castle for the night. There's a hundred places to hide... inside these little passages, the towers... it's a bloody honeycomb.'

It actually looked like a honeycomb, all yellow and orange in the evening light. The main gates were wide open, a young uniform Mumford didn't recognize guarding the entrance.

You forgot how big this castle was. Inside the perimeter walls there was a green open space where they had sideshows and medieval-type displays in summer, and then the Christmas Fair. From here a stone footbridge took you over the moat, which was all dried up now, leading into the main fortification with this huge gatehouse tower that had been the old Norman... keep, was that the word?

Robbie would know.

Couldn't be. One fourteen-year-old boy looked much like another – trainers, baseball cap. This would turn out to be some tourist kid larking around.

Mumford went back to being observational, like he hadn't retired two days ago and this was still his job. Some part of him knowing that if he was to keep from losing everything that had ever meant anything in his life, he needed to start off how he meant to go on, and that was not as just another member of the bastard public.

Walking with his uniform counterpart, Sergeant Steve Britton, towards another...

... another death scene.

Just another death scene. Nothing to do with him. A mistake.

Red spears of sunlight were bouncing off the ambulance parked near the footbridge. A couple of paramedics were bending over the edge of the dried-up moat.

'Visitors can go right to the top, see,' Steve said, talking rapidly, a bit hoarsely. 'Good... good views.'

'Robbie Walsh knows his way blindfold, Steve.'

The square tower seemed awful high now, the size of a big block of flats in this part of the world. A St George's flag was hanging limp up there against the amber sky. The stone bridge had a wooden handrail, and even from here Mumford could see there was blood on it, like a splash of spilt creosote. Should've been taped off.

He could see into the moat now, something humped and twisted on the bottom, the fact that they'd left it down there saying everything.

'Must've come down on the handrail, bounced off,' Steve said.

'Broken neck?'

'And the rest.' Steve swallowed. Likely never had to do this before to one of his own. 'Andy, I… I hope it's not. I hope I'm mistaken, that's all.'

'Sure t'be,' Mumford said. 'Let's get it over.'

'We used to see him all over town. Walking up Broad Street, and down Old Street, and past the station. You'd think he'd get sick of it, same streets, day after day.'

Steve making it clear he knew what Robbie Walsh looked like.

'He never got sick of it,' Mumford said. 'Always finding new things, so they reckoned. He loves it here. History-mad. Goes to all the lectures, all the exhibitions. Has some kind of season ticket for this… for the castle. So he can come in and out.'

'People knew him, Andy. All the local people and the shop-keepers knew him. Always polite. Not like most of the little sods.'

Steve keeping up this street-corner chat routine to delay the moment, prepare Mumford for the worst. One of the para-medics was on his feet now, talking to the cops and shaking his head, likely telling them what they already knew.

'Witnesses?' Mumford said.

'Feller seen it from over the river, top of Whitcliffe. Artist bloke. Paints pictures of the castle. Watching a buzzard through binoculars. Said it was… Ah, you don't wanner know this stuff…'

'I wanner know everything.'

'Just make sure first, eh?'

'I wanner know everything,' Mumford snarled, knowing that he was shaking like a civilian.

That night, Angela, his sister, did some screaming.

The Hereford boys had finally found Ange and her partner in the Orchard Gardens, the city's most misnamed pub, out on the edge of the Plascarreg. So it was getting on for midnight when they got to the Community Hospital, and Ange must have drunk a fair bit, which didn't help.

In the hospital mortuary, Mumford, for all his experience, had turned away, biting his lip. Lying there, with only his not-too-damaged face exposed, the boy had looked all of eight. Ange had taken one quick glance and then it was the full hand-wringing dramatics: *It's him, it's him… oh shit, shit, shit, look what they done to him!*

During this performance, Mumford had found himself watching the scumbag partner, Lennox Mathiesson, hunched up with his hands in his pockets, nodding his head, half-fascinated, ear-trinkets clinking. It sickened Mumford that Angela was three months pregnant with this rubbish's baby.

Tomorrow morning, the body of her first child would be taken to Shrewsbury for the post-mortem. Tonight, outside the hospital, Ange shelved her grief and set about doing what Mumford reckoned she'd been doing since before she could walk, which was generously apportioning the blame so that there was none of it left for her.

'That selfish ole bitch, I just hope she's satisfied. I gotter come all this way to see my son lying dead, killed, because she wasn't fit to look after him. She robbed me… robbed me of my son. I hope she's fuckin' satisfied now.'

Ange in the car park, legs apart, arms folded and a sawn-off top advertising her navel and her condition. Thirty-nine years old.

'I reckon you better get off home, Angela,' Mumford said. 'I'll phone for a taxi.'

'Happier yere than he ever was with you? You remember when she come out with that one? What did you say? Nothing, as usual.'

'She's not right,' Mumford said quietly. 'You know that.'

Except on that occasion, Mam had been dead right. Mumford drew away from the alcohol fumes, stumbling back into a tree trunk as his sister stuck her wet, smudgy face up to his.

'She en't fit to look after a child, that's for sure. And you never said a word, so I hope you're satisfied too, mister smart-arse fuckin' detective.'

9

'He en't a detective no more.'

Knowing smirk from Lennox Mathiesson, ten years younger than Angela, two convictions for burglary, one aggravated, plus an ABH. Well, Mam's mind might be on the blink but she could still recognize a bad bastard when she saw one, and that was why her and Ange hadn't spoke for the best part of two years, since Ange had left Robbie's dad – decent enough bloke, worked at Burton's men's-shop – for Mathiesson.

Mumford got out his mobile, putting in the number of this taxi firm he knew in Leominster. It'd cost, but he just wanted an end to this night.

'Oh yeah, get me out.' Ange staring at him with contempt. 'Get me out, 'fore I makes trouble. Well, we're gonner make trouble, mister, you count on it. We can sue that castle, for a start.' Hands on her hips now, body arched, belly swelling out. 'Letting him run wild all day in dangerous ole ruins that oughter be fuckin' pulled down.'

Run wild? Robbie? Mumford was thinking of all the times he'd heard her say, I wonder sometimes where he came from, hiding away with his books, no proper friends. It's not like having a normal child, is it?

'Angela,' he said, 'obviously you're terrible upset, but let's just get one thing straight: there's no case to sue the castle. Robbie was there illegally, when it was closed for the night.'

'Well, we'll fuckin' see about that, won't we, mister smart-arse fuckin' *ex*-detective.'

Mumford nodded, standing with his heels in a flower bed, taking it. What else could he do?

'And what's disgusting, like I say, is she never knew where he was. I bet she even forgot he was stayin' yere.'

Laughable, that, coming from Ange. It had always been Mumford himself who'd picked Robbie up and brought him over to Ludlow for his holidays, and his most sorrowful image of the boy was not the lolling body under the tower but the pale kid with a suitcase waiting like an orphan at the top of the steps at the Plascarreg.

10

Different boy altogether when he got to Ludlow, but Ange was never going to want reminding of that.

He got the taxi firm on the mobile. 'Soon's you can, Paul, eh?'

'And I'll tell you what, mister – you can tell the ole bitch she can pay for the fuckin' funeral…'

'God almighty, Angela!'

It had been like this for as long as he could remember. Mam had been forty-five when she'd had Ange, and the gap was always too wide – Mumford always in the middle, covering his ears.

'Wasn't fit to look after nothin', and you never seen it, or you pretended not to, more like, 'cause you was always too busy persecuting folks just wanted a bit of pleasure outer life.'

Meaning the time he and Bliss had had Mathiesson's brother for enough crack to lay out half the estate. Personal use. The balls they expected you to swallow. Mumford had never set foot in Ange's flat from that day to this.

'You bloody let her take him away from his own mother just when I needed the help. You robbed me, she robbed me, every—'

Ange had started to cry again then, tottering across to Lennox Mathiesson, who gathered her into his tattooed arms, giving Mumford this thin smile over her quaking shoulders.

Time he was off. Needed to pick Gail up from poor bloody Mam's. Gail in her best frock for the celebration dinner. Christ.

'Anyway, you know where I am,' Mumford said and walked away, Angela screaming at his back.

'You tell her I hope she never sleeps again!'

All the lights were on in his mam and dad's house, the last neighbour walking away. They were good to her, the neighbours in this short, terraced row down at the bottom of the town, between the station and the new Tesco's.

Mumford sat in his car and just wanted to stay there. He could see Gail and his dad through the extended front window, its curtains still drawn back. His dad had a hand on his forehead, likely with exasperation by now; his dad had never had much patience with female emotions. Gail had a cardigan over her new frock, and she was bending down, like she was bending over a sickbed. Below the level of the window frame, his mam would be sitting in her chair and the TV would be on with the sound turned down.

He could feel the atmosphere in that room coming out at him like radio static.

Gail was a nurse and knew how to handle people in grief; all Mumford knew was how to catch the people who'd caused it. Which didn't apply in this case, whatever Ange said, and, even if it had, he wasn't allowed to do anything no more.

Unless Ange was halfway right, and he was the guilty party.

He leaned his sweating forehead against the back of his hands on top of the steering wheel and let the breath come out of him. Feeling beyond exhaustion.

Aye, he'd known the state she was in, the ole girl, but he'd also known how much it had meant to her having Robbie around. Didn't know much about degenerative brain disease but he did know his mam would have gone downhill a whole lot faster without the boy.

When he looked up, he saw how pale the night sky was, the big tower of St Laurence's looming out of the body of the town. And became aware of another person standing out on the edge of the Tesco's car park, still as a post, looking across the road at the house.

A woman, it was, with pale hair escaping from the hood of a long grey cape that hung to the ground. The night was so still that the cape didn't move, its folds like the stone pleats of the robe of some religious statue. The only movement was a white flickering like a candle on an altar. And it *was* a candle, Mumford saw, in a metal lantern that hung from the woman's hand emerging from a slit in the cape.

Mumford experienced a moment of superstitious fear – like he was seeing the angel of death outside the house – and then a bigger fear that he, like the ole girl, was losing his marbles, and he got out of the car in a near-panic.

As he reached the edge of the car park, the woman turned to face him, and there was enough light for him to see that she was entirely human and that she'd been crying.

'You all right, madam?' Mumford said.

She didn't reply, just walked away with the candle-lantern swinging like a captured star in a cage, and Mumford shook his head and crossed the road to his parents' house.

PART ONE

Robbie

'I talked to one of the officials and he told me that he was always getting reports of odd happenings in and around the castle.'

Peter Underwood, A Gazetteer of British Ghosts *(1971)*

'It is well recorded that those left behind often do experience feelings of closeness to their dead loved ones during the months immediately after their loss.'

Ian Wilson, In Search of Ghosts *(1995)*

1

Into the Loop

'No – please – I want to understand this,' Siân said. 'You're telling us that you yourself have seen one.'

Her pewter hair hung like a warlord's helmet. She'd found her way to the head of the table, and she was sitting there in judgement. Her expression was like, Say it... say that word again.

The word that Merrily was realizing should be avoided.

'I once had an experience, that's the only way I can describe it,' she said. 'A series of experiences, if you like, that I couldn't rationally explain.'

In the vault-like vicarage kitchen, beeswax candles burned low in their saucers, and the empty ashtray mocked her. She'd been trying to tell herself she'd guessed it was likely to turn out this bad, but the truth was, no, not in her worst dreams.

'And so I went to the Church for advice, and the Church wasn't exactly helpful. Felt I was being treated like some kind of hysterical loony.'

Siân's grey eyes blinked once, like the steel shutters on the little windows of a police cell. Merrily stared into them. Sorry – I meant, like some kind of emotionally dysfunctional person with advanced learning difficulties.

'And where exactly did you have this... series of experiences, Merrily?'

'Here. At the vicarage. Upstairs. Just after we moved in, a couple of years ago.'

'This is rather a big house,' Nigel Saltash said.

'Huge – certainly compared with anything I'd lived in before.'

'Just you and your daughter?'

Saltash tilted his head fractionally, as though he needed this slight motion to activate his enormous brain. It also turned his smile on. He had an all-purpose smile: questioning, explaining, sympathizing, patronizing. For many years, he'd been a psychiatrist; some things didn't change.

'Just the two of us, yes,' Merrily said. 'Me and Jane. Like now.'

'So, if I were to humbly suggest – and you could say I'm simply playing devil's advocate, if you like – that you were feeling terribly insecure at the time... a stranger in the village, not yet fully licensed or formally installed as vicar... and you'd been thrown into this enormous, ancient, echoing... rather spooky old house...'

'Plus, I was not that many years widowed. And we had very little money. Also like now.'

'And have the experiences stopped now?'

In the candle-glow, Nigel Saltash's face was taut and tanned from skiing somewhere. His light grey hair was cropped tight and fitted flush into his beard. He was long and lithe and living proof that seventy was the new fifty.

'Yes, it was all over very quickly,' Merrily said. 'Once we'd got certain things sorted out.'

'You're playing into my rationalist's hands, Mrs Watkins. Deliberately, perhaps?'

'Well, I suppose I'm making the point that someone like you can turn anyone's circumstances to your professional advantage.'

'But am I necessarily wrong?'

Merrily shrugged. 'I'm always going to say "I know what I saw," and you're always going to say "But you didn't really see it at all." '

'And that way, surely, we arrive at something approximating to the truth,' Siân Callaghan-Clarke said.

'Do we?'

'Nine times out of ten, yes.'

'Anyway,' Merrily said, 'that was the main reason why, when I was offered the post of exorcist – Deliverance Consultant – I would have found it hard to say no.'

'I still cannot believe you've been allowed to go on for so long… alone.' Siân was shaking her head. 'The danger you've been in…'

'Sorry?'

One of the candles sputtered out, and Merrily ran a fore-finger nervously around the rim of her dog collar.

She'd been naive; she'd misread the signs.

Huw Owen had told her at the start what she'd be up against. If women priests were seen as soft plaster patching up the already crumbling walls of the Church, a woman exorcist—

Might as well just paint a great big bull's-eye between your tits, Huw had said memorably.

A month or two ago, when the Bishop, Bernie Dunmore, had said, *I'm afraid that, once again, I've been asked what you're doing about establishing a Deliverance advisory panel*, she'd shrugged it off.

Realizing that, OK, sooner or later there was going to have to be a support group within the diocese, but it had to involve the right people, didn't it? People who were sympathetic, who didn't have an agenda, political or otherwise.

Only, the ones she'd thought of as the right people hadn't wanted to know – Simon St John, vicar of Knight's Frome, backing away in mock terror when she'd asked him, making the sign of the cross with both hands. But the point was, she knew that he would always be there for her, like the wise old owls outside the diocese, Huw Owen and Llewellyn Jeavons. It just wasn't official; some of these people didn't do official.

Whereas people like Siân Callaghan-Clarke and Nigel Saltash didn't do anything else.

Saltash was a good friend of the Dean, and giving his profes-sional services free – no better reason for the Dean to take him to meet the Bishop and the Bishop to introduce him to Merrily. In any modern Deliverance circle, a qualified psychiatrist was now fundamental. A free one was a godsend.

Thank you, God. Thank you so much.

'You mean I'm in spiritual danger?' Merrily said. 'As a woman in a male tradition?'

Now Siân was staring at her, leaning back in her chair like Merrily must be deliberately winding her up. Siân's mother was a New Labour baroness; she wore her feminist credentials like defiant tattoos. Within five years she'd either be a bishop or out of the Church. Spiritual danger, political danger – all the same to her.

'I meant, like, the first exorcist having been Jesus himself,' Merrily said lamely.

She let the silence hang, recalling the reported mutterings of her predecessor, Thomas Dobbs, as he'd prowled the cathedral cloisters trying to engineer her resignation. At the time, she'd been probably the first – certainly the youngest – woman diocesan exorcist in Britain, operating under the customized title Deliverance Consultant. Appointed, it later became evident, largely because the former Bishop of Hereford had wanted to get into her cassock. Siân Callaghan-Clarke, already a well-placed minister in the diocese, would have heard the rumours and stored them away.

Payback time for bimbo priest?

Martin Longbeach carefully relit the candle with a taper. Martin, tubby and camp, wore an alb and an outsize pectoral cross and was known to covet the south Herefordshire parish of Hoarwithy because of its exotic Italianate church. It had been his idea that they should light candles tonight, to 'aid concentration'.

'By danger,' Siân said, 'I meant the danger of being compromised and exploited… and of having to make instant decisions that you're perhaps not…'

… qualified to make, experienced enough to handle.

Siân left this unsaid. Merrily sat in the candlelight, images of the past couple of years encircling her like pale smoke – fears, anxieties, faltering hopes, tentative joys. And also the most bewildering and stimulating years of her life.

There was a stillness in the air. Was this it? Intimations of the end, on a cool April night?

Siân Callaghan-Clarke clasped her long hands and leaned over them across the table.

'Tonight we've tried to go over what we understand by the term "Deliverance", and the multiplicity of conditions we're expected to examine – from perceived ghosts and poltergeists, to perceived curses, possession and so-called psychic attack. We've considered the cases Merrily has to deal with, day to day: the deluded, the disturbed, the fantastical, the pathological liars—'

'Not forgetting those in need of prayer and non-judgemental understanding. And the ones afflicted by what seemed to be genuine... intrusion,' Merrily said.

'Seemed to be.' Nigel Saltash smiled.

'Seemed to me to be. A conclusion not lightly reached.'

'The point is,' Siân said, 'that deciding who is deluded and who – however remote that possibility might be – is, ahm, genuinely afflicted... has been Merrily's sole responsibility. An impossible situation for just one person, who also has a parish to run.'

'I've not been without back-up. Huw Owen's always on the end of a phone.'

Merrily felt the outline of the unopened packet of Silk Cut in a pocket of her denim skirt. The other back-up.

'Ah yes,' Siân said, looking over her half-glasses. 'Huw Owen.'

'I'm sorry,' Saltash said. 'Who is Huw Owen?'

'Nigel, I'm not sure you'll want to know.'

Siân's eyes were still and neutral. Merrily was furious but bit down on it. She really, really needed a cigarette. They were all looking at her.

'Huw was my primary tutor. Me and a bunch of others. He runs training courses for the Deliverance Ministry in a former Nonconformist chapel in a remote part of the Brecon Beacons.'

'Where nobody can hear you scream,' Siân said. 'My understanding is that Huw Owen, while living the life of a fourth-century hermit, has himself been in such a precarious psychiatric state for so long that—'

Merrily felt herself arch like a cat. 'That's ridic—'

'—that not only can he no longer be relied upon to remain au fait with current thinking—'

'And fucking defamatory!' Merrily said.

In the silence, the phone rang in the scullery, which she used as her office.

Siân looked up, said mildly. 'You want to get that?'

'I'll… let the machine take it.' Merrily glanced at the scullery door, which was ajar. 'If it's not urgent…'

They all sat there uncomfortably as the machine in the office played Merrily's outgoing message through the open door, Nigel Saltash giving her a look that was professionally wry and sympathetic.

It was Saltash who'd introduced Siân, who'd worked with him when she was standing in as a hospital chaplain. She said she'd been wary of Deliverance work up to now, but if Nigel was going to be involved…

Siân, in turn, had brought in Martin Longbeach, once her curate, who was clearly a placid and malleable guy. And, no doubt, guaranteed not to fancy Merrily.

This was a nightmare.

There was a bleep from the answering machine and a cough.

'Mrs Watkins. Mumford. Andy Mumford. I'll… call you later, if that's all right with you.'

The line went dead, the machine rewound, Merrily nodded. 'I can call him back.'

'Would that have been Sergeant Mumford?' Siân asked. 'From Hereford CID?'

'I think he's about to retire, actually. May already have…'

'You've had some interesting dealings with the police, haven't you? I was talking the other day to Sergeant Mumford's superior – DCI Howe?'

'Oh? Yeah, our paths have… crossed.'

'So she tells me. I get on very well with her.'

Figured. If glacial Annie had opted for the Church rather than a fast-track police career, Canon Callaghan-Clarke would have been her ideal spiritual director.

'I'll make some more tea,' Merrily said. Nobody had referred again to Huw Owen. Nobody had reacted to her outburst.

'No, I think we should say goodnight at this point.' Siân folded her document case, took off her glasses. 'Given ourselves quite a lot to consider.'

'Yes.'

'I think we've all accepted that, having inherited a basically medieval structure, our task is to turn it into something practical, efficient and geared to the demands of the twenty-first century. To formulate a set of parameters, so that changes in, say, personnel will not damage the efficacy of the essential Deliverance module.'

Merrily gripped the cigarette packet on her thigh. Deliverance module?

Siân stood up.

'I think the main decision we've made is that, to ease the very obvious pressure on Merrily, all of us should immediately be brought into the loop – the Deliverance e-mail loop, that is. And that each and every new case should be submitted for observations before any action is taken. Correct?'

'It makes sense,' Martin Longbeach said. 'We might not always be able to make a contribution, but it's a question of sharing.'

'I'll… tell Sophie at the Bishop's office,' Merrily said.

'And in my case,' Nigel Saltash said, 'in these formative days, I do think it might be rather a good idea for me to tag along and observe some of the people you're dealing with, Merrily. I mean, purely from an educational point of view?'

'Sorry?'

'I want to learn. See how you operate. Had more time on my hands since we sold half the land. Always thought I could settle down, in retirement, as a farmer, but I'm afraid that once a shrink... Would that be in order? I want to understand how you see Deliverance.'

Merrily took a big breath. 'Nigel, how I see Deliverance... I'm supposed to be a priest, right? I have to operate on the basis of there being a spiritual element – that we've got used to calling God – in everything. So I actually believe that things can happen on more than one level.'

'Indeed,' Martin Longbeach said. 'The holistic approach is essential. All aspects of life are interconnected.'

'And the fact that there are certain things that I'm never going to be able to explain scientifically or psychologically... that doesn't bother me one way or the other. And I think we should be there to say to the people affected: no, you're not necessarily going mad—'

'But if you are' – Nigel Saltash smiled hugely – 'we can also help you with that.'

Merrily sighed. 'As I tried to say, when I was having problems the Church looked at me sideways and raised its eyebrows pityingly. I don't want anybody out there to feel I'm writing them off as disturbed or deluded.'

'And I'd absolutely hate to cramp your style, Merrily,' Saltash said.

Merrily stood up. Her legs felt weak.

'We'll see what we can work out.'

'Of course we will,' Saltash said.

Dear God.

2

Vice-rage

LOL HAD A bunch of new-home cards. He'd put them in the deep sill of the window overlooking the bathroom-sized garden and the orchard beyond. Jane began to read them, holding the first one up to the hurricane lamp hanging from the central beam.

'Alison, eh? Wooooh!'

The card had a pencil sketch of horses on the front. Alison Kinnersley, who bred them, had lived with Lol for a while before taking up with James Bull-Davies, whose family had once run this village before they ran out of money. Two years ago, even a struggling squire with holes in his farmhouse roof had been a better bargain than Lol.

But now Lol had Mum and a career back on course, and the village more than accepted him, and even Alison was being generous.

It's definitely the right thing to do, she'd written. *You can't hide it for ever. Even James thinks that now, and I don't need to tell you how conservative James is.*

'Wow,' Jane said, 'if it goes on like this, they'll be inviting you to run for the Parish Council.'

Lol looked down from the stepladder, the overloaded paint-roller in his hand dribbling burnt orange onto the flagstones. Jane had chosen the ceiling colour; it looked wrong now, but she was never going to admit that. Lol just looked uncomfortable. He had orange smudges down the front of his Gomer Parry Plant Hire sweatshirt, tiny spots on his round, brass-rimmed glasses.

'Then again,' Jane said, 'maybe not.'

There was a card from the Prossers at the Eight till Late and one from Gomer Parry and Danny Thomas – *Welcome back, boy* – with a sheep on the front driving a JCB.

Finally, one from Alice Meek. *God bless you in your new home, Mr Robinson.* Big letters full of stroke victim's shake. Alice was only alive because of Lol, and the village knew it, and that was why he was so welcome here now.

And, of course, it was making him wary. Lol didn't wear medals. Finding the old girl half-frozen over a grave in the churchyard, carrying her into the vicarage, and all the heavy stuff that had happened afterwards... he didn't even like to talk about any of that. It could easily have ended so differently.

The verdict at the inquest on the guy who'd wanted Alice dead had been Accidental Death – totally correct – although most of what had happened had not come out, the villagers closing ranks around Lol. No longer an outsider, even if it wasn't publicly acknowledged that he was Mum's... whatever.

Couldn't have worked out better, really. His first album in many years was out, he had respectable gigs scheduled. And he was about to abandon his temporary flat at Prof Levin's recording studio at Knight's Frome – like, thirty miles away – for this little terraced house a one-minute stroll from the vicarage. So, like, if his star, for once, was accelerating towards the high point of the heavens... well, nobody could say it had been easy.

Jane looked up at him. It was getting too dark to paint, and the electricity was still disconnected, but he was going at it like, if he stopped, somebody would come and take the house away and maybe take Mum, too... and then the tour would be cancelled and the album would be savaged in the *Guardian* or *Time Out*, and...

'Come on down, Lol. Tomorrow is another day.'

'Need to finish this corner.'

'You can't even see the corner. Let's go and get some chips, otherwise I won't get to eat till breakfast. If Mum gets through with the po-faced gits on the Deliverance Committee before eleven, it'll be a certifiable miracle.'

'Hate going in the chippie now,' Lol said. 'They won't let me pay.'

Jane laughed.

'It's not funny, Jane.'

'Lol, they like you. That's—'

'Unsettling.'

Jane sighed. 'When's the next gig?'

'Next Thursday. Bristol.'

'Wooh, bigger and bigger. Glastonbury next year?'

'Jane, you trying to make me fall off?'

Oh God, Nick Drake Syndrome; it never really goes away.

'Bad enough that there's this guy from Q magazine coming to interview me on Saturday,' Lol said. 'I mean, if I'd thought—'

'What?' Jane went to the foot of the ladder, shouting up like he was on a mountain. 'Did you actually say… Q magazine? Like, did I hear that correctly? And did you say, "That's bad enough"? And are you insane?'

'Just there are things I don't necessarily want people to read about.'

'So like' – Jane spread her hands wide in frustration – 'don't talk about them! Talk about any old crap. Lie. They won't care, they're a music mag. When will it be in?'

'Dunno. It's a monthly. Guy said they work weeks in advance. Maybe it won't be in at all. They probably do a lot of interviews that get overtaken by better stuff.'

'This diffidence is worrying.' Jane shook her head. 'I think I preferred the paranoia.' She went to put Alice's card back on the window sill, and found another one lying face down. 'What's this, Lol?'

Actually, this one wasn't a card, as such: it was a folded paper, lined, like from a writing pad. She opened it out and held it up to the lamp, saw crude line drawings done in thick fibre-tip, of a big house and a little house with two parallel lines between them, suggesting a road. Across the big house was scrawled:

VICERAGE

Jane looked up at Lol. 'Vice-rage?'

'Vicarage.' Lol started rolling hard at the ceiling. 'Could be a double meaning there, I suppose, but I wouldn't think whoever sent it was that smart.'

There was a double-pointed arrow connecting the two houses across the road. Underneath the drawing was written:

RECKON YOU CAN FIND YOUR WAY IN THE DARK?

'Bloody hell,' Jane said. 'It's a poison-pen letter.'

She looked up the ladder. Lol went on painting.

Jane smiled thinly. So this was the problem.

Well, there was always going to be one spiteful bastard, somewhere. Mum got along with most people in Ledwardine, but not everybody approved yet of women priests. And it was a safe bet that not everybody who did approve would accept the idea of the female clergy having intimate relationships unsanctified by marriage – like the clergy was supposed to stay in the Victorian era, Mum and Lol walking out together, with a chaperone.

This would be one of the areas of his life that Lol would prefer to be kept out of Q magazine.

'Who sent it?'

'I don't think that's supposed to be obvious, Jane. That's possibly why it isn't signed.'

'But there's an element of threat. I mean, I realize it's probably just some semi-literate tosser…'

Lol came down from the stepladder, ducking under the beam that divided the room. The beam was dark brown oak, well woodwormed – a big chocolate flake. The hurricane lamp swayed, shadows rolled. Jane wanted to crumple up the paper, but on the other hand…

'Can I keep it?'

'What for?'

'Might be an opportunity to compare the writing. Like with the parish noticeboard? The cards in the shop window? Or even the prayer board in the church. I mean, it's always useful to know who your friends aren't. Anyway' – she folded the paper – 'nothing really to worry about. I don't think Mum's worried. I mean, the Bishop knows.'

Jane picked up a paint rag and dabbed up some blotches from the flagged floor, recalling the first time she'd seen Lol, when he was looking after Lucy Devenish's old shop, Ledwardine Lore. Lol peering out between racks of apple-shaped candles in the orchard-scented air. Like a mouse. He'd been really messed up back then.

Jane had been fifteen, just a kid. Now she was facing A levels and a driving test, and she wasn't a virgin, and Lol and Mum were some kind of tentative, nervous item.

And Lucy Devenish was dead.

Hard to accept that, even now. No matter what colours the crooked walls and sloping ceilings were repainted, this was Lucy's house and always would be. When you stood in the hall you could imagine you still saw her old poncho hanging over the post at the foot of the stairs. If it was really dark when you came in, you could imagine Lucy herself there, wearing the poncho, her arms lifting it like batwings.

The people from London who'd agreed to buy the house when it first came on the market last year had given back word after their five-year-old asthmatic kid had asked who the old woman was on the landing.

Scary. Lucy hadn't been scary, not really. Formidable, certainly. Maybe a little witchy, in the best, most traditional sense, and…

… OK, she *had* been a little scary. But she'd liked Lol and supported him when he needed it, and she'd been some kind of mentor to Jane, and…

… And this was OK. Lol finally getting the house – this was meant. Everything finally was going to be OK for Lol and for Mum, who'd been a widow for long enough. Yeah, in one way it was ridiculous, Lol living in this little house and Mum across the road in the huge vicarage, with seven bedrooms, but it was an arrangement that would work, for the time being.

And it would have Lucy's blessing. Lucy who, though dead, still somehow spoke for Ledwardine.

Jane allowed herself a shiver. Lol carried the roller and paint tray into the kitchen and put them in the sink.

'How about you get the chips?'

'Lol, you wimp.'

'Wallet's on the mantelpiece.'

Jane found it and took out a tenner.

'Mushy peas?'

'Why not? Just don't say they're for me.'

Jane shoved the tenner down a back pocket of her jeans, along with the vice-rage note, and shrugged on her fleece.

'You'll be all right on your own for a few minutes, then? You and Lucy?'

Lol said, 'Sometimes – did I tell you? – sometimes I try out a new song on her. If she likes it, she joins in. A bit croaky and out of tune, of course, but you can't—'

Jane threw the paint rag at him.

3

Pebbles

NEXT MORNING, WHEN Jane had left for school, Merrily phoned Huw Owen. She hadn't slept well, was feeling frayed and edgy, sitting in the scullery in the kid's old pink fleece. Outside the window, the day was crazed with April chemistry: white sunlight soaking through holes in the foaming cloud.

'So when did this happen, lass?'

Huw had been up north on what he liked to call a retreat, working with a gang of hard-nosed clerics in the badlands of south Manchester. She wasn't yet ready to hear his horror stories.

'Think it happened when I wasn't looking. Can't say you didn't warn me – if you don't pick a team, somebody picks one for you. Just that my guys didn't want to be picked.'

He was silent. She could hear the kindling detonating his living-room fire. Pictured his feet in peeling trainers on the hearth, the volatile sunlight in his old hippy's shaggy hair. She was getting the feeling that his Manchester time had left him energized rather than wearied.

Precarious psychiatric state. Bitch.

'I feel pathetic,' she said, 'ringing you with this stuff. I just wondered if you'd – you know – heard anything.'

Huw had been born in rural Wales but brought up in Yorkshire, returning to the Beacons in middle age as a parish priest and a personal trainer in the practice of exorcism. Where

31

nobody can hear you scream. Merrily heard the creak of his chair as he stretched, thinking.

'Callaghan-Clarke. Wasn't she one of the bints who did a circle-dance round the tombs of the old bishops in Hereford Cathedral to celebrate the ordination of women?'

'If she was, she's calmed down now.'

'The calming power of naked ambition. Get their feet under the table, next thing they want's a bigger table. Where exactly does she stand in your... Deliverance circle?'

'Given herself a title: Diocesan Deliverance Coordinator. We voted on it. Every case we get from now on has to be submitted to the group before any action's taken. We voted on that, too. Three in favour, one bemused abstention.'

'Bugger,' Huw said.

'Quite.'

'A little focus group. It's just what you need, isn't it?'

'We light candles and concentrate. I'm not kidding.'

She told him about Martin Longbeach, and Huw laughed – the noise milk would make if you could hear it curdling.

Merrily looked up at the wall clock: nearly nine a.m., and a difficult funeral to organize – an elderly woman who'd moved to the village no more than a fortnight ago to live with her daughter and son-in-law, themselves comparative newcomers. And Andy Mumford was due here around ten. It was looking like another day when she wouldn't see much of Lol.

'Back-up's one thing,' Huw said. 'You need a witness some-times, no question, and somebody to watch your back. But an ill-matched committee operating in an area where nothing, at the best of times, is ever a bloody certainty...'

'We all accept the need for a psychiatrist...'

'There are good shrinks,' Huw said, 'and there are dangerous shrinks.'

'You come across Nigel Saltash before?'

'Never.'

'Me neither.' Merrily gazed out of the window at the unmown lawn, vividly green against the grey sky with its seeping sun.

'He's a regular churchgoer, however.'

Huw laughed again. 'You know your problem, lass? Had your picture in the papers once too often, and you take a very nice picture. They don't like that. And they weren't happy at all when you were cosying up to the pagans against Ellis.'

'Oh, Huw, Ellis was the kind of humourless, dangerous, fundamentalist bigot who brings the Church into—'

'Ellis was part of the Church,' Huw said. 'Whereas pagans are pagans. Any road, I'm just planting the thought.'

'Who doesn't like it? Not the Bishop?'

'Dunmore's a time-server. He wouldn't even be consulted. Think higher.'

'Huh?' She was thrown.

'You want a list of all the embittered, back-stabbing bastards who hate the whole concept of Deliverance? Hey, God forbid that priests should meddle in metaphysics. Somebody's happen saying, we need to keep an eye on that little Watkins in Hereford... could be getting carried away... too much, too soon. Needs a steadying hand...'

'Hang on. Let me get this right. You think Callaghan-Clarke may have been nudged into place as a... an instrument of restraint?'

Merrily heard Huw sniff. She was thinking of what Siân had said about his precarious psychiatric state. Would it help to tell him about that? She stared out into the garden, at the pale buds on the apple trees.

'And the bottom line,' she said, 'is that nothing much gets done, right?'

' "But how can we be certain?" ' Huw doing this delicate, disapproving, posh voice. ' "We could so easily look ridiculous, couldn't we?" And this lad with the candles sounds like window dressing. Bumbling New Ager. Whimsical, but essentially nice and harmless.'

'Making us seem a little woolly?'

'That's a good word, aye.'

'Let me get this right. You actually think—?'

'Leave it with me,' Huw said. 'I'll ask around, see what I can find out.'

Merrily made a call about the funeral. Hereford Crem: two p.m., Monday. She'd go and see the family over the weekend. It was always a problem when you didn't know either the dead person or the bereaved: gently quizzing them about their mum, looking for the one little jewelled detail that would make it meaningful before you slid her through the curtains and the next one came through – another priest, another set of mourners. A line of sad trains on the last platform.

Andy Mumford turned up ten minutes early.

On the phone last night he'd sounded agitated. When he walked in, she was shocked.

He was wearing a fawn-coloured zipper jacket over a yellow polo shirt. She'd never seen him without a suit before, and he looked all wrong. He'd always seemed comfortably plump; now he was sagging and his farmer's face was less ruddy than red.

'You had breakfast, Andy? I can do toast—'

'No, no…' He waved a hand, said he'd have tea. Weak. No sugar.

So she'd been right: he'd retired from the police.

'When?'

'Three weeks back.' Mumford pulled a chair from under the pine refectory table. 'Three weeks and two days. CID boys bought me a digital camera.'

'Oh.'

'Now I'll have to get a computer.' He sat down with his legs apart, hands bunched together between his knees. 'Like having your leg off.'

'Sorry…?'

'People thought I was looking forward to it. Like you look forward to having your leg off. Wake up in the morning and you think it's still there, and then you realize.'

It was why his clothes didn't fit; he'd lost the kind of weight you could never quite put back. Poor Andy. She'd seen a lot of

34

him over the past two years, most recently as bag-carrier to Frannie Bliss, the DI. Bag-carrier and local encyclopaedia: an essential role.

'You'll get another job?' Merrily filled the kettle. 'Security adviser somewhere, or…?'

'To be honest, Mrs Watkins, I'd rather *not* be a night-watchman at some battery-chicken plant.' Mumford looked down at his hands. 'Might get some chickens of my own, mind. Beehives. Dunno yet. However—' He looked up at her. 'How're you?'

'I'm all right.'

She smiled. Along the Welsh Border it was some kind of etiquette that you took ten or fifteen minutes to get around to what you'd come about. You tossed pebbles into the pond and, at some stage, the issue would float quietly to the surface. Must have been fascinating to listen to Mumford interrogating a suspect.

'Your mother don't live round yere, Mrs Watkins?'

'Cheltenham. She has a lot of friends there now. We don't see each other that often.'

'But you did have some relations yereabouts?'

'My grandad had a farm and an orchard near Mansell Lacy when I was a kid. All gone now.'

Mumford nodded. 'My folks moved north into south Shropshire, after my dad retired from the Force. Ludlow. They had a little newsagent's and sweetshop for a while, then it got too much for them.'

'Nice place. Historic.'

'Pretty historic themselves, now, my mam and dad. They'll expect me to do more for them, now I'm retired.'

'No brothers… sisters?'

'Sister. Twelve years younger than me, lives in Hereford with this low-life idle bugger. Her…' He paused. 'Her boy, from when she was married, he never got on with this bloke. Always an oddball kid. Used to spend the school holidays with his grandparents. In Ludlow.'

He looked at Merrily, and she met his baggy-eyed gaze and detected ripples in the pond, a circular movement, something coming up.

Mumford said, 'My sister's boy, my nephew – Robson Walsh.'

The name broke surface, lay there, the water bubbling around it. *Robson Walsh.*

'Suppose you'd still be… dealing with the funny stuff, Mrs Watkins?' Mumford's face was a foxier shade of red now, but she saw that his eyes looked anxious.

'When it comes up.'

She sat down opposite him. Never the most religious of professions, the police. Saw too much injustice, degradation, few signs of divine light. Even Frannie Bliss, raised a Catholic up in Liverpool, had once said that if he ever made it to heaven he wouldn't be too surprised to see a feller with a trident and a forked tail sitting on a cloud and laughing himself sick.

Whatever this was, it was hard for Mumford.

Robson Walsh. Robbie Walsh, Robbie Walsh…

'Oh my God, Andy.' TV pictures: old mellow walls, police tape. A school photograph. 'The boy who fell—'

'From Ludlow Castle, aye. I was there.'

'At the castle?'

'In the town. Come to pick up the wife – she was working at Ludlow Hospital. We were going out for dinner, celebrate my… celebrate…' He looked down at the table. 'Station sergeant at Ludlow spotted me in the street, took me into the castle. Boy's still lying there, waiting for the pathologist.'

'God, I'm so sorry, Andy, I just never—'

'I've spent time with a lot of families lost a child.' He looked up at her. 'But at the end of it, Mrs Watkins, you always gets to go home.'

'You said your sister's son?'

'Slag.'

'Oh.'

'Lives in Hereford with a new bloke – toe-rag. Only too happy to let the boy spend his holidays at his gran's. Now she blames me.'

'Your sister? Why?'

''Cause we covered up, Robbie and me, covered up how bad the ole girl was getting. He couldn't stand the thought that he wouldn't be able to go and stay there. He loved it, see. Ludlow. The history.'

'They called him The History Boy – in one of the papers.'

'That's right.'

'You and he covered up that your mother was…?'

There was a knocking from the front door, where the bell had packed in again. Merrily didn't move.

'What's the point of putting a long name to it?' Mumford said. 'But her mind's going, and it en't no better for this.'

'But didn't your sister know what your mother was like?'

'They don't speak. Not since she went off with the toe-rag. I usually got to take the boy to Ludlow. Hell, he was all right there. Better than at home on the bloody Plascarreg, with a latchkey.'

'Your sister lives on the Plascarreg?'

Not the best address in Hereford.

'He was capable and intelligent,' Mumford said. 'I never had a son, but I couldn't've complained if I'd got one like him. Anyway, Gail works at Ludlow Hospital three days a week, so she pops in, sees they're all right.'

'What about your father?'

'Not the most sympathetic of men. Tells you about all the death he's seen in his time, how you gotter put it behind you kind of thing. Meanwhile, ole girl goes over and over it in her mind, what's left of it.' Mumford glanced over at the door to the hall – more knocking. 'You better get that.'

'It's OK.'

Probably just the postman with a parcel. He'd leave it in the porch.

Robbie Walsh. She recalled the case throwing up questions in the papers. How had he managed to conceal himself in the castle? Had he been alone?

'So has the inquest…?'

'Opened and adjourned after medical evidence. Boy was cremated at Hereford. No proof of anything more than an accident. Most popular theory is he got totally absorbed in whatever he was checking out inside the castle, got hisself locked in and went up the tower to try and signal for help. Mabbe leaned over too far.'

'That feasible?'

'It's feasible. But there's ways out of there for an agile kid, and if anybody knew 'em he would. But... nothing iffy sitting on a plate, the police don't go looking for it no more. Not enough manpower to handle what they got on the books already. Verdict of misadventure, most likely.'

'And what do you think?'

'I reckon it should be an open verdict. Mabbe I'm just saying this on account of it's destroyed what was left of my bloody family, but I reckon there's stuff we don't know. Meanwhile, my mam... this is gonner be hanging over her for the rest of... whatever she's got left.'

There was more knocking at the front door, insistent.

'In more ways than one, it looks like,' Mumford said.

'Sorry?'

'Hanging over her. It's why I've come. You better get that this time, it en't gonner stop.'

Merrily went to open the door.

Just what she needed.

'Sorry if I got you out of the bath or something, Merrily.'

Nigel Saltash smiling his all-purpose smile.

4

Routine Pastoral

ON HIS TRAINING courses at the disused chapel in the Beacons, Huw Owen liked to invent pet names for the unquiet dead.

Insomniac, hitch-hiker, breather, groper...

Exorcist jargon, a touch of black humour for the troops.

Merrily brought over an extra mug, poured three teas and sat down at the head of the table, her back to the window. The sun laid a creamy sheen, like an altar cloth, on the pine table top.

Huw would have called Mumford's mother's problem a parting-caller or a day tripper. Throwaway terms for a commonplace phenomenon – loved ones dropping in just to show their faces, let you know they wouldn't be far away. They tended not to stay long. She remembered Huw saying that, nine times out of ten, they were none of his business.

'The technical term is "bereavement apparition",' she told Mumford. 'If anybody bothered to do a survey, they'd probably find that at least fifty per cent of bereaved people have similar experiences.'

Usually widows or widowers, or the children or siblings of someone who had recently died. But it could equally be a favourite teacher or a long-time colleague. You'd be doing something mundane around the house when suddenly you'd feel a sharp awareness of whoever had died. Or you'd actually see them passing through the hall or maybe sitting in a favourite chair. Just a glimpse, and then they'd be gone.

'What we're saying, Andrew,' Nigel Saltash said, 'is that this tends to happen with a person one is used to having around. It's something I've encountered many, many times.'

He was wearing a tracksuit the colour of his hair, and his tanned skin shone. At the door just now, on auto-smile, he'd told Merrily he'd thought they ought to have a chat one-to-one. Didn't want her, after last night, to run away with the wrong idea. And as this was his day for early-morning jogging with Kent Asprey, the fitness-freak Ledwardine GP... Oh yes, old mates. Hammered the country lanes together every Friday.

Terrific.

So there'd been no alternative to bringing him in and explaining to Mumford about the new Deliverance Advisory Group – giving Mumford an opportunity to say nothing, make an excuse and leave, call her later.

But, of course, it turned out that he and Saltash knew each other from way back, when Saltash had worked at the Stonebow Psychiatric Unit in Hereford. Reminding Mumford of all the times he'd been called across to Police Headquarters to assess some drugged-up prisoner self-harming in the cells. What days, eh? And now both of them retired. Or entering a new life-phase, as it were.

Saltash watched, with a smile conveying mild pain, as Mumford dumped three white sugars in his mug of tea.

'Essentially, what you're looking at, Andrew, is grief-projection. The bereaved person is carrying an image of the departed one very close, as it were, to his or her heart. We don't want to have seen the last of them. A part of us desperately wants them still to be around, in the old familiar places. And so an area of our consciousness responds to the need. This is almost certainly what's happening with your mother and her visions of the boy. Are we together on this one, Merrily, would you say?'

The tilted head. The smile that was a well-oiled explanatory tool.

But he was probably right. Huw Owen's advice had always been to leave parting-callers, in general, alone. Didn't matter whether they were hallucinations or psychological projections or something less explicable, they usually brought comfort rather than fear or distress, and so they were part of the healing mechanism, part of a phase that would pass. And if Mrs Mumford's mind was on the slide...

'Can I...?' Merrily conspicuously sugared her own tea and stirred it noisily. 'Can I just briefly go over some of it again, Andy? Your mother says she... saw him, first, in the kitchen, right?'

Mumford nodded, glanced at Nigel Saltash, then glanced away.

'Out of the corner of an eye. Said he was standing by the fridge, like he was about to help himself to a can of pop. When she turned towards him, he... vanished. This was before the funeral.'

Nigel Saltash was nodding eagerly. Merrily wondered, despondent, if he was going to call in every week after jogging with Dr Asprey, to discuss the many areas where so-called spiritual guidance overlapped with nuts-and-bolts psychiatry.

'And the second time?' she said to Mumford.

'In the back garden. Robbie's standing by the bird bath, looking up at the house. Mam was in the bedroom, says she saw him through the window. But it was... you know, it was like a reflection in the glass. When she stepped back he wasn't there any more.'

'A reflection,' Saltash said. 'Yes, of course.'

'Same in the town.' Mumford was mumbling now, like he wanted to get this over. 'Near the Buttermarket. Shop window.'

'Oh, really? Another reflection?'

'Kind of thing. She was with my dad. He didn't see anything. She was looking in the window and Robbie, he was behind her, but when she turned round...'

Merrily said, 'Did she think he knew she was there?'

'I don't... I don't know.'

'I mean, does she ever think he wants to communicate with her?'

Mumford shook his head. 'Don't know.'

41

'Does it frighten her at all?'

'Frighten her?' The corner of Mumford's mouth twitched. 'Robbie?'

'Right.'

'I see what you're getting at, Merrily,' Nigel Saltash said. 'There's clearly a contributory element of perceived guilt here – whether or not that guilt is misplaced. And also' – he leaned across the table, holding his hands like bookends – 'a desperate need to know exactly what happened.'

'Does she know you were coming here, Andy?' Merrily said.

'I…' Mumford shook his head. 'She don't like a fuss. Like she was very embarrassed at the size of turnout for the funeral – people from the castle, councillors, the Press. Like they were sitting in judgement, she thought. But all it was… it's still a small town, see. They take something like this to heart. Bishop insisted on conducting the funeral hisself—'

'David Cook?'

The Suffragan Bishop of Ludlow. Number two in the Hereford diocese. Bernie Dunmore, now Bishop of Hereford, had previously held the post. But surely David Cook…

'—Even though it was only about a week before he went in for his heart bypass,' Mumford said. 'Not a well man, and he looked it.'

Mumford didn't look a well man, either. His hair was grey and lank, his eyes baggy and wary, small veins wriggling in his cheeks. He had to be about twenty years younger than Nigel Saltash, but he seemed older. Just a civilian now – no longer Detective Sergeant, while Saltash was still Dr Saltash.

'Look, I…' Mumford came to his feet. 'Might well be like you say, Mrs Watkins, imagination playing tricks.'

'Well, that wasn't necessarily what I—'

'Old girl's had a shock. She don't want no fuss, neither do I. I just thought, as I knew you… You've cleared things up a bit. That's fine. And the doc here…'

'Glad to help an old mate, Andrew.' Nigel Saltash sitting back, with his arms folded. Like when the driving-test examiner had told you to park and sat there making notes on his clipboard.

Merrily said on impulse, 'I think I should probably talk to her.' She saw Saltash raising an eyebrow. 'So, if you want to ask her, Andy…'

'You think you could, ah, get rid of it, Merrily?' Saltash's smile expressing professional curiosity.

'Wrong terminology, Nigel.'

'Ah, sorry. Help it on its way?'

'Even that might be counter-productive.'

'So you have this general policy of non-intervention, unless there's a clear threat to the patient's mental health.'

Patient. God.

'Something like that,' Merrily said.

She hated this. She hated it when lofty consultants exchanged viewpoints at the foot of the bed, like the third party was already brain-dead.

'I have a lot to learn, don't I?' Saltash said. 'On which basis, if you go to see this lady, might I perhaps tag along?'

She could see Mumford was uncomfortable about this. Saltash evidently picked up on it, too, smiling down at him.

'Andrew, old boy… I'm retired, OK, like you? This is observation only.' He was doing this windscreen-wiper gesture with both hands. 'No reports, no referrals.'

'I'll talk to her about it.' Mumford seemed less than reassured, which was quite understandable.

'I'll call you, Andy,' Merrily said.

Coming up to midnight, she was lying full-length on the sofa at Lucy's old house, with Lol sitting at one end, her head in his lap. Low music was seeping from a boombox beside the glowing hearth.

'I suppose I'm going to have to do something,' Merrily said, 'before it all falls apart on me.'

The sofa, delivered that day, was the only furniture in the parlour. It was orange, like the too-dark ceiling – never trust Jane in Linda Barker mode.

'Psychiatrists,' Lol said.

The weight of his own experience turned the word into some kind of lead sarcophagus full of decomposing remains.

'I think I want to kill him,' Merrily said.

The sofa smelled of newness and showrooms, but the scent from the fire in the inglenook was of applewood, the kindest, mellowest aroma in the countryside.

'Well,' she said. 'You know…'

Oh, he knew… She was thinking of 'Heavy Medication Day', the only angry song on the new album. It was about his experiences on a psychiatric ward with a doctor who… over-medicated. *Someone has to pay, now Dr Gascoigne's on his way.* A lot of residual bitterness there.

Last year, before they were a unit, he'd enrolled on a training course for psychotherapists, with the feeling that he could maybe, in some way, alter things from the inside. Discovering fairly soon that mere psychotherapists weren't anywhere near the inside and, like all therapists and crisis-counsellors, they were ten-a-penny nowadays. And so Lol had walked away from it, back into music.

He slid a hand under her hair. 'How necessary are they?'

'Shrinks?'

'I mean in Deliverance.'

Merrily thought about it. 'You could probably say they're only actually essential when you're dealing with someone who thinks he or she is possessed by something… external. A psychiatrist would be able to detect symptoms of, say, schizophrenia.'

'Symptoms of schizophrenia don't necessarily prove the person actually is schizo,' Lol said.

'No, but it's something that needs to be eliminated.'

'How often have you had a case of demonic possession, then?'

'Never. As you know. Never had a case where it was down to schizophrenia, either.'

'So the idea of having a psychiatrist as a permanent part of your Deliverance group…'

'Could be overkill,' Merrily said. 'If you consider that most of what we're dealing with are what you might call non-invasive psychic phenomena... then if you have your resident psychiatrist insisting that it's always down to delusion, hallucination, comfort chemicals in the brain, et cetera...'

'... Then what's the point of people like you?'

'Listen to us, we're finishing one another's sentences,' Merrily said. 'How cosy is that? What's this music?'

'Elbow. *Cast of Thousands.*'

'It's lovely.'

'It's bloody terrifying. I don't know why I bother.'

'Never mind, they were probably influenced by you.'

'You vicars can be so patronizing.'

Merrily looked around in the firelight, among the paint cloths and the ladders, for a clock. Jane was out with Eirion, as usual on a Friday night. By agreement, she was always home by one.

There wasn't a clock anywhere yet. She guessed she'd been here about an hour and a half.

'So, anyway, I called Andy before I came out,' she said. 'I'm going over tomorrow to see his mother. Not being much help around here, am I?'

'You're crap at painting anyway. You told the shrink you're going?'

'I really don't know what to do. I mean, this is routine pastoral stuff. I wouldn't be going if it wasn't Andy Mumford – I'd refer it to local clergy. It doesn't need a psychiatrist, so why set a precedent? You're right, it's overkill. All this belt-and-braces stuff, the Church covering its back, never sticking its neck out...'

'Can you cover your back and stick your neck out at the same time?' Lol bent and kissed her, one hand pushing her face into his, the other hand...

'Mmmmph...' It suddenly struck her that there were no curtains in this room and one window overlooked Church Street.

'You've gone stiff,' Lol said.

She sat up. 'You should talk.'

'We could go upstairs, take some cushions. Merrily, people know…'

'I need to get home. Jane'll be back. Besides, if you've got to drive back to Knight's Frome—'

'I'm going to sleep here on my nice new sofa,' Lol said. 'There's this guy from Q magazine coming tomorrow, quite early.'

'He's coming here?'

'Prof didn't want him poking round the studio. We've got Tom Storey in, mixing his album. Prof's a very private producer, Tom hates the media. I won't say a word about you, you know that.'

'It shouldn't be like this.' Merrily stood up and straightened her sweater. 'I'm sorry. I mean, there's probably no real reason for…'

'We'll get there,' Lol said.

Would they? Within a few weeks, when his intermittent tour was over, he was going to be living here permanently. She supposed that what the new-home cards on the window sill were saying was that it was time to stop being coy and covert.

'Oh hell, Lol, let's – I don't know – put a notice in the window at the Eight till Late or something.'

'Uh…' Lol went over to the window where the cards were. 'You should know about this.'

Handing her a folded paper. She took it to the hearth and opened it out. It wasn't hard to read it by the firelight. Big letters.

FIND YOUR WAY IN THE DARK?

'Oh.' Not a universal welcome, then.

'I'd have said it was somebody having a laugh,' Lol said, 'but I can't think of anybody… I mean, it's not that funny, is it?'

She refolded the paper, annoyed. 'You might as well tell the guy from Q. It would at least end this kind of stuff.'

'Not in the context in which they'd run the story. It'd have to be from my side… the arrest, the loony bin. My Years of Hell. Now finding happiness at last, with a good woman in every sense, and letting it all come out in the music.'

'God.' Merrily shuddered. 'Let me think about this.'

When she left, she went by the back door, reaching Church Street via the alley. Keeping to the shadows until she was approaching the square, where security lamps lit the front of the Black Swan and only two cars were still parked.

What was coming back was what Huw Owen had said.

Had your picture in the paper once too often.

He was right, of course. Deliverance was the Church's secret service. Essentially low-level. Publicity was seldom helpful. No room at all for the cult of personality.

Maybe the Deliverance group/panel/circle/whatever was a good thing. Good for her. Prevent her becoming proprietorial. A question of sharing, Martin Longbeach had said.

Always painful lessons to be learned about yourself, your attitude.

So why was she deciding, as she padded quietly across the cobbled street to the vicarage, that she would not ring Nigel Saltash about tomorrow's appointment with Mumford's mother?

5

Saturday Sun

Nigel Saltash came to pick Merrily up at ten.

Jane spotted him from the landing window on her way down from her apartment in the attic, calling down the stairs.

'He's got one of those cool little BMW sports cars.'

Merrily widened her eyes. 'Like… gosh.'

'He's getting out. He's wearing jeans and a cream sports jacket that could be Armani. He looks a smooth old bastard, Mum.'

Merrily said nothing, stepping into her shoes at the bottom of the stairs, sliding her slippers under the hallstand. She was still feeling resentful, manipulated. What Saltash had done was phone Andy Mumford himself last night, saying he'd tried to call Merrily but she was out. Finding out the time of this morning's proposed visit to Mumford's mother and then leaving a message on Merrily's machine suggesting he pick her up: no point in a convoy.

'So how badly do you think he fancies you?' Jane said.

'He's seventy-one, flower.'

'The new dangerous age. They're getting in as much sex as they can before it's too late. Apparently, at that age they can only hold an erection for five minutes max, and it's counting down all the time, did you know that?'

'Oh, Jane…'

'And, listen, you've got to stop calling me "flower". You've been calling me "flower" since I was seven.'

'I'll try.' Merrily pulled her coat from the peg. 'What are you doing today?'

'In the absence of his girlfriend, I'll probably help Lol finish painting Lucy's living room.'

'I don't think so.'

Jane peered down at her, hands on hips. 'I'm sorry?'

'The guy from *Q* magazine's coming to interview him. Teenage girl walks in, the guy remembers Lol's history.'

'Oh, that is…' Jane bounded downstairs. 'That is like totally ridiculous. It was twenty years ago. He was a kid. And he was fitted up, and if the guy from *Q*'s done his research he'll know that.'

'No smoke, flower. Just stay away until he's gone, OK?'

'Hah!' Jane stopped, with an arm wrapped around the black oak post sunk between the flags like a tree stump at the foot of the stairs. 'Now I understand. If the journalist sees me, Lol will have to explain whose daughter I am. And we can't have that coming out, can we?'

Merrily sighed. 'It's a music magazine. They wouldn't be interested anyway.'

'Yeah, but doesn't the same firm publish *Heat*?'

'Jane, please? Humour me?'

Feet crunched the gravel outside and the front door was rapped. Merrily unbolted the door, telling herself that some Deliverance teams worked like this all the time, in tandem with a bloody shrink.

At the Eight till Late, now the only worthwhile shop in Ledwardine, a partitioned strip along the side of the main window was full of handwritten notices.

PUPPIES. Border Collie/Lab cross. Good working strain. Parents can be seen. £40… RESPECTABLE CLEANER NEEDED TWO DAYS A WEEK… MOUNTAIN BIKE, NEARLY NEW. EIGHTEEN GEARS.

That kind of stuff. Even the personal columns of the *Hereford Times* were loaded now with ads like: *Live Adult-fantasy Chat… Venus's 24-hour Wankline*. But village noticeboards never changed – unless 'respectable cleaner' was some little-known rural euphemism for bondage-supervisor.

This window was Jane's last hope, anyway. She'd checked out the prayer board in the church. She'd even, for the first time ever, been through the parish register to see if, by chance, somebody had endorsed their marriage vows in the hand that had also scrawled VICERAGE.

She'd photocopied the poison-pen note before giving it back to Lol. OK, maybe it wasn't that poisonous. It was just that they all had to go on living here, and Lol and Mum had been through all kinds of crap already, and it just really pissed Jane off that there was some mean-spirited git in this village who begrudged them a hint of happiness.

And Mum was the vicar and therefore too nice to deal with it, and Lol was too timid, and so…

Mobile hairdresser. Women and men catered for.

She pulled the photocopy from her jeans, held it up to the window. Close.

Jim Prosser, who ran the shop, waved to her from inside. Jane put away the paper, waved back. Jim knew everybody in Ledwardine, must have seen a fair few handwritten shopping lists and weekly orders, for delivery. And he knew all about Mum and Lol.

Maybe not. And the lettering wasn't that close.

She walked off down Church Street. Sharp Saturday sun slanting on Ledwardine, the black and white cottages and shops all tarted up for the early tourists looking for pseudo-antiques and maybe a weekend cottage to display them in.

Predatory Londoners on the spree. Jane had read in one of the Sunday property supplements that, now you couldn't find a garden shed in the Cotswolds for much under half a million, the Welsh Border was no longer considered too remote for commuters. So Ledwardine, this classic calendar village still enclosed by ancient orchards, was well in the cross-hairs. Even its one-time council estate no longer looked like a council estate, with its new hardwood windows, rendered brickwork, conservatories bulging out like transparent blisters.

Hereford's estate agents were doing faster business than Venus's Wankline.

Lol had somehow squeezed in, though Jane guessed that his mortgage on Lucy's house was crippling. And knew that when she got round to needing a place of her own there'd be like no chance here. And she liked Ledwardine, didn't want it to become Beverly Hills with a botox population and Jim Prosser forced to stock disgusting pâté de foie gras to stay in business.

But unless you had a farm or something to inherit, you were stuffed. At least when the Church kicked her out of the vicarage Mum could move in with Lol. If that was acceptable to Mr Vicerage.

Who might be here right now on the square, watching.

Jane wandered around, keeping an eye open for Eirion's car. After Mum had put her off going to Lol's, she'd called Eirion at home in Abergavenny, and he'd said, yeah, OK, he could probably try and cobble together a few quid for the petrol; he'd come over. Less enthusiastic than he might have been. Was something cooling off? It was true that there were times when she felt she needed some space, maybe go out with someone else, just to, you know, compare. But the thought of Eirion with another girl... she couldn't handle that.

She stopped in front of the two-up, two-down terraced cottage, separated from the pavement by a ridge of new cobbles. Lucy's house. A little black Nissan was parked outside behind Lol's clapped-out Astra. The man from *Q*? She thought of going round the back and letting herself in through the kitchen door that Lol never locked. Just sitting in the kitchen, listening.

But she knew that if Lol was being too self-deprecating she'd just get annoyed and give herself away. And she was annoyed enough already, at the carrion crows from Off scooping up Ledwardine. And at herself for being so insecure.

* * *

'You must feel I'm rather on your back,' Saltash said, cruising onto the Leominster road.

He had dark glasses on and his leather seat eased well back. There was a buttermilk sun, and the hedgerows on either side of the road were greening up almost in front of their eyes.

'Well, I... tend to think that if you arrive with a psychiatrist most people feel a bit threatened,' Merrily said. 'Some of them have really had to steel themselves to approach someone like me, and so... we probably need to think of a way around that.'

Saltash chuckled. 'Just as well I'm no longer a psychiatrist, merely a new member of the team who wants to learn.'

'Probably a few things I could learn, too,' Merrily said, being diplomatic for the moment. She was wearing civvies, jumper and skirt. In another parish, you didn't make a show of what you were.

The BMW was swallowing miles in small, easy sips. When Saltash slowed for the Leominster traffic island, the engine made a thick and fleshy sound, as if it was powered by rising sap. With the size of insurance premiums and the cost of petrol, you peered into a sports car these days and almost invariably saw white hair and driving gloves. Merrily tightened her seat belt.

'So what exactly do you want to know about ghosts, Nigel?'

'Ghosts?' Saltash twisted his head towards her, the cords in his long neck like piano wires. 'Oh, ghosts are terribly interesting. Don't you think? I doubt there's ever been a wholly convincing study, though.'

'That mean you're thinking of making one?'

'Be awfully time-consuming, but perhaps worthwhile. I'd certainly be quite interested in examining apparitions as subjective – or reflective – phenomena.'

'I'm sorry?'

'A study of perceived apparitions to discover what they're telling us about the perceiver.'

'The ghost as a psychological projection of someone's inner condition?'

'Inner guilt, inner torment.' Saltash joined a tailback of cars from Leominster's town-centre lights. 'Sense of loss. Repressed sexual desire. Is the perceived ghost, for instance, shadowy and quiescent? Is it urgent, or aggressive?'

'So I can take it you don't accept the possibility of ghosts as an objective reality.'

'Merrily, the very word "ghost"' – Saltash's smile broke out – 'is surely an antithesis of the word "real".'

'So, even as a Christian—'

'I don't think the Bible has a lot to say on the subject. Or am I wrong?'

'Well, it... occurs, here and there.'

'But probably without a hard and fast definition of the term ghost. You see, I don't know how far you personally go with this. I'm not going to ask you about your personal "psychic experience" – highly subjective, therefore rarely helpful, and not a can of worms I'd want to open at this stage of our relationship.'

This stage?

Merrily had the feeling of being worked, becoming the subject of some kind of private thesis. And guessing that whatever she said next would seep, at some strategic point, back to Siân Callaghan-Clarke.

There was that mellow, new-car smell inside the BMW, a discreet No Smoking sign on the dash. She wished she was alone, in her rattling Volvo.

'Look, I... I don't have a particular problem with psychological projection. Probably does account for a lot of ghost stories. But it doesn't fully explain the traditional haunted house, does it? Where something is seen again and again, by more than one person. How would you deal with that?'

'Where do you want to start?' The lights turned green; Saltash turned left. 'Preconditioning? Folie à deux on a grand scale? If I were a physicist, I might even be drawn to seek a more scientific explanation of the trace-memory theory. But that's not my backyard. The mind's where I live. Edging, a touch warily for the moment, however, around Jung's collective unconscious.'

'So I'd be safe in assuming that the whole idea of the unquiet dead... would be well over your belief threshold.'

'Merrily...' Nigel Saltash wore his smile like a gold medallion. 'Do you think we know each other well enough yet to even raise that question without the risk of permanent damage to an otherwise promising relationship?'

Promising? Promising how?

They were leaving Herefordshire now, and the personality of the countryside was changing. She saw the plains and ridges and escarpments of Shropshire: a bonier landscape, a lighter green, a bigger sky.

She saw, far in the east, the sawn-off slope of the Clee Hills. And then, momentarily, in the middle distance, fading out of the morning mist to the north-west, the tower of the church that was sometimes called the Cathedral of the Marches.

St Laurence's, Ludlow. The ancient town clustered below it, an island in amber. A small town with an antique lustre and a bigger history than the whole of Herefordshire.

No town that ancient is unhaunted, Merrily thought, irrationally.

At first, Lol had thought, *He's too young*.

Too young to know the background. Too young to understand how difficult it had been to get anywhere in the 1980s with music that was soft and breathy and woven into a mesh of acoustic guitars, when everything else was shiny and synthesized and nobody had heard of Nick Drake, and the Beatles were archaeology.

Jack Fine sat on the shorter stepladder, his microphone between his knees, wired to a mini-disc recorder in his jacket pocket. He had floppy hair and sulky lips and looked like he could be about nineteen. But then so did a lot of blokes that Lol learned later were in their mid-twenties. A sign of age, but he tried not to worry about this any more. And it became clear that Jack Fine did know the background. Maybe too much of it.

'So, as I understand it, Lol, this goes back to when this other guy in the band – Karl Windling? – was hot for this groupie, and he roped you in to keep her mate occupied. And they were both under-age, and you got stitched up?'

'I was eighteen,' Lol said patiently. 'I was very naive.'

'But you were the one who finished up getting arrested and taking the rap—'

'For something that never even happened.'

Oh God, how many times was he going to have to tell this wretched story? Even Karl Windling was history – dead in a road accident two years ago.

'Leaving you with a police record,' Jack said.

Lol nodding wearily. 'And then my parents… they were tied into this fundamentalist religious sect, and they disowned me. And everything went downhill from there. Got the wrong kind of help, cracked up, wound up in a psychiatric hospital, and… Listen… Jack… I'm not trying to cover anything up or tell you your job or anything, but would it be possible to maybe not go into all this again?'

'Lol…' Jack leaned over his mike, his fair hair falling over his forehead and covering up one eye. 'Look, man, OK, I can gloss over it. I can deal with it in, like, a couple of paragraphs? It's just that you seem to be putting this experience into a few of the songs on the album?'

Lol sighed. No way round this.

'The song "Heavy Medication Day",' Jack said. 'The one that goes, "Someone's got to pay, now Dr Gascoigne's on his way." What's that about?'

'It was just a particular doctor who was – how can I put this? – liberal with the medication. Anything for a quiet life. And probably so people wouldn't know what he got up to on the side.'

'Go on.'

'Uh-huh.' Lol shook his head. 'He knows and I know, and all the rest is… just a song.'

'There's real anger in that song, though, isn't there? Which is

56

unusual for you – it's usually more sort of resigned. It's as if this guy did something really bad to you.'

'Not to me personally.'

'So, what—?'

'Can we leave this one, Jack?'

'Seems to me this whole album is about your journey, through the system… back into the light, kind of thing,' Jack said. 'Like an exorcism.'

'Not exactly the word I'd use.'

Jack grinned, like maybe he knew about Merrily. He couldn't know.

'So how did you wind up out here in the sticks?'

'Well, I… came here originally with a woman. She eventually went off with someone else. And then, um…' Lol leaned back on his sofa and paused for a few seconds while he worked out what it was best to leave out – like him leaving the village and then coming back, because of Merrily. '… Then I met Prof Levin, just as he was setting up his studio on the other side of the county. And I've been working there, helping Prof out, doing a bit of session stuff. And then Prof kind of persuaded me to do the album. So I owe it all to him, really.'

Lol got out a copy of the CD and put it on the boombox, and they sat there, amid the paint cans and the dust sheets, discussing the songs and people who'd played on the tracks.

'Including Simon St John on bass and cello,' Jack said. 'That's a real name from the past. And he's a vicar now, right?'

'He's been a vicar for years.'

'Cool.'

'Yeah, he's cool.'

'But you're nothing to do with the Church…'

'Oh no.'

''Cause, like, your parents…'

'It can put you off, when your parents are… extremists.'

A lorry full of gravel went clanging down Church Street, and Jack was silent for a moment, seemed to be thinking what else he could ask.

'How long have you been in music-writing?' Lol asked.

'Oh, not long. My old man – he publishes specialist magazines now, but he used to be a newspaper reporter when he was young. But my grandad thought this was a really disreputable thing to be and he tried to persuade him to pack it in and get into the management side. My old man's really encouraged me to go into cutting-edge journalism. Go for it, you know? Don't look back.'

'Music's, er, cutting edge?'

'I do other stuff. Anything that comes up, really. Anyway, Lol… I mean, you were really fucked up for a long time, weren't you? It was like with Nick Drake – how long's he been dead now, thirty years? I mean, like him you couldn't cut it on stage, face an audience.'

'I identified a lot with Nick Drake, from the beginning. Hence the name of the band, Hazey Jane.'

'Huh?'

'The Nick Drake song, "Hazey Jane"?'

'Oh yeah, sure. Sorry, I thought you meant… So like, how did you get over that? 'Cause you did this amazing comeback gig… at the Courtyard in Hereford?'

Lol told Jack about all the help he'd had from Moira Cairns, folk-rock goddess, who happened to have been recording at Prof's. How Moira had literally pushed him out in front of that audience. Scary? Oh yeah, cold-sweat situation. All those lights, all those faces.

'And you're still doing a few gigs as support for Moira, right? But you and her…?'

Jack moved his hands around.

'Oh no,' Lol said. 'Nothing like that.'

'But you're with somebody?'

'No, I live alone. A rural idyll.'

'Right,' Jack said. 'Right.'

Still waiting for Eirion, Jane saw Lol and the guy from *Q* come out of the front door of Lucy's house and walk up the street to the village centre. They seemed to be getting on OK. She didn't know why she felt so responsible for Lol. He was just that kind of guy – vulnerable.

The journalist was a surprise. He didn't look any older than Eirion, for God's sake. He had a camera with him – a Nikon, digital-looking. Doing his own pictures, too. Jane slid behind one of the thick oak supports of the old market hall as they came onto the square. A few shoppers and tourists were glancing at them by now, and Jane saw that Lol was looking a bit unhappy.

''Course I won't say where it is,' the Q guy said.

'Only the market hall's fairly well known,' Lol said. 'Be a give away.'

'No problem – we'll face you the other way. Better for the light, too.'

The guy lined Lol up on the edge of the square, with the church in the background and people walking past, and Jane wondered if he was trying to simulate one of the famous black and white street-scene pictures taken for Nick Drake's first album, *Five Leaves Left*.

And she wondered, not for the first time, if that was a good thing. Nick Drake's music was wonderful but he surely represented the old Lol. He had, after all, killed himself with an overdose of antidepressants.

Jane saw Eirion's car arrive – little grey Peugeot with the CYM sticker, identifying him as a Welshman abroad. Eirion drove slowly around the square to park in front of the vicarage gate, and Jane stopped herself from running across, waving. A measure of cool might be more appropriate. Try and cobble together a few quid for the petrol, indeed.

She strolled casually over the cobbles as Eirion climbed out. He spotted her at once and did his incredible smile – the kind of smile that said you were the only person who could make it happen.

Smooth bastard.

OK, he wasn't. Eirion wasn't smooth. He didn't even know he had any charm.

When they'd finished kissing, he said, 'Is there something wrong?'

'Why?'

'It's very busy here today, isn't it? I've never seen it like this.'

'It's Saturday.' Jane looked back at the square. Lol and the guy from Q had gone already. Not a major photo-session, then.

'Didn't used to be like this on a Saturday, did it?' Eirion said.

'Tourism. It's like tourists have suddenly discovered the area.'

'Good for the shopkeepers.'

'I suppose.'

Jane imagined the figure of Lucy Devenish, the ghost of Ledwardine past, standing in the shadows under the market hall. Lucy looking very old, the way she never had, and the poncho drooping. Something feeling wrong.

'Let's get out of here,' Jane said.

6

On the Slippery Slope

MERRILY FOUND THE atmosphere stifling. Too much heat, food-smells, a sense of something out of everyone's control.

She exchanged glances with Saltash from opposite ends of the sofa. Saltash raised an eyebrow. Mrs Mumford seemed to think he was some kind of priest. And the wrong kind, at that.

'Where's the Bishop?' she kept shouting at her son. 'You said you'd bring the Bishop. You never does what you says you's gonner do.'

Mumford sat, impassive, on a hard chair by the TV, which was silently screening some Saturday-morning children's programme: grown-ups wearing cheerful primary colours and exaggerated expressions, smiling a lot and chatting with puppets.

Soon after they'd arrived, Mumford's dad had walked out. 'Can't stand no more of this. I'm off shopping. She won't face up to it. You talk some sense into her, boy, else you can bloody well take her away with you.'

'I'm cold.' Mrs Mumford was hunching her chair dangerously close to the gas fire. 'Fetch me my cardigan, Andrew.'

'You got it on, Mam.'

Mumford looked down at his shoes. The room felt like the inside of a kiln. His mam wore this winter-weight red cardigan and baggy green slacks. She had one gold earring in, and that wasn't a fashion statement. She looked from Merrily to Saltash to Andy. She'd done this twice before, as if she was trying to work out who they all were.

'Why en't the Bishop come?'

'He en't well, Mam, I told you. He had a heart operation.'

Her eyes filled up. 'You'll tell me anything, you will.'

'Mam—'

'He was always nice to me, the Bishop, he never talked about God and that ole rubbish. Used to come in when we had the paper shop. Used to come in for his *Star* nearly every night.'

'Mam, that was the old bishop. He don't live here no more.'

'He can't tell me why, see! That's why he don't wanner come.' She turned to Saltash. 'Can't tell me.'

Mrs Mumford stared at Saltash in silence. Merrily looked away, around the room. The walls were bare, pink anaglypta, except for a wide picture in a gilt frame over a sideboard with silverware on it. But the picture had been turned round to face the wall. All you could see was the brown-paper backing, stretched tight.

What was it a picture of? Ludlow Castle?

'What would you like the Bishop to tell you?' Saltash asked.

Mam kept on staring at him, like she knew him but couldn't place him. You could feel her confusion in the room, like a tangle of grey wool in the air. Her voice went into a whisper.

'Why did God let her take him?' Starting to cry now. 'Why did God let that woman take our boy?'

Saltash leaned forward. 'Which woman is that, Phyllis?'

'You're supposed to be a policeman!' Mam rounding on Andy, chins quaking. 'Why din't you stop her?'

Andy Mumford drew a tight breath through clenched teeth, the veins prominent in his cheeks.

'The Bishop, when he come round, he sat on that settee with a cup of tea and a bourbon biscuit and he never mentioned God nor Jesus, not once.'

Merrily said softly, 'Mrs Mumford, who was the woman?'

Mam didn't look at her. 'I can't say it.' She pulled a handkerchief from her sleeve and blew her nose. Saltash caught Merrily's eye.

62

Andy said, 'Mam, you can say anything to Mrs Watkins, and it won't go no further.'

'What... this girl?'

Mam snorted. Mumford looked helplessly at Merrily.

'Phyllis,' Saltash said. 'I think you were starting to tell us about Robbie.'

'Oh...' She smiled suddenly, her face flushed. She sat up, centre stage. 'He loves it here, he does.'

'He felt safe here.'

'He loves it.'

'He was interested in history, wasn't he?'

'He loves all the old houses. He's always walking up and down, looking at the old houses. He knows when they was all built and he knows who used to live in them. You can walk up Corve Street with him, and he'll tell you who used to live where, what he's found out from books. Reads such a lot of books. Reads and reads. I says, you'll hurt your eyes, reading in that light!'

'Phyllis,' Saltash said. 'Can you see Robbie... reading?'

'No!' She reared up, nodding the word out, hard. 'I don't need to see him no more. I said, please don't let me see him. I don't wanner see him like that...'

'Like that?'

'All broken. I don't wanner— I just hears him now. Nan, Nan... Sometimes he's a long way away. But sometimes, when I'm nearly asleep, he'll be real close. Nan...' She smiled. 'And he draws them, the old houses. He's real good. Draws all them old houses. And the church. And the ca—'

She stopped, her mouth open. And then her whole face seemed to flow, like a melting candle, and a sob erupted, and she clawed at her face and then – as Merrily stood up – kicked her chair back, dropping her hands.

'She took him off.'

'Mam!' Andy knelt by the side of the chair, steadying it. 'You mustn't—'

'She pushed him off, Andrew.'

63

'No,' Mumford said. 'Now, that didn't happen. Did it?'

'Pushed him off,' his mam said. 'He told me.'

'What do you mean?' Mumford staring up into his mother's swirling face. 'What are you saying?'

Outside, the sun had gone in and there was a cold breeze. Merrily stared across the car park at the Tesco store. Its roof line had a roller-coaster curve, and she saw how this had been formed to follow the line of the hills beyond the town.

Some town – even Tesco's having to sing in harmony.

She felt inadequate. Something wasn't making sense. Or it was making the wrong kind of sense. There was an acrid air of betrayal around the house where the Mumfords lived, in the middle of a brick terrace, isolated now on the edge of one of the new access roads serving Tesco's and its car park. When they came out, Nigel Saltash had spotted Andy's dad walking back across the car park with a Tesco's carrier bag, a wiry old man in a fishing hat.

'Think I'll have a word, if that's all right.'

Mumford nodding glumly, sitting on the brick front wall of his parents' home, looking out across what seemed to be as close as Ludlow got to messy. The train station, small and discreet, sat on higher ground opposite the supermarket. Lower down was an old feed-mill, beautifully preserved, turned into apartments or something. Then tiers of Georgian and medieval roofs and chimney stacks and, above everything, the high tower of St Laurence's, like a column of sepia smoke.

'The doc says she needs assessment,' Mumford said. 'Should have had assessment some while back. See the way he looked at me?'

'It's how he looks at everybody,' Merrily said. 'He's a psychiatrist.'

Her hands were clasped across her stomach, damming the cold river of doubt that awoke her sometimes in the night – the seeping fear that most of what she did amounted to no more than a ludicrously antiquated distraction from reality.

'Checking out the old feller now, see,' Mumford said. 'Next thing, he'll have the bloody social services in. This is—' His hands gripping the bricks on either side. 'She's got worse, much worse, since the boy died.'

'A dreadful shock can do it. Reaction can be delayed. It doesn't necessarily mean she's on the slippery slope.'

'At her age,' Mumford said, 'what else kind of slope is there?'

Merrily paced a semicircle. She saw Saltash, just out of ear-shot. His head was on one side, and he was pinching his chin and nodding, flashing his mirthless smile as Mumford's dad talked, his carrier bag at his feet. She was remembering Huw Owen's primary rule: never walk away from a house of distur-bance without leaving a prayer behind.

Had she left without a prayer because she was afraid it might have inflamed the situation? Or because Nigel Saltash was there?

'Just because I'm working with a psychiatrist doesn't mean other possible interpretations go out of the window.' She bit her lip, uncertain. Hoping she wasn't just fighting her corner for the sake of it. 'What do you think she meant about a woman pushing him off the castle?'

Mumford shook his head. 'She never said that before.'

'Does it make any sense?'

'There was a witness – bloke lives over the river. Steve Britton showed me the statement. Bloke saw him fall. Nothing about anybody else. I… Where's she get this stuff from? Never said nothing like that before. I don't… Christ, I need to check this out, now, don't I? You're right, it's easy enough to say she's losing it.' He sprang up from the wall. 'I dunno… at every stage of your bloody life you become somebody you said you was never gonner be.'

'In what way?'

'Ah… you'd be on an investigation: murder, suicide, missing person, and there'd always be some pain-in-the-arse busybody relative – never the father, always someone a bit removed from it – who'd be trying to tell you your job. Have you looked into this or that aspect, have you talked to so-and-so, why en't you done this? You wanted to strangle them after a bit. But the truth is there aren't enough cops to do half of what needs doing. And so things don't come out the way they should, things gets left, filed, ignored...'

'Be careful, Andy,' Merrily said, for no good reason, knowing she wouldn't be careful in a situation like this.

'Airy-fairy sort of feller, apparently – writes poems and publishes them hisself.'

'Who?'

'The witness. I'll mabbe go see him. Got time now, ennit? Got time to be the busybody pain-in-the-arse uncle. Nobody bothered about the kid when he was alive, except for one ole woman.'

'Andy, I'm hardly the person to be disparaging it, but if she does think she's been given this information by a... by Robbie...'

'Could be something he told her days before, ennit? Before he died. Something that's suddenly clicked. I been agonizing about Robbie's death for three weeks now. Thinking, leave it till after the funeral, wait for the inquest. Now even Mam's on at me to do something. *Why din't you stop her?* Where the hell did she get that from, Mrs Watkins?'

On the edge of the car park, Mumford's dad had picked up his carrier bag and he and Saltash had started back towards the house in the wake of Saltash's all-concealing smile.

'Andy.' Merrily beckoned Mumford into his parents' tiny front garden. 'I think we should try and deal with this... Go back in. But not with him. Think of something.'

7

I'll Be Waiting

THERE WAS ANOTHER clear reason why the implications of retirement were terrifying Andy Mumford.

His dad.

Reg Mumford was taller than his son and held himself stiff-backed and upright, but it was hard to believe now that he'd ever been a policeman. Still wearing his fishing hat, he was standing with his hands on the shoulders of his wife's chair, as if it was a wheelchair. Merrily's feeling was that this was because he didn't want to look at her.

'I reckon they've started watering the beer again, Andrew.'

'You said.'

'Have you found that?'

'No, Dad.'

'Always start doing it this time of year when the tourists come.'

'I don't think so.'

'Prices goes up, too. Don't seem two minutes since it was one and six a pint.'

'Before my time, Dad.'

'Hee, hee!' Reg Mumford pointed at Andy, who was standing uncomfortably up against the sideboard near the picture that was turned to the wall. 'You en't gonner be saying that for long. Now you're retired, see, time's gonner speed up, time's gonner flash by, you mark my words, boy.'

'Mrs Watkins would like to talk to you again,' Mumford said.

'I'd be delighted to talk to this young lady, Andrew. Shall we go out for a drink, the three of us?'

'She wants to talk to Mam, Dad.'

'Won't get no sense out of her,' Reg said. 'I can tell you that much.'

Merrily, still standing by the door, glanced at Andy Mumford, watched his lips retract, a sign of extreme frustration. They were getting nowhere here. Nigel Saltash had suggested lunch in one of the splendid new restaurants which, he said, now made visits to Ludlow such an unexpected pleasure. At least she'd got out of that, saying that she had a sermon to write, and then Mumford telling Saltash he had to pick his wife up in Dilwyn, not far from Ledwardine, so he could give the vicar a lift back.

She came over from the door and knelt on the rug in front of Mrs Mumford's chair. Mrs Mumford contemplated her for a while and then began to nod, light graduating into her eyes as if the action of nodding was powering a small dynamo.

'Now then. Now. I know who you are. I was a bit confused, the way that man kept smiling at me, but I know who you are now, my dear.'

Merrily smiled back. Somehow she didn't think Mrs Mumford was going to get this right.

'You were at the funeral, weren't you?'

'Erm…'

'You're the teacher. Yes. Robbie's teacher. You was his favourite, you're…' Mrs Mumford started to prise herself up. 'You're his… history teacher!'

'Well, I—'

''Course you are.' Reg Mumford was leaning over the chair from behind and pointing a forefinger at his own head, making screwing motions. 'And we're very glad to see you, aren't we, Phyllis?'

'He loved history,' Mrs Mumford said.

'Yes,' Merrily said. 'Yes, he did.'

'Much bloody good it did him.' Reg snorted. 'Should've been out playing football. If he'd played football like a normal boy he'd still be alive. I've always said that.'

'Dad, for Christ—'

'Andrew, we gotter face facts. We're all terrible sorry 'bout what happened, but it en't no use blamin' ourselves for ever and a day, is it? Boy was a bloody dreamer, head in the clouds, no gettin' round it.'

'All right, Dad,' Mumford said, desperate. 'We'll go to the pub, you and me, eh? Half an hour, Mrs Watkins, will that be all right?'

Merrily nodded, grateful.

'Now, I know I had something to show you,' Mrs Mumford said. 'Where did I put it?'

Merrily had made tea for them both. The kitchen wasn't as clean as it might have been; she'd wondered if there was a home help. Mrs Mumford didn't seem to be disabled, but she was very overweight.

'Look in that top drawer, would you?' She seemed to be accepting Merrily, now they were on their own, but not as a priest; she wouldn't be ready for that. 'No, no, not that one... the long one... that's it.'

'This?' Merrily opened the drawer and found a hard-backed sketch pad inside.

'There it is. Will you bring it over?'

'Phyllis... why's this picture turned to the wall?'

'Eh?'

'The picture.' Merrily touched it.

'No! You leave that alone!'

'OK.' She drew back, took the sketch pad to Mrs Mumford who put it flat on her knees. Merrily pulled up a dining chair. An envelope fell out of the sketch pad and she caught it and put it on the chair arm.

'Don't know what that is,' Mrs Mumford said. 'Now, look at these. He spent hours on these. You've got to be careful not to

69

touch them or it'll all come off. He had a spray, he did, but it still comes off.'

They were charcoal sketches. The first one was clearly of St Laurence's Church, but its size was exaggerated so that the townhouses seemed like dog kennels. The second had been drawn from directly below, so that the tower resembled a rocket about to blast off. The perspective looked, to Merrily, to be spot on. There was light and shade and he'd smudged the charcoal to produce mist effects.

'He was very talented, Phyllis.'

'Sit there for hours, he would, drawing pictures of the church and the black and white houses. The others... we never sees them, they never comes to see their ole gran. Only Robbie.'

'He loved being here with you, didn't he? What's this one? Is that what they call the Buttercross? With the little clock tower on top.'

'Town council meets there. That one's the Feathers Hotel.'

Mrs Mumford was much calmer now, leafing through the drawings, some identified underneath: Castle Lodge, The Reader's House, the Old College.

'Did he sit outside with his sketch pad?'

'Too shy. He went out, see, and he looked at the old houses for a long time and he'd walk all round them and then he'd come back and he... you know... what do you call it?'

'Drew them from memory?'

'That's it.'

Either Robbie had had a photographic memory or he'd really studied these buildings, come to know them intimately. Whichever, it was remarkable. Merrily said this to Phyllis, and Phyllis began to cry silently, the tears just coming, her cheeks swollen and shiny like the pouches that fed hospital drips, and Merrily held her hand, and Phyllis said, 'He's dead,' looking up at her, as if pleading for a contradiction.

'You'll see him again, Phyllis.'

'No.' Phyllis's fingers tightening in a spasm, flooded eyes gazing past Merrily now, at the picture turned to the wall.

The atmosphere in the room seemed brown and felt dense, as if the air was flecked with clouds of midges. The sketch pad slid to the carpet.

'Phyllis, will you say a prayer with me?'

'The only one of 'em ever come to see his ole gran,' Phyllis said.

Did she mean still?

'Can I say a prayer?'

'When's the Bishop coming?'

'I'll make sure he comes,' Merrily whispered. 'I'll bring him. I promise.'

'Can't see the Bishop like this.' Phyllis pulled her hand away. 'State of me.'

'You're upset, and you've got every reason to be.'

'Going to the bathroom.'

'OK.' Merrily helped her up. Phyllis had a bandage on one leg, rumpled, and it wasn't clean. 'Will you be all right? Does that dressing need…?'

'I'm all right. That woman will come… my… Gail, is it?'

'Andy's wife.'

'She's a nurse.'

Her daughter-in-law of… thirty years, was it? Merrily held open the door that led to the hall. 'Have you got a down-stairs…?'

'I'm all right, girl.'

Merrily left the door open, went to pick up the sketch pad. It had fallen open at a drawing of what looked like a high stone wall with a jagged white hole in it the shape of a figure, like when a cartoon character crashed through brick-work. She picked up the pad, took it back to the open drawer, listening for Mrs Mumford's movements down the hall.

Problems here, and nobody would challenge Saltash's assessment.

When she was putting the pad away, light from the front window showed how she'd misinterpreted the drawing. It wasn't a hole in the wall, it was a white figure in the foreground, a vaguely female figure with the charcoal smudged around it to suggest a glow, a halo. It was two-dimensional, without contours, featureless.

It seemed to be the only figure in any of Robbie's drawings.

Merrily closed the sketch pad, put it away in the drawer, went back to plump up the cushions on Mrs Mumford's chair and spotted the white envelope that had fallen from the sketch pad.

It seemed legitimate to open it.

Inside the envelope was a picture postcard, an atmospheric filter photo of Ludlow Castle in a pink and frosty dawn light, the message written in black fibre-tip across the full width of the card.

Dear Marion,

I am in Ludlow again as I told you and it's brilliant here even on my own altho when I am walking through the castle I feel you are there with me and then I feel really happy.

Sometimes I pretend you are walking next to me and we are holding hands and it's brilliant!!!! Everything is all right again, and I never want to leave cos this is our place.

I was so miserable I didn't think I could stand it till the end of term. Its worse than ever there. I hate them, they are stupid and ignorant and they are trying to wreck my whole life. The nearer it gets to the end of the holidays the sadder I feel and don't want to go back there and I wish I could stay here with you for ever.

Please come like you promised you would.

Please, please, please come.

I'll be waiting.

On the way back, in Mumford's car, coming down from Leominster towards the Ledwardine turning, Merrily said, 'I did a brief house blessing, no fuss, a prayer for Robbie to be at rest, and the Lord's Prayer.'

'She even realize what you were doing?'

'She's not that far gone, Andy. Although I don't think she

quite got the point that I was a priest. Hard to say. Erm… look, I'm going to talk to the Bishop, OK? I mean, she asked for him, right?'

'All that was…' Mumford looked embarrassed. 'They both knew him quite well, the Bishop, Mr Dunmore, back when they had the paper shop. Hardly ever went to church, mind, certainly not the ole man, but it didn't seem to bother him. But, hell, he's Bishop of Hereford now. We can't just get the Bishop of Hereford to an old woman who—'

'What… like, if it was the dowager Lady Mumford it wouldn't be a problem? Of course we can get him. You got me – I mean you were concerned enough to think it might be something we could help with.'

'Wish I'd never bothered. The ole man, he don't give a toss.'

'He's not making her feel any better, is he? Do you think he even notices?'

'Mrs Watkins, the fact is he's been treating her like she's daft for half a century.'

A stray spatter of rain landed on the windscreen. Merrily took a breath.

'Well, I'm not sure she is.'

'What's that mean?' He almost turned at the wheel, but the old Mumford set in and he kept on looking at the road.

'It's a feeling. Based on this and that. Who's Marion?'

'Who?'

'Did Robbie have a girlfriend?'

'Too shy.'

'That's what your mother said. But there was an unfinished message on a postcard. In an envelope in Robbie's sketch pad. Begging someone called Marion to meet him at the castle. He said it was their special place. He said he was imagining them holding hands.'

'Written by Robbie?'

'He hadn't signed it yet, but the handwriting matched the titles he'd put on some of the drawings. Also, was he having a bad time at home?'

'Not according to his mother, but that don't mean a thing. If I had a home like his, I'd've been having a bad time.'

'Perhaps you should read the card,' Merrily said. 'I put it back in the sketch pad, next to a rather strange drawing.'

'Strange how?'

'Difficult to explain.'

Cole Hill came up in the windscreen, and the church steeple, and rain came on for real. Two o'clock in the afternoon, and it felt like dusk.

'Marion,' Mumford said. 'Don't mean a thing. You ask the ole girl?'

'I didn't mention it. She was already upset, so I just did the prayers.'

'She seemed calmer.'

'Final point,' Merrily said. 'The mirror turned to the wall.'

'Couldn't fail to notice that, could you?'

'I thought it was a picture, so I had a quick look while she was in the loo – thinking maybe it was a picture of the castle or something.'

'Mirror.' Mumford sighed. 'Dad wouldn't let her take it down. Nothing to straighten his tie in.'

'I'm not happy with this, Andy.'

'No,' Mumford said.

Sermons: every week another one hanging around your neck like a penance, supporting the traditional assumption, from the days when the priest was the only person in the village who could read, that you could stand up there in the pulpit having universal truths channelled through you, when all you really had were questions.

An hour after Merrily got back to the vicarage, the computer in the scullery was still switched off, Ethel the cat curled up in the tray next to it. On the sermon pad she'd scrawled a number of questions, including: old people – why have we stopped listening to them?

Maybe, one day, something unexpectedly profound would

get pushed between the lines, a surprise parcel in the spiritual letter box. One day.

The phone rang.

'Merrily, this is Siân. Just a very quick call. Nigel and I had lunch – apparently, you were late with your sermon.'

'Well, I always like to leave it till the last minute. Keeps it fresh, like... like a salad.'

God, why does this woman always make me talk bollocks?

'Anyway, Nigel was impressed with your handling of a rather difficult situation.'

Huh?

'Inevitably, when people we've known for years, like ex-Sergeant Mumford, are involved, we feel we have to go through the motions, don't we? But I do think this case underlines the usefulness of having someone like Nigel who can confirm our own suspicions with some authority.'

'Suspicions?'

'He tells me he's already given ex-Sergeant Mumford his own initial assessment, along with suggestions on how it should be followed up with his mother's GP as early as possible next week. He's also going to write up a short report for Sophie to keep on our database. And I think that concludes our involvement.'

'That's what you think, is it?'

'Except, of course, as a discussion point amongst ourselves. I've given this a lot of thought, and I have to say there's a danger that, by our very existence, we may, ahm, sometimes be actively encouraging people to inflate their feelings of paranoia or persecution, or their reactions to sudden and shocking bereavement, into something altogether more fanciful.'

By our very existence?

'You're suggesting we shouldn't exist?'

Siân laughed. 'Essentially, I'm merely saying that we – the Deliverance Ministry – if we are to lose the unsavoury aura of medievalism, should not be seen to bolster people's protective fantasies. Encouraging them to deny personal responsibility by projecting it into something separate and amorphous over which they have no control. I'll put this on the agenda for our next meeting, shall I?'

'Erm…'

'But thank you, all the same, for going to Ludlow with Nigel – although I gather he did the driving.'

'Evidently.' Merrily felt rage clogging her chest. 'Siân, are we becoming a fu— focus group?

'That's becoming a derogatory term, I think.'

'Because focus groups appear to be designed to obliterate the individual intuition by which something as inexact as Deliverance often stands or falls.'

'One viewpoint, certainly,' Siân said. 'We could discuss that issue, also.'

Afterwards, Merrily sat watching the wind in the apple trees.

She folded up the pad and rang the Bishop at the palace behind Hereford Cathedral. Answering machine. She left a message asking what he was doing tonight, anticipating his groans, but this was important, even if she wasn't sure exactly why. Intuition, maybe.

She rang Andy Mumford on his mobile.

'Hold on one minute,' Mumford said, and she heard him apologizing to someone else, and then he came back with a different acoustic – outside. 'I was in with Mr Osman. The witness. Feller who saw Robbie fall?'

'You went back to Ludlow?'

'En't far.'

'Oh God, what are we doing, Andy?'

'Think I've found a woman,' Mumford said. 'Mabbe two.'

8

Imbalance

'HARD TO CREDIT,' the Bishop said. 'My God, how it's changed.'

The street had narrowed, closing around the crawling Volvo. Merrily couldn't see how the town centre could have changed much at all in about five centuries.

She had her window wound down. The dusk was dropping over Ludlow like muslin on antique trinkets, the cooling air singed with woodsmoke. The medieval timbered buildings on either side seemed to be reaching for each other, gables bent towards a creaking kiss under the dusty copper sky.

'Not the buildings,' the Bishop said. 'Most of this town's in aspic. Lay a finger on a brick and English Heritage will crucify you.'

'With antique nails?'

'Goes without saying. No, I meant the people. Even when I was living here, on a Saturday night you'd have the pub trade and not much else. Now look at them – listen to their accents. TV actors live here now, you know – and news-readers, politicians. And what are they all doing? Where are they all going? They're going to dinner. Now call me a puritan…'

'Inappropriate. You haven't got the waistline for it.'

'You're very frivolous tonight, Merrily.'

'Actually, I'm nervous,' she said, 'and I'm not sure why.'

The plan had changed. Andy Mumford wanted them to meet up at the spot where the man had seen Robbie Walsh fall. There were some things that Mumford thought Merrily should know before she took the Bishop to see his mother.

The Volvo was stuck in an unexpected queue of vehicles on the bottleneck corner near the Buttercross. She tapped the accelerator as the engine began to falter, recalling reading somewhere that Ludlow now had more Michelin stars than any other town its size in the country.

'What exactly started this invasion of restaurants, Bernie?'

'I think they had a food festival, which was a huge success. Perhaps someone realized there was something irresistible about expensive meals served in crooked oak-framed rooms with sloping floors. I don't really know why it took off. All I know is that it's virtually destroyed my chances of ever moving back one day. Nowadays, if you're going to even look in an estate agent's window in Ludlow, it's advisable to swallow a Valium first.'

Bernie Dunmore was probably the first Suffragan Bishop of Ludlow ever to be given Hereford – safe pair of podgy hands after a difficult period. All the same, he was often heard to say he wished they'd left him alone; seemed to have personal history invested here.

'Which is how we arrive at a possibly dangerous imbalance,' he said. 'It's always been a friendly town, but there'll be resentment, inevitably, from people who were born here and have been thoroughly priced out. Even the likes of me – I wasn't born here, but there's nowhere quite like it. Once you've been here, you never want to leave.'

'You do the Lottery, Bernie?'

'Is that a sin, do you think, in my position?'

'Only if you pray for a result.'

The traffic broke and they emerged into the market square, turned sandy by the last of the sunset. There were shops either side of the square, and a wider street sloped down to the left: warped and tangled medieval timbers giving way to graceful Georgian terraces with their soft lights, and the wooded hills behind.

Serene, timeless, secure in itself. All of that.

The Bishop shaded his eyes against a sudden sunset flare before they drove back into shadows.

'Straight on, Merrily. And then, just as you think you can't go any further, follow the wall to the left.'

The wall. Directly ahead, across the square, flat as a film-set in the muddy dusk, was the reason, maybe, this town had survived to become so cool and comfortable in the twenty-first century.

By day, as Merrily remembered, the castle was more obviously ruined: sunny sandstone, like a big play area. Now, in fading light, it was seizing power again, dragging its history around it like a heavy military cloak. It was a royal history.

'Didn't Catherine of Aragon live here for a while?'

'With the short-lived Prince Arthur,' Bernie said. 'And then she married his brother, who became Henry VIII, and the rest is… Oh, and the two ill-fated sons of Edward IV, they were here. The Princes in the Tower. Here in happier times – presumably. People tend to be happier here.'

She headed left, where he'd told her, along the walls. Ludlow Castle: lost and won, besieged and battered, but still hugging this craggy site, as if to stop the town crumbling into the river below.

'I suppose hundreds of people must have died here.'

'It's just that most of us thought the deaths were over,' the Bishop said.

Steeply down through Dinham, another ancient piece of town with a small medieval chapel dedicated to the martyred St Thomas of Canterbury, and across the bridge over the River Teme, with the castle behind them – from this side, as much of a fortress as it had ever been. She supposed that the highest tower was the keep, from which Robbie Walsh had fallen.

'I suppose I ought to have come to the funeral,' the Bishop said. 'But it was David's show and, with the TV cameras and everything, I knew there'd be scores of people there. Anyway, I didn't think the Mumfords would remember me. I just bought my papers there.' He sighed. 'Suppose that's why I felt obliged to come with you tonight, even though I'm not entirely sure what this is about or why she'd want to talk to me, especially.'

'She liked you because you didn't have much to say about God.'

Bernie grunted. 'Limited opportunity to bring the Almighty into a transaction involving a packet of Polos and the *Shropshire Star*.'

She smiled, guessing he'd used the Mumfords' shop as an information bureau, picking up on local gossip. He could look jovial and vague, but Bernie didn't miss much. When he'd asked her how she was getting on with the Deliverance panel, she'd been glad it had been too dark for him to see her eyes while she was murmuring that this was something they perhaps ought to discuss. When there was more time. Like several hours.

'Phyllis and Reg must have been well into their seventies when I knew them,' the Bishop said. 'I remember when they sold the shop we sent them a good-luck card.'

'You ever see the boy?'

'I've been trying to remember. I don't think so. But he didn't live here all his life, did he?'

'Only the best bits, apparently.'

Across the river, the land gave in to ranks of dark conifers and the lane took them uphill. Cottages and a hotel had been flung into the hillside, lights coming on in them now. The road kept on climbing, and they did almost a U-turn and emerged, unexpectedly, onto a natural parapet.

Merrily slowed. 'Gosh.'

'Never been to Whitcliffe before, Merrily?'

'It's... incredible.' She stopped the car at the side of the lane.

It was like arriving in the circle at a theatre, and the whole of Ludlow was the set... the best, most focused, most enclosed view of a whole town she'd ever seen – this fairyland of castle and ancient streets, like a richly painted wheel around the spindle of the church tower, haloed by the molten glow of evening.

Another car was parked a few yards away, two men getting out of it, one of them Mumford. The other man was taller and wore a big hat. Merrily eased the Volvo up behind them.

'This chap happy to talk to us, Merrily?'

'I think Andy kind of used you to square it with him – if the Bishop's involved, it must be kosher. As it were.'

Merrily zipped up her fleece over the dog collar. It was cold now, for the end of April. Cold enough for frost. Mumford and the big-hat guy came over. Mumford wore a dark, heavy jacket.

'Mrs Watkins, Bishop – this is Mr Osman.'

'Gerald.' The guy shook the Bishop's hand and then Merrily's. He was wearing a Barbour, and his wide-brimmed hat was waxed, too. An incomer, then. Pinched face, prominent teeth.

'Mr Osman's a writer,' Mumford said.

'Well... illustrator, mainly, and book designer. I produce local watercolours, with accompanying verse. A new career, in retirement, and a chance to immerse oneself in the place. And calendars. I also produce calendars. Gerald Osman.'

'I think someone sent us one at Christmas, actually,' the Bishop said. 'Watercolours, yes. Keep it in my office.'

'Do you really? You must come up to the house for a glass of wine afterwards. We're at the bottom of the hill, this side of the river. My wife used to think it was so lovely having a house with such a wonderful view of the castle, but not so sure any more. Rather wishes it would all go away.'

'Yes,' Mumford said. 'Perhaps you could show us, sir, where you were when you saw the... my nephew fall.'

'Well, as I told you, it's just... just here, actually. Quite a remarkable view of the castle, as you see. And it was earlier in the evening, therefore so much clearer.'

The sky was darkening fast now, a sharp shaft of burnt orange over the keep, getting duller, like a spearhead cooling after the forge.

'I've painted it many times, at different times of day and night,' Mr Osman said. 'Often from this actual spot – so I do know this angle pretty well. As you see, it can look rather sinister in the last of the light, and in the rain it often has a faintly dolorous air. But in the early evening, on a fine day, it's mellow – like the crust of a mature Cheddar. Everything very clear: every ridge, every fissure.'

'If there'd been two people up there, do you think you'd have known?' Mumford said.

'Well, it's rather further away than it looks from here, so human figures are very small, and I didn't manage to focus my binoculars until I saw him fall – couldn't believe it, obviously. Terrible shock.'

'But you've spent a lot of time in the castle,' Mumford said. 'You've been up that tower.'

'Of course. I've been everywhere, making sketches – which is why I recognized your nephew. I mean from the photographs on the TV, not when he was... falling... The moment the face came up on the screen I said to my wife, Good Lord, I've seen that boy several times. I've even talked to him.'

'In the castle?'

'When it was quiet, I'd sit in the castle grounds, make some watercolour sketches. I'm sure they come out just as well when I do them at home, from photographs, but I always felt I was honouring a tradition – all the distinguished artists who painted Ludlow Castle. Turner, for heaven's sake! Not one of his best, I grant you.'

'And the boy...'

'Would come and watch me. From a distance at first. Normally, I'm quite wary of children, especially teenagers, with some of the malevolent little tykes around nowadays. But this boy was genuinely interested. Eventually telling me he did some drawings himself. And his extensive knowledge of the castle was apparent from the start – knew the names of all the towers, their history, the various stages of development. I was impressed.'

'Knew his way around,' Merrily said.

'Absolutely. Rather a pleasant boy. Shy at first – I find shyness something of a virtue these days.'

'And the woman,' Mumford said heavily. 'You were telling me about the woman.'

'Ah. Yes. Mrs… Pepper? Lives in that rather splendid old farmhouse down from the bottom of The Linney.' Mr Osman pointed somewhere to the left of the castle ruins. 'Well, it's a bit of a fraud, actually, was built up from very little by some professional restorer – who, incidentally, cut down a wonderful old oak tree, allegedly by mistake.'

'And the woman herself…'

'She bought the place earlier this year. She's supposed to have been quite well known at one time – afraid I don't know very much about that kind of music myself. She's… like a number of people living here now, I suppose, somewhat eccentric.'

'And you saw Robbie with her,' Mumford said.

'Oh yes.'

'How many times?'

'Well, twice, certainly. She's quite distinctive, with the varying colours of her hair and the way she dresses.'

'Dresses how?'

'Oh… like out of a Victorian melodrama. Long coats. Swirly cloaks.'

'I see. You ever talk to the boy when he was with her?'

'Never. Some people one instinctively…' Mr Osman cleared his throat. 'But the boy would follow her around, and they'd be pointing things out to one another. If I hadn't known she lived here, I would probably have thought they were tourists, a mother and son.' He looked at Bernie. 'I gather you're a friend of the family, my lord.'

'Just, ah, Bishop… please.' Bernie had dressed down tonight – golfing jacket, corduroy trousers. 'Yes, we're all trying to help them come to terms with what happened.'

'Dreadful thing. I did telephone the police station the next day to tell the sergeant I now realized this was a boy I'd seen in the castle. And about the woman. He didn't seem to think that was very important.'

'Oh?' Mumford's tone didn't alter. 'What did he say, exactly?'

'He just said something to the effect that Robson Walsh was a familiar figure to a great number of people. Boy was clearly obsessively interested in the history of Ludlow and would talk to anybody who seemed to know something about it. Though why that particular woman would be considered a fount of local knowledge—'

'I'm sorry,' Merrily said. 'Did you say she was a musician?'

'Some sort of singer, I gather, at one time. Mrs Pepper. Hasn't lived here two minutes – well, say six months. Admittedly, we've only lived here permanently for about three years ourselves, but it was our holiday home for seventeen years before that, so I think we're permitted to feel a touch proprietorial.'

'And you said she was eccentric...'

'I try not to listen to gossip.'

'You don't happen to know her first name, do you?' Merrily said.

'I don't think I do, no.'

'Couldn't be Marion?'

'Doesn't ring any bells. Well, not in that context.' Mr Osman turned to Mumford. 'You asked me that, didn't you?'

'Do you know anyone called Marion who... frequents the castle?' Merrily asked.

'Well, not...' He laughed. 'As I told Mr Mumford here, not someone I've ever seen.'

'I'm sorry?'

Mr Osman didn't reply. Over the town, the sky was turning a luminous acid green with early moonlight.

'Ah,' the Bishop said. 'I think I understand. You mean Marion de la Bruyère. But that wasn't the keep, was it, Mr Osman?'

'It was the Hanging Tower, Bishop. I wrote some verse about her, for my calendar the year before last. Marion, whose endless death... is poised upon a midnight breath. Not... not awfully good, really.'

'I'm sorry,' Merrily said. 'Three of you seem to know what this is about, but one of us doesn't. Who are we talking about here? What does she do?'

'She haunts,' Bernie Dunmore said. 'Allegedly.'

9

The Bishop's Tale

THE BISHOP SAID he was confused: too much, too fast.

'Why did you want to know if Osman had seen anyone else on the tower? I mean, surely you don't imagine that someone actually killed the boy?'

The ornate lamps in the square were white, like magnesium flares.

'We have' – Merrily slotted the Volvo into a corner, down by a darkened delicatessen and well away from the castle – 'a kind of reason to try and eliminate the possibility.'

God, she was thinking, *do we*? She had her window half-down, collecting music and laughter draining from a pub in a nearby street no wider than an alley, the sounds disconnected, somehow, as though on the tape-loop of a separate but parallel time-frame.

Eras overlapping: a disconcerting town.

All she'd told him earlier was about the supposed bereavement visions – that Phyllis Mumford had been in a distressed and confused state, that he was the only priest she seemed likely to open up to. There hadn't seemed much point, at that stage, in going into what Phyllis had said about a woman.

But it was unavoidable now.

'I see.' The Bishop breathed in slowly. 'That's rather a difficult one, isn't it?'

'Only for a Deliverance consultant,' Merrily said. 'The rest of you are free to roll your eyes.'

'If I could just say…' Andy Mumford was a bulky shadow on the back seat. 'The fact that Osman didn't see another person don't mean there wasn't someone up there with the boy. Just they didn't hang around afterwards.'

The Bishop shuffled. 'You do know what you're saying here, Andrew?'

'After many years as a detective, Bishop, I think I got a basic idea.'

'Yes, but what are you actually suggesting – kids fooling about and one falls off the tower? Or what?'

'I was ready to believe,' Mumford said, 'that it was an accident. At first. Mabbe it's what we all wanted at the time – no stigma with an accident. But now' – he leaned forward between the front seats – 'now it's like something's telling me, real strongly, that something en't what it seems. You understand?'

'Story of my life,' Merrily said.

'The night Robbie was found, after my sister ID'd the body, I go back to my mother's house. There's a woman outside. Long cape. Just standing there, looking across at the house. When I tried to talk to her, she walked off.'

'What?'

'What I could see of her face, she'd been weeping.'

'Andy, you never even mentioned this before.'

'Didn't think too much of it afterwards. Spooked me a bit at the time, OK, but I was tired. Lot of neighbours been in and out the house. Lot of people dress funny in Ludlow these days – people going out to dinner.'

'So the chances are your mother knows this woman?'

'She was carrying a lantern – with a candle in it. Well, there's a few shops in town now selling tat like that. You think, some crank, don't you?'

'We'll certainly ask Phyllis about her,' the Bishop said. 'Perhaps clear it up.'

'Meanwhile,' Merrily said. 'Can we…' She squirmed a little. 'Can we talk about Marion now?'

* * *

The 'Dear Marion' postcard. She talked about that.

'When we go over there, I'll ask Mrs Mumford if I can show it to you.'

'Needs to be photocopied, I think, Merrily,' the Bishop said.

'Good idea.'

'Then Andrew has to decide if the police should see it. Meanwhile, let me... let me get this right – this is a postcard, with a photograph of the castle on the front, written by Robbie Walsh to someone he actually addresses as... as Marion.'

'Someone he imagines he's walking with in the castle grounds, holding hands. And there's a drawing of what appears to be a spectral female figure. Pleading with her to come to him. "I'll be waiting," he says.'

'I see.' Bernie Dunmore was silent for a moment. He seemed agitated. 'What are your conclusions about that?'

'The psychological one first?'

'Please.'

'Shy, solitary kid, fascinated by medieval history, besotted with Ludlow...'

'You're thinking fantasy-girlfriend,' the Bishop said.

'I don't know. Is she fantasy-girlfriend material?'

He sighed. 'All right... look... I do, as it happens, know something about this story. Goes back to the twelfth century. Or, in my case, about thirty-five years, to when I was a young curate. Here, as it happens.'

'I didn't know you were a curate in Ludlow.'

'Not something I've ever emphasized on my CV. A bishop is expected to have been around. Unfortunately, once I'd lived here I didn't want to end up anywhere else. Moved on, drifted quietly back. I've been, ah, fortunate.'

'You jammy sod, Bernie.'

'Yes, that's another way of putting it. So... I happened to be a young curate at St Laurence's when a chap called Peter Underwood – doyen of British ghost-hunters, though I didn't know it at the time – was researching a book called, if I remember rightly, *A Gazetteer of British Ghosts*. It has quite an extensive entry on Ludlow – most of which, as it happens, is taken up by the story of Marion de la Bruyère. Marion of the Heath.'

She was usually described as 'a lady of the castle', Bernie said.

Which could have meant anything – possibly she was a lady-in-waiting, if there were such creatures in the reigns of King Stephen and his successor, Henry II.

Turbulent times. Less than a century after the Norman conquest, and the ownership of the new and highly strategic Ludlow Castle was in dispute. Stephen had put the fortress in the charge of a Breton knight, Joce de Dinan – arguably the source of the name Dinham, for the community under the castle's perimeter wall, to the south-west. But the powerful baronial de Lacy family thought it should be theirs, and it was the conflict between Joce and the de Lacys that led to a young knight called Arnold de Lisle, a de Lacy man, being taken prisoner.

'While not exactly established history, it's certainly well-documented in a medieval epic known as *The Romance of Fulk FitzWarrin*,' Bernie said. 'Seems that Marion de la Bruyère – described by one source as "a guileless damsel" – had fallen in love with the prisoner, Arnold, and helped him escape from the castle either down a rope or knotted sheets.'

And then – her fatal mistake – Marion had arranged to let Arnold back into the castle, on a later occasion, by means of a rope ladder.

'While the two of them are otherwise engaged in Marion's bedchamber, a large number of armed men from the de Lacy camp come swarming up the ladder to capture the castle. Now we know that happened – de Lacy did get the castle. Appears to have slaughtered a lot of people and set fire to property in the streets of Ludlow that night to make it clear that he was now running the show. In fact, some of the killing and the burning would have happened exactly where we're parked now.'

'Thanks for that, Bernie.'

'Anyway, when she finds out what's happening, Marion – full of remorse and fury at his betrayal – snatches Arnold's sword and kills him with it. And then – not seeing, presumably, much of a future for herself – she throws herself from a high window in the Hanging Tower.'

Merrily said, 'But that—'

'No, it's not where Robbie fell. It's a tower at the rear of the castle, facing the river. And the present Hanging Tower doesn't seem to have been built until two centuries after these alleged events took place.'

'But Marion…?'

'Yes. Marion. There's certainly quite an extensive section in Underwood's book relating to her activities, post-mortem. It, ah, it was said that people could hear her final screams for many years, but the more recent stories relate to a sort of heavy breathing – supposedly as she psyched herself up either to dispatch Arnold or herself. Underwood told me he'd talked to a local man who'd heard it several times and researched it pretty thoroughly, disproving to his own satisfaction the theory that the noise was caused by a nest of young owls. Not possible in January, apparently.'

'Nothing seen?' Merrily said.

'Ah… there was talk of a… a white lady. Nothing on record.'

'But it seems likely that Robbie Walsh would have heard the stories.'

'Best-known ghost story in Ludlow, Merrily. And there's no shortage of competition in this town. There's a chap now who conducts ghost-walks at least twice a week in the season. Marion, I'd guess, would be his star attraction.'

'From what little I know about medieval history,' Merrily said, 'an unattached female, in those days, wouldn't be far into her teens.'

Bernie coughed. 'If at all.'

'Robbie would have known that. He wandered the town alone. He might well have fantasized a relationship – maybe, at that age, no more than a rather romantic friendship – with a girl from the past, rather than a supernatural entity. The guileless damsel. The kind you rarely encounter today.'

Merrily thought about Jane, who wouldn't have fitted the description 'guileless' since turning eight.

'And written to her?' Bernie said.

'Gives a kind of substance to the fantasy. Makes her seem more real to him.'

'Pleading with her to meet him? Saying he'll be waiting?'

Merrily shrugged.

'If that's your psychological explanation,' the Bishop said, 'I'm not sure I want to hear the other one.'

'I haven't fully worked out the other one yet.'

They were silent for a few moments. A bunch of kids were whooping and kicking a lager can in the square. Merrily wound her window up.

'Andy, isn't it likely, given what Bernie says, that your mother would have heard the story of Marion?'

Mumford grunted. 'I hadn't. But then I en't from yere.'

'Could she be subconsciously associating it with Robbie's death, is what I'm wondering. She's seen his drawing. She's probably read the letter, even if she's forgotten about it. And in her confused state of mind…'

Out on the square, one of the boys who'd been kicking the can, shouted out, for no obvious reason, 'Fuckin' shiiiiite!' Merrily thought of the cries – somewhere on the tape-loop – of slaughtered citizens, hacked to death by de Lacy's men, while the broken body of Marion de la Bruyère still lay at the foot of the tower.

'And also, Andy, given that the card suggests a depth of unhappiness at home, doesn't this open up another possibility?'

'You're saying suicide.'

'In which case' – Merrily looked over her shoulder at the shadowy Mumford – 'would you really want to take it any further?'

'Wrong tower,' Mumford said stubbornly. 'You heard what Osman said: boy knew that castle like the back of his hand. He wants to kill himself the way this girl did, why would he jump off the wrong tower?'

'I don't know.'

'Tell you what,' Mumford said. 'If you wanner stick with this ghost stuff, mabbe I'll check out the real woman. The living woman. The one he was seen with. Mother and son.'

'Mrs Pepper.'

'If her name turns out to be Marion, what we gonner be looking at then?'

'Look, it's getting late,' the Bishop said. 'Perhaps we should go and do what we came for – see how we can comfort your mother. Perhaps hear what Phyllis has to say. And then… little prayer-circle, do you think, Merrily? Proper blessing of the house? How's your father, Andrew?'

'He's all right.'

'Probably showing less than he's feeling if he's the Reg I remember, but I'll persuade him to join us. All right, Andrew, how about you drive down and prepare the ground? Merrily and I should perhaps… discuss tactics.'

'Thank you,' Mumford said. 'Aye, I'll go and talk to them. Thanks.'

He had to put his shoulder to the rear offside door, which jammed most times. When he'd gone, the Bishop turned to Merrily, his arms folded, his legs stretched out into the well.

'So what's all this really about?' he said mildly.

She asked if she could have a cigarette, so they got out and walked down towards the centre of the town. There was a greenish sheen on roofs and a glare in window-glass as a near-full moon came up like stage lighting, sharpening the medieval gables and creaming the appropriately buttery stonework of the Buttercross with its neo-classical portico and its clock tower.

Eras overlapping like double exposures on a film.

'Don't say I didn't warn you,' Bernie Dunmore said. 'I warned you last summer, before that trouble at the hop kiln nearly backfired on you. I said that, when dealing with matters that can never be verified, you needed to cover your back. Had to get some support around you.'

'It just wasn't as easy as you thought. The people I was hoping to get are not… joiners.'

'Yes, well, unfortunately, in the Church of England the joiners are usually the ones trying to further a political agenda. I don't know Siân Callaghan-Clarke very well, and I'm sure the hint of dominatrix I sometimes see in her eyes is pure illusion—'

'Bernie, I never wanted a cosy life.'

'—Whereas Saltash is someone I have had dealings with over the years, and the man has an ego the size of a Hereford bull's balls, to put it bluntly. And, incredibly for a psychiatrist, he doesn't appear to listen. So you have my sympathy there, Merrily. However…'

This was difficult. If Merrily wasn't careful, the Bishop was going to think she'd generated this whole situation to bend his ear on the subject of control-freak Deliverance advisers, brought him out here to get him on her side.

'Bernie, if you're thinking—'

He lifted a hand. 'We do share a secretary. Sophie gets e-mails from Callaghan-Clarke. Endlessly, it seems. Questioning this, questioning that, usually about the way we conduct Deliverance.'

'She hasn't complained to me.'

'Hasn't complained to me, either. Sophie doesn't complain. Just hasn't concealed the computer traffic. I mean, obviously, as soon as interest in using Saltash was expressed from the Dean's office, of all places, I suspected we'd have problems, if only because I knew he'd rather like to repossess your office for general Cathedral admin.'

'I didn't know that.'

'You knew he was hardly a Deliverance, ah, groupie, Merrily.'

She followed him across the narrow medieval street into the wide street that glided gracefully down to the Georgian era and the river.

'How close is the Dean to Saltash?'

'Not sure, Merrily, but I have the feeling he was once chaplain at a mental hospital somewhere. Oh, they're going to try and tie your hands, between them, that's not in doubt. As to Siân – whether it's personal ambition on her part, or she's firing someone else's bullets, I wouldn't know. But remember, whatever they try to make you do, you're still the only officially trained Deliverance minister in this diocese.'

'She's certainly doing her best to discredit the man who trained me.'

'Oh, don't worry about old Huw – been there before, loves it. And you don't have to do what you're told. In fact, resisting the rationalists is probably an important part of your role. Tightrope, obviously, I'm not denying that, but then the whole job's a tight-rope.' He pushed his hands into the pockets of his golfing jacket, watching his plodding feet in the moonlight. 'Of course, you'll never prove Saltash wrong, because to do that you'd virtually have to prove the existence of ghosts, wouldn't you?'

'Hadn't thought of it quite like that,' she lied.

'I...' He stopped under the awning outside the ancient and cavernous De Grey's restaurant. 'There's something I didn't tell you, Merrily.'

'Oh?'

'When the Underwood ghost book was published, I... All right, I was a curate, but I was still a young chap, played rugby, had some mates, and we used to go drinking on a Friday night. Not to excess, in my case, obviously, but we enjoyed ourselves. And I happened to have a copy of the book, and we... I mean, you know what young chaps are like...'

'Do I?'

'We're in the pub one night, half a dozen of us, discussing this business of the heavy breathing in the tower – giving it somewhat salacious overtones, I'm afraid. I said it was all a load of rubbish, probably dreamed up to attract more visitors to the castle. Someone said, how can you say that, all the nonsense you've got to swallow and regurgitate every Sunday? Anyway, the upshot, there was a bet... ten quid.'

'Lot of money back then, I'd guess.'

'Curates were paid even worse in those days, and I was engaged at the time, so, yes, ten pounds... well worth having. There were five of them, and they threw in a couple of quid each. One of them, you see, knew a way into the castle at night, over one of the walls, Dinham end, and then... anyway...'

'You didn't...'

'If it had been for a whole night, I definitely wouldn't have, but it was quite a warm evening – warmer than tonight – and we agreed on two hours. I had to swear on the Bible that I wouldn't sneak out. The deal was two hours, absolutely on my own in the Hanging Tower, and if I was still there when they came to get me, around half past midnight, the money was all mine.'

'You astound me, Bernard.'

'Wasn't going to tell you in front of Mumford, that's for sure. Anyway, we all went in together first. I'd never been in the Hanging Tower before. You have to go across the Inner Bailey – there's a wonderful Norman chapel in the middle, dedicated to St Mary Magdalene – and then into a sort of great hall, which is rather eerie because it has these sculpted stone faces on the walls. One of my friends had a torch and he kept lighting up the faces, making woo-woo sort of noises. All pretty juvenile.'

They were walking downhill now, towards the old town gate, where the roadway still passed under an arch with lighted rooms over it.

'The so-called Hanging Tower protrudes from the rear of the castle – must have been two or three storeys high originally, but there's no roof now, so you can just see the windows in recesses, one above the other, and then the sky. Small rooms now – six of us filled the space, but when the others had gone... most unpleasant.'

'Well, *I* wouldn't have done it.'

'It was a boy thing, as they say. Castle's a very different place at night, hadn't realized that – all that nice, mellow, honey stone. But when you're absolutely on your own inside an enormous walled ruin, it's... black. Smells... the thought of rats. And cold as hell in there, a clammy damp in the air. I spent the first hour at the window – least I thought it was an hour, probably ten minutes – looking out at the few visible lights. Night mist coming off the river, and I couldn't see the ground, or the sky, and it felt... I gather it's commonplace if you're on a high building and suffering from vertigo to want to... you know...'

'You wanted to jump?'

They were alone on the street, no cars for a few moments, and Bernie's voice was resonating as though in a small church as they passed under the short tunnel which had once been Broad Gate.

'Probably couldn't squeeze through now, but I could have then. Didn't like it, anyway, so I had to move back into the dark. In the end I found myself hunched up in a corner, in near-total darkness, which was like being entombed, and I... at some point I became aware of an unhappiness. Almost a physical thing, rather like when you feel the beginnings of a sore throat and it's no more than an unpleasant taste. Have you ever tried to pray and you couldn't?'

'Not sure.' Merrily lit another cigarette. 'Been times I'm ashamed of when I just couldn't do it because it seemed worthless... useless. Slippage of faith.'

'No, we've all been there. This was an actual physical inability to pray when I very much wanted to. The way an asthmatic can't find breath. Here I was, a fairly recently ordained minister of the Church, and I... could not pray.'

'That would be scary.'

'Panic. The unthinkable. The feeling that it just didn't work here, that God had been excluded from this place. I remember – it seems laughable now— No, actually, none of that night seems remotely laughable – I remember thinking of the ten quid at stake, and how despicable that had been. How what was happening to me was a direct result of that. That what I'd done – taking that bet – had been almost evil. I... when you asked me earlier tonight if I did the National Lottery, no, I don't. I've avoided anything approximating to a bet ever since.'

Merrily stopped on the wide pavement, under the first street lamp beyond what had been the town boundary, the road sloping to the River Teme at Ludford Bridge.

'What happened?'

'I ran away, of course. Or *stumbled* away would be more accurate. When I realized I was actually cringing into the stones, like a cornered animal, I… threw out a prayer, like a sort of yelp. Just God help me! Just praying that I could move. And I did move. Like the clappers. And you're probably smiling.'

'I'm not, honest, boss.'

'I'll cut it short. There are two ways out of that tower, and I took the wrong one at first and came up against some steps that led nowhere any more, a blank wall, and that was horrifying, as if whichever way I went I'd come up against a wall that hadn't been there when I went in. Imagination, in these situations, becomes so unbelievably powerful. So I scrambled back down and back into the chamber and… well… that's when I saw her. I bloody saw her.'

'What?'

'She was— Look at me…' The Bishop held his hands out under a street light. 'After all these years… still shaking.'

'You saw Marion?'

'Oh, for heaven's sake, I don't know who or what it was, but I remember I did know, with a quite awful certainty, that something was going to happen as soon as I re-entered the chamber. Partly because of the cold – yes, I do know that's a cliché. But it wasn't a normal cold, not a healthy cold – not like rushing wind or crackling frost. It was a negativity, an absence, a hollowness… an area in which warmth couldn't exist. Any more than normal prayer.'

Bernie held the lamp-post, like a drunk, Merrily feeling chilled now. One of those attic moments, when you opened an old chest to expose ancient rotting fabric.

The Bishop's tale. She wondered when he'd last told it to

anyone. And she wondered why, in all the discussions they'd had about the nature of Deliverance, he'd never even hinted at a personal experience.

'She... it was... as I re-entered the chamber, there was a paleness. I can see it now, but I still can't properly describe it – only my own reactions to something that seemed to be made of nothing more than the cold air and the damp unfurling from the stone. I wasn't aware of a face, but I was sensing a horrible smile that was more like an absence of smile. A smile so cold, so bleak, so devoid of hope... only this perpetual, bitter... terminality.'

Merrily brought the cigarette to her mouth. It had gone out. As she fumbled for her lighter, the Bishop stepped away from the lamp-post, rubbing the warm blood back into his hands.

And then, as Merrily's lighter flared, so did bigger lights – flashing white and orange and wild blue, bouncing from pale walls and darkened windows.

10

Leave God Out of It

THE ROAD HAD already been closed below Ludford Bridge, which explained the sparseness of traffic on Broad Street.

Not so sparse, though, at the bottom of the hill, where there had once been mills and the distinctive Horseshoe Weir sent the River Teme rushing over flat rocks – a beauty spot on the edge of town, now a garish confluence of hysterical light: an ambulance, police cars, blue beacons still revolving, inviting an audience like bleak neon.

'Road accident, looks like,' Bernie Dunmore said. 'Funny we didn't hear it happen. Better turn back, I suppose. Last thing they need is—'

'Andy.' In the full-beam headlights of a static vehicle, Merrily could see the stocky figure climbing over the lower wall towards the river. 'Down there, look, by those—'

Two policemen were going after Mumford, close to the shimmering sheet of the river.

'Poor chap can't seem to walk away from it, can he?' the Bishop said.

But Merrily was already running down the hill, the throbbing voice inside her chest keeping time with her pounding feet, going, No... no... no... no...

They were bringing him back over the wall, one pushing him to the other who'd leapt over onto the pavement, Andy shouting,

'Don't you stupid bastards ever listen?'

The cops had an arm each. At the side of the road, a third shone his torch on them.

'Andy? Andy Mumford?'

'Get them off me!'

'It's all right, boys,' the third cop said. 'Who told you?'

'Small town, Steve.' Mumford shaking them off, brushing at his arms where they'd gripped him.

'Did you see…?'

'Didn't get a chance, did I?' In the torchlight Mumford's face was smooth and cold, like washed grey stone. 'These cretins—' He looked up, saw Merrily. 'Mrs Watkins.'

'Andy, what's—?'

'Better go and make sure, hadn't you?' the third cop said.

Merrily found herself following Mumford over the wall, nobody blocking his way now they knew who he was. It was a longer drop the other side than she'd been expecting, and she stumbled, Mumford catching her arm.

'Couple of neighbours waiting for me outside the house, with Dad. One was walking his dog by the river when he seen these boys come out of the pub by the bridge and go wading into the water.'

The policeman called Steve came alongside.

'Can't believe this, Andy.'

Mumford said nothing. They reached another cop and two paramedics in luminous jackets. There was a stretcher, and two wide-beam lamps were sparing them nothing. Merrily looked once and then turned away, fists tightening, watching the moonlit river washing under Ludford Bridge, hearing the hard questions, the terse replies.

'No mistake, Andy?'

'No.' Mumford moving round the body. 'No other injuries?'

'Not that we can see.'

The swab of froth on Phyllis Mumford's mouth had made it look as if she'd swallowed soap. Had made it seem, at first, like she was still alive, blowing bubbles. The bandage on her leg had been hanging loose, like a pennant.

Mumford grunted, hands in his pockets, shoulders hunched.

'Nothing anybody could've done,' Steve said.

'Didn't go off the bridge, then?'

'Be more damaged, wouldn't she, Andy? Looks like she got over that wall, same way we just came in, just started wading out from the bank and then slipped on the rocks. Anybody'd fall over in a minute, in the daytime even. No chance at all at night, see.'

'Not at her age.'

'No. What can any of us say? If those boys had got there five minutes earlier... I'm real sorry, mate.'

'Aye.'

Merrily turned, and Mumford was there. They walked back slowly towards the wall, Mumford clearly coping with it the only way he knew how – like he hadn't retired and this was someone else's mother. Someone else's mother, someone else's nephew, someone else's life.

'Cold water,' he said. 'They always reckon a heart attack gets them first.'

'I'm sure it... must,' she said. 'Andy—'

'A mercy. Under the circumstances.'

'—Why? Why would she come out in the dark, on her own?'

'You tell me.'

'This is just...' Standing there, stupidly shaking her head. 'I should've...'

Didn't know what she should've done. This was altogether beyond comprehension.

'My fault, ennit?' Mumford said. 'Should've noticed the way she was going. Should've had her assessed. Couldn't expect the ole feller to see it, he en't noticed her for years.' His arm came back and he smashed his right fist into his left palm. 'Christ!'

'It's not...' She caught his arm on the rebound. 'It's not your fault.'

'Look, Mrs Watkins, I got a long night...' He turned away.

'Long night ahead of me.'

Sounding like what he was really talking about was the rest of his life.

Someone helped Merrily back over the wall: the Bishop.

'Saw a chap I knew. Merrily, this is beyond all—'

'Aye,' Mumford said, calm again, as if that one slam of the fist had been like a pressure valve.

'Andrew. Look… where's your father?'

'One of the cars, last I seen. With Zoë – policewoman. Dunno which one it is.'

'I'll find it. I'll talk to him.'

'Only I'd leave God out of it, if I were you, Bishop,' Mumford said and turned to Merrily. 'These accidents will happen, won't they? Ole women shouldn't play by the river at night.'

Merrily thought, *Accident?*

As they stepped onto the pavement, several people were trailing past and, as they faded into the lights, she saw that they were wearing old-fashioned evening dress, two women in long black frocks and two men in tailcoats and top hats. She thought of posh restaurants, the new and affluent Ludlow, Phyllis Mumford dying alone, on the edge of all this.

'Need to call the wife.' Mumford had his mobile out. 'Pick up the ole feller, take him back to our place.'

'I could—'

'I'll see to him. You get off home.'

She wanted to scream, For God's sake, you're not a copper now, you're one of us!

'Come over to the car, Andy,' Steve the policeman said. 'We better sit down, sort some things out.'

Merrily was left alone. The party in evening dress had stopped, gazing down to where a knot of police and paramedics were concealing the body. They were not what she'd thought, these decadent revellers. A ruby glistened like a bubble of blood in the cleft of the chin of one of the women and one of the men in top hats wore eye make-up and his hat had ribbons hanging behind, like an old-fashioned undertaker.

'Come on…' A policewoman came over, arms spread wide. 'Don't hang around, please.'

'Is she dead?' one of the girls said, like she was asking about the time of the last bus.

'You can read about it tomorrow. Come on.'

'I won't be here tomorrow.'

'Good,' the policewoman said.

'Was it suicide?'

This was an older, quieter voice. Merrily saw that there was a fifth person in the group, this woman wrapped in a grey cape so long that it was touching the pavement.

The policewoman said, 'Do you have anything to tell us about this incident, madam?'

The woman smiled faintly, with a shake of the head, as the blue beacon light passed over her face, brushing like a strobe effect over an eagle nose and causing a glistening like hoar frost in hair that was like strands of tarnished tinsel. And Merrily recognized her. Partly from Mumford's description, but mainly…

Pale arms outstretched, fingers clawed, sleeves of a black robe slipping back. A copper bangle like a snake…

Merrily froze, hands clasped, catching a long-ago devilish reflection of herself in a mirror: white lipstick and a black velvet hat and mascara caked on like chocolate. Heard her own mother, appalled: *You're not walking out of this house looking like that…*

'No, I thought not,' the policewoman said. 'So would you mind not blocking the footpath, please?'

She's quite distinctive, Mr Osman had said, *with the varying colours of her hair and the way she dresses.*

And then Andy Mumford in the car: *If her name turns out to be Marion, what we gonner be looking at then?*

From what Merrily could remember, her name had never been Marion.

She saw Mumford getting into the back of a police car with his friend Steve, heard the church clock strike almost softly. Ten o'clock and all so very far from well.

She stood in the middle of the road, the dog collar under the zipped-up fleece tight to her throat like a stiff admonishment. Furious at herself for failing to foresee something like this and, to a lesser extent, at Saltash whose flip diagnosis had probably been right, although it could be no more proven now than the existence of ghosts.

11

Nightshades

MERRILY DIDN'T FEEL any better in the morning, Sunday. She awoke with the light and lay watching the red dawn surfing the ceiling, where the oak beams were like beach barriers. Wondering what difference it would make to a suicidal world if she just didn't bother to get up.

Unless anyone specifically asked, she hadn't been in Ludlow last night, and neither had Bernie Dunmore. They'd agreed this as she dropped him, around one a.m., at the Bishop's palace in Hereford.

Bernie had told her about his time with Reg Mumford. He'd taken Reg to the Angel, in Broad Street. 'As a damn bishop, you get out of it,' Bernie said. 'Out of real people. You've forgotten the conclusions you once came to about what this job's about – not preaching, just pure, concentrated listening.'

In the bar, he said, Reg had been remembering his wife as she used to be and a lot of other people Bernie didn't know. Memories dripping into the beer, most of them from a long time ago.

Reg hadn't mentioned his wife's death – as if that was something he wasn't yet ready to process, Bernie said.

As for Robbie, Reg didn't understand how the boy had come to get himself killed, didn't see any use dwelling on it. Kids did daft things, and sometimes they ran out of luck, and that boy... face it, he wasn't entirely normal. Reg never knew how to talk to him, never had since he was little. Phyllis, however...

Reg had been trying to lose himself in daytime telly. Looking up every so often and seeing Phyllis gazing into the mirror, where she'd found a new channel of her own: the Robbie Channel. Robbie still sitting scrunched up over the table, drawing his black and white buildings, hands all black with charcoal – holding up his hands, Phyllis said, and grinning at her through the mirror. Phyllis weeping through her mad world, which had reflections of Robbie everywhere. Sometimes trailing aimlessly around the shops – Reg embarrassed, striding ahead, then looking back and seeing Phyllis staring in some window. Look, there he is again… do you see him? Reg buying her bits of things in the shops – it was only money – but when they got home the packages were never opened.

Would have destroyed Reg, too, if he'd given in to it. But Reg had seen too much death in his time, and he'd lost all patience with her – only so much a man could take. It was Reg who, in a fury, had turned the mirror to the wall before the Bishop came, because he hadn't wanted the Bishop to see Phyllis going insane. Only it hadn't been the Bishop at all, it had been Andy and some strangers and Reg didn't want to meet any more strangers. This bloody smiley feller coming up to him in the street, all chatty, then asking who his doctor was – what right did they have, treating you like a kid?

Merrily got out of bed and knelt under the window, with its view over the village towards wooded Cole Hill, under a shiny salmon sky, and prayed for Reg and whatever remained of Phyllis and Robbie. When she stood up, her eyes were wet, and she found herself thinking, irrationally, of Lol and had this image of herself running down the drive and across the cobbles in her nightdress and banging on the cottage door, screaming, Let me in! for all the village to hear.

At breakfast, Jane said, 'Mum, you look like sh—'

'I know, all right?'

'You turn up for Communion looking like that, they'll all lose their faith.'

'Oh hell, what time is it? And what are you doing up so early?'

'Just curious about why you were out so late. On the other hand' – Jane put a pensive forefinger to her chin – 'if you were to turn up at the altar in your dressing gown, a soupçon déshabillé, it might bring in more blokes, and— You're not in the mood, are you? What's happened?'

'The elderly lady.' Merrily brought her mug of tea and sat down opposite Jane, morning sunlight piercing the top window, over the sink. 'The woman Saltash and I were supposed to be helping? She drowned herself last night in the River Teme.'

Jane blinked. 'Mumford's mother?'

'Must have happened while we were no more than half a mile away, talking to a bloke who saw Robbie Walsh fall. Her lying in the water, us theorizing about some bloody stupid old ghost story and wondering—'

'What old ghost—?'

'Not important. No more important than me going on to the Bishop about Saltash and Callaghan-Clarke and feeling sorry for myself.'

'Oh God, Mum…'

'Deliverance – the fourth emergency service. Have to laugh, don't you, flower?'

'I'm not laughing. Was she, you know… confused?'

'We always assume that, don't we? That's what everybody would have assumed last Christmas if Lol hadn't got to Alice Meek before the cold did. But even if Mumford's mum was on the slide, there might have been a part of her I could have got through to, with perseverance. And I didn't really try.'

'But you did try. You pressured the Bishop into going back with you because he was an old mate of the Mumfords.'

'Putting the responsibility on someone else.' Merrily's head felt congested; she found a tissue in her dressing-gown pocket, blew her nose. 'Should have tried harder, instead of half-thinking, Yeah, Saltash could be right, this is probably more his show than mine. I don't know, maybe I just—'

'Mum, don't keep doing this to yourself. You did what you thought was best at the time. You always do. So just, like, finish your tea, have a wash, brush your hair, get your kit and… off to work.'

Merrily looked at the kid, who was no longer a kid, and dug out a smile from somewhere.

'There you go,' Jane said. 'Why, there could be as many as, like, four people in that church, just gasping for Holy Communion. Get down there and give 'em… wine.'

So she got through it. No big state of eucharistic grace, no all-enveloping peace, but she got through Holy Communion and Morning Worship – doing the sermon about listening to old people, the real meaning of honouring your father and mother. Not very convincing, really, and she was having problems staying focused. When she closed her eyes, she saw Phyllis Mumford's drowned face and heard her wispy, untethered voice: *Now then… I know who you are… I know who you are now, my dear.*

Back in the scullery, she rang Lol, explaining about last night. About the two women who had faded into the picture, one dead, one on the streets of Ludlow in a full-length cape, accompanied by younger people in decadent goth costumes. The shock of recognition.

'Belladonna?' Lol said. 'Are you sure?'

Just after lunch – priests always knew when other priests were most likely to surface on a Sunday – Siân Callaghan-Clarke rang. She'd heard about Phyllis Mumford from Nigel Saltash, who'd heard it on the radio.

'It's terrible, but I'm afraid Nigel wasn't entirely surprised. There's an area psychiatric support team that ought to have been told about Mrs Mumford. But human resources are terribly stretched these days, largely as a result of increasing addiction problems. Awfully sad, though, because Nigel was going to talk to their GP first thing tomorrow.'

'Was he?'

'But thank heavens, Merrily… thank heavens, in a way, that you didn't take it any further.'

'Sorry?'

'From a Deliverance point of view. When you think of the kind of adverse publicity if the media had discovered that you'd performed what they would have seen as some sort of exorcistic rite at this poor woman's house just hours before she died.'

'A home-blessing?'

'It's not what's been done, Merrily—'

'A few prayers?'

'—It's who's done it. You've become fairly widely known now, not least to certain sections of the media, as an exorcist. Certain people would put two and two together and make six.'

'But suppose that – after this exorcistic rite – it hadn't happened. Suppose Mrs Mumford hadn't wandered into the river. Was therefore still alive…'

But then she *had* done it. She'd returned, behind Saltash's back, and done her rudimentary blessing, and Mrs Mumford had still died.

'We could play the "what-if" game for the rest of the day, Merrily,' Siân said, 'but I doubt exorcism has ever been hailed as a cure for senile dementia.'

'So, do you think it's time for me to quit, Siân, before I bring the Church into even more disrepute?'

'Let's not be silly,' Siân said.

Sunday evening, the Bishop rang. Something he thought Merrily should know.

'Old Reg Mumford phoned me today. Encouraging, really, that he was able to do that.'

'How is he?'

'Staying at his son's house, but insisting on going home tomorrow. He… seemed more focused. And resigned. And in his resignation, behind the loss, one could almost sense, I'm afraid, an exhausted kind of relief. Said he knew Phyllis would never have come to terms with what had happened to Robbie, however long she lived.'

Merrily was taking the call on her mobile, alone in the church, preparing for the Quiet Service. She lowered herself to the edge of a pew opposite the west window, where the evening sun made a ruby in the apple held by Eve.

'You mean he'd actually thought she might want to die?'

'Not exactly,' Bernie said. 'She was so convinced the boy was still there, in the town, that Reg said he was half-expecting to hear she'd been knocked down in the traffic after spotting Robbie across the road or something and rushing to him.'

'His... reflection.'

'Reflections. Exactly. Look... ah... Reg said that, in happier times, he and Phyllis often used to walk by the river. And one fine evening last week, she got him to take her back there.'

'Oh no.' Merrily closed her eyes.

'And it was early evening, and the water was fairly still, even so close to the Horseshoe Weir, and she went and stood near the wall, looking down. And of course...'

'Robbie.'

'Looking up at her from the water.'

'Oh God.'

'Reg couldn't take it. He pulled her away. They walked home in silence, nothing to say to one another. The last thing she said to him last night – therefore the last thing she said to him ever – was, "I can't feel him in here any more. You've driven him out."'

'Meaning the mirror – turning it to the wall?'

'Who knows? And then she walked out, and she was standing at the front of the house, and he could hear her talking to one of the neighbours for a while. When he looked for her, she wasn't there.'

'He didn't tell you this last night?'

'I think he had to get it clear in his own mind. Anyway, thought I should tell you, that's all. So that we can draw a line under it, as it were.'

Merrily heard soft footsteps, opened her eyes to the sight of Lol padding into the aisle. Sometimes he'd come to the Quiet Service, though never any of the others. He was wearing his old Roswell-alien sweatshirt. He'd worn this in church before, possibly a signal that he wasn't yet fully integrated.

'You really think a line can be drawn, Bernie?'

'I think we have to. This Marion business... that's always going to be a mystery.'

'Why have you never told me about that before?'

'Didn't seem relevant. And anyway—'

'You mean, not relevant to, like, what I do?'

'Put it this way,' he said, 'you're the only person I've ever told. Including the friends who got to keep their ten quid. And I trust you'll keep it to yourself. Are you in the church, Merrily?'

'You want me to swear on the Bible, over the phone? Sorry. Yes, I'm just rearranging the furniture.'

Lol was pulling movable pews up to the front to set up a rough circle.

'Ah,' the Bishop said. 'Your meditation service. That going all right?'

'We just call it the Quiet Service now. Yeah, going very well, since we managed to cool the rumours of miracle healing. We'll do prayers for specific people sometimes, but strictly no hands-on. I know my level. We get about twenty most weeks.'

Including Jane, occasionally, and now even Lol.

Merrily beckoned him down the aisle and into the vestry, soon to be converted into a gift shop. Its walls had been freshly painted in yellow and some cheap pine shelving had been fitted. A faded Victorian sofa, now looking for a new home, had been pushed against the wall under a window, and Lol sat on that.

'Well, this is nice, but wouldn't it be some kind of sacrilege?'

'I just want to talk, you fool.' Merrily shut the door behind them.

'Sacrilege could have been exciting.' Lol lifted his hands. 'Kidding.'

'I know.'

Couple of years ago, the church organist had openly fantasized about slowly unbuttoning Merrily's cassock. Lol, however, after the experience with his parents, was still wary of the Church and its trappings. Another reason he preferred the Quiet Service, when Merrily wore only her pectoral cross over a dark sweater and jeans.

'So,' she said. 'Belladonna?'

'You could be right.' Lol sat forward, hands on his knees. 'I rang Prof. He said he'd been warned a few months ago that she was living in the area and possibly working on a new album. Consequently, he was putting it around that the studio was booked up for the foreseeable.'

'She's not changed, then?'

'Don't go there,' Lol said.

'Hey, I've been there. When I was Jane's age, it would have been. It was at a wrestling stadium – she wasn't very famous then, but she had a cult following. We all wore black tights for the gig and I had this kind of funeral coat I'd bought for a couple of quid from Oxfam, and a black velvet hat and a lot of cheap stage make-up. Thank God all the pictures have disappeared.'

'You really were a goth?'

'A phase. We all linked arms under the stage and stood very still, like mourners around a catafalque. I didn't like the music that much, to be honest. Too slow, a bit dismal. Occasional bursts of hysterical screaming. No tunes to speak of.'

'What does she look like these days?'

'Hardly any different. This long grey Victorian kind of cape that trailed in the mud. Same slightly beaky nose, same slightly crooked teeth.'

'But in an attractive way. That strange kind of uneven beauty,' Lol said.

'Mmm.' She tossed him a suspicious look. 'So how close did you get all those years ago?'

He smiled. 'Nice of you to imply I might have been brave enough at eighteen. No, we once played a very badly organized one-day festival in this half-flooded field in Oxfordshire. We were near the bottom of the bill – eleven a.m. – and she was in the prime sunset spot. We didn't actually stay for her gig. But I did hear the discussion she had with the organizers about the level of facilities. Scary.'

'Formidable woman.'

'Hadn't realized she was so posh until then. You don't expect it. No, I never actually met her. She…' Lol's gaze had turned watchful. 'She came down to the river last night because she'd heard there'd been a death?'

'She asked a policewoman if it was a suicide. I thought that was a curious question. Suggested she knew who it was. Or maybe I was just thinking that because I realized this was probably the woman seen with Robbie Walsh. She certainly knew where he lived because Mumford saw her standing outside the house. Ironically, we were going to ask Mrs Mumford if she knew this odd woman personally. Thought that might solve something.'

Merrily could hear voices and footsteps from the nave. And laughter, which was good.

'This gig I went to,' she said, 'when I was seventeen – the band were all dressed as undertakers and they wheeled Belladonna on stage in a coffin, on a bier.'

Remembering the album: *Nightshades*. Fairly sure she didn't have it any more, or Jane would have found it. Maybe that was why she'd got rid of it. On the cover, Belladonna had been sitting in some kind of dusty chapel cradling a mandolin like a baby, a strap of her dress pulled down as if she was about to breastfeed the instrument. Subtly profane.

'This guy you spoke to,' Lol said. 'He said the woman's name was Mrs Pepper?'

'Mmm.'

'Prof told me Belladonna was married at one time to her producer, Saul Pepper.'

'That's it, then. I'll phone Andy Mumford when I get home and confirm it.'

Whatever her connection was with Robbie Walsh, Mumford would find it. *If you wanner stick with this ghost stuff, mabbe I'll check out the real woman. The living woman.* His mother's drowning was hardly going to make his inquiries more restrained.

'Lol…' He was leaning back on the Victorian sofa, exposing the big-eyed alien on his sweatshirt. Lol the former psychiatric patient, drop-out psychology student. 'You were an imaginative kid, right?'

'What makes you think that?'

'Did you never fall in love with someone who didn't exist? Seriously.'

'With me, it was always serious.' Lol stood up. 'Even the real ones, you turn them into something that doesn't exist. You start with a beautiful face and you build around it something that might actually love you.'

She told him about Robbie Walsh and Marion de la Bruyère.

Lol said, 'If he saw Ludlow as a refuge from something very bad… It was the end of the holidays, wasn't it, when he died?'

'Virtually.'

'Maybe he really couldn't bear to go back this time. Maybe he just wanted to stay with Marion.'

'Suicide? Mumford's given no indication that his home life was that bad.'

'Everything can seem very closed-in at that age,' Lol said. 'The future's like staring down the wrong end of a telescope. You can't envisage anything more than a few months ahead, at most, and if you're having a very difficult time you don't see a way out, ever.'

'He killed himself in Ludlow, dying the way she died, because that was the only way he could stay there?'

She looked into Lol's eyes. Lol shrugged.

Slipping back into the nave for the Quiet Service, Merrily was trying to see this unlikely triangle: Robbie, Marion, Belladonna. The kid's connection with a 1980s goth rock singer was the hardest to envisage.

'Frankly,' Lol whispered in the vestry doorway, 'if it turns out he was suicidal, I can think of more suitable people to administer counselling.'

114

12

Esoteric

MERRILY SOMEHOW SENSED it and looked up maybe half a second before it was dismissed… and Sophie's face was blank again.

Outside the gatehouse office window, muscular clouds were hanging over Hereford like a street gang closing in. Maybe it was the sudden darkening of the room that had caused her to raise her head; nothing to do with Sophie, the only person she knew who could convey disapproval without any change of expression – probably went with her breeding.

'What's wrong, Soph?'

'I'm sorry?'

Sophie looked up from her computer. She was wearing a dark red woollen suit over a cream silk blouse. The Bishop of Hereford's lay secretary over many years and several bishops. Worth her weight in pearls.

'You scowled,' Merrily said.

'I don't think so, Merrily.'

There was a muttering of thunder from Dinedor Hill or somewhere. Merrily got up from her desk. On Mondays she usually tried to come in for a couple of hours to review the Deliverance schedule, although lately there hadn't been much of one. She was late today because of the afternoon cremation. A difficult funeral: people she hadn't known before, and so it was all the more important to make it resonate. Huw wasn't the only Deliverance minister to suggest that cursory, conveyor-belt funerals were leading to disquiet on both sides of the grave.

'I'd better put the kettle on before the power goes.'

'This isn't Ledwardine, Merrily, the power isn't going anywhere.'

'It's my turn, anyway.'

She filled the kettle and plugged it in, spooned tea into the pot then swiftly backed up and peered over Sophie's shoulder at the computer. There was an e-mail in the frame.

Sophie, Re the 'sample' of Deliverance files that you mailed me this morning, this is not what I meant. I feel it is important that the whole team sees all correspondence before it is filed. I also think we should be able to access the database at all times of day, rather than having to trouble you during office hours. Please get back to me with your thoughts before close of

Sophie clicked it away.

'Ah,' Merrily said. 'I see.'

Sophie gazed into the screen-saver photo of swans on the Wye, impossibly blue.

'I tend to receive instructions most days from Canon Callaghan-Clarke.'

Outside the window, the sky was solid now, like a rock formation over Broad Street.

And, oh dear, you didn't do this. You didn't treat Sophie Hill as a servant. What you had to learn, if you wanted to avoid trouble in the workplace, was that Sophie served only the Cathedral.

'And will you be getting back to her with your, er, thoughts?'

'What do you suggest? For instance…' Sophie went back into the e-mails. 'Should I have sent her a copy of this?'

* * *

116

Happy Beltane, Ms Exorcist! Yes soon be Walpurgis Night!!!
Why don't you come out and let your hair down. ha ha ha.

( )

* I * Lucifer

'This came through the website?'

'Yesterday. When exactly is Beltane?'

'April the thirtieth… Saturday? May Day Eve, anyway. When all card-carrying Satanists perform their blood sacrifices.'

'Ah, yes. Probably mailed from an Internet café.'

'Just some kid who's learned how to construct a devil on the keyboard. With a website, you're bound to get a percentage of this sort of crap.'

'Unless, of course' – Sophie looked up – 'one decides to dispense with the facility.'

'Scrap the message line? She wants to do that?'

'The entire website, actually,' Sophie said.

'What?'

'I've been asked, initially, to supply a list of all the e-mails it's stimulated in the past year.'

Merrily went to the window, exchanging hard looks with the sky. This time, there had to be a mistake. The website was about offering straightforward advice to people experiencing problems they thought might be of paranormal origin. It included self-help procedures and useful prayers. It advised them to contact their local clergy if the problems persisted or, if they preferred to, e-mail, phone or write direct to this office.

She turned back to Sophie.

'So how many people *did* contact us in the past year through the site?'

'Not a great many. Perhaps thirty.'

'And what percentage, would you say, were jokes or try-ons?'

'I'd say about twenty per cent. A few were from children who genuinely thought they had a problem, but turned out to have seen too many episodes of *Buffy the Vampire Slayer*. A couple came from Women's Institutes asking if you could address their meetings. We had, I think, four from people thanking us for the prayers and the advice and saying they'd actually worked and they were now sleeping better – that sort of thing.'

'And how many requiring follow-up action?'

'Seven. Mainly poltergeist-related, all subsequently dealt with by the local clergy – prayer and counselling.'

'It's a substantial number, when you think about it, for a largely rural diocese. What exactly has Siân said?'

'She said she'd placed the issue of the website on the agenda for the next meeting of the Deliverance Panel and, as I say, went on to ask for detailed background information as to the site's usage.'

'What do you think her argument's going to be?'

'I suspect she's going to dismiss the whole thing as costly and trivial. If anyone wants this essentially... esoteric service badly enough, they'll go to the trouble of finding us. Of course, I may be quite wrong—'

'Esoteric – that was her word?'

'Unless I misheard.'

'So we're minority stuff. They're pushing us into a back room and switching the light out.'

'Or possibly a cupboard,' Sophie said.

'If that website has saved just one faintly timid person from—'

'You don't have to convert me, Merrily.'

'No.'

They looked at one another in the dimness of the afternoon. The kettle rumbled towards the boil, distant lightning glimmered. Merrily sat down at the desk, her back to the window, and switched on the lamp.

'Sophie, what am I going to do about this bloody woman?'

This morning she'd phoned Huw Owen, leaving a message on his answering machine. He'd come back to her just after twelve when she was getting into her black coat for the funeral.

He hadn't found out very much and none of it was encouraging.

Except that there appeared to be no hidden agenda. No worthwhile conspiracy theory. No credible faction, in or out of Canterbury, with a mission to destroy Deliverance.

Which, of course, didn't mean it wasn't bubbling under, somewhere.

Huw told her what he'd learned about Siân Callaghan-Clarke: fifty-one years old, formerly a barrister – which would explain her need to work with professionals like Saltash, the resident expert witness. Born in Winchester to an upper-middle-class, High Church, landowning family.

'Word is,' Huw said, 'that the father was a traditionalist. Her younger brother would have the career, Siân was expected to marry well, raise kids – women's stuff.'

Not a good time to impose those values. Siân had not only not married well, she hadn't married at all, moving to Worcester as a criminal barrister and managing to raise two sons inside a comfortably loose arrangement with her head of chambers. He was still around, still in Worcester, and the sons were both at Oxford.

The Church?

'Well, it was in the family,' Huw said. 'Uncle became Bishop of Norwich. Her brother – who she appears to have resented from an early age – is now an archdeacon, Exeter or somewhere. Siân, commendably enough, began to help some of the youngsters she was defending and concluded that the Church had the facilities to operate a support network for addicts and suchlike and wasn't using them. It's not that simple – as I've just been finding out up in Manchester – but it was enough to get her involved. And that was the time when the battle for women priests was on, and her younger brother, apparently, was strongly anti.'

'That would do it,' Merrily said.

'Oh aye. That were the red rag, all right. She'd get into the Church and she'd leave the brat behind.'

As a priest, Huw said, Siân was exactly what she seemed: a modernist and a politician. Known to be tolerant of Islamic fundamentalism while deploring its equivalent in Christianity. Suspicious of evangelism and Alpha training. Considered opposition to gay clerics to be irrational to the point of superstition.

Talking of which…

'Aye, well… there were rumours of her having a bit of a thing in Worcester with a bloke I trained with, Keiran Winnard – younger than me, charismatic in all senses of the word. She'd certainly be his type: striking blonde, plenty of style and fancy footwork in debate. Liked a woman with a bit of intensity, Keiran, as I recall.'

'Risky, though, in the Church. In the same diocese?'

'Wouldn't be the first. Pure physical attraction, not necessarily a meeting of minds. Anyway, it must have burnt through quickly enough, leaving her even less well disposed towards the miracle-and-wonder lads than before. Happen that was the reason she got out of Worcester. Or she just thought she could rise faster in Hereford – smaller pool, bit of an outpost. Either way, looks like Hereford's got her for the foreseeable future. And so have you.'

'So maybe she sees Deliverance as a method of exercising control,' Merrily said to Sophie.

'You mean, over the wilder elements within the diocese? The charismatics, the evangelicals?'

'If you consider that, in certain hands, exorcism itself can be very rigid and repressive… keeping the lid on the cauldron, as someone once said. Taking a dim view of the Charismatic movement, arm-wavers, happy-clappies, speakers in tongues, because of what they might be opening themselves up to. Look at my predecessor. He hated all that.'

'But from a different perspective, surely.' Sophie leaned into the lamplight. 'Canon Dobbs lived an ascetic life – self-denial, fasting, long hours of prayer. A deeply spiritual man. Bitterly opposed to women priests, as we know, and I have no doubts at all where he'd have stood on the issue of gay clergy.'

'With his back to the altar and a big cross in front. You're right, it works both ways. Rationalism can be even more repressive, in its way: all possession is mental illness, all ghosts are psychological projections. Siân is potentially more restrictive than Dobbs.'

'Then why…' Sophie pinched her chin, forefinger projecting pensively along her cheek. 'Why would she want Martin Longbeach on the Panel? A… well, a tree-hugger.'

'Window dressing, Huw reckons. I mean, he's harmless, isn't he? And gay. Probably an excellent source of information from the lunatic fringe. And doubtless so deeply honoured to be chosen that he's more than happy to pass it on.' Merrily smiled. 'Is Siân a gay icon, do you think? Or maybe Martin's being groomed as my successor…?'

The phone rang. Sophie snatched it quickly, probably to kill the image of Martin Longbeach here in this office with his thinking-candles and his herbal teas.

'Gatehouse.'

Merrily heard a man's voice on the line. Pale sheet-lightning brought the office up in shades of grey.

'One moment, I'll see if she's in.' Sophie covered the mouthpiece. 'It's former-Sergeant Mumford, are you—?'

'Sure.'

She'd spoken to him very briefly last night, telling him about the woman who had proved to be Belladonna. It had meant nothing to Mumford, who said his knowledge of rock music began and ended with the Rolling Stones. Sophie passed the phone across the desk.

'Andy, I was going to ring you tonight. How are—?'

'You got a TV, switch it on.' Mumford's voice, flecked with storm crackle, also loaded with the kind of urgency you didn't expect from him. 'Just caught the headline, called you at home, your daughter said you'd be there. You got a television in the office?'

'Well, we have…'

Looking up at the portable collecting dust on the filing cabinet.

'Switch it on. Central News, it's on now, don't hang around. I'll call you back.'

Thunder trundling, like a heavy goods vehicle over the horizon, as he hung up.

PART TWO

Jemmie

'People who will accept an apparition because it is a visual experience will tend to reject the conviction of a sense of a presence because the experience is not externalized... I am convinced that this sense of a presence is experienced far more often than is reported.'

Andrew Mackenzie, The Seen and the Unseen
(1985)

'And who that lists to walk the towne about
Shall find therein some rare and pleasant things.'

Thomas Churchyard (on Ludlow, 1578)

13

Extreme

'… Remains a possibility, but, yes, very unlikely to have been accidental.'

The stonework, in jagged close-up, was hard against the patchy sky. Then the picture pulled back, and you could see that the shot had been done from the ground.

This was as near as they could get because the tower was taped off, two police protecting the site. Old videotape from coverage of the Robbie Walsh tragedy, Merrily thought.

They cut back to the policeman who'd been talking over the shot. She didn't recognize him. '… Just about possible to survive that kind of fall, but unlikely,' the policeman said.

Now Robbie Walsh's face came up, the school photo, Robbie with his hair brushed and his tie straight, his mouth in an unsure smile, his eyes flicked to one side. The reporter's voice over the picture:

'… weeks since the town was shattered by the death of fourteen-year-old Robbie.'

They'd been too late to catch the link into the story and had also missed the first part of the report. It looked like Central News was going heavy on the death of Mrs Mumford, rehashing the events preceding it.

The boy's photo had been replaced by another one, a poignantly blurred holiday snap of a woman in a sundress leaning – bitter irony now – against a lifebelt hanging from a sea wall.

Merrily bit her lip.

'And then, at the weekend, came news of the shocking death of Robbie's grandmother, Mrs Phyllis Mumford, whose body was pulled from the River Teme, flowing just below the castle here. Eighty-three-year-old Mrs Mumford was said by neighbours today to have been inconsolable after the death of her grandson, who'd been staying with her and her husband at the time.'

Shot of the river, a police barrier, two sheaves of flowers lying up against it, the cellophane flapping.

'The town is in mourning once again. But absolutely nothing could have prepared the people of Ludlow for what was to happen today.'

'Huh?'

Merrily looked at Sophie. The phone on Sophie's desk started to ring. Sophie opened a drawer and put the phone in and shut the drawer up to the wire. Merrily moved closer to the TV.

'... Hard to take in. We're shocked... shattered.'

Man in his sixties, hair like wire wool and hollow cheeks. George Lackland, Ludlow Mayor, the caption read.

'... Gather she wasn't local,' George Lackland said. 'We don't know where she came from, but the thought that she came here – a girl that age – specifically to... you know, to die, in this horrible way... that really doesn't bear thinking about, does it?'

'Christ,' Merrily said.

Long shot of the tower. The reporter saying, 'And that's the terrible question that just about everyone here is asking tonight...'

The camera finding the reporter – evidently live, picking up off the back of his taped report – standing outside the castle, on a walkway halfway down the banks above the river, his spread arms conveying universal incomprehension.

'... Did the girl come here to kill herself in a macabre imitation of the death of Robbie Walsh? There was nothing to suggest that Robbie's death was anything other than an accident. But two identical accidents at the same castle? As the Mayor said, the implications of this are, to say the least, disturbing.'

In the studio, the presenter, a blonde young enough to be the reporter's daughter, said, 'Paul, do we know yet where exactly the girl had come from – how far she'd travelled?'

'Tammy, my information is that the police do have a name, and the parents of a fifteen-year-old girl are, at this moment, being brought to Ludlow in the hope of a formal identification. But it could be several hours before that name is formally released.'

'Is there any connection with Robbie Walsh?'

'It's a question that's been asked, but there's no reason to suppose there was any connection between them at all – except, of course, the circumstances of their deaths.'

'And what does that say about Robbie's death, Paul?'

'Well, there's no particular suggestion that it throws a different light on Robbie's death. There'll always be an element of mystery about that. What I'd guess police and townsfolk are asking is: was this girl, in some awful way, inspired by… by the way he died and, of course, the dramatic location?'

'Obviously, Paul, this is something nobody could have predicted. But how could it possibly have been prevented?'

'Tammy, it's an impossible situation. This is a major tourist attraction that gets hundreds of visitors every day, many drawn in by its dramatic location, at the highest point of the town, with these high walls, these ruined but still very tall towers and this steep drop almost to the river. Yes, of course it's dangerous, but so are hundreds of beauty spots all over the country and what's being said is, well, if someone's determined to die, there's no shortage of places to go.'

'But *two* teenagers – both at Ludlow Castle?'

'Why here, particularly? Yes, that's a question a lot of people are now trying to answer. Children do have to be accompanied by an adult and, with the number of tourists increasing daily as we move towards the main holiday season, there's no doubt at all that attendants here are going to be exercising considerable extra vigilance.'

'Paul, thank you,' Tammy said. Turned back to camera. 'And if the girl's name is released, we'll update you on our late-night bulletin.'

Merrily switched off the set. The phone had stopped ringing, and Sophie brought it out of the drawer.

'A girl,' Merrily said. 'A fifteen-year-old girl. What's it mean? Another one.'

'Children are impressionable,' Sophie said.

She used to teach.

Merrily reached for the phone. 'I'll ring Andy. He mustn't've known anything about it, either, until he switched the news on.'

Mumford's line was engaged.

'Probably ringing the sergeant he knows at Ludlow. Poor guy must feel right out of the loop when something like this happens and he finds out from the news like the rest of us. Especially when it's going to add a lot of fuel to his own suspicions.'

'Merrily, as the reporter said, there's no reason to think Robbie Walsh's death was anything other than accidental. Children have always been impressionable. Now they've become horribly... extreme. They want extreme experiences, extreme sports, sensations...'

'Death?'

'They see death on TV, and it's usually rather exciting.'

Merrily pulled the Silk Cut from her bag. 'Bloody hell, Sophie.'

Sophie frowned at the cigarettes.

'When I was a child, the country had just come through a world war, and people were simply grateful to have survived, and we children were aware of that. Today... some of them seem to treat life almost like an unwanted present that they might as well take back. I'm sorry, Merrily, if I seem to be losing my Christian compassion. I'm sure there'll be a thoroughly heartbreaking story behind it.'

The phone rang. Merrily grabbed it.

'Andy?'

'Ah, you are still there,' the Bishop said. 'I suppose you've heard the news from Ludlow.'

'Just caught the last part of the TV piece.'

'Tragic,' the Bishop said. 'Awful… wasteful. Three deaths, three… and in fact it's more than tragic, it's nightmarish, now, in ways I…'

'We don't know where she's from?'

'Other side of Herefordshire. Ledbury, I think. That is, George— I rang an old friend in Ludlow, George Lackland, the Mayor – you saw him on the TV thing. Used to be my senior churchwarden. George says the police are saying she seems to have hitch-hiked across.'

'Thirty-odd miles? Forty?'

'Something like that.'

'Do they know why?'

'Will they ever?'

'Witnesses?'

'Someone on the bowling green below The Linney appears to have seen her fall. No one inside the castle was aware of it, although it must have happened while the place was open to visitors. So easily done, you see. You can't follow everybody around. She apparently paid to go in and just… never came out. Nightmarish.'

'Was she dead when they found her?'

'I'm not sure. George thinks there may have been complications. But if she was alive when they found her she didn't survive long.'

Outside, the rain had started, like nails on the window.

'Bernie… erm, should we be… involved in any way?'

Merrily heard his breath, slowly expelled.

'I don't know. Something did strike me when I saw the TV pictures. Actually, I feel rather foolish and trivial even mentioning it at a time like this, but you just know that some people in the town are going to be talking about it. This sort of gossip… one can't do anything to stop it. You, ah… Marion. You remember Marion.'

129

'I think I can just about remember Marion, yes.'

'And we were all thinking, yes, but... wrong tower.'

'The keep, as distinct from the Hanging Tower.'

'Precisely. Well, you wouldn't know the layout of the castle, but I do. And there it was, on the news.'

'Sophie and I missed the beginning of the report,' Merrily said cautiously.

'Well, they didn't make a point of it, but they wouldn't know either. However...' The Bishop coughed. 'They showed it from the outside. Unmistakable. This time, it *was* the Hanging Tower.'

14

Black Poppies

THAT NIGHT, LOL boiled some water for tea, using a Primus
stove in his kitchen, leaving Merrily to finish dressing by firelight. He had something to tell her, but it could wait.

When he came back into the living room with the tray, she
was sitting on the end of the sofa, small and demure, with –
unless he was deluding himself – the same glow on her face that
he'd once seen by the light of altar candles, and her hair tied
back with a rubber band. But, too soon, the glow was fading.

'OK?'

'I'll go up to the bathroom later, with a torch and a mirror, to
check the fine details.'

'That's not exactly what I meant,' Lol said.

As so often, it had been a touch furtive. Curtains surrepti-
tiously drawn. Cushions from the sofa, this time, on top of
freshly washed paint cloths on the flagstones. Like teenagers,
when the parents might come in... only the parents were the
parish.

'Jane kept a straight face,' Merrily said, 'when I said it was my
turn to help you with the painting. And then she spoiled it by
murmuring something I didn't quite catch, about brushes and
paint pots.'

Lol smiled. Merrily looked around the fire-lit parlour with its
bounding shadows. There were always shadows. Lol thought
about Lucy Devenish, who'd made him read the poems of

Thomas Traherne, the seventeenth-century Herefordshire minister who believed that God wanted you to be happy. *Sitting there listening to your mournful, wistful records. It's spring! Open your heart to the eternal! Let the world flow into you!*

Lucy's last spring, as it had turned out. Suddenly, he could almost feel her in the room with them – Lucy sensing Merrily's underlying gloom and frowning, and turning, now, towards him, poncho aswirl, eyes like the smouldering core of the fire.

Do something, Lucy commanded.

Lol gazed into the top of the chromium teapot.

'I see three male presences looming over you.'

'Mystic Laurence, huh?'

'One's a retired detective, who hates the way his world is being fragmented. One's a bishop, for whom retirement is looming, and he doesn't want his longed-for haven spoiled. And the third is a retired psychiatrist, who... Actually I don't think there's such a thing as a retired psychiatrist. They never give up analysing.'

'Wrongly, of course,' Merrily said.

'But the message is: retired people are the new delinquents – too much time, nothing to lose. Beware of them. Essentially, the teapot is saying this is not your problem.'

'Easy for the teapot to say.' Merrily went to sit on the hearth. 'Last night, when he rang me in the church, Bernie was, "Oh, let's draw a line under it." Tonight, he's virtually saying, "Sort this out." '

' "Sort this out for me." '

'He does seem to feel a spiritual responsibility for that town.'

'Because he used to work there. And hopes to retire there. So maybe nothing spiritual about it at all, really,' Lol said.

'Not sure about that.' She took the pot away from him and poured tea for them. 'Anyway, he thinks this girl's death is going to cause a lot of dangerous speculation. And he's probably right. The legend of Marion de la Bruyère is very well known in the town, and this is her tower. The idea that the girl didn't know about that seems remote.'

'Might have a terrible appeal for a certain kind of teenager in despair, sure.'

'More so, probably, than the accidental fall of a fourteen-year-old boy, from a different tower. I just… There has to be a connection we can't yet see.'

'Had the girl been seen in Ludlow before?'

'We're not going to know that until they confirm her identity and issue a picture.'

'You keep saying "we". It's not your problem.'

But Lol knew already that this was a lost cause.

'I looked up Belladonna on the Internet.' Merrily sugared the teas. 'Just to see what she's doing these days. What she's doing in Ludlow.'

'And?'

'Didn't find out. Learned a lot of history. For instance, the name Belladonna isn't actually much of an affectation. Her name was Arabella Donnachie. So she was always carrying Belladonna around with her in the middle of her name.'

'Wonder if her parents intended that.'

'Says not on her website. Says it was fated… all that kind of stuff. She was born in Banbury, Oxfordshire. Father a well-off accountant. Educated at Cheltenham Ladies' College. Walked out at seventeen to form a band, for which she was apparently later considered too weird.'

'In what way?'

'Didn't say. I, erm, tried to call Mumford tonight. No answer at home, mobile off. Suppose he's gone after her?'

'She can take care of herself,' Lol said, and Merrily looked up. He shrugged. 'I had a call from Prof.'

'Relating to…?'

'Well… Belladonna.'

'And you weren't going to tell me?'

'Choosing the moment. Did I mention that Tom Storey was at Knight's Frome, mixing his album?'

He didn't know if she'd ever been a Tom Storey fan. Always more of a boy's hero, Tom – like Jeff Beck, Peter Green, Mark Knopfler and Eric Clapton before he recorded 'Wonderful Tonight'.

'Normally, I keep out of the way when Tom's there,' Lol said. 'He's, um… irascible. His hair's all white now, and his moustache seems to cover half his face. It's like the studio's being vandalized by the Abominable Snowman, and yet at the end of it all those guitar licks – fluid, economical, delicate—'

'He knows Belladonna?'

'—And, underneath it all, a sensitive man. I mean *sensitive* sensitive. And sensitive about discussing it, because he's in permanent, neurotic denial. Tom will tell you – just like your friend Saltash – that it's all crap and all in your mind. Except that Tom knows it isn't. So when Prof said, hang on, I'm going to put Tom on the line…'

'Belladonna.' Big voice filling the mobile phone, making it feel twice as heavy, like an ingot. 'Bella-fucking-donna.'

Lol had had to sit down.

'You know what that woman did, Laurence? She had a baby. She's in maternity when she learns she's finally got herself a recording contract. The longed-for break. What's she do? Kid's born, she gives it up for adoption.'

'At that stage?'

'Might have arranged it earlier, I'm not brilliant on details, I'm giving you the sense of it. Gives the father up, too. Dead now, poor sod – smack. That's the kind of woman. Carries death around like a tray of black poppies. Gives up a child for a recording contract.'

Hard to be sure how accurate this was. Lol knew that Tom felt strongly about anything child-related. His daughter, Vanessa, was Down syndrome. He treated her like a goddess.

'But that was a long time ago,' Lol said. 'She couldn't have been much more than a kid?'

'A woman, take my word – then. Gawd knows what she is now.'

Tom talked about the albums – biggish over here, for a while, but in the States… mega. Which was rare for a British punk or New Wave artist.

'American punks, at least they knew a few chords and they didn't gob on the audience. British punk, Americans just didn't get the joke. But, see, Belladonna was never funny. And she wasn't like the rest. She talked posh. Talked like bleedin' Julie Andrews. They loved that in the States.'

Because America had quite taken to her, Tom said, Belladonna had made a huge amount of money very quickly. And because she'd looked after it – with Daddy's assistance – she never wound up on some sad, end-of-the-pier, 1980s nostalgia trip like some other poor bleeders Tom could name.

'They put the loot into property. Old houses. Bought this dump looked like the Bates Motel, done it up, sold it for triple, never looked back. Daddy saw the value, Bell only bought the place on account of – what's this tell you about her? – on account of she reckoned it was haunted.'

Lol had asked, hesitantly, what it had told Tom.

'Tells me she don't… she ain't got it. She don't feel. Haunted, to her, was like romance. This fucking, irresponsible, dilettante bitch.'

They were close to Tom's barrier here. He'd let go of a huge but unstable laugh at this point, like a big tipper-lorry dumping gravel.

'The house… the house wasn't haunted enough, apparently. Or the bleedin' spooks couldn't stand the company and pissed off.'

'She didn't feel' – Lol took a chance – 'the way some people… feel. But she wanted to?'

Tom was quiet, Lol half-expecting him to ring off. And then,

'Story is, she had meningitis as a kid. Teens, anyway. Came close to checking out, had some death's-door experience, changed her life. Kept wanting to tell me about it, following me around. Sent me a card wiv… you know, a picture inside. Of her. *That* kind of picture. I don't fink so. Outta my face, you crazy woman!'

'So when was the last time you actually spoke to her?'

'Gawd… few years ago? She wanted to work wiv me this time. Like I'd be that insane? Didn't seem to be able to decode the phrase piss off. Kept ringing, bending Shelley's ear, the missus – I wasn't gonna talk to her, no way; it's why we was. ex-directory, Gawdsake. We had the number changed, in the end. Mad, sick, stupid woman. And the music… atrocious.'

'Where was she living, the last you heard?'

'Moves around. Always moved around, couldn't settle. I fink – Shelley would know this – I fink, the last we heard, she was on her daughter's back. Nah, nah, not her daughter, Saul Pepper's daughter. The poor bastard she married. He had a daughter already. Bell went to live near the daughter, that's the last we heard.'

'Would that have been in Ludlow?'

'Where?'

'In Shropshire.'

'Shit,' Tom said. 'That ain't too far away from here, is it? Listen, you ever run into the mad bitch, you never spoke to me in your life, Laurence.'

Lol put a log on the fire.

'The marriage to Saul Pepper ended, apparently, about six years ago,' Merrily said. 'He went to America to work. Has a new family now. One website says the split was amicable. Pepper said she was too' – Merrily sighed – 'too weird for him. In the end. Seems to have been too weird for people all her life.'

'But not too weird for Saul Pepper's daughter.'

'Nor, it seems, for Robbie Walsh. Erm… what Tom Storey told you about the near-death experience – that's interesting. The Church has a strange attitude towards all that. The most common perceived experience of an afterlife, but we're oh so wary.'

'You?'

'Me, no. I'd love to have a near-death experience. Well, not *too* near, not just yet, but I mean most people who've had them

136

– the long tunnel, the glorious light – they immediately seem to lose all fear of dying.'

'I thought the clergy naturally would have no f—'

'You're kidding.'

Lol smiled. 'Doesn't really explain Belladonna's music, though, does it? Her old stage act. Which was not about the delights of the afterlife as much as the trappings of death itself: coffins, biers, all that. What kind of near-death experience accounts for that?'

'Good point. None of this adds up, does it? I mean, that's the problem… nothing here adds up. Nothing quite connects. Pieces missing, everywhere.'

'What about the dead girl?'

'Especially that. That's… horrific.' Merrily stood up, steadying her mug of tea. 'I'm going to suggest that Mumford talk to Frannie Bliss, see if he can find out what the police have uncovered. I think what Bernie's saying is that it needs to be sorted – explained – before local people start putting a superstitious slant on it.'

'Does that really happen any more, in our secular society?'

'*Especially* in our secular society,' Merrily said. She reached out for Lol's hand. 'Nothing wrong, is there?'

'I… no.'

'You're OK about the Bristol gig?'

'I'll just take lots of drugs,' Lol said.

She peered at him to see if he was smiling. He smiled.

A few minutes later, he watched from the front window as she moved across the edge of the cobbled square to the vicarage gate. He felt vacant, spare. She was working seven days a week, letting herself be used to further other people's agendas. In the past week, he'd written about half a song that was never going to be more than a filler track on the next album, if there was a next album. He felt incomplete, worthless.

The fire was burning low and the room was laden with shadows as dense as old clothes. It was time he got the electricity connected.

15

Ghost-Walk

MUMFORD DIDN'T WANT to talk to Frannie Bliss.

Well, it wasn't that he didn't want to talk to Bliss, he said on the phone, just that he didn't want to put the DI in a difficult position.

Mumford, reluctantly, as Joe Public: a crisis of confidence.

'You do want to find out about this?' Merrily said. 'How this girl's suicide ties in. If it does.'

'Suppose I wouldn't mind, aye.'

Almost certainly Welsh Border-speak for, *Yes, I will never rest again until I know.* Outside the scullery window, the apple trees' budded branches dangled uncertainly, and the grey-green moss gleamed coldly on the stone wall between the vicarage garden and the churchyard. Spring had stalled in frosty spurts of morning mist, the exhaust of winter.

'You heard the local radio, Mrs Watkins?'

'Some of the early stuff.'

The breakfast lead on Radio Hereford and Worcester had been an extended report live from Ledbury. Not unexpectedly, the parents weren't talking. Anonymous neighbours said that the dead girl, Jemima Pegler, used to be a helpful, friendly kid, once, but she'd changed. Neighbours in small towns didn't like to use words like *sullen.* They said more *withdrawn* lately.

'You leave it on for the studio discussion?' Mumford said.

'Didn't have time.'

'Your friend Dr Saltash?'

Merrily gripped the wooden arms of her chair, Ethel the cat taking off from the desk and raking up a page of the sermon pad.

'Introduced as a retired consultant psychiatrist with Hereford hospitals, special consultant to the Departmeat of Health, and the author of a paper on self-harming in children and teenagers.'

'Andy, was this man always bloody ubiquitous, or is it just my paranoia?'

'Said he couldn't really comment on an individual case but in the general way of things this particular method of suicide – public place – it was usually a cry for attention. A child saying, You're all gonner know who I am now, kind of thing.'

'And two near-identical deaths in more or less the same spot?'

'Didn't make much of that. Once a place gets known for it... like scores of folk jumping off Beachy Head, ennit?'

'He mention your mother?'

'Not in so many words. Old folk, that's not so emotive, is it? Not like kids.'

'And we still don't know what the police think.'

Giving Mumford another opportunity to say he'd contact Bliss.

'Look,' he said, 'I gotter go into Ludlow this afternoon, see about the inquest, get an undertaker on standby for the ole girl. Might talk to some other people while I'm there. Let you know what I find out, all right?'

'Please.'

''Course,' Mumford said, 'no partic'lar reason why you shouldn't give the boss a call.'

'Bliss?'

'Always got time for you, as I recall.'

'And then, like... tell you what he says.'

'I wouldn't mind,' Mumford said.

'Andy Mumford,' Frannie Bliss said nostalgically. 'Merrily, I just can't tell you how much I miss the miserable bastard. The faded rugby-club ties, the knackered tweed jackets he probably inherited from his dad...'

'His dad's still alive, Frannie.'

'Figure of speech, Merrily.'

'Unlike his mother.'

'Ah... Jesus.' Over the sounds of phones and fractured laughter in the Hereford CID room, she heard the side of his fist bump the desk. 'I'm not thinking, am I? I'm sorry. I was gonna ring him, Merrily, it's just...'

'Difficult?'

'Yeah. Strangers, I can handle the sorry-for-your-loss routine, and when it's a working copper, you all go out and get drunk together. But a retired DS who never wanted to go. Never even got pissed when he left – you know that? We're in the pub for his presentation, and he's shuffling about a bit, trying to pretend he can't wait to see the back of us. And then I look around and he's like... just not there any more. Gone. Evaporated. Always that bit of distance, mind: him local, me incomer.'

'Been trying for two years to get him to stop calling me "Mrs Watkins".'

'No chance,' Bliss said. 'So... Andy's slumped in his garden, like a bloody old smouldering bonfire, thinking the Shropshire cops are sitting on information that could reveal the truth about his nephew's death, right?'

'And there's also the question of his mother. And now...'

'The girl. Listen, I've gorra say at the outset, this is not really my case. True, both kids came from this division, but it's Ludlow's headache, for which we're frankly quite glad. I mean is it a case? I don't know. Has it been a case for you, as it were?'

'I've never yet had anything so clean-cut as "a case", you know that.'

'Go on, then,' Bliss said, resigned. 'Tell me why you're interested.'

So Merrily told him about Mrs Mumford and the bereavement apparition/delusion/hallucination. Well, he knew what she was about. He was a Liverpool Catholic, tended not to laugh at her. Not often, anyway.

'Funny, I remember me ma, when me uncle got killed on the railway, she swore she'd seen him walking up our front path. Didn't know he was dead, then. Opens the front door, nobody there. Family's a funny thing, Merrily. What did you do?'

'Nothing. I had a psychiatrist with me. Not an entirely happy situation, but I won't go into it now. Bottom line is, what she subsequently said, in front of Andy and me, was that a woman had taken Robbie. Later, she appeared to be suggesting that a woman had pushed him off the tower.'

'How did she know that?'

Merrily sighed. 'He'd told her.'

'Ah,' Bliss said. 'The old phantom-witness scenario.'

'I knew you'd be impressed.'

'Don't get me wrong—'

'I'd have been dubious, too, Frannie, except we talked to someone who'd seen the boy with a particular woman on two occasions. Once in the grounds of Ludlow Castle.'

'And?'

'What do you top detectives call it these days when you've got a feeling?'

'We call it time to keep very quiet, Merrily. Because, in the modern, computerized, CCTV, DNA, CPS-conscious, politically correct, focus-group fuckin' police service, we do not do individual feelings any more.'

'And there was me thinking you were the last maverick cop under forty. Man who needed to live life on the edge.'

'That was before I was back with Kirsty. Now I'm a husband and father again, with a mortgage and a career path.'

'I see,' Merrily said. 'Well, then... thanks very much, Frannie. Erm... have a nice life.'

The rest of the morning, she didn't think about any of it. She had parish matters to deal with, not least the fortnightly Ledwardine magazine which, in recognition of the need to sell a few hundred copies to people who didn't go to church, had become a general community newsletter. Edited in this parish, inevitably, and somewhat crudely, by the vicar.

It usually carried a few paragraphs on newcomers to the village, and Jane had left a piece on Lol in the file, which Merrily got around to just before noon.

We are delighted to welcome to the select end of Church Street Mr Robinson, who many of you will no doubt remember as the young, good-looking and talented one in the almost-famous 1980s folk-rock band, Hazey Jane. Mr Robinson, who spends some of his spare time with the vicar, has recently relaunched his musical career after a difficult period in his life, but wants it to be known – although far too shy to say so himself – that he will not be available for the Ledwardine Summer Festival or any other piece of crap planned by his fellow incomers to 'put the village on the map'.

Also in the file was a copy of a letter from an outfit calling itself Parish Pump which had apparently gone to every community in the diocese.

Do YOU want to make your parish magazine into a genuine going-concern – a professional publication that every parishioner will want to buy? If so, we can help you. We can show you how to turn your parish notes into something lively, gossipy and compulsively readable. We can even DO THE WHOLE THING FOR YOU! And if you aren't satisfied with the increase in income, we'll refund your fees. Parish Pump guarantees to pump up your income. Contact us NOW.

You had to hand it to them for enterprise, but the idea of turning the *Ledwardine Community News* into something resembling *Hello!* magazine somehow didn't appeal. Still, she put it back in the file; perhaps she'd show it to the parish council. Jane's contribution, however… she cremated that slowly over the ashtray, with the Zippo. Because the magazine was usually laid out and printed in a hurry, you could never be too careful; it just might get in.

The phone rang. She burned her thumb reaching for it.

'This woman,' Mumford said. 'Sorry – you got time?'

'Where are you?'

'Ludlow. On the mobile, in a lay-by. Edge of the town centre, below the castle. Looking at a pair of locked gates. Mrs Pepper's house, what you can see of it behind all the trees.'

'I can imagine she wouldn't want to be too public,' Merrily said. 'Some of her old fans could well be slightly disturbed people.'

'That's what the feller does the ghost-walk said.'

'Sorry?'

'Ludlow Ghost-tours.'

'Ah. Right.'

'Don't stop her roaming the street in the early hours, mind. Sometimes on her own, sometimes with her followers. From out of town, mostly. Weird clothes. Like Dracula.'

'I saw them, Andy, down by the river.'

'Been street fights between local boys and these creeps, did you know that?' Mumford said. 'A stabbing one time.'

'In Ludlow?'

'Like anywhere else at closing time. Local yobs don't work for the tourist office.'

'This is what the ghost-walk guy said?'

'Eventually. Took some time to get anything from anybody. Most folk won't hear a word against her. I asked around in shops… cafés… the tourist information office. Helpful at first, then they clammed up. Without exception. Either they din't know or they said it was rubbish, telling you to take no notice of any malicious gossip you gets told, it's all lies. Woman lives quietly, does nobody any harm. Bit eccentric, that's her business. What d'you make of that?'

'That it's a nice town, where people don't like malicious gossip?'

'Shops, Mrs Watkins, businesses. Good customer, mabbe? Rich woman, big spender?'

'Or maybe they thought you were a reporter.'

'No,' Mumford said, 'they didn't think that. So, finally, I'm in this café, and an elderly woman having a cup of tea overhears me talkin' to the proprietor, leaves the money on the table, follows me out.'

Mumford paused; Merrily heard faint voices in the background, passers-by. When it was quiet again, he came back, his voice tight to the phone.

'Whispers to me, do I mean the woman who walks the back streets, the alleys, very late at night, early morning?'

'Ah.'

Mumford said the elderly woman lived in one of the discreet courtyard retirement flats between the church and the top car park – new housing cleverly built into the oldest part of town, ancient stone walls merging with new brick, almost the colour of the old. Desirable dwellings, if you didn't mind a few curious tourists, the occasional drunk.

And the night walker.

'Walking the back streets dressed all in white, sometimes carrying a candle in a lantern.'

'That's your woman.'

'So I went back to see the ghost-walk boy. Taking what you might call a slightly firmer line with him.'

'I hope that's not understatement, Andy.'

'Only language they understand, his sort. Anyway, he opens up eventually. Telling me how this woman hired him to take her on his walk. This was not long after she moved in. Just him and her. Nearly three hours, questions all the way. Ghosts: when was this one seen? Is it still seen? Have you seen it? I reckon he wasn't too upset, in the end, at being kept out most of the night, mind.'

'He was well remunerated?'

'One way or another, I reckon.'

'Unfair. People change. Presumably you asked the ghost-walk guy about Mrs Pepper and Robbie?'

'Nat'rally. Well, first thing – he knew Robbie. All right, no surprise there, they all knew Robbie, all the shopkeepers, the coppers. But the ghost-walk feller, they had an arrangement. He'd come along on the walks, tell folks about the history of the various buildings. Very useful for the ghost-walk feller. People liked him, see – Robbie.'

'The History Boy.'

'Exactly.'

'Would that be how he met Mrs Pepper?'

'I'd say. Anyway, figured I'd go over to her place down lower Linney, ring the bell, ask her straight out. Come up against a pair of locked gates. No bell, no speakerphone. Just an expensive mailbox. So I climbs over.'

'That wise?'

Mumford snorted. 'Walks up the drive, fully visible from the house. Farmhouse, looked like – pretty old. Bangs on the front door. Nothing. But, see… she was in there. Thirty years a copper, you just know when they're in. And she was… She was in.'

'You tried phoning?'

'Ex-directory. Which wouldn't have been a problem, few weeks ago.'

'No… maybe not.'

Merrily could sense his frustration. He was panting a bit now. She had the impression that years of bitterness were being funnelled into this, like petrol into a generator.

'Folks finding candle stubs on walls, tree stumps, where she's been. Been going on for months. And me – even I seen it. Hovering round Mam's house with her bloody candle. Why didn't I go after her?'

'Because you had no reason to. Because whenever there's a public kind of death, a big funeral, there's always someone like that around – leaving flowers, burning candles. I see it all the time. And she was crying, wasn't she?'

'Was she crying at the river?'

Merrily paused. 'No.'

'I en't gonner make a mistake like that again,' Mumford said grimly.

* * *

Merrily shoved the parish-magazine file into a drawer, lit a cigarette. This could get out of hand. With the death of his mother – an unnecessary death, a second public death – Mumford wasn't going to stop.

When the phone went again, she thought it was going to be him ringing back, having cooled down, but it was Bliss. He sounded relaxed or maybe that was just in comparison with Mumford.

'You remember Karen? Merrily?'

'Huh? Sorry…'

'You all right?'

'Yes. Sorry. Karen…?'

'Big farm girl? WPC. Acting DC now. With Mumford gone, I campaigned very strongly to get Karen on the team. Another real local country person, somebody who can work a baler and drain a slurry pit – can't get along with these poncy law graduates. Now then, earlier today Karen brings in a personal computer. Lifting it around like it's a toaster, what a woman.'

'Good to hear you have a new bag-carrier worthy of the term.'

'The computer's original owner: Jemmie Pegler. Jemima.'

'I thought you said it wasn't your case.'

'Yeah, well… you ringing up like that, out the blue, got me thinking. I always hate it when me mates are talking over me head. And Karen, despite having pigshit on her boots, is also our resident computer expert – bit of a natural, so they sent her on a course for stripping down hard disks, all that – so Shrewsbury asked if she could do the necessary with Jemmie's gear. And I thought I'd have a peep.'

'Nice to have you back, Frannie.'

'Yeah, that really hurt me feelings. Still the last maverick cop under forty, and proud of it.'

'So what did you find on the computer?'

147

'Upsetting.' Bliss didn't sound upset. 'Hard disk is full of links, for instance, to these horribly scary teenage-suicide chat-lines. Would you like to see?'

'Shall I come now?'

'Leave it till late afternoon, when the DCI has a meeting at headquarters with some tosser from the Home Office. And no dog collar, eh? I'd really hate it to get back that I still talk to dangerous cranks.'

16

Kindred Spirit

THAT EVENING IT rained again. Hard, brutal, nail-gun rain, like in winter.

For the first time in about a week, Merrily had built a fire of logs and coal in the vicarage sitting room. She sat watching Jane cuddling Ethel on the hearthrug. There was a lot to be chilled about tonight, but it was cosy enough in here, if you averted your eyes from the damp spreading under the window.

'What is this?' Jane said. 'Suddenly, everybody wants to talk about suicide.'

'Never mind,' Merrily said. 'We don't have to. Put the CD back on.'

'Not the Belladonna album again.' Jane put the cat down and made as if to get up, staging a startled glance at the door. 'Anything but that... in fact, let's talk about suicide. What do you want to know?'

Jane being self-consciously frivolous, but she really hadn't liked the CD – *Nightshades* – that Merrily had found in Woolworths. *If you ever do come across that woman in Ludlow, just don't invite her here.*

'Teenage suicide,' Jane said sweetly.

'All I said, flower, was that it seems to have—' Merrily shook herself. 'Sorry, did I call you "flower" again? It's no good, doesn't seem right saying "Jane" all the time.'

'Not my fault you wanted a kid called something basic just because *you*'d been landed with a silly name.' Jane slumped

149

back down. 'Just call me whatever makes you happy. And yes, I do know people my age who've been into suicide chat-rooms.'

'Why?'

'How do you mean?'

'I mean, is it suddenly seen as cool or something?'

'Is it cool to die?'

'OK,' Merrily said. 'Jemima Pegler was habitually sullen and uncooperative and didn't talk to her parents.'

'Hmm. That does sound like a particularly curious case—'

'Jane.'

'OK, sorry...' Jane leaned back, hands clasped behind her head. 'It's like one of the uncles said on the news – how were they to know she was seriously depressed when she wouldn't talk to them?'

'You don't sound too sorry for her.'

'Sorry?' Jane said. 'I'm supposed to feel sorry for her? Look, suicide chat-rooms, it's like it's the final taboo. The great unknown. The ultimate experience. Because nobody you know – all the cool guys who've been there, done that, washed the T-shirt again – it's the one thing, the one place – death – that they haven't... do you know what I'm getting at?'

'Possibly,' Merrily said. 'In fact... yes.'

Jemmie Pegler had been fifteen years old. Reading her e-mails, you had to keep reminding yourself of that.

Merrily had left the Volvo in the Gaol Street car park, to find Frannie Bliss waiting for her in the street with an executive briefcase. Annie Howe, the DCI, had been delayed, was still in the building. Bliss had rushed Merrily off to a café in a mews at the opposite side of the car park. On a discreet corner table, he'd laid out a sheaf of printout material from the dead girl's computer.

But first he wanted to talk about Mumford.

'Merrily, why the... why didn't you tell me?'

He'd had his red hair cut tight to the skull, maybe because it had been receding or maybe because he thought it made him look more dangerous. Which it did.

'I did tell you—'

'No, you didn't. You totally did not tell me, Merrily.'

'I don't understand...'

'Mumford's been in Ludlow today, right?'

'Right.'

'Talking to people all over the town about Robbie Walsh and this woman?'

'Did I mention—'

'And the reason I know about this is that the DCI told me. And the reason the DCI knows is that she was telephoned by her opposite number in Shrewsbury, a shiny-arsed admin twat called Shaun Eastlake, who was clearly chuffed as a butty at being able to tell her about a... a member of the public stamping around his patch interrogating other members of the public, having identified himself as Detective Sergeant Mumford?'

'Oh God,' Merrily said.

'Now, I think you can probably imagine how the Ice Maiden is reacting to this.'

'Mmm.' Danger signals in Merrily's head blinking amber and red. Before Bliss had been promoted to Inspector and Annie Howe to DCI, Mumford had been her bag-carrier and local-knowledge man – history which, in the present circumstances, would matter not a damn.

'Frannie, look, I didn't know. Should have realized, of course... should have realized, if only from personal experience, how hard it is to get information out of people if you haven't got the weight—'

'Merrily!' Bliss's fist came down on the table, a woman behind the counter glancing anxiously across. 'It's an offence. Impersonating a police officer? And if you've been a police officer, does that make it better? No, it makes it wairse.' The Mersey in his accent bursting its banks. 'Is it conceivable the fat bastard's forgotten that?'

'Frannie—'

151

'You think I'm kidding? This is Annie Howe we're talking about, not a human being, and her face is as close as it gets to being pink with embarrassment.'

Merrily sat back. 'One of the people he talked to told the police?'

'No, they told George Lackland.'

'The Mayor, right?

'And county councillor? And vice-chairman of the West Mercia Police Committee?'

'Oh God, really? But, apart from the element of deception, why would he – or any of the people Mumford talked to – not want the truth to come out about Robbie Walsh and a woman who—?'

'I don't know. Maybe she's well connected. Let's just say that Ludlow's one little town where Mumford would be well advised to walk like the streets are tiled with antique porcelain. Bearing in mind that when it comes to bailing-out time, Steve Britton will no longer be his friend. Best to assume he doesn't have any friends any more, in or out of uniform, at Ludlow nick.'

'Policemen don't just drop their mates.'

'Times change, Merrily. We didn't used to have divisional chiefs like Howe. So you tell Mumford: any officer spotted discussing the weather with him, it's a red-card situation. Do you think you could convey that to him?'

Merrily nodded. There was nothing to be said. Mumford was so far out of line he probably couldn't even discern a line any more.

'Good,' Bliss said. 'Now let's talk about poor Jemmie Pegler.'

it was realizing i just did it to keep him quiet and so he'd keep paying for the drinks. what's that say. im anbodys after a few drinks and they just laugh at the desperate worthless fat bitch and when your worthless thats the bottom. your never gonna come back from that are you

Merrily winced. 'Who's this one to, Frannie?'

'Girlfriend. Found it on the end of a reply from the other girl.

Karen went to talk to the other girl. She seemed genuinely shattered. Said Jemmie Pegler's e-mails always went over the top – wanted her mates to think she was a woman of the world who'd had so many men she was bored with sex. Girl thought it was all bullshit.'

'Doesn't seem like that to me.'

'In which case...' Bliss put a stiff-backed photo envelope in front of Merrily with another e-mail on top of it. 'The girl said she thought this was bullshit, too.'

they've gone out again so i looked in the bathroom cabinet just now and im thinking what would happen if i emptied every packet and every bottle in there and swallowed the lot. well just be sick as a dog most likely. how sad is that, sam. im not going out sad. im not. when i go theyll fucking know ive gone.

Merrily read it a second time, then opened the envelope.

It was a flash photo, in colour: a party pic of a fleshy girl, laughing. Short black hair gelled into gold-tipped spikes. A nose-stud with an implausible royal-blue gemstone. She was gripping a bottle by its silvery neck.

'When did the computer come in, Frannie?'

'Soon after we got a firm ID. Last night.'

'And would Karen have been working on it last night?'

'She was certainly on last night, and it's much nicer tucked up in an office with a computer and mug of tea than going out on the cold streets, so probably. Why?'

Merrily went back to the e-mail. 'This line about not going out sad. Seems to echo what someone apparently said on the radio this morning – that this kind of public suicide was a way of saying, "Now you're all going to know who I am." '

'Who said that?'

'I'm probably being paranoid. Dr Saltash, interviewed by Radio Hereford and Worcester. Is he officially assisting the police?'

'Possibly. He's done it before. The Ice Maiden's fond of psychological consultants, profilers, all these buggers who're supposed to be doing our job for us.'

'Mmm. And Siân Callaghan-Clarke.'

'Who?'

'Colleague of mine.'

Callaghan-Clarke on DCI Annie Howe, the night of the Deliverance Panel: *I get on very well with her.*

'Why paranoid, Merrily?'

'Sorry?'

'You said you were probably being paranoid.'

'Oh, it… it's just that Nigel Saltash has been inflicted on me as a psychiatric consultant.'

'He probably volunteered when he saw your picture.'

'Do you have a reason to say that, or…?'

'Hmm.' Bliss did a wry smile. 'If he is a mate of the Ice Maiden's, forget I spoke. Have a look at this one.'

i want to go away. want US to go away where they cant get at us do you know what im saying. im sick of *guys* im sick of *going to london* in nicked cars only it always turns out to be Worcester and im sick of loading the poxy dishwasher. i want to GOOOOOO AWAYYYYYYYYYYYYYYYYYYYY FOR GOOD!!!!

Merrily went back to some of the earlier e-mails about Jemima not wanting to go to school any more, but not wanting a job either. Jemima professing to despise girls who stuck with one boy longer than a few weeks – suggesting that boys usually dumped her within that time-span.

'Doesn't want to live at home, but she thinks it must be crap to have a place of your own and have to clean it. So… she's overweight and has a reputation as an easy lay because she must be desperate. Self-esteem at rock bottom. Bored with going out with blokes who nick cars because there's nowhere worth driving to in them. Was she ever diagnosed as clinically depressed?'

'Parents say not.'

'Drugs?'

'In normal life... possibly. Hard to say. When she died, however— This is well off the record, right?'

'Absolutely.'

'The window in the ruins we're fairly sure she went out of is not actually that high up. Certainly not compared with the top of the tower that Robbie Walsh came off. You can't get to the top of Jemmie's tower without a ladder – it's hollow. So you're going out of one of the reachable windows – quite a drop the other side, and it *could* kill you, but it's not a foregone conclusion. Unless, that is, you've already shot yourself full of enough heroin to make Keith Richards play the wrong chords.'

Merrily looked up, blinking.

'She shot up before she jumped,' Bliss said. 'Threw the syringe out the window first, it looks like. SOCO found it underneath a yew tree, with her mobile a few feet away, both some distance from the body. PM this afternoon showed cardiac arrest.'

'Is that—?'

'Common enough, with an inexperienced user. More often than you'd think, the first fix is the last. Sometimes they don't even have time to take the needle out before they've gone. Dr Grace thinks she might've been dead before she hit the ground, but we'll never know that.'

'God.'

'So for all the drama, it's a sad little death, Merrily. Mobile shows she tried to call her mate, Sam, before she did it. See, we know she wouldn't have had any problem at all getting the stuff. A useful by-product of getting into Jemmie's computer was it led us directly to a dealer we didn't even know about in Ledbury. She'd had Es and dope from the same guy. So delightfully indiscreet, these kiddies.'

Ledbury: pleasant, picturesque old place at the foot of the Malverns. You didn't think of it happening there. But then, it happened more or less everywhere now.

'And some links to bigger players in Hereford,' Bliss said. 'For all she never spoke to her parents, she's chatting away to us, from the other side of the grave. Talking of which...' Bliss spread out some typescript. 'Read this.'

with a plastic bag u can tie it round your neck but its not really necessary and it will take u much longer to get it off if u change your mind!!! Wot is good about plastic bags is that u dont look really horrible when they find you like with some methods of suffocation cos your eyes dont come out all bloody.

'You can also read about the delights of hanging yourself,' Bliss said.

'This is an Internet chat-room, right?'

'A specialist suicide chat-room. Adults advising unhappy kids on how to top themselves. Can't describe what I'd like to do to these bastards with a few plastic bags, but then a few of us Catholics still think suicide's a sin.'

'Did Jemmie Pegler join in the discussions in the suicide chat-rooms?'

'Just eavesdropped, I think. Lurking, as they say. Been doing it, on and off, for weeks, it looks like. Downloaded quite a lot. So we know she'd been dwelling on the possibility of suicide for quite a while.'

'But no clues as to why she chose this method, this place? No mention of Robbie Walsh? Or Ludlow Castle?'

'Nothing.'

'You see, the point is that Robbie fell from the big tower, the Norman keep. No history to that. But Jemima wasn't the first to go off the Hanging Tower.'

'Tell me,' Bliss said.

Merrily told him about Marion.

'Long time ago, that.' Bliss reached down to his briefcase.

'You've already indicated this particular tower isn't best suited to suicide, yet Jemima was determined to go that way.

Did she use all that heroin to give her courage, or was it to make sure she died if the fall wasn't enough?'

'Interesting question,' Bliss said.

'How about Robbie Walsh – did he have a computer?'

'Apparently not. Karen checked this afternoon.'

'You're having second thoughts about Robbie Walsh because of this?'

'You got me thinking,' Bliss said. 'However, according to his mother, he wasn't the computer type. An old-fashioned reader. Certainly enough books around the place, according to Karen. History books. No personal CD collection, either. Very old-fashioned little lad. An old-fashioned family, the Mumfords. Well, most of them.' Bliss laid a folder on the pile in front of Merrily. 'There you go. All ends tied?'

It contained a colour printout from a website.

LUDLOW GHOSTOURS

'You knew,' Merrily said.

'Just thought I'd see if you did. It's all there. Marion of the Heath. For a small fee, this feller will even guide you to the spot.'

'She'd downloaded it.'

'And more besides. Plan of the castle. She knew exactly where she was going and what she was gonna do when she got there.'

'Anything else you haven't told me because you wanted to see if I knew it already?'

Bliss smiled.

Before leaving Hereford, Merrily had called Mumford on his mobile, from the car, sitting in the Gaol Street car park with the rain beginning.

'Aye,' Mumford said wearily. 'I know.'

'Who told you?'

'Doesn't matter.'

'Pointless me asking why you felt you had to pass yourself off as still a copper.'

There was silence. She thought she'd lost the signal. The rain pooled in a dent on the Volvo's bonnet; when Mumford's voice came back it sounded dried-up, like a ditch in summer.

'Can't talk to people. Simple as that. Never could. Can't do small talk. Walk into a shop, I can just about ask for what I wanner buy. What do I say? "I'm Robbie Walsh's uncle and I'm feeling guilty as hell and please can you help me?" Can't do it. Never could.'

In the same way he could only call her Mrs Watkins. In the same way he'd addressed Gerald Osman as 'sir', but not out of politeness. His whole identity had been written on his warrant card.

'What did Bliss say?' Mumford asked.

'He said you should stay out of Ludlow. He was probably hyping it up a little.'

'Mabbe not.'

Merrily sighed. 'OK, here's what else I found out.'

She told him about Jemmie Pegler's computer and the suicide chat-rooms. Emphasizing that, although his name had appeared briefly on the chat pages, there had been no obvious personal connection with Robbie Walsh. Hopefully, this would keep Mumford out of Ledbury.

'Computer, eh?' He let out a slow hiss. 'Never thought. Damn.'

'Bliss said Robbie didn't have a computer.'

'Of course he had a computer. His grandparents bought it for him. Had me collect it from PC World. Packard Bell.'

'Well, he hadn't got it any more, Andy.'

'We'll see about that,' Mumford said.

Driving home, with the rain starting up, Merrily wondered how much was actually known about Marion de la Bruyère, 'a lady of the castle'. You thought of flowing robes, one of those funnel-shaped headdresses, with a ribbon.

But Bernie Dunmore had been right. You were probably talking about a child. Those precious teenage years were also very much bypassed in the Middle Ages; by Jane's age you could be a mother of three. Marion was probably about fifteen herself when she died, or even younger. Young enough, certainly, to be fooled by a smart operator she thought was in love with her.

Jemmie Pegler, staving off chronic emotional starvation, maybe profound loneliness, had been in very much the right mental state to imagine that Marion, disaffected, betrayed – a kindred spirit – would be holding her hand as she jumped.

Merrily said to Jane, 'What sort of state do you imagine someone would have to be in for the idea of suicide to become appealing... exciting?'

'Look,' Jane said. 'Suicide chat-rooms – my basic feeling is that most people who go into suicide chat-rooms are never going to top themselves. It's just titillation. Like running across railway lines, bungee-jumping. Real suicide, that's when you just no longer want to be alive. When it seems like there's absolutely nothing worth hanging on to. You don't care how you do it, do you? As long as it works.'

'Jemmie Pegler went through with it. In a way that suggests she cared very much how it was done.'

'Yeah, that's weird. And what about Robbie Walsh?'

'Possibly killing himself? Mmm. I think we're all starting to have second thoughts about poor Robbie.'

'Well, thanks, anyway,' Jane said.

'For what?'

'For not saying, "Look, flower, if there was ever a deep source of depression in your life, I hope you wouldn't hesitate to—" That's the phone.'

Merrily pointed a menacing finger. 'Don't go away.'

By the time she got to the scullery, the answering machine had caught the call – as was intended, to ambush the people who made a point of phoning at night because it was cheaper, to bend your ear for an hour on some parish issue of awesome triviality.

'Mrs Watkins, if you're there—'

She sighed and picked up, switching on the anglepoise lamp. 'Andy.'

'I'm at my sister's. Robbie's mother?'

'Andy, do you think maybe you need to relax, just a little?'

'I got Robbie's computer.'

'Oh.'

'Thought you might wanner know. When my sister told Karen the boy hadn't got a computer, she lied, nat'rally. Which Karen would've guessed, of course, but she was hardly in a situation to push it.'

'I'm sorry – why would your sister lie?'

'Two reasons. One, they was worried about what he might have on there that p'raps a good, caring parent ought to have known about. Two, they thought they could sell it for a couple of hundred. Taking it to a car-boot sale, along with the rest of his stuff. 'Course, she also tried to tell me they'd already got rid of it, but I remembered the lock-ups.'

'Sorry?'

'Garages – a number of which don't contain cars but serve as storage for various items that residents of the Plascarreg might not want found inside their houses. Sometimes using each other's garages – or the garage of some harmless old lady with no car – to confuse the issue.'

'The Plascarreg. Of course. Are you bringing the computer out?'

There was a pause. 'I could spell this out, but you're an intelligent woman. My sister's here on her own. The boy-friend's down the pub. I got till he comes back to check this over. Not that he scares me, but if I can get away without a scene, that's best. So I'm gonner go over the hard disk on site, as it were.'

Merrily looked up at the wall clock: 9.05 p.m. Over the phone, she could hear vehicles revving, the tinny sound of hard rain splattering a car roof.

'Would it help if I came over?'

'Couldn't ask that, Mrs Watkins. Not the Plascarreg.'

'This is Hereford, Andy, not Brixton. What's the number of the flat?'

'One thirty-seven.'

'OK.' She wrote it down.

'I can't ask you to do this,' Mumford said. 'Not at night.'

'You didn't ask. I'm electing to come. I'm interested.'

'You're stupid,' Jane said. 'You can't see what he's doing to you.'

Merrily standing in the hall, pulling on her coat, Jane in the kitchen doorway, doing the slow head-shake that conveyed superior knowledge.

'Make this very quick,' Merrily said.

'OK. Lol will doubtless confirm the psychology at a future time, but essentially Mumford is a subordinate, officer, right? He never rose beyond sergeant... because he was totally reliable but never had the spark of inspiration that make guys like Bliss – and don't you ever dare tell Bliss I said this – into a bit of a star.'

'No worries there.' Merrily unbolted the front door. 'Bliss would not believe you'd ever said that.'

'And now Mumford's lost Bliss, right?' Jane came into the hall. 'He's floundering. He's out of his depth. He can't make decisions. He can't function without a governor. And so, like, whether he realizes this or not, he's put you into that essential role...'

'Jane, that's—'

'It's spot on, vicar, I'm telling you.'

Merrily stepped outside, then turned back. 'Would you actually like to help?'

Jane's eyes half-closed. 'What?'

'Go on the Net and see if you can find any links between Ludlow and suicide sites and, erm... anything else.'

Jane looked surprised. 'Yeah, OK.'

'Thank you, flower.'

'Any time. I'll, er... I'll see you later, then... guv.'

Outcast

IN THE CITY the rain had stopped, leaving the roads blurred and gleaming, the white-lit restaurant complex in Left Bank Village like an ice palace beside the River Wye, as Merrily drove across Greyfriars Bridge.

This was tourist Hereford, only seven minutes' drive away from the Plascarreg Estate, where no tourists went except by mistake.

Plascarreg: Welsh for place of the rocks. If what she'd read some months ago in the *Hereford Times* was still valid, the only rocks here now were crack-cocaine. Plascarreg was flat-pack brick and concrete housing blocks just off the road between Belmont and the Barnchurch Trading Estate, its windowless backs hunched against the west wind and the city. Half-lit in sour sodium, it looked like a vague idea half-thought-out.

Merrily drove in slowly, on full beam. The derelict land opposite had been scheduled for an extension of the Barnchurch site, suspended through lack of investment or perhaps because someone thought derelict land reflected the Plascarreg ethos better than fields.

The second block was three storeys high: flats behind covered walkways. There was a parking area crammed with vehicles, with just one space free if you put two wheels on the kerb. She reversed in, next to an abandoned van with a stack of crumbling bricks under one rear wheel-arch. It would have been stupid to tell herself she wasn't feeling vulnerable here, but when you'd started out as a curate in a particular area of Merseyside it wasn't exactly a fear of the unknown.

Mumford hadn't said whether his sister's flat was on the ground floor or if there was a stairwell involved. Nobody liked stairwells at night. She started walking along the edge of the roadway, looking up at dull lights behind tight-drawn curtains, edging round puddles, hands in the pockets of her waxed jacket that was hanging open. The air was damp and chilled and sharp, and there seemed to be nobody—

'Mrs Watkins.'

'Andy…?'

Moving softly in the shadows, and it was all shadows here, Mumford took her elbow.

'Should've told you on the phone, we en't going to the flat. It's just over yere.'

He led her to a low concrete block, separate from the flats: garages, with up-and-over metal doors. Stopping outside one with a thin rim of yellow light around it, pulling up the door with a clang that echoed like machinery in a quarry. The light came from a caged circular ceiling lamp, reflected in an oil-pool on the concrete floor where a car would have been.

'You better make this bloody quick, Andy.' A woman moved out of the shadows and pushed in front of Mumford. 'And remember, you don't take nothing.'

She was about Merrily's age, maybe a bit older, with Mumford's small features surrounded by a lot of dark hair. Her red leather coat was open, showing that she was pregnant.

'My sister, Angela,' Mumford said. 'This is Mrs Watkins.'

'Merrily.'

'Good job you didn't come in your dog collar,' Angela said. 'They eat priests on this estate.'

'They wouldn't enjoy me,' Merrily said. 'I'm more chewy than I look.'

Angela gave her a glance, unsmiling. So maybe this wasn't the time to offer condolences.

'Remember what I said,' Angela said to Mumford. 'You don't take nothing away.' She tossed him a key on a chain. 'You got half an hour, no more. Lock up when you've finished, key through the letter box.'

Angela walked out without looking back. Mumford tried to pull down the door from the inside but the handle was missing.

'I would say she's changed.' He left a gap under the door, so they could get out again. 'But she en't.'

At the far end of the garage, the computer sat on a work-bench, already switched on, casting a somehow baleful blue light over stacks of cardboard boxes. Mumford nodded at the boxes.

'Take a look, Mrs Watkins. See what's left of Robbie Walsh.'

Merrily walked around the oil. There were about a dozen wine boxes from supermarkets. Warily, she opened one.

Books. She pulled one out, large-format: *Everyday Life in the Middle Ages, in Pictures*. Heraldic symbols in each corner. Once a paperback, its covers had been stiffened with card, the way you did to prolong the life of a book that you really loved, one that was well used, day after day. It flopped open where a page had been torn out, none too carefully, fragments of it still flapping from the spine. The facing page was headed: TRIAL BY ORDEAL.

Mumford prodded a box with his shoe.

'All his books are yere. Stuff on castles… armour… weapons. Guide books to historic houses people gave him… all off to a boot sale at the weekend – outside of town, they en't daft.'

'They're selling all his stuff?'

'Need the space. Another baby on the way – boyfriend's this time, just to prove he can.'

Merrily put the book back in the box and closed the flaps. It felt like pulling a sheet over a body.

'What happened to Robbie's father?'

'He came to the funeral. Not a bad bloke.' Mumford opened another box, pulled out a turquoise baseball cap, put it on his own head, where it almost fitted. 'This was always too big for

Robbie, see. Poor little devil never realized why folks were laughing. Tried for street cred, never got close.'

'You've got kids, haven't you?'

'Two girls. One in New Zealand, one a veterinary nurse, living with a vet down in Newport. They done OK, considering.' Mumford took off the cap. 'When you make CID, you're as good as lost to your family. "Oh Dad, you're not working again, we never sees you." "Look," I'd say, "I'm protecting you and your mother, that's what I'm doing." Any old excuse. See this?'

He'd opened up a book he'd evidently been using as a mousemat for the computer. *The Tudor Household*. Something had been scribbled on the front and then scribbled over. Through the top scribble they could still make out crude black letters: Walsh is gay.

'Jane tells me the word's become an all-purpose term of abuse now, among kids,' Merrily said.

'Abuse,' Mumford said. 'Aye.'

'What are you thinking?'

Mumford reached into the book box, pulled out a paperback with a white and sepia cover: *Castles and Moated Sites of Herefordshire*. It looked new, except for the brown tape holding the spine together. A pamphlet fell out: *South Wye History Project*.

'Looks like the book was ripped in half, ennit? He was real careful with his books.'

'What you're saying is he didn't do this.'

'That's likely what I'm saying.'

'The boyfriend?'

'Or it could be Ange. When he was little, if he left toys around after she'd told him to put them away, she'd throw them on the fire. I've seen it. This was when she was still with his dad and they were living out at Kingstone. Marital tension. Always felt I... oughter do something for the boy. Couldn't think what.' He put the book back carefully in the wine box. 'Hell, he was never abused, I'm not saying that. Just never encouraged. Which is how he became a loner, up in his room with his books.'

Mumford turned away, stood very still, hands in the pockets of his dark tweed jacket.

'Andy—'

'Let's have a look at the computer.' Mumford brought out his glasses case; his hands were shaking very slightly. 'Never got to see the boy much since she moved in with Mathiesson. They never liked me coming round. Not with both neighbours on probation. No excuse, is it? I could've done something.'

He put on his glasses and gripped the mouse, began dragging the cursor over icons on the computer desktop. Mumford – Merrily had noted this before – was surprisingly at home with computers.

'Seems likely the only time the boy ever went out on his own was in Ludlow. Just walking the streets. In his element.' He clicked on an icon, bringing up a photograph of the ornate oaken façade of the Feathers, in Corve Street, against an improbably Mediterranean blue sky. 'What he'd do, see, he'd download documents and photos from the Net, compiling his own files. Switch on his computer, straightaway he's back in Ludlow. Street maps, architectural plans, the lot.'

'Virtual heaven,' Merrily said, aware of her own voice giving way. She coughed.

'Aye. Look…' Mumford brought up a series of short histories of different buildings; some, like The Reader's House, she'd heard of. 'This is what I wanted you to see.'

THE WEIR HOUSE
Name adopted, since recent major restoration, for this one-time farmhouse on an elevated site below the castle and overlooking the Teme. Origins believed to date back to the early fourteenth century, when it was acquired by the Palmers' Guild, or earlier. Timbers extensively replaced, but one original cruck-beam is preserved and the central fireplace, believed fifteenth-century, remains a significant feature.
NOT OPEN TO THE PUBLIC.

'That's her house,' Mumford said. 'Mrs Pepper.'

There was sweat on his forehead, a small mesh of veins like a crushed insect twitching below one eye.

'But it… Andy, it seems to be one of over a dozen old buildings he's got listed there.'

He shook his head. 'All the others are key historical buildings. This Weir House, it's just been done up from a shell. It's the only one on the list that's not important. And not really in the town itself.'

'But…'

'It's only there 'cause it's hers.'

'You think?'

'Ludlow. The one place he thought he was safe…' He clicked to a photo of the Buttercross, staring at it as if he could get the full story out of the stones.

'Safe from what?'

'Where he thought he was free, then.' He stepped away from the monitor. 'You have a look, see if anything occurs to you.'

Merrily went over to the computer keyboard. 'You checked his e-mails?'

'Nothing.'

'No e-mails at all?'

'I reckon they been wiped – by Ange or Mathiesson, just in case.'

'In case of what?'

'I'm not sure.'

'You been through the deleted mails?'

'Bugger-all. See for yourself.'

Under *deleted mails*, Merrily found one that said *GHOSTOURS. Re half price*. She clicked on it.

Hi Robson!

Thanks for your mail and your interest in GHOSTOURS. Yes, it certainly is half-price for children. However, we don't usually allow anyone under sixteen to go on the walk unless accompanied by a responsible adult. Mind you, it's usually the adults who are most scared!

*Is there a parent or relative who would come with you? If
so, we usually gather in the Bullring on Friday and Saturday
evenings, at 8.00 p.m. But pop into the shop when you're here
and we'll see what we can do!*

Cheers,

Jonathan Scole,

Ludlow Ghostours.

'That's months old,' Mumford said. 'Boy making plans for
his holiday. This is the ghost-walk feller the Pepper woman paid
to take her round. Would she have made a responsible adult for
Robbie, you reckon?'

'Andy, that—'

Merrily turned round. A boy had squeezed under the metal
door. He looked about ten or eleven. She tapped Mumford on
the shoulder, gave the kid a quick smile.

'Hello.'

The boy said nothing.

Mumford eyed him with naked suspicion. 'What d'you want,
sonny?'

The kid moved further into the garage, baseball cap pulled
down. 'What you doing?'

'What's it look like we're doing?' Mumford said. 'We're
playing computer games.'

'What you got?'

'Sonic the Hedgehog,' Mumford said. 'Before your time. En't
you got something violent to watch on TV?'

'That Robbie Walsh's stuff?'

Mumford clicked off the e-mail. 'Makes you think that?'

'Their garage, ennit?'

'You knew Robbie Walsh?'

'You his grandad?'

'No I en't, you cheeky little sod.'

'Ange said we could have a look at his stuff, see if there's
anything we wanted.'

'Aye, I bet she did.'

'Honest!'

'All right, goodnight, son,' Mumford said. His tone had hardened. His hands hung by his sides. Mumford still had police presence. The kid backed off, ducked under the opening, then stuck his head back in.

'Don't want none of that shit, anyway. Robbie Walsh was gay. I'd get Aids or some'ing.'

And disappeared, laughing. Mumford said nothing, but went over and pulled down the metal door, leaving a much smaller gap at the bottom this time.

'He probably doesn't even know what it means, anyway,' Merrily said when Mumford came back to the computer.

'I know what it means.' He didn't look at her. 'Means the boy was different. Sensitive. Bit academic and didn't hang around with whatever gangs operated on the estate. An outcast, in other words.' He picked up the book with the damaged spine. 'Therefore a target.'

'He was being victimized? Bullied? That's what you think?'

Mumford didn't reply. He put the book back and laid a hand on the mouse, running the cursor from icon to icon.

'Try Internet Explorer and click on History,' Merrily suggested. 'Find out where he's been lately.'

But Robbie's most recent ventures on the Net amounted only to Ludlow tourist sites, Ludlow historical society documents. Nothing unexpected. Nothing that looked like a suicide chatroom. After about fifteen fruitless minutes, Mumford went back to the desktop, where nothing looked promising unless you were seriously into medieval history.

It was cold in here, and Merrily was no longer sure what they were looking for. It all came down to Mumford's feeling that the boy had been in need of help and he hadn't noticed. Perhaps thinking he'd got off too lightly with his own daughters, to whom nothing bad seemed to have happened.

'School Projects,' she said. 'Try that. Sounds boring.'

Mumford looked at her. A vehicle went slowly past the garage.

'Maybe a bit too boring,' Merrily said. 'Do you think?'

Mumford clicked on it. An e-mail appeared at once.

Dear Robbie,

Thanks for the stuff you sent me. It was great. It's cool that we're interested in the same things and OF COURSE I won't stop writing to you.

But DON'T WORRY! I know things can seem really bad but like my nan says it's always darkest before the dawn and I know this is going to work out for you and you'll get away from that awful place. Just HANG ON IN THERE and thanks for sharing this with me, I feel really privileged.

Look, Robbie, I've got a lot to do with exams and stuff coming up, so if you don't hear from me for a bit don't think I've forgotten, all right. Love and GOOD LUCK!

Merrily read it again. There was no signature.

'Well done, Mrs Watkins,' Mumford said.

'It looks like he's copied the e-mail onto a document, deleting the signature and the e-mail address. He's hidden it away where nobody's likely to look for it and if anyone finds it they won't know who sent it.'

'Mabbe scared of his mother or Mathiesson getting into his computer when he en't around.' Mumford scrolled up. 'Hang on, here's another.'

Dear Robbie

You've made me cry. I just wept when I read your mail. Those bastards! You can't let them do these things to you. You have to tell someone, do you understand? You could even tell the police, never mind about your stepfather or whatever he is. You've got to do something, do you understand? I'll tell the police for you if you want, I don't mind. Just DO SOMETHING!

love

'I take it all back,' Merrily said.

'You didn't say anything.'

'I thought it. I thought you were making something out of nothing.'

Mumford scrolled up again. No more e-mails.

'We need to go through everything, Mrs Watkins, no matter how unpromising. He's probably got stuff scattered all over the place.'

Merrily read the last one again. 'Obviously a girl. A boy would never admit to crying. It's also someone close to his age...'

'Because she talks about exams.'

'And if we assume the last one was sent first...'

'Then he's replied to it, obviously,' Mumford said. 'He's replied and deleted his reply from his own computer. He's upset he's made her cry, and so he's saying, Oh, things en't that bad. And he's told her something. And he's sent her something.'

' "Thanks for sharing this with me"... what's that mean?'

'Sounds like he's told her about some plan for getting away. Right.' Mumford straightened up, rubbing his hands. 'I'm taking this computer home. Then I'm gonner come back tomorrow and talk to Angela. You agree? I en't overreacting?'

'No, you're not overreacting.'

'Accident – balls,' Mumford said. 'That boy killed hisself.'

'It's starting to look more like it.'

'And if I—'

Mumford spun round as the garage door came up suddenly and violently, like a car crash. Breath shot into Merrily's throat and she toppled a box with her elbow, spraying books across the floor. She saw still figures in the gaping night.

Silence except for a metallic chink.

There were four of them. One, in a hooded top, had something like a dog-chain doubled up and stretched between his fists, and he kept pulling it tight, letting it go, snapping it tight.

Chink.

18

Departure Lounge

THE CLAUSTROPHOBIA IN the Departure Lounge was so intense that Jane had to go into the kitchen for a glass of water. Didn't like this at all any more.

Dipping into the Internet was sometimes like lowering yourself into hidden catacombs or potholing. Going down... click, click, click... one site dropping into a deeper site, crawling through narrow tunnels, until you found you'd sunk so far that, when you looked up, the patch of light over your head had totally vanished, and the air was too filthy to breathe.

Of course, she knew what this was: too many bad experiences with confined underground places linked with death – the cellar at Chapel House, the crypt of Hereford Cathedral. It was close to phobic, and she resented that but it still didn't mean she could handle it.

She filled a tumbler with sparkling water. All she needed now was a bottle of old-fashioned aspirin to wash down. Twenty should do it, right?

Naw, twenty is nowhere near enough, Karone the Boatman, from Nevada, had written for the benefit of Dolores, from Wisconsin. *Ya don't just wanna be sick...*

Jane had started with the new teen-oriented search-engine I Wanna, which dealt mostly with shopping wannas. Shopping to topping yourself was quite a long and tortuous trip and meant circumnavigating all the agony-aunt sites that wanted to talk you out of it.

But she was getting better at this, nearly as good as Eirion now at knowing what to look for. Which was how she'd wound up with the disgusting Karone the Boatman in the Departure Lounge.

Welcome to the Departure Lounge. Take a seat. You are among the best friends you have ever had, perhaps your last good friends. Help yourself to a drink (see our wine list, left). Listen to some music (see our selection, right).

As you can see, the Departure Lounge has two doors. You may leave at any time, through the door on the right. Or you may choose, if invited, to enter, through the left-hand door, into the Inner Lounge.

If invited? It was confusing. The walls of the Departure Lounge kept shrinking and expanding, and the doors on both right and left would alternate from black to white, and sometimes they were both grey. This was technically quite a sophisticated site. More sophisticated, at least, than some of the sickos who hung around in the virtual lounge like virtual pimps.

Karone the Boatman, from Nevada? Jane guessed he'd taken his name from Charon, the boatman who ferried the dead across the Styx in Greek myths... only he'd never read any Greek myths; someone had probably just told him the name, mispronouncing it, and he'd never even bothered to check it out. She pictured some earnest, humourless, semi-literate, burger-munching git in a sweaty baseball cap, who was arrogant enough to imagine it was his mission in life to help other people end theirs.

Karone kept printing up a link to his personal website, on which Jane had tentatively clicked, thus learning how to make a foolproof noose. Shutting down the site at this point, before slime could start oozing through the monitor.

She went back and perused the music selection: some classical stuff and a few names Jane hadn't heard of. Plus Leonard Cohen's 'Dress Rehearsal Rag', which it said Cohen had banned himself from singing – was this a joke? – and a song called 'Gloomy Sunday', which definitely was not a joke.

God.

'Gloomy Sunday' – also known as 'The Hungarian Suicide Song' – had been written and recorded in 1933 by Rezso Seress after breaking up with his girlfriend.

In the song she dies and he decides to follow her. The actual girlfriend later killed herself, leaving a note saying only 'Gloomy Sunday'. Rezso Seress himself jumped to his death from his apartment in 1968.

'Jumped to his death.' Jane found that she'd whispered it.

She was starting not to like this. She learned that the song had been banned by the BBC and other broadcasters because it had been linked to so many suicides, some within the music business – one of the more recent had been one by the Scottish duo, The Associates, who'd recorded it in 1980.

But the most sinister version remained the original, which had recently been cleaned up. It was said to promote nightmares, depression and irrational fear in listeners, but was not available for downloading on this particular site.

However…

The cleaned-up version was not available in 1999, when 'Gloomy Sunday' was covered by Belladonna, and the singer insisted that the crackles and scratches on the 1933 recording be scrupulously duplicated on her own version. Record company executives refused to include the Belladonna version on the album The Pervading Dark *– for which it had been recorded – after a spate of suicides, including an assistant engineer, a secretary and the singer's former lover, the session musician Eric Bryers, who threw himself from high up in a block of flats in south London.*

Jane drank some water. Christ, another one. Did Mum know about this? Somehow she suspected not.

One theory was that the music was part of an occult ritual devised by Seress for purposes unknown, in which his girlfriend was expected to take part. But the implications of it terrified her, and this might have been linked to her suicide.

The words 'Gloomy Sunday' were blinking at Jane from the monitor.

Uh-huh. She drew back and clicked away the panel.

Belladonna. There were some artists who'd been big in the 1980s that it was still cool to kind of like: Elvis Costello, Julian Cope and XTC, of course, who would have been totally celestial if they hadn't stopped touring and been forced to compete against dreary synth bands. But Belladonna...

Belladonna had embraced synthesizers. Her voice even sounded like it had been produced electronically, thin and screechy with occasional pulses – part of the machine. Belladonna was distant, lacked any kind of intimacy. But in its dismal-as-January way, the music did, Jane was forced to concede, sometimes carry you away. Just not to anywhere she could imagine ever wanting to be carried.

Actually, she was being particularly wimpish tonight. Could be something to do with being alone in the vicarage. She really should download Belladonna's 'Gloomy Sunday'. It was almost certainly a scam – that whole story sounded phoney.

On the other hand, she was pretty sure The Associates had existed. The trouble with the Net was that it was always very good at half-truth and conjecture.

Jane clicked back to the music panel. Immediately, 'Gloomy Sunday' began to flash. Her hand hovered over the mouse.

Mumford calmly put his glasses in their case, tucked it down the inside pocket of his jacket. He stood there, turning his head slowly from face to shadowed face, as if he was matching each one to a mugshot. Then he straightened up, hands by his sides, cleared his throat.

'Help you boys?'

And Merrily realized that they *were* boys. Mainly young teenagers, plus the kid of eleven or so who'd been here earlier.

The tallest and presumably the oldest of the teenagers peeled himself away from the others. 'So what's happening, dad?' He was about a head taller than Mumford.

'Heard you was having a garage sale.' The beefy kid with the chain grinned from inside his hood, like some kind of malevolent gnome. He pulled the chain tight. *Chink*.

'Con,' the tall kid said, 'will you put that fuckin' thing away?' He looked mixed-race, had prominent teeth, a stud in the cleft of his chin. His silky black jacket had zips everywhere, like ridged operation scars. 'Sorry about my mate, dad, he's seen too many old videos.'

'Don't apologize,' Mumford said mildly. 'Just take him back to the home and we'll say no more about it.'

'Good one, dad. So...' The tall kid with the zips looked around. 'This is it, then, is it? The official Robson Walsh closing-down sale? Everything must go, yeah?'

'Knew Robbie, did you?'

'We was only his very best mates, dad. We had some awesome laughs with Robbie.' He turned to the others. 'Am I right?'

The eleven-year-old giggled. The other small kid – yellow fleece, combat trousers, watchful eyes – looked down at his trainers.

'You had some laughs.' Mumford's voice was a thin, taut line. 'With Robbie.'

'So, like, basically, we thought we'd like to buy something to remember him by. Not the books, though. The books are shite.'

'What kind of laughs you have with Robbie?'

'See, I was thinking that computer. How much?'

'Not for sale,' Mumford said.

'Tell you what, dad... forty quid.'

'You en't listening, son.'

'All right – sixty. You en't gonner get sixty for a second-hand computer that old, are you?' The tall kid unzipped his jacket, felt in a pocket of his jeans, took out an amazingly dense wad of notes. 'OK, I'll go seventy. Seventy quid. How's that?'

Merrily saw that the boys had arranged themselves in a rough semicircle around Mumford and her, the width of the garage, so that nobody was going to get past them.

'Lot of notes you got there, Jason.' Mumford's face was set like cement, his eyes steady on the tall kid. 'Been nicking little children's dinner money again, is it?'

Jason? Mumford knew him? Merrily kept quiet, staying in the corner beside the workbench. They were only boys, after all. The eleven-year-old... he could even be ten. The other younger one, maybe twelve or thirteen, kept glancing nervously at the tall kid, as if he was worried about where this was going.

Merrily felt the heat of sweat on her forehead.

'You talking to me?' the tall kid said. 'Is that my name, dad?'

'Ah well...' Mumford reached up and unplugged the computer from a socket over the workbench; the screen sighed and faded. 'Could be I made a mistake. Just you reminded me for a minute of Jason Mebus, star of a whole stack of CCTV nasties – urinating in High Town... nicking *Big Issues* from a disabled man. Jason's just waiting for his seventeenth birthday, he is, so he can be in prison videos.'

'Fuck are you?' the tall kid said.

He might as well have pinned on a lapel badge that said *Jason*.

'Then again, it's a bit dark now.' Mumford looked into the black screen. 'So I might've been mistaken. And if you was all gone from yere 'fore I had a chance to get a good look...'

Good. Merrily breathed slowly. That was sensible.

Jason didn't move. The gnome with the chain stifled a laugh.

Merrily saw something dance into Jason's eyes. He reached out a hand, laid it on Mumford's shoulder.

'You a cop, dad?'

'Take your hand off me, boy,' Mumford said mildly.

Jason's grip tightened. 'No, come on, dad... are you a c—?'

Mumford came round faster than Merrily could have imagined, had the boy's arm down behind his back, had him swinging round and rammed up – smack – hard against the side wall, squashing his open mouth into one of its concrete blocks.

'No. For your information, I en't.' Mumford's forearm in the back of Jason's neck. 'Which means I can do what I like to you, ennit, boy?'

Merrily saw a bloody imprint on the wall where Jason's mouth had kissed it.

'Andy...' She came out of the corner. If Mumford had smashed this boy's front teeth, they were in trouble. 'Let's just—'

'You can start by explaining why you want the computer, Jason,' Mumford said, 'or mabbe who sent you in to get it for them, and then—'

And then Merrily was dragged aside from behind, and stumbled to her knees, and saw across the bench that the boy in the yellow fleece had hold of the plug on the computer lead and had started to pull on it, his face red with effort and a kind of panic in his eyes.

By the time she was back on her feet, the dog-chain was around Mumford's throat, the fat kid tugging on it from behind, swinging on it, both feet leaving the ground, and Mumford's eyes bulging out of his veined, florid face.

19

The Joy of Death

SADGIRL. OK, IT wasn't sophisticated, but it was simple and it sounded vulnerable and inoffensive: SADGIRL, HEREFORD, ENGLAND.

It would do.

So Sadgirl left a message in the Departure Lounge.

i lost my baby, and i lost my fella. i'm seventeen and i dont want to get any older. dont want to do any of this again. i listened to belladonna and shes given me the courage to do what i have to do. i want to rest for ever with my child. this is serious.

Rest for ever with my child. Jane thought this was moving and resonant. She felt better hiding behind Sadgirl. Putting her own name in there would have been awful: planting some part of herself in the electronic depths – a suicide seed.

Sadgirl was cyber-bait. It just needed someone to come through and harden the link between Belladonna and suicide. Jane had a picture of the dragon lady lurking, logged on from Ludlow, waiting to entrap damaged people.

Which wasn't entirely ridiculous. She instinctively didn't like this woman. OK, she hadn't even been born when Belladonna was famous, and she hated almost all 1980s music on principle, but it went beyond that now. She'd logged on to the Belladonna websites – surprised at how many there were, mostly unofficial

– and they were all creep sites. You had an immediate sense of something unhealthy, sexually perverse and kind of slick and clammy, like those things people put up to catch flies.

And the woman – her music, at least – was sharing the same cyberspace as Karone the Boatman, sultan of sickos.

Maybe – and the idea wasn't total fantasy because anything was possible in cyberspace and everyone was equal – Sadgirl could lure Belladonna into the open. She just needed to know more. Mum had not divulged enough to give her much of a handle, and Mum was out of reach, which left…

Lol.

It was useful, not to say comforting, to have Lol just across the street. Jane stayed connected to the Net and phoned him on her mobile.

Lol said, 'She's out with Mumford? At this time of night?'

'It's not a date, Lol. And like, I'm sure that, while a certain kind of woman wouldn't be able to resist that gruff, monosyllabic—'

'I'm backing off, all right?' Lol said. 'Just because I'm across the road—'

'No, I like you to be concerned about her. It's old-fashioned.'

'Meanwhile, what exactly is bothering you about Belladonna?'

'Just need a clearer picture of where she fits in. Like, why is she in Ludlow? What's she doing there?'

'Everybody's got to live somewhere, Jane. It's a very sought-after place these days. However… apart from the fact that her stepdaughter's in the area, we really don't know.'

'But there *is* a definite connection between her and Robbie Walsh, right?'

'Seems that way. However—'

'Therefore, if I was to firmly link her with Jemmie Pegler, as well…'

'You haven't…?'

'Got to be close. Mum says Pegler was visiting suicide chat-rooms, and if they're the ones I've just peered into, they're more or less recommending Belladonna as, like…'

'Music to slash wrists by? That's no surprise. It doesn't mean she's authorized it.'

'She could have, though.'

'It, um... sounds like you've been having an interesting night.'

'Educational. I tell you, Lol, if I was ever contemplating an exit, it's the last place I'd go for help.'

'That's the idea, isn't it?'

'Ha ha. No, listen, there's this guy who comes on like, are you cool enough for it? Like, do you have what it takes to be a statistic? You can imagine people who are really, really depressed, and this creep's sneering at them, like it's a challenge – are you hard enough to top yourself?'

'Could be reverse psychology.'

'Not that subtle. It's telling them that if they can't find the balls to do it, they really will have failed. You know?'

'Out of interest, which Belladonna songs?'

'Well, she – this is probably some kind of sick joke – but she's supposed to have done a cover version of something. "Gloomy Sunday"?'

Lol said, with no hesitation, 'The Hungarian Suicide Song.'

'Shit, Lol...'

'It's fairly well known. Billie Holliday did a version.'

'And survived?'

'For a while. She didn't have a very nice life.'

'Did you know that Belladonna had recorded it?'

'No, I didn't. Doesn't surprise me, though.'

'See, there's supposed to be an original version from 1933 that if you hear it...'

'I've heard that, too. Not the song. I've heard what it's supposed to do. The music business is full of ghost stories.'

'They only had the Belladonna version on the Departure Lounge recommended listening list. Along with a Leonard Cohen song he apparently doesn't play any more.'

'And Nick Drake's "Fruit Tree"? That's usually among the top ten suicide songs.'

'I didn't see that. Lol, the Hungarian guy who composed it and Belladonna's ex-lover, Eric…'

'Bryers.'

'You knew him?'

'I know people who I think did.'

'They both committed suicide by, like, throwing themselves off buildings. Did you know that?'

'It's a popular method, Jane.'

'Especially in Ludlow, apparently,' Jane said.

'Jane, let's not… Like I say, Belladonna might not even know they're using her songs.'

'Nah, I think she's there. I can feel her lurking like an evil presence. And Jemmie Pegler was definitely into those sites.'

'Let's not get carried away, Jane, OK?'

'Hey, when did that ever happen?'

Lol was silent. She could picture his expression.

'You had any more anonymous letters, Lol? You *would* tell me?'

'You'd be the first to know.'

'I bet.' Jane leaned into the computer screen. 'Hey, something's come up. I'll have to go.'

'Jane, you didn't listen to—'

She cut the line. This could be significant. But how would she handle it if Belladonna herself had left a message for Sadgirl? Well, it was possible.

But it was Karone the Boatman who'd come back, and he was not sympathetic.

Sadgirl, u r in the wrong room, babe. Nobody here wants to know about ya problems. Come back when ya ready to DO THE THING.

The heartless bastard! You'd lost your baby, got dumped by your guy, and this scumbag…

Jane started to laugh. Oh God, she must really be overtired. She finished the fizzy water, thinking how it would be best for

Sadgirl to react now. She knew how she wanted to react, but that wouldn't achieve anything outside of personal satisfaction.

She switched off the desk lamp, sat back in the chair and closed her eyes to think this out.

Standing in the wreckage of Robbie Walsh's torn-off life, Merrily lit a cigarette and smoked half of it and then threw it down on the concrete and stamped on it. When she put a hand to her face, it sent up a hot wire of pain. Afterwards, her fingers were slicked with blood and water and mucus.

'Should mabbe see a doctor.' Holding his head at an angle, Mumford bent and picked up a cardboard box. Books were scattered all around, oil soaking into the pages, the turquoise baseball cap crushed flat. 'Shouldn't've let you come, Mrs Watkins. Should've realized.'

'What about you, for God's sake?' Merrily could see the flush on his neck, a glaze of blood where the chain had bitten.

'I'm fine.'

'Oh sure – that's why your voice is like a penny whistle someone's trodden on.'

She tried for a laugh, but she was still too shaken, the scene replaying itself from when she'd thrown herself at the fat kid, trying to get a grip on his gelled hair – at the same time aware of the kid in the yellow fleece pulling the computer, by its cord, towards the edge of the bench. She remembered seeing Mumford turning into the chain, his hand crabbed across the face of the fat boy, thrusting him away. Merrily feeling grateful that he'd found the strength... until, at the same time as the computer hit the concrete, the boy's elbow had pistoned back into her face.

Sitting on the floor, semi-stunned, she'd heard one of the younger kids crying out, 'Car coming!' and been aware of Jason Mebus lurching away, eyes flashing hate at Mumford, blood from his mouth forming twin channels either side of the stud in his chin.

In the next memory-frame, there was just her and Mumford amid the wreckage.

He stood over the computer for a moment before lifting it back on the bench where it sat lopsided, looking like a badly fractured skull.

'Andy, we have to tell the police.'

He laughed.

'Andy, come on... Blood on the wall? You half-garrotted? God knows what I look like. We're supposed to just walk away?'

Mumford sighed. 'Mrs Watkins, you know how these things work. They appear in court in their school uniforms, hair all neatly brushed. Look real scared and helpless. One's got a missing front tooth. They got Mr Ryan Nye representing them, on legal aid, making references to my mental state following the death of my nephew – who these boys will deny they ever met – and then my mother. I need to paint you a picture?'

'Suppose I phone Bliss at home?'

His expression was enough to shut her up. He put out a hand and tipped the computer lightly. Something inside it collapsed.

'Got what they wanted, then.'

She remembered Jason Mebus, on his way out, putting in two vicious, hacking kicks, splintering the back of the computer.

'Probably won't fetch much at the car boot sale now, Andy.'

'No.'

'What are you going to tell your sister?'

Mumford bent down, picked up Robbie's baseball cap. 'Not a thing.'

'Sorry?' Merrily had found a tissue in her coat pocket; she brought it cautiously to her face, winced, looked up at him through one eye. 'Is there something here I'm not understanding?'

'I was thinking at first it was the boy told the others we were yere,' Mumford said. 'But then I'm thinking, wouldn't Ange stay with us? Wouldn't you stay with somebody wanted to mess with your dead boy's stuff? Make sure they didn't find anything you didn't want found?'

'What are you saying?' She had a full view of his throat now, red and purple and swollen and lacerated. At least his wife was a nurse.

'Funny Ange en't come back, ennit?' he said. 'Funny we en't seen nothing at all of her feller, Mathiesson.'

'You think they put those kids...?'

'Could be they all had reasons for making sure we never got to see what was on that computer. The kids too.' Mumford's eyes were pale and hard. 'Tells us why Robbie was afraid to come back from his gran's, mabbe?'

We was his best mates, dad. We had some laughs with Robbie.

'As someone trained always to see the best in people, I confess to having a problem with those kids,' Merrily admitted.

'Let's not dress this up, Mrs Watkins,' Mumford said. 'They killed him. As good as.'

And she was in no position to dismiss it. When they left, stepping under the door into the dark and the damp, she noticed Mumford stuffing the crushed turquoise baseball cap into his jacket pocket. Then he picked up the computer.

'Long shot,' he said. 'But it's possible the hard disk might not be totally destroyed.'

Jane woke up so suddenly that Merrily had to hold on to the chair to stop it tipping over.

'Sorry...' She held on to the kid's shoulders. 'I didn't realize you were—'

The scullery was lit only by the computer. Merrily felt she'd had about enough of computers for one night. She had to have a bath. She felt exhausted and aching and soiled and useless.

'Why haven't you gone to bed?'

'Where've you been?'

'How long have you—?' She saw what was on the screen. 'You fell asleep online?'

'Oh shit... listen, it's been twenty minutes max. Anyway, it doesn't cost much at night.'

'Forget it, it's my fault.' Merrily switched on the anglepoise lamp and turned off the computer. 'I should've rung – except I thought if you'd gone to bed— Don't look at me like that. Things were... difficult. I realize it's unlikely I'm looking my best.'

'Shit...' Jane breathed.

'Jane—'

'Things really were bloody difficult, weren't they?'

'I'm OK. I'll tell you about it in the morning. In confidence.'

'So, like, did Mumford do that?'

'Huh?'

'Was it Mumford gave you the black eye?'

'What?'

Merrily stumbled out of the study, through the kitchen to the mirror in the hall, slapping lights on. From the framed print, Holman-Hunt's Jesus Christ regarded her with sorrow and pity and eternal understanding.

'Oh shit,' Merrily said.

When she came back to the study, holding a cold sponge to her eye, the computer was back on and Jane was in front of it. Didn't even turn round to reinspect the injury.

'Mum... take a look at this.'

'You know what time it is?'

'Yeah, yeah. Listen... The suicide chat-rooms, OK? I got into this one, and it seemed to be just, like, crap. There was this guy in Nevada, and— Anyway, I logged on under a false name—'

'Sadgirl?' Merrily leaned over the desk. 'That's you?'

'And Belladonna was there. Or least her music was, but Lol said somebody might have just ripped that off. And there was a song she covered, a famous suicide song, where lots of people connected with it topped themselves. It was Hungarian originally, composed in 1933.'

Merrily dabbed at the eye, wishing now that she hadn't brought Jane into this. 'Sounds a bit tenuous.'

'Except Belladonna's boyfriend also committed suicide, just like the original composer, by – get this – jumping off a high building?'

'Well, that's… it's tragic and everything, but it's not exactly an uncommon method.'

'Yeah, well, I was trying to find a stronger connection. I dropped in the name Belladonna and got a nasty reply from this bastard, Karone, which is what he seems to specialize in, and then – this must've come in while I was asleep, right?'

'OK, let me see…'

Merrily eased Jane away from the screen. Sneery message from someone called Karone the Boatman, and then someone called Dolores had written,

Sadgirl, you have to understand Karone is a technical adviser and inclined to be abrupt. i think what he's saying is you need to go back and think things out. this is the biggest thing you have ever done or will ever do. i myself know, because of my condition, that i'm going to have to do this thing sometime, and all that is important to me is that when the time comes i do it efficiently and quickly and without leaving an unsightly mess for my folks to clear up. you sound like your problems are emotional and i beg you to go away and think again because it will surely pass.

'Sorry, that's not the one.' Jane scrolled down. 'I feel really bad about Dolores. She's obviously got something really horrible wrong with her.' She put a forefinger on the screen. 'This one.'

REVENANT
Sadgirl, Belladonna understands.
Death is eternal life without pain.
Know that we must make our own eternity.

20

Old Ludlow

'CANON CALLAGHAN-CLARKE is looking for you,' Sophie said, without glancing up. 'She's rung here twice already. Claiming your answering machine isn't switched on.'

'Can't believe how inefficient I am sometimes.'

Merrily dumped her bag on the desk, pulled out the chair opposite Sophie, who was addressing an envelope by hand with a fountain pen. Glasses on the tip of her nose, Sophie put the envelope in a tray, for the ink to dry, and started on another.

They'd talked on the phone soon after nine, when Jane, clear-eyed and superficially undamaged by minimal sleep, had carried off a slice of toast and marmalade to the bus stop. Merrily had told Jane a certain amount, not everything, about last night. She'd told Sophie – because there were probably confessionals less secure than this office – the whole situation. More or less.

'Oh yes,' Sophie said. 'On the filing cabinet – this morning's *Daily Mail.*'

'Oh.'

The paper was folded at page five and a fuzzy picture of Jemima Pegler at a party, collapsed in laughter, with two other girls holding her up. The circumstances of her death had come to light too late for yesterday's morning papers to indulge in more than straight reporting.

What a difference a day made: on the other side of the page from Jemima was a line drawing of a woman in a medieval robe and headdress.

A leap across time… Eight centuries separated them. But now Jemima Pegler and Marion de la Bruyère are united in tragic death.

Obvious the media would discover Marion. And nobody waited for an inquest any more; the police line 'no suspicious circumstances' was a strong enough pointer to suicide. The story said Jemima's death had the hallmarks of a copycat suicide, but who was she copying – Robbie Walsh or the death-plunge of the twelfth-century woman whose ghost was said to haunt the castle?

The story is certainly well known in Ludlow, according to Jonathan Scole, who runs Ghostours, which organizes lectures and guided walks around the town's haunted buildings.

'Our tours are getting increasingly popular, and this poor kid may well have come to one. We do occasionally get groups of teenage girls.

'Marion is a very romantic figure, and one of the highlights of the tour is gathering under the castle wall at the precise spot where she fell.

'It's intended to be pure entertainment, and I'm afraid I do tend to ham it up a bit.

'Naturally, it horrifies me that the story could have had this kind of impact on someone, but I doubt it did. If we'd had a multi-storey car park, it's quite possible she would have jumped off that.

'I think if someone's determined to die, they're going to do it somehow, aren't they?'

But an experienced psychiatrist who is studying the Ludlow deaths, said that a second fatal fall at the castle was

*disturbing because it indicated the formation of a
behavioural pattern.*

'Saltash.'

'He does seem to be cornering the market in what one might
call soundbite psychology,' Sophie said.

'He might be right, actually – the teenage pack-mentality, the
need to feel that, even in death, you're not alone. Anyway,
someone has to be around to do the psychobabble.'

'How far have you read?' Sophie murmured.

'What?'

*and teenage girls are particularly susceptible to the fantasy
world of ghosts and the supernatural as an escape from the
ordered world of school and the prospect of exams,' said Dr
Saltash, who is also a special adviser on mental health to the
Diocese of Hereford, which includes Ludlow.*

'Special adviser on mental—?' Merrily let the paper drop to
the desk.

'You notice he doesn't neglect an opportunity to file psychic
phenomena under the general heading of fantasy,' Sophie said,
'thus detaching it from the Church's official area of belief.'

'This isn't going to stop, is it?'

Merrily slumped down next to the window. It wasn't warm
out there, but there was enough early-afternoon sunshine for a
few people on Broad Street to be wearing dark glasses. She took
hers off just as the phone rang and Sophie looked up.

'Ah.' Sophie's hand froze over the receiver. 'I thought there
might be some minor aspect of last night that you hadn't
mentioned.'

'Impressive, isn't it?' Merrily tilted her head to the window.
The sunlight hurt. 'Purplish last night, now a delicate bottle
green.'

'What are you putting on it?' Sophie picked up the phone.

'Just the glasses.'

'Gatehouse.' Sophie tucked the phone between shoulder and chin, just above the pearls, leafing through her letters. 'Yes, Bishop, I'm doing them now, they'll be in the lunchtime post... Certainly... Well, yes, she's here now as a matter of fact... I will.' Sophie put down the phone. 'He's coming over later. He wants to talk to you.'

Merrily had started to roll up the *Daily Mail* into a stiff, tight tube. She stopped, sensing the change, and saw that Sophie's face had hardened and darkened in a way that... just didn't happen.

'God almighty, Merrily! What the hell are you getting into?'

'It was— OK, it wasn't exactly an accident, but it—'

'You do know that's what's known as assault causing actual bodily harm? What did they do to Mumford?'

'Some...' Merrily let the paper unroll, shaking her head help-lessly. 'Some damage. Nothing serious. We hope.'

Before leaving home, she'd talked on the phone to Mumford's wife, Gail, who'd sounded cold and guarded, saying Mumford could hardly turn his head this morning. Hardly the first time he'd brought injuries home, but that was supposed to be all over now, wasn't it?

Sophie wasn't letting it go, either.

'Did he even think about what might happen to you last night, when he took on these savages?'

'I don't suppose he did.' Merrily reached for her bag; a woman with a painful black eye was allowed a cigarette. 'With hindsight, I think he was quite happy when they invaded the garage. He was on home ground. Recognized one.'

'Can we at least assume this will bring him to his senses?'

'Sophie, we both know it's going to make him worse.'

Blokes like Mumford – the bag-carriers, the local-knowledge men, the stoical, taciturn, imperturbable, down-beat, low-key, salt-of-the-earth types – when those guys started to come apart, it was like landmines: you were never sure where the next one was going to explode.

'We now have – or we had last night, it's destroyed now – evidence that Robbie Walsh was scared to go home to Plascarreg.

We have it from his e-mail correspondence. Also his letters to… We also know he fantasized about Marion de la Bruyère. Saw her as some kind of a confidante and wrote to her.'

The postcard she'd seen, next to Robbie's sketches, was now making perfect, heartbreaking sense.

Sometimes I pretend you are walking next to me and we are holding hands and it's brilliant!!!! Everything is all right again, and I never want to leave cos this is our place… I was so miserable I didn't think I could stand it till the end of term. Its worse than ever there. I hate them, they are stupid and ignorant and they are trying to wreck my whole life. The nearer it gets to the end of the holidays the sadder I feel and don't want to go back.

'If there's anything that makes me feel a very unchristian hatred, it's bullying. From cruelty to animals to…' Merrily drew in too much smoke, suppressed a cough as colliding clouds sucked a sunbeam from the desk between her and Sophie. 'We even know who some of them are, now. They as good as admitted it. But bullying's not quite a crime, and neither's suicide any more. Three people dead, and none of them crimes. Doesn't make them any less dead.'

'This woman,' Sophie said. 'Mrs Pepper…'

'I don't know what to think about that any more, Soph. She's a woman who makes mournful music, evidently chosen as a suicide soundtrack by people who run unsavoury websites and chat-rooms. There's undoubtedly a cult – or cults – of suicide operating on the Internet. If she is into all that and she talked to Robbie Walsh – as we know she did – and he was suicidal, is it remotely conceivable that she would actually have encouraged him to jump off that tower? I mean, I hate bullying, but I can understand the spiritual vacuum it comes out of. But this…'

'There are Internet sites that are actually urging people to take their own lives?'

'That's the implication, according to Jane. And chat-rooms. Bit like the Samaritans in reverse, isn't it?'

Sophie's expression didn't alter. Sophie was a Samaritan.

'Merrily, if you think this woman might be connected with

one of these organizations, it's surely our duty to expose it.'

'In what capacity? It's not a Deliverance issue, is it?'

'Isn't the woman fascinated by ghosts?'

'That isn't, in itself, a Deliverance issue, either. Anyway, if I follow agreed procedure and consult the Deliverance Panel, are they going to let me get within ten miles of Mrs Pepper? Mumford's already been warned off by Annie Howe, with whom Siân Callaghan-Clarke says she "gets on well". Probably attend the same kick-boxing classes.'

'This is a mess, Merrily.' Sophie folded her reading glasses, snapped them in their case. 'Everything seems to be a mess at the moment.'

The Bishop arrived before lunch. He looked pensive. He sat on the edge of Sophie's desk, picked up a pen and kept tapping its top into the palm of his left hand.

'George Lackland, Merrily. You haven't met him, have you?'

'Mayor of Ludlow.' She had her sunglasses back on. 'Vice-chairman of the Police Committee.'

'That's the one.' He unbuttoned his jacket, and his purple shirt strained over his stomach. 'Long-standing county councillor, magistrate. George is… the epitome of Old Ludlow.'

'And your old friend.'

'Yes. An honourable man. Conservative in every conceivable sense of the word, of course. Retails traditional furniture, as distinct from so-called antiques.'

'He sounds… very influential,' Merrily said.

The Bishop looked pained. 'I realize that, to you, attaining power and influence means being as bent as… as…'

'A crozier?'

'Thank you, Merrily, I'm all too conscious of the opportunities for personal gain afforded to an unscrupulous bishop. But some of us do our best, and so does George Lackland.'

'Sorry, Bernie.'

'Anyway, he's been in touch. Called me last night, and we spoke again this morning. As you can imagine, George is very concerned – as are many people in the town – about these deaths at the castle. Everything that happens in Ludlow, he takes personally, always has. It's that kind of town – people feel privileged to belong to it.'

'Mmm.'

'That part of the castle – the Hanging Tower – has now been closed to the public, for obvious reasons. But already, sightseers have been turning up on the other side of the wall – where this girl fell. Can't do anything about that: it's a public right of way.'

'What sort of people?'

'Young people, mainly. A group of them were observed last night. They'd gathered with candles. Singing and chanting. There's an old yew tree. They were clustered around it. Near where she fell.'

'Jemima.'

'And, ah, the other one.'

'Robbie?'

'Marion,' the Bishop said.

'Why would they gather there, Bernie?'

'Would you expect a coherent reason? Everything seems to become a shrine these days.'

'Well, perhaps if they knew the full facts, they'd find it less romantic.'

There'd been nothing in the *Mail* or anywhere else, presumably, about the heroin overdose.

'They'll draw their own conclusions, anyway. As some people in the town are now doing.' The pen was going tap-tap on the Bishop's palm again: agitation. 'You see, George Lackland's always been a man of the Church. Senior churchwarden until his civic duties became too onerous. Seen by many of the older residents as something of a figurehead, and not only in a temporal sense, especially with David Cook still in convalescence. So George has... been approached.'

'Oh.'

'Don't look at me like that, it's how things are done there.

People worried about the town's reputation have made... approaches.'

'Tourist association?'

'Well, yes, but also church people. All kinds, not just us. The RC church, various Nonconformist chapels. Individuals who fear for the spiritual health of the community. People who might feel happier talking to the Mayor than to each other.'

'And what are they saying?'

' "Hinting" would be a safer word. No more than whispers. Undercurrents.'

'Mmm?'

'You're not getting me to say it, Merrily.'

'Some people are suggesting that the recent spate of tragedy is somehow rooted in... whatever happened on the same site over eight hundred years ago?'

'Ah...' The Bishop cleared his throat, uncomfortable. 'I don't imagine anyone's expressed it with that degree of... exactitude. Rumours trickle through the streets about a place becoming unlucky, and they gather momentum. Even when I was there, you'd get people saying the town was becoming ungodly, selling out to Mammon – new restaurants, rich incomers.'

'How does that relate to two teenagers and an elderly woman?'

'Well, it... That is, George says some people were suggesting the Walsh boy had become a little too obsessed with the past. Aspects of the past, that is, that should be left to, ah...'

'Has he seen the papers this morning?'

'For once, it seems, the papers are only echoing what's already been whispered. It'll die down in the press, probably before the week's out. The media always treat these stories as a joke. Not in the town, however. Things will be blamed on it that have no connection whatsoever.'

'So what's the Mayor want?'

'A meeting. He's asked me to go and see him. Tonight. I've told him I'd like to bring someone with me who knows more about the elements being, ah, hinted at. Are you free tonight, Merrily?'

'I could be.'

'Good. Excellent.'

'Right, then,' Merrily said. 'So, do you want me, or Sophie, to inform the Deliverance Panel?'

The Bishop looked blank.

'Procedure,' Merrily said. 'All possible cases must be referred to the panel for assessment before any action is taken.'

'Who decided that?'

'The panel.'

'Well, I think' – the Bishop stopped tapping and closed his hand around the pen – 'that we ought to regard this as a preliminary and essentially informal discussion. Don't you?'

'If that's what you think, Bishop.'

'Oh yes. I do.' He placed the pen carefully on the desk. 'I… your eyes, Merrily. Is there something wrong with your eyes, or are you trying to look sinister?'

21

Tradition

THE MAYOR CLOSED his heavy front door, and they stepped into a hall that was cream-panelled and bright with shards of crystal light from an electric chandelier. Through Merrily's new glasses it glowed amber and pink, like a rose garden at sunset.

'This is the Reverend Mrs Merrily Watkins,' the Bishop said. 'Merrily is my, ah, Deliverance Consultant.'

'Oh yes?' The Mayor shook hands stiffly. He wore a mid-brown three-piece suit, with a watch chain, and you didn't come across many of those any more. 'I see.'

He obviously didn't see at all. You could be close to the church your whole life without being aware of what went on in the crypt. Bernie Dunmore didn't explain; Merrily felt he was still faintly embarrassed, even in Ludlow, about perpetuating a tradition as medieval as hers.

'Come on through, Bernard,' the Mayor said. 'Let's sit down in the drawing room and hope to discuss all this in a civilized manner.'

George Lackland's home was above and behind Lackland Modern Furnishings, midway down Corve Street. The Corve was the more modest of Ludlow's two rivers, and this ancient street sloped steeply down from the town centre to meet it. The shops here didn't look like shops at night; most were fabricated inside historic buildings, and the owners hadn't been allowed to enlarge windows or put up new signs. Much of Corve Street was frozen in various eras, all of them pre-neon.

Even the Mayor looked like part of the façade. His forehead jutted like a mantelpiece over the deep-set embers of his eyes. He looked more like a bishop than the Bishop.

'Nancy sends her apologies, Bernard. Meeting of the festival committee. Some very big names coming to town this year.'

'You mean the few who don't live here already?' Bernie said. He was still in his episcopal purple shirt. He'd told Merrily that George would expect this.

She followed the Mayor down the hall to his drawing room, unbuttoning her black cardigan so that the dog collar was fully on view. She wasn't insecure about the women's priesthood any more, but he might be.

'This is nice,' she said.

Well, it probably had been, once. The room was lodged in the era when cream leather three-piece suites were cool, and carpets were always fully fitted because bare floorboards were a sign of penury. There was a high ceiling, with mouldings and another crystal chandelier. French windows revealed a moon-bathed sunken garden, and that really *was* nice.

'Yes, we're fortunate – if that's the word – to have quite a number of famous folk living here now.' George's voice had an Old Ludlow roll, Shropshire easing into Hereford. 'We seem to have become a bit of a refuge from London – actors, television personalities, political people…'

'Singers?' Merrily said.

'Aye, singers too.'

The Mayor put on a cautious smile, showing Merrily to a chair near the hearth, where a log-effect gas fire fanned out tame flames. He opened a drinks cabinet, glancing towards the French window – perhaps, by daylight, you'd be able to see the castle ruins from here. Then he looked back, with uncertainty, at Merrily.

'I'm sorry, Mrs Watkins… what exactly was it that you said you did? I don't fully…'

'Perhaps…' Bernie coughed. Sweat had pooled in the centre of his expanding male-pattern tonsure. 'Perhaps I ought to explain, George, that Deliverance Consultant is the modern term for what we used to call Diocesan Exorcist.'

A silent moment, flames flickering emptily among the artificial logs. Conscious of what the Bishop had said about her looking sinister, Merrily had dived into Chave and Jackson on Broad Street and picked up this pair of less-dark glasses that might even be taken as ordinary tinted spectacles. On the outside, the glasses looked light brown, but they turned these flames bright red, like a miniature synthesis of hell.

'Merrily's our adviser on the paranormal.' Bernie sank into the leather sofa. 'That is, the person who advises people who believe they're having problems with... what we loosely refer to, George, as the unquiet dead.'

There. He'd said it. His hands came together in his lap as the cushions broke wind with a soft hiss.

'This young woman?' George said. 'Oh dear.'

And then he changed the subject and went to get them drinks.

Merrily saw, against a far wall, an elderly radiogram: polished mahogany case with gilded fabric over the speakers. She could imagine the records: nothing later than Elvis.

She sipped her tonic water. 'Mr Mayor, is there any history of... disturbance, unrest... around the Hanging Tower?'

It had taken half an hour to get to this point, via the new restaurants (a good thing in general, better than nightclubs) the new Tesco's (there was demand for it, and it could have been worse, long as it didn't put the traditional butchers out of business) and the new people.

The new people? Well, they had money, which they spent in the new shops. Buying the sort of old rubbish that George and Nancy, not so long ago, used to throw out. But at least the new people appreciated the town. Sometimes too much.

'Disturbance?' the Mayor said. 'You mean these young people dancing around?'

'No.' Merrily looked at the Bishop. 'I mean paranormal phenomena.'

'Of what... nature?'

The Bishop avoided her gaze and said quickly, 'Merrily knows about the breathing, the gasping sounds. Alleged.'

Alleged, huh? *When I realized I was actually cringing into the stones, like a cornered animal, I... threw out a prayer, like a sort of yelp.*

George Lackland came to sit down opposite Merrily, a leather-topped coffee table between them, with a hard-backed loose-leaf file on it.

'Look,' he said, 'there's always been stories. You expect it, don't you, in an old place? Different stories all over the town. Catherine of Aragon's been seen, some say. There's an old woman who walks through the churchyard – that's a regular one. But Marion, aye, she's probably the oldest. The breathing, like someone in a deep sleep, quite a few folk reckon they heard that. Nobody's said they seen her lately, mind – not in years.'

'People used to?' Merrily said.

The Bishop's chin was sunk into his chest.

'The White Lady,' the Mayor said. 'Marion of the Heath. Walked the ruins. And the path around the walls. And people who used to live in the flats at Castle House used to talk about strange noises and... what do you call it when things misbehave?'

'Poltergeist phenomena?'

'Aye. But, like I say, nothing about that lately. Although somebody did blabber on about strange lights round the old yew tree, year or two back.'

'What kind of lights?'

'Hovering lights.' The Mayor made a ball shape between his hands. 'Orbs of lights.'

Routine stuff. Low-key energy-fluctuation.

The Mayor's eyes narrowed. 'What are you looking for, exactly?'

'I'm not looking for anything that isn't there... at some level,' Merrily said. 'It's just that what you've told me doesn't sound as if it's particularly bothering anyone.'

'I don't know what you mean.'

'You see, we don't consider it our function to investigate all inexplicable phenomena just because they're there. We like to think that we're here to try and help people who are frightened or upset by what's happening to them.'

'Well...' George Lackland leaned towards her. 'Top and bottom of it is, if you don't mind me saying so, Mrs Watkins, that a great many people have been very gravely upset by these deaths. Folks remember Mrs Mumford in the shop, and they were fond of that boy, too. Walked into my shop one day, asked if he could look at the old fireplace in the back, and the cellar. Very polite, very knowledgeable. All the little tearaways as breaks your windows and writes on your walls, and the one who falls to his death has to be the decent one.'

'He didn't fall from the Hanging Tower, though.'

'He was the start of it. The start of something.' The Mayor looked into her eyes; maybe he could see the discoloration through the glasses. 'See, I truly love this old town, Mrs Watkins. We're not from here; my family's roots are in East Anglia, but we've been here nigh on two centuries – wool merchants originally.'

'That sounds... pretty local to me, Mr Mayor.'

'We're settled, but we don't feel we own it. Been selling furniture here for over seventy years – real furniture, hardwood, none of your stripped-pine rubbish. We believe in solidness and quality – what this town always stood for. Solidness. We can be relaxed about the side-effects of the tourism and the new people – because we've got a solid heart. And the Church... the Church has always played an essential role here, and still does.'

George turned away, staring fiercely into the gas flames.

'What about the owners of the castle?' Bernie said. 'What do they have to say about all this?' He turned to Merrily. 'The Earls of Powis, the Herberts, have owned the castle for many generations. Edward Herbert was MP for Ludlow in the early nineteenth century, prior to inheriting the earldom.'

'Bit of a silence so far,' the Mayor said. 'Apart from taking the obvious steps to ensure it don't happen again – plans to get that window barred, that kind of measure. It's a question of what other steps might be taken. On what you'd call a spiritual basis.'

'We'd have to go carefully, George.' Bernie took a hurried sip from his brandy balloon.

'Let me put it to you directly,' Merrily said. 'Do you personally really believe that the two deaths at the castle are in some way connected with a paranormal presence dating back to the twelfth century?'

George Lackland grimaced at the stupidity of the question.

'Top and bottom of it is, it don't matter what I believe, Mrs Watkins. I'm the Mayor. My role is to go along with the will of the people. And among the older residents there's a strong sense that something's very wrong. Very bad.'

'Is there a history of suicide here?'

'Well, obviously—'

'I mean in the rather lengthy period between the twelfth century and a few weeks ago.'

The Mayor didn't reply. Bernie Dunmore shot a warning look at Merrily, to which she didn't respond.

'I mean, what actually happened, do you think, to make two teenagers take—' She bit off the sentence: no suggestion of suicide in Robbie's case, although after last night... '*Lose* their lives in a place that had been the scene of just one suicide, over eight hundred years ago?'

George Lackland looked at the Bishop. 'Am I supposed to be able to answer that?'

'George, I think what Merrily's saying is that we have levels of response. Perhaps in the old days, the – let's get the word into the open – the rite of exorcism was enacted without many preliminaries. Today, with the, ah, levels of bureaucracy within the Church...'

'Is this lady going to help us, Bernard, or not?'

'Of course she is,' the Bishop said.

Help us? Merrily had the sense of being woven into someone's fabric. It was time to tease out George Lackland's agenda. This was the man to whom the traders and tourist operators had gone when Mumford had started questioning them about Belladonna. This was the man who, as vice-chairman of the police committee, had leaned on the head of Shrewsbury CID, who in turn had contacted Annie Howe to get Mumford warned off.

Right. She took a sip of tonic. 'Erm... the strange people gathering around this yew tree below the Hanging Tower. With their candles, and their chanting. Who are they, Mr Mayor, do you know?'

'Not local.' As if this was all that needed to be said about them.

'What did they look like?'

'Oh... stupid. Horror-film clothes. You know the kind of thing.'

'What I heard,' Merrily said, 'was that there'd been quite a few of them around the town recently. Possibly before the deaths.'

The Mayor spread his hands. 'It's possible. We get all sorts comes and goes.'

'And there was a bit of a fight with some local boys.'

'More of that than there used to be, regrettably – street violence. Too much drink about.'

'And someone got stabbed?'

'First I've heard of that, Mrs Watkins.'

But she'd seen the twitch of a nerve at the corner of an eye.

'Perhaps people like this were... attracted here by the ghost stories?'

'I wouldn't know about that.' He smiled apologetically and shook his bony head. 'To be honest, I feel a little bit daft sitting here in this day and age talking about ghosties and ghoulies and things that goes bump.'

'Oh, I get used to it,' Merrily said. 'But the thing is, before we can organize any kind of remedial action, we have to eliminate all the possible rational explanations. For instance, somebody told me that these kids in fancy dress are probably just fans of... one of your rich settlers? A singer?'

George Lackland said nothing. Nothing twitched this time, but she was sure that she saw a quick glitter of anguish in the hollows of his eyes, and he planted levering hands on his thighs as if his instinct was to walk out.

'Can't remember her name… used to sing these mournful songs all about death and… and things like that.' Merrily smiled ruefully at George. 'Not your cup of tea, really, I suppose.'

The flame-effect gas fire gasped, the Bishop's brandy glass chinked on an arm of the sofa as he sat up, and she felt his curiosity uncurling in the air.

'No,' the Mayor said at last. 'Not my cup of tea at all.'

He came to his feet, screwing his eyes shut for a moment and swaying slightly, rubbing a hand wearily over the back of his neck.

'Ah, that's the trouble with public life,' he said. 'Always some malcontent ready to shoot his mouth off.'

'Something here you should be telling us, George?' the Bishop said.

22

Stepmother

THE BISHOP'S GAZE swivelled back to Merrily, and in it was incomprehension... and suspicion.

Well, she could understand it. The hour-long journey here had been filled with an explanation of her bruised eye and everything that had led up to it: Jemmie's sordid e-mails, Mumford and Robbie's computer and the history books and Jason Mebus. Not reaching the Departure Lounge until they were leaving the bypass at the Sheet Lane entrance into town, with the moist blue night dropping over Ludlow like the lid on a jewel box.

And so not quite getting around to Belladonna.

'I've got nothing to hide about this,' George Lackland said. 'Nobody could possibly expect me to like the woman.'

He was standing up now, behind his cream leather chair, both hands gripping its wings. One of the bulbs in the chandelier had blown and was hanging there like a bad tooth, making the room seem just slightly tawdry.

'When the boy came home with this girl, Susannah, she was everything you'd want for your son – respectable, steady, nicely spoken. And a solicitor, too, of course. Always useful to have a solicitor in the family, especially with a firm like Smith, Sebald and Partners.'

Merrily glanced at Bernie, both eyebrows raised to convey that she had no idea what the hell the Mayor was talking about.

'Sorry, George,' Bernie said, 'I'm a bit out of touch – which boy is this, Douglas, or, ah…?'

'Stephen, the younger one. The one who went to university. Like Nancy said, when you think of the girls he might have brought home from that place…'

'He's, ah, engaged, is he?'

'To this girl from Smith, Sebald, as I say. Very well established firm, as you know – offices in Ludlow, Bridgenorth and Church Stretton. She'll be a partner one day, Bernard, no question of that.'

'I'm sorry, George – who exactly are we talking about?'

'Susannah,' the Mayor said. 'Susannah Pepper.'

'Ah,' Merrily said.

Of course.

Bloody hell.

'Your… future daughter-in-law… her father would be a record producer called Saul Pepper?'

The Mayor looked at her with keen interest. 'That's quite correct, Mrs Watkins. But how could you—?'

'I have a friend in the music business. I gather Saul Pepper lives and works in America now, since the break-up of his marriage to… Mrs Pepper.' She turned to Bernie. 'Who lives in the renovated farmhouse at the bottom of The Linney – and was seen in the castle with…?'

The Mayor's hands tightened on the chair wings, and then he turned away. Merrily could tell that getting the story out of him was going to be like dredging a pond – a lot of discoloured water and sludge, and the bottom never quite exposed.

But enough had now been clarified – particularly the warning-off of Andy Mumford – to make the exercise well worthwhile, no matter how long it took.

'They were engaged before you met her mother, then,' Merrily said.

George spun round. 'Stepmother!'

'Of course.'

'But yes, you put your finger on it there all right, Mrs Watkins, we had not met her before the engagement.'

'George, do excuse me,' Bernie said, 'but my own knowledge of the, ah, the stepmother is somewhat scant.'

'Aye, and if my knowledge was as scant as yours, Bernard,' George said, 'I'd count myself a happy man.'

Of course, when Susannah Pepper had told them her stepmother was coming to stay, George hadn't known who this woman was, let alone why she was considered notorious. He knew that Sue's mother had been deserted by her father for the woman, whom he'd proceeded to marry. It hadn't lasted, however, and he'd moved to America, starting a new family over there.

Well out of it, as George now realized, although the divorce had been amicable.

'She has… considerable assets, Bernard. Could probably buy my business twice over. Susannah's her solicitor and financial adviser. And nursemaid, now. And, by God, she needs one. Day and night. Particularly at night.'

Merrily said nothing. Let this come out in its own way.

'Whenever they needed to discuss her financial affairs, Susannah used to travel to her stepmother's home,' the Mayor said, 'wherever it happened to be at the time. She moved around a lot, London one year, Paris or Rome the next. And then… she came to Ludlow.'

Well, that first visit of the stepmother… George didn't think much of it. Not an event he was ever going to keep gilt-framed in the formal gallery of his memory. And nothing particularly amiss at first. They weren't contemporaries, George and Bell, not by ten or more years, yet for that first meeting she'd been dressed decently and conservatively, if a little eccentrically, in an Edwardian-type summer dress, her blonde hair neatly styled, Nancy had noted. Quite girlish, rather attractive.

And clearly besotted with the town, from the start.

George should have spotted the danger signs: the woman tripping and gliding around the Buttercross, this delighted smile on her face, upturned to the sun. And then breaking into almost a dance. He was quite gratified, at first, in his proprietorial way. Not having any idea then that she was already planning to stay…

… For good.

George looked at the Bishop. 'Do you know that she tried to get one of the flats at Castle House?'

'Was she eligible?' Bernie turned to Merrily. 'We mentioned this earlier – there was a large house built onto the outer walls in, I think, the nineteenth century. Later turned into council flats, would you believe? Not quite sure what the situation is at present.'

'There was a couple living there, halfway through a forty-five-year lease,' George said, 'and she tried to take it over. She was besotted with the idea of living inside the castle. I think she thought if she could get that apartment she'd soon have the whole house – maybe feel like she owned the castle, who can say?'

'What happened, George?'

'Oh, the Powis estate managed to stop it. They have other plans for Castle House. But she has money, my God, she has. The people she tried to bribe! Fortunately, the Earl of Powis is a man of strong Christian principles and I reckon he saw the danger. Eventually, she settled on The Weir House – so called. I don't know what she gave for it, but the people who rebuilt it seemed to have been well satisfied. As for Bell— Hold on a minute, would you?'

George went over to a long mahogany sideboard, opened a drawer, took out a slim box file, brought it back and emptied out the contents in front of Merrily, as if he was putting all his cards on the table.

'This is one from the *South Shropshire Journal*.'

He spread out a photocopy of a press cutting.

Ludlow is my heaven,
says rock diva Bell.

***

In the colour photo, Belladonna sat on the steps of the Buttercross in a filmy cream dress, arms folded. She looked graceful and calm and strangely demure.

'She'll only ever speak to the local papers,' George said. 'Reckons this town's her whole world now, and nothing outside it matters. Oh, they all had a go, when she first moved here – national papers, television. None of them got close.'

'Don't suppose they tried too hard,' Merrily said. 'She isn't as famous as she used to be.'

'If they all knew what I knew, Mrs Watkins,' George said, 'she'd be in every paper there is. That's the top and bottom of it.'

'And are you ever going to tell us, George?' The Bishop sat cradling his brandy balloon, with its last quarter-inch of spirit. 'Merrily's not exactly one of the Little Sisters of the Assumption. She's been around, you know.'

'Thanks very much, Bernie.'

'George knows what I mean.'

'What's ironic,' George said, 'is that she's become a bit of a heroine to many people here – 'specially the new folk, the well-off folk. Ever a bit of timely cash needed to conserve some historic building, she's in there with her chequebook. Made plans, apparently, for her own trust fund, to protect the old places. And then there was the housing business. You remember the development plan for the Weircroft fields, Bernard?'

The Bishop shook his head. 'After I left here, I imagine.'

'Owner of a couple of rough fields not far from The Weir House – bit of a wide boy, you ask me, had the look of a gypsy – he was trying to get planning permission to put houses on them. And there was a fifty-fifty chance he'd get it, too, eventually.'

'Down by the river?' the Bishop said. 'Surely not!'

'Under the castle walls, near enough. Council opposed it, and so did all the residents nearby, naturally. But the way this government is on housing now – build more and more, ignore the green belts – chances are he'd have won on appeal, especially as he was promising more than the usual quota of low-cost homes which are hard to get in Ludlow now. Then she made him an offer for the land.'

'Did she indeed?'

'And a very meaningful offer it was, too, but he had to decide now. Now or never. Well, he couldn't afford to risk it, and so she bought the ground and declared it preserved. And now none of her neighbours will have a word said against her, because, if she moves, that ground's gonner be up for grabs again. So all the folk in that vicinity, from Upper Linney to Stanton Lacy, turns a blind eye and a deaf ear.'

'To what, George?'

'To a good deal more than rumour, but I've never been one for gossip, Bernard, you know that.'

'Erm...' Merrily thought that one day she might meet someone who actually admitted to relishing tittle-tattle. 'She walks the streets, right? At night. With a candle, sometimes.'

George Lackland folded his arms and sucked in his lips.

'Like a ghost,' Merrily said.

George dropped his arms. 'Like a whore.'

'Oh, really, George,' the Bishop said.

'You were here long enough, Bernard. You know what's what. The prostitutes in this town... they knows their place. And you will agree that place is not, for instance, St Leonard's graveyard.'

'Oh, come now—'

'We manage to keep it all under wraps one way or another. The police – well, if she's broken the law, it's not much compared with what else they have to handle nowadays. Can a woman be done for indecent exposure? Minor theft?'

'I'm sorry,' Merrily said. 'What—?'

'She stole a prayer book from St Laurence's. Maybe other things, too, but someone saw her put the prayer book in her bag and walk out. And there was more, but we couldn't tell David Cook, with the state of his health.'

'More of what, in particular?'

'We didn't exactly hold on to the evidence.'

Merrily waited. Bernie Dunmore took a precautionary sip of brandy.

'What she left in the church' – George spoke tightly, as if his throat was closing up – 'back of one of the misericords. Well, you don't keep… articles like that.'

'Perhaps I'm somewhat naive,' the Bishop said.

'Corey House in Broad Street, Bernard? The decorators?'

'Architectural Interior Designers and Restorers, I believe they call themselves now.'

'Decorators,' George said. 'The son, Callum, he went to finish off a wall for her at The Weir House. Had some very peculiar requests made of him. His father's on the town council, and he had a word with me. They're newcomers, but they're a decent family. Thought I should know.'

'What were the requests?' Merrily asked. But George shook his head in a shuddery kind of way.

'And there's the parties. The young people. The singing.'

'What kind of singing?'

'I only use that word out of politeness,' George said. 'Sounds like a tribe of tom-cats.'

'You've heard it?'

'Just the once. I was advised to walk down The Linney and have a listen. There was something resembling a song, but I couldn't distinguish the words. I think it was her and some other people.'

'Possibly the ones who gathered under the Hanging Tower after the girl's death?'

'Aye. The neighbours… they look the other way. Some of the local boys are less tolerant, 'specially when they come out the pubs.'

'Was it… one of these local boys who was stabbed that time?' Merrily asked.

George took a long breath, said nothing.

'But nobody was charged, right? Perhaps somebody was persuaded not to make a complaint?'

'Probably wasn't serious,' George said quietly.

'As a leading member of the Police Authority,' Merrily said, 'I suppose it's a bit difficult for you.'

The Mayor's eyes flared with anger, like coals far back in an old kitchen range. Merrily came back quickly, before he could clam up again.

'Did you know that Mrs Pepper had been seen with Robbie Walsh not long before he died?'

'Well, of course I knew. She was seen all over the town with him – in the church, the path by the yews as leads down to the back entrance of the Bull, the old alleyways…'

'Do you know what brought them together?'

'No. But then, I've not had what you'd call lengthy conversations with her. Wisest not to.'

'Do you have any idea at all why she does… the things she does?'

George didn't reply. He began scratching at the back of his hand as if he'd been stung.

'You've evidently been covering up for her, George,' Bernie said. 'For quite some time, it sounds like. For, ah, Susannah's sake. And Stephen's, naturally.'

The Mayor went to the French windows and pulled a cord to draw the velvet curtains. Stood with his back to the dusty pink folds, as if he was keeping something out.

'And the good of the town, of course,' Bernie said slyly.

'She's a sick woman, she's…' George Lackland reached up and pulled the curtains together at the top, where one had slipped off its glider, and Merrily thought she heard him say 'evil' but couldn't be sure. He turned around. 'Pressure of wondering what she's gonner do next is getting to me a bit, have to say that. Top and bottom of it is, I wish she'd never come, and I wish she was gone.'

'I might be slightly off course here,' the Bishop said, 'but it seems to me that all your problems might conceivably be part of the same one. Do you think?'

George Lackland didn't reply.

'And you can't involve the council, George, and you can't

involve the police. Therefore, I suppose that's why we're here.'

'Maybe I just wanted to talk to somebody who knew the town and could see the picture,' the Mayor said. 'Even if they thought there wasn't anything they could do. At least they'd understand a few things.'

'Some things are not easily understood.'

'Likely I used the wrong word. I'm not an educated man, as you know. But there's areas of... areas of experience where education don't help that much.'

The curtains were swaying a little in a draught from somewhere. George Lackland watched them with a faint smile.

'I remember a young chap thought he was up for a bit of easy money – just spend a couple of hours on his own in the Hanging Tower.'

'Oh now, George, that was a long, long time—'

'Never seen a man more scared, from that day to this. Comes running across the old inner bailey, stumbling and tripping – didn't think his pals could see him, and they didn't like to rub it in at the time.'

'What?'

'Didn't want you trying to escape, Bernard, so we took a few bottles of pale ale into the old Magdalene Chapel and kept very quiet. Sobering, though, in the end. We all thought you were faking it, at first.'

Merrily smiled. The Bishop saw her and scowled.

'Bastards.' He finished his brandy. 'All right, George, suppose someone was to look into it. All of it. Discreetly. Someone sympathetic but, ah... knowledgeable in all the necessary areas. And, of course... utterly reliable.'

'Then I would be most grateful to that person,' George Lackland said, 'and provide what assistance I could.'

Down by the fake logs, Merrily froze.

217

23

Duality

THE ROAD TO Hereford was due south, more than twenty
moon-washed miles. For the first three or four, neither of them
said a word. Merrily's black eye was pulsing. Her new sunglasses
lay on the dash. Somewhere behind its facia, the old Volvo was
ticking like a time bomb.

Eventually, the Bishop coughed.

'Mother-in-law from hell, eh? Well... stepmother-in-law.'

Merrily glanced to her left: moonlight bathing the Bishop's
brow. At the Little Chef at Wooferton, the lights had gone out.

'What have you done, Bernie?'

'I think the word "evil" passed old George's lips at one point,
but I'm afraid he had his back to me at the time.'

'And that justifies it, does it?'

'We have nothing to justify, Merrily.'

'Not yet.'

'It's all quite legitimate.'

'So you'll send an official memo to the Deliverance Panel first
thing in the morning, saying you're personally authorizing me
to investigate a cluster of deaths and their possible connection
with a woman who's causing considerable embarrassment to
the Mayor of Ludlow.'

'We can deal with that,' the Bishop said. 'And surely... you
want to, don't you?'

'I think I'd want to know why I'm doing whatever I'm supposed to be doing. I mean, let's establish, first of all, what your

long-time friend the Mayor is after. For instance, when he was close to advocating exorcism, which woman do you think he was talking about, the dead one or…?'

That duality again. It had been there from the start: *Why did God let her take him? Why did God let that woman take our boy?*

'Look, I had no idea,' the Bishop said. 'I didn't know there was any connection between George and this woman. Until that chap who makes calendars brought her up, I'd never even heard of her.'

'Because bloody George is using his position to hush it all up! He's already had Andy Mumford warned off. Plus, a guy who was stabbed in the street has probably been given a bung to keep quiet about it.'

'You don't know that—'

'Ha! I mean, sure, I can see the Mayor's problem – she's landed like an alien being from a world he can't even comprehend – but there's no way I want to appear to be working on behalf of someone who works the system like good old George.'

'Merrily, he hadn't even mentioned Mrs Pepper. It was you who introduced the subject.'

'You think? You know what, Bernie? I think he was talking about her all along. From the beginning. I think she's what's causing unrest among the older God-fearing folk of Ludlow, far more than the possible influence of a silly little girl who got taken for a ride in the twelfth century. On which basis, by the way, I'm buggered if I'm going to even consider exorcizing the Hanging—'

'Merrily!'

'Sorry. Didn't get much sleep last night. Got elbowed in the eye by a psychotic teenager.'

'How come you know so much about this Mrs Pepper?'

'Lol. And Jane on the Internet. It doesn't take very long to find out about anything any more. Also, I saw her, when I was on the river bank with Mumford and you were in the pub with his dad. I recognized her… realized this was who Osman meant.'

'Well, I don't know anything about her, as I said, but I do know that George Lackland, while he may work the system, is a decent man who thinks his beloved town is being contaminated, if only by having its moral tone lowered. Is he exaggerating this? I don't know.'

'Personally, I just can't see a wealthy middle-aged woman going in for wholesale alfresco sex in a town she regards as heaven. And I don't want to get involved—'

She braked, catching a movement on the grass verge: badger about to scuttle across the road.

'—get involved with a witch-hunt.'

'Witch-hunt.' The Bishop leaned his head back over the passenger seat, from which the headrest was long gone. 'How simple things were in those days. The mob would have dragged her in front of some judge who thought he was God, and then taken her out and hanged her at Gallows Bank.' He turned his head towards Merrily. 'Still there, you know. Still this patch of open space, in the midst of modern housing. You can see where the actual gibbet stood, so that executions would be visible all over town. Ludlow, you see, looks after its past.'

'Unlike Hereford?'

'We try. Unfortunately, I think our old execution site is underneath Plascarreg.'

'Really?'

'Don't you dare make anything of that.'

Merrily smiled.

'And try not to hang George. He's an old-fashioned civic leader. Middle Ages, he'd have been the sheriff. When they eventually come to lay him out, they'll find the imprints of chain links on his chest.'

Of course, he'd know exactly how George felt because it was how *he* felt. If Ludlow was tainted, George was tainted, and if Bernie let George down he would probably feel he'd forfeited his right to come back and live out his sunset years in the benign shadow of the Buttercross.

'Of course, the woman's obviously mad,' he said. 'Too many chemicals in years gone by, one assumes.'

'You think we should inform the Diocesan Director of Psychiatry?'

She felt him staring at her, working this out. He shifted, something clicking ominously under his seat.

'Saltash.'

'You read the *Mail*, then.'

He grunted. 'It was in *The Times*, too, actually. Yes, that man did rather exaggerate his role, didn't he?'

'Glad you think so.'

'Heavens, Merrily, last thing we want is worried people avoiding Deliverance for fear of being considered eligible for assessment under the Mental Health Act.'

'But under our new, agreed working practices, I'm supposed to report – for instance – what we've just been told, for consideration by the panel before any action is taken. Like I said earlier, I shouldn't even have come tonight without clearing it with them.'

'It's preposterous, Merrily.'

'It's what we agreed.'

'What *they* agreed, you mean.'

In theory he could, as Bishop, overrule any of it. In practice, it would be impossible without dispensing with the panel and making lifetime enemies of Siân and Saltash, and the Dean who had brokered the deal. She left all this unsaid, but it was drifting between them as Leominster appeared over to the right, an island of lights.

The Bishop sighed.

'Merrily, let's not fool ourselves. Look at me: overweight, over sixty and not up to much in the pulpit. I've never been under any illusions. I'm a caretaker here and I suspect my time's already running out.'

'Come on, Bernie, people like you.'

'Like? What's that got to do with it? There are those who could have me quietly retired in no time at all, if they chose to whisper in the right ears. And I rather suspect Ms Callaghan-Clarke's one of the potential whisperers.'

'You think Siân wants you out?'

'I don't know what I think. Hereford's not the most exalted of dioceses, and nicely out on a limb. Good place for a woman to have a chance at the helm, wouldn't you say?'

'Siân Callaghan-Clarke?' Was that the wheel shaking, or her hands? 'Bishop of Hereford?'

'I'm simply saying it's a possibility that's occurred to me, that's all. May be years off, yet. Then again…'

'Christ,' Merrily said.

'And there's… something else. I'm not supposed to tell you this yet, but… the Archdeacon came to see me this afternoon. You know Jeff Kimball's moving to St John's at Worcester, leaving a major vacancy at Dilwyn?'

'I didn't.'

'Well, he is. And with Archie Menzies retiring in the autumn, your area of north Herefordshire's going to be stretched. Inevitably, the Archdeacon's looking at the possibility of a shake-up – introduction of a collaborative ministry in that area: rector, team vicar, et cetera. And, as all this would be happening very close to the Ledwardine parish boundary, it's been suggested that Ledwardine should be included in the review.'

'Oh.'

Her hands slackened on the wheel. She could see where this was going. Only a matter of time.

'And, of course, someone pointed out that you had only one parish,' the Bishop said.

'Inevitably.'

'Something of a rarity these days, you will admit.'

'Who, er… pointed that out?'

'No idea, but I expect you could make a solid guess. My opinion, as I've frequently stated, is that, with an expanding Deliverance department to run, one parish is quite ample, and I do know you're working seven days most weeks. But when I pointed this out to the Archdeacon, he said it had been suggested to him that perhaps Deliverance was something that, ah, expanded according to the time and the manpower – or, indeed, womanpower – available.'

'The Archdeacon's been got at.'

'So it would seem.'

'Someone wants me to have a bunch of extra parishes. Thus leaving very little time for Deliverance work.'

'Draw your own conclusions. The thinking, I would guess, is that Deliverance would itself then become something of a team-ministry.'

'And the post of Diocesan Exorcist – under whatever title?'

'Would disappear.'

'Well, I suppose that's neither here nor there.' Merrily kept her eyes on the road. 'Except that the end result would probably be that Deliverance itself – as a specialist field – would eventually also disappear.'

'I can see that happening, yes,' the Bishop said. 'It's a political thing, isn't it?'

They hit the Leominster bypass, picking up speed and extra rattle. The Bishop seemed tired, almost defeated. Merrily wondered how close he was to pre-empting attempts to remove him while a suitable property in Ludlow was still within his price range.

'I'm sorry,' he said. 'I didn't want to tell you tonight.'

'I'm glad you did.'

'I may be misinterpreting it.'

'I don't think you are. It explains a lot. Well...'

'Quite.'

'If I fight it, it's going to look like pure self-interest, extreme selfishness – some ministers struggling to support seven parishes, while I'm poncing around with a flask of holy water.'

'There's so much resentment in the Church now. I'll hold out against it, of course...'

'You can't. I wouldn't expect you to. Anyway... let's see what happens. Meanwhile, there's the Ludlow situation to sort out.'

'Look,' he said, 'if you think you should take it to the Deliverance Panel, do it. If they say leave it alone, leave it alone.'

The parish church of St Mary, Hope-under-Dinmore, rose up on the left, separated from its parish by the fast road. Our Lady of the Bypass. Merrily slowed; this stretch had a bad record for deaths.

'Stuff them,' Merrily said. 'I'll do it. But if anything rebounds on George I won't try to catch it first, OK?'

'Of course not. Merrily, look, I've been thinking about this whole situation. Why don't you take a week or ten days off from the parish – get Dennis Beckett in as locum. Then you can look into the situation and you won't be responsible to anybody, will you? You won't be there. You'll be working... what's the word?... not plain clothes?'

'Undercover?'

'That's it. Afterwards, you produce a report for me, and I inform anyone who complains that this seemed to me to be the best way of dealing with a delicate and rather nebulous situation.'

'Bernie, have you really thought this through?'

'And it's not a witch-hunt, Merrily, it's pastoral care. It's very clear that this woman needs help. Women don't behave in this way because they're happy and fulfilled. They don't leave used sanitary towels down the back of a fifteenth-century misericord, they—'

She turned to him. 'I don't remember him telling us that.'

'He didn't. He got halfway and became embarrassed. The incidents – it happened three times in successive, ah, months – were mentioned as a whimsical footnote in a report on church maintenance I was obliged to read.'

We didn't exactly hold on to the evidence.

'That's weird, Bernie.' She followed a pale grey ribbon of road up the long hill towards Hereford. 'Not to say faintly ridiculous.'

'Play it by ear. Follow your conscience.' The Bishop loosened his seat belt, settled back with his hands folded on his stomach.

'Do have a cigarette, Merrily, if you want.'

'You're a true man of God, Bernie,' Merrily said.

Merrily didn't have the cigarette until she'd dropped Bernie Dunmore at the Bishop's Palace, behind Hereford Cathedral. It was about nine-thirty p.m., a few people about. She parked for a few minutes on the corner of Broad Street and King Street, opposite the cathedral green, took the Silk Cut from her bag and thought about Belladonna and Marion de la Bruyère.

About ghosts.

In the 1930s, a cowled, monkish figure had been repeatedly seen in the cathedral close. Seen initially by policemen. The whole town had been hugely excited, apparently. Excited rather than frightened. As many as two hundred people would gather here on the green, night after night, in the hope of spotting the ghost. Like a football crowd, someone had observed at the time.

Merrily smoked and gazed out at the green and the Cathedral and the soapy spring moonlight splashing through the trees, where all those people had stood in anticipation of… a multiple psychological projection, a shared hallucination on a grand scale?

The existence of ghosts, the nature of ghosts. At least half of the raison d'être of Deliverance.

She rang Jane to say she was on her way home. The kid sounded tired.

'I'll probably have an early night. Take it nobody beat you up or anything?'

'Not so's you'd notice. Look, I'm sorry I had to go out again.'

'Save it for Lol. He's off to Bristol tomorrow.'

'Oh my God, I forgot!'

'You always forget.'

'I'd better go round.'

'Stay the night, I'll be OK.'

'I'll be back by midnight,' Merrily said.

'Yeah,' Jane said morosely. 'I expect you will.'

She parked the car at the vicarage and let herself in. A kitchen lamp had been left on, but there was no sign of Jane. She gave Ethel a foil pack of Felix and then, out of habit, went quietly up to the attic apartment, just to make sure.

'Er... night-night, Mum,' Jane said from the other side of the door.

Merrily smiled. Forgiven. Kind of.

She managed to catch the Eight till Late just before it closed, picked up some cigs and a bottle of white wine, carrying the bottle openly down Church Street. The village was deserted, but there were a lot of windows on either side. It was the darkened ones you had to worry about – not all of them were holiday homes.

However, the darkened ones did not, tonight, include Lol's.

He'd seen her coming. He was standing in his doorway.

'You've had the electricity reconnected!'

'No going back now,' Lol said.

He still seemed bewildered at finding himself a man of property. The hall behind him was lit by a low-wattage bulb dangling over the newel post where Lucy Devenish used to hang her poncho.

Merrily felt a rush of emotion.

'No,' she said. 'Definitely no going back.'

In full view of all the darkened windows in Church Street, she stepped up to the doorway and kissed him on the mouth. Saw his eyes widen close to hers as he manoeuvred her inside, throwing the door shut behind them.

'What have you done?'

Oh God, her glasses! They were still in the car.

'I...' She swallowed. 'Would you believe it if I said I'd walked into a lamp-post?'

'No.'

'Thought not.' She put the bottle on the floor, felt at her dog collar. 'Look, I'm sorry I'm still in the kit. It's coming off tonight, for... for at least a week. I've been told to get a locum in, so I can be a... an ordinary person.' She shook her head. 'I'm probably demob happy, Lol, that's what it is.'

A lock of hair brushed her bruised eye like a bird's wing. She pushed it aside with a hand and winced.

'Tell me what happened,' Lol said.

She looked up the stairs and imagined Lucy Devenish standing at the top, watching them with a weary disappointment, her poncho drooping. And then caught a sudden mental image of Belladonna down near Ludford Bridge, wrapped in her floor-length cape, electric-blue light on her beautiful, predatory face.

Thought about Marion de la Bruyère – a young girl who had reacted to betrayal in the manner of the times, now a ghost more than eight centuries old – and what the Mayor of Ludlow might be asking.

Probably her last task as a Deliverance minister.

And it wasn't even official.

'Actually,' she said, 'to be honest, I'm not so much demob happy as demob... very pissed-off.'

Could have done a deal with Bernie, Merrily told God later. I could have said save my ministry, get those two bastards off my back, and I'll help you in Ludlow. That was the obvious thing, wasn't it?

But, like, playing politics – that's not what the Church is supposed to be about, is it? Yeah, yeah, the Church has been deep into politics from the start, but that didn't make it right. Or did it? I mean, it survived, didn't it? Would it still have survived if there hadn't been political popes, reformation, renewal and... and...

I don't want it to end. That's what I'm trying to say. Deliverance. I don't want it to be over.

Thought I was starting to get it... to get *some* of it right. Maybe helping people. Sometimes. OK, I was too late to help some people, like Roddy Lodge, and too blind to help others – Layla Riddock? But I had a strong feeling You were using me to

give Nat and Jeremy a chance at Stanner last winter. That was…
I mean sometimes it's been amazing.

And, sure, I've felt desperate because it didn't seem to be
working, or I wasn't getting it right. And guilty when it was
fulfilling, when it felt like I was wielding light… guilty because
I only had one parish and didn't have to go on the road on
Sundays and learn how to preach properly.

Have I been guilty of pride? Are there ministers in this diocese – there surely are – who could do this so much better than
me? Did YOU send Siân and Saltash? Am I stupid and naive
and blind? Is it Your will that I give this up, let it be taken from
me, stop meddling in the affairs of the dead, run five, six, seven
parishes instead, watch it all falling away for all of us…?

I'm sorry. I don't know. I don't know. Do I fight this or lie
down? Which is worse, cowardice or pride?

And do You ever listen any more?

Merrily opened her eyes, standing by the window, moonlight
sugaring the trees on Cole Hill, no easy answers written in the
sky.

PART THREE

Bell

To 20th-century eyes such colossal expenditure on unproductive religious ritual may seem strange, but in the 13th, 14th and 15th centuries most people were in no doubt that what kept mankind from both spiritual perdition and temporal catastrophe was an incessant flow of prayers to God from the priesthood and from religious orders. It was more vital expenditure than commercial investment or relief of poverty.

Michael Faraday, Ludlow, 1085–1660 *(1991)*

Ludlow had become the elite leisure centre of the middle marches in the 18th century and the castle was the focus of this burgeoning tourist industry... John Byng thought it was 'one of the best towns for a genteel family of small fortune to retire to... Ludlow was thus one of the first tourist "honey pots" in England.'

David Whitehead – 'Symbolism and Assimilation', chapter in Ludlow Castle, Its History and Buildings, *ed. Ron Shoesmith and Andy Johnson (2000)*

24

Ancient Incense

MERRILY FELT VERY small and exposed.

She was wearing jeans and a green fleece with a torn pocket. She had a canvas shoulder bag with her cigarettes inside and her phone. Around her neck was a chain with a tiny gold cross on it that was hidden by the neck of her grey T-shirt.

Demob-disorientated in an old town like a pop-up book, coming at her from all angles in wedges of carrot-coloured antique brick and twisted timbers and thrusting gables.

Cars and trucks laboured up Corve Street and down Old Street, or were funnelled, squealing like pigs, into the Bull Ring and King Street which must have been designed for donkey carts. And the sun slithered overhead like a soft-boiled egg trailing clouds of bloodied membrane. Or that was how it looked, through the rose-tinted glasses.

And she felt very small, especially next to Jon Scole of Ghostours.

'Drinks,' he said. 'Right. OK… OK… I've got to think about this. Which one of these tarted-up piss-parlours threw me out last?'

Ethereal he wasn't. He wore a motorbike jacket with extraneous chains. He seemed about seven feet tall, and he had long hair and a beard and a Manchester accent that could split logs. He winked at Merrily, tossed back his blond ringlets.

'Only kidding, Mary. They love me, really. I bring 'em

customers they'd never see as a rule: old ladies who want coffee, or a bitter lemon if they're feeling daring – soft drinks and beverages, that's where the real money is. 'Sides, you need a clear head for ghosts, I should know. OK, the Feathers it is, then. Top place. You did say the Feathers, didn't you? They always do.'

'I didn't say a word,' Merrily said.

'Hey, you thought it, though? Nobody can resist going in the Feathers at least once. Hang on…' He lifted a finger as if he was testing the wind direction. 'Now. Right. Feathers Hotel… OK! Now, we don't normally get to this until last 'cos it's not what you'd call typical. As ghost stories go, it's a bit off the wall, but still…'

He led her across the road, weaving through the traffic, drivers letting him through: Jon Scole looked like he could damage small cars. He stopped at the opposite kerb, gazing up at the ornate Jacobean fantasy that looked as if it had been sculpted out of Cadbury's chocolate flakes and marzipan. The last time she'd seen the Feathers Hotel was on Robbie Walsh's computer.

'I mean, classic haunted inn, right? What would you reckon, Mary: a highwayman in a black mask? No… well, maybe, I dunno… but the most interesting phenomenon in this particular location is – get this – young girl in a miniskirt and a see-through blouse.'

'Really?'

'Fact. Usual time, about now – no, later, around noon. Comes sashaying straight across where we just come… right through cars… fades through the bloody cars and out the other side… up onto this very pavement, and then – poof! Vanishes! Seen, not once, but about a dozen times, back in the 1970s when I were still learning to walk. Go in there, luv, ask the staff. Come on, I'll prove it to you.'

'No… Jon… I'd rather not ask anyone. I don't want to—'

'Sorry!' He put up his hands, as though the spectral girl had just glided out of the Telecom van parked up on the kerb with its hazard warning lights on. 'Got you. You don't wanna make a thing of it. I'm with you. Let's just go in, grab a drink.'

At a round table in the Comus Bar of the Feathers, she made like the old ladies and asked for tea. Jon Scole grinned at her through his curly copper-wire beard.

'Vicars and tea, eh? Sorry! Just can't get over you being a… you look so little and…' He puffed his lips out. 'Sorry, I'm a bit direct, me.'

'No, that's— It's always nice to know where you are with people. Makes quite a change. But if you could just, like' – Merrily patted the air – 'reduce the volume?'

'Right, OK.' He brought down his boom to a loud whisper. 'And that's the last time I'll mention religion in public, swear to God. Don't worry about the folk you get in here, though – unless it's Rotary day, it's guaranteed to be mostly tourists.'

'Why's it called the Comus Bar?'

'Milton's play, *Comus* – first performance 1634 at Ludlow Castle. Little Robbie Walsh told me that, God rest his soul. Everywhere you go, this town, you're wading through 'ist'ry. Come in off the street, you got to scrape it off your shoes like dogshit.'

He took off his motorbike jacket, hung it over the back of his chair. Underneath, he wore a leather waistcoat. He pulled it straight.

'Used to wear a watch and chain, then word reached me Councillor Lackland thought I were taking the piss. Didn't want to offend dear old George. He could make things very difficult for me, could George – all the official buildings I need to take people through. And the shops – George runs the Chamber of Trade. He could wipe me out in a month, no shit.' A gap appeared at the bar; Jon Scole stood up. 'Pot of tea, please, Ruth, and a pint of the good stuff.' He sat down. 'So, Mary… you want to meet Bell, eh? Tough one, that. Not impossible, but certainly tough.'

It was George Lackland who'd set this up.

The Bishop had talked to George on the phone from the Deliverance office early this morning, setting the ball rolling. Perhaps whatever she turned up could be filtered through Sophie during office hours, Bernie said. Best if they were not seen to be collaborating, although she was welcome to ring him at home at night. Merrily didn't imagine it would make much difference now. There were times when you felt it was all out of your hands, a Will of God situation. She'd never actively sought out the deliverance role, so if it was taken away... what right did she have to feel furious, embittered, isolated, stabbed in the back?

'You all right, Mary?' Jon Scole said.

'Yes... sorry...'

'You looked like you suddenly wanted to kill somebody.'

'No, it was just...' She felt the blush. 'Had a late night.'

This morning, she'd sat in the office and listened to Bernie giving George Lackland the spiel, Important Man to Important Man: *George, we have to work this out between us, you and I, and I think our priority is essentially the same – that is, preserving the spirit of the finest, most precious little town in the country. But if we're tampering with heritage, George, we have to tread softly. I'll be frank, what I've said to Merrily is this: go into Ludlow, talk to people, take the spiritual temperature, come back to me and we'll make some sort of decision. Sooner rather than later, I promise.*

Not spelling anything out. Never once mentioning Belladonna.

And then George had been talking for a while and Bernie had been nodding and glancing at Merrily and giving her small, confidential smiles, finally telling George that of course he understood. *We decoded your messages, old friend. We'll keep your confidence, and you'll keep ours?*

The parish details had all been arranged surprisingly easily. Merrily and Sophie had fixed up for Dennis Beckett, retired minister, go-anywhere locum, to take on the Ledwardine church services for the next two weekends and handle any routine parish business that came up. Merrily would still be at home at nights, but she'd leave the answering machine on the whole time, directing any calls on urgent parish business across the county to Dennis. She'd tell Uncle Ted, senior church-warden, tonight. He wouldn't be happy, having to work with

Dennis at such short notice, but when had Uncle Ted ever been happy since she'd taken on Deliverance?

As for Siân Callaghan-Clarke and the Panel, Sophie had already dealt with that. Sophie accepted that part of her role was laundering clergy lies; she'd told Siân that Merrily's favourite aunt – not her mother, who could easily be traced – had fractured a hip and, as Merrily had holidays owing... Where was this? Sophie wasn't entirely sure, but somewhere not too far away, as Merrily would be coming home some nights, when another relative took over – Sophie making it complicated enough to forestall questions.

Then George Lackland himself had phoned Merrily, telling her he'd arranged for her to meet Mr Jonathan Scole. A volatile young man, but he could give her information that it wouldn't be right for George himself to come out with. And, because of what Jonathan did, he'd spent some considerable time in the company of a certain person, George said.

Now, the only problem here is that I might have to tell him who you are and what you do. I have every reason to think he'll keep it absolutely confidential. Every reason. My wife works a good deal in tourism and Jonathan's business depends on a certain amount of goodwill, if you understand me. No, he's a good lad, really, he's kept us well informed about matters that might have proved embarrassing. Top and bottom of it is, I think he'll be quite thrilled to work with someone like you... Now then, is that all right for you?

Well...

You tell him what you want him to know and what he's to keep to himself, and you tell him he's got me to answer to if he don't. Not that that'll be necessary.

The mood swings of last night had no longer been in evidence. George Lackland had a town to run, and it had been like talking to some avuncular Mafia don whose ethos had long since transcended all moral values.

'So I'm in your hands.' Jon Scole sucked the top off his beer. 'Whatever you want. And I might seem a bit of a loud-mouthed bastard, but I can promise you, Mary' – Jon tapped his nose, froth on his beard – 'nothing gets out.'

Mary? Well, why not? He knew she was a vicar with the diocese. But he didn't know her surname, and now he'd got her first name wrong. Perhaps even George Lackland had heard it as Mary.

She was working undercover. She would be Mary. Fine.

She'd met up with Jon Scole at his shop in Corve Street. The shop was called Lodelowe, a medieval spelling of the town's name. It was a darkly atmospheric gift emporium, with lamps made from pottery models of town houses, misty framed photographs, paintings and books: books on the history of Ludlow and books about the supernatural.

Jon Scole understood from the Mayor that, unlike some people in the Church he'd had dealings with, Mrs Watkins wasn't averse to discussing ghosts, which had seemed to be the clincher for him. They could talk about ghosts. Jon loved to talk about ghosts. And also about the strange ways of the exotic Belladonna – Bell Pepper.

'Oh yeah, I get on with Bell… as far as anybody does. Bell loves ghosts. I mean, that's it. Mystery solved. I could lead you along, make a big thing out of it, but that's what it comes down to. That woman bloody loves ghosts. And you know what's so funny about that – I mean considering all those spooky albums? You know the big joke? Bell can't see 'em. She cannot see ghosts.'

'That's what she's said to you?'

'I tell you' – Jon pointed down the Comus bar, which was unexpectedly modern, not at all rustic – 'if the bint in the see-through whatsit drifted through here now, she'd carry on with her gin and tonic, tequila, whatever— Oh, listen, I never finished that story, did I? That was a strange one. A bloke investigated it, found this actual young girl who, every week, she used to visit her auntie, or her great-auntie – anyway, they were close – and when the auntie died suddenly and the girl moved away, she used to imagine herself going back along the same route, reliving it – a happy time. And they reckon that's what people saw.'

'A phantasm of the living?' Huw Owen called them extras or walk-ons.

'Blimey, you do know your way around my backyard,' Jon said. 'I tell you, Mary, this town's heaving with ghosts. I can do well here, if they leave me alone.'

'You've not been doing this long?'

'Came here not long before Bell. Parents died – got killed in the car.'

'I'm sorry. Was it—?'

'Bit of a shock. Year or so ago now. They had a restaurant – well, more of an upmarket transport caff, to be honest, south Man. – Cheshire, they liked to say. I couldn't face taking it over, so I flogged the lot to the bloody Little Chef – opportune, really – and took to the road, looking for something interesting.'

'So, you own the shop?'

'No, I'm renting – ridiculous bloody rent – but it's still at the experimental stage. This bloke Roy Liddle, who did the ghost-walks before, it was more of a hobby for him. I'm afraid I'm a little bit more of a businessman, don't want to invest all I've got in it if it's going to flop, do I?'

'The ghost-walks?'

'Ties in with the shop: mysteries of old Ludlow. Not doing badly, but it's early days yet – I only opened last Christmas, still feeling me way. Can't afford to tread on too many toes at this stage. So when the Mayor sent for me…'

'Sent for you?'

'Well… asked if I'd drop into his furniture shop – it's only fifty yards up the road. You should've heard him. He'd been asked to assist "senior clergy" investigating "certain incidents". Absolutely confidential, Jonathan. Me trying to keep a straight face. What is that about?'

'It's about what you might call the spiritual spin-off from two very similar deaths at the castle.'

'One an accident. Unless…'

'Mmm?'

'Unless you and George know better?' Little smile there.

'Did George indicate that?'

'Well...' Jon Scole thought for a moment. 'I should tell you – if he hasn't already – that there's a certain issue on which old George and me swap confidences.'

'Belladonna?'

Jon grinned. 'Bane of his life. Lovely lady – undermining every bloody thing he thinks he stands for: moral decency, all this stuff. And he can't do anything, 'cos very soon she's gonna be at the very heart of his eminently respectable family. Respectable! He's an old crook, like all bloody councillors. You ever know a councillor who was in it for the public good?'

'But why would he share confidences with—? I'm sorry...'

'A yob like me? Because I mix with the kind of people who come into contact with Bell. And even Bell herself, now and then. Better placed than anybody, me, to keep an eye on her. I mean, I can see his problem – it must be scary having a woman like that around.'

'A woman like what?'

'A woman with enough money never to have to give a shit for people like Councillor Lackland. A woman who's fascinated by the mysteries of life and death, and is open to... experiments.'

'What kind of—?'

Jon tapped his nose. 'All in good time, Mary. Tell me about yourself.'

'Well...' She'd spent some time working out what she wanted to say and what it was best to conceal. 'I work for the Diocese of Hereford...'

'You're a real, actual priest.'

'I... yeah.'

He frowned. 'See, that's not good, Mary. She doesn't like priests, Bell. Likes churches but she doesn't like The Church. If you get me.'

'Mmm.'

'So what's The Church's angle on this?'

'Good question. All right... I work for the division of the Church that investigates hauntings and... things of that nature.'

'That's more or less what George said, but I wondered if he was having me on, so I said I'd talk to you. So you're actually an exorcist, right?'

'Well, I... yeah.'

'You don't look a lot like Max Von Whatsisname.'

'I'm a disappointment to everyone.'

'There isn't some silly bugger wants you to go in and exorcize the castle, is there?'

'Nothing formal, as yet.'

'Because that...' Jon was lifting his glass. He put it down with a bang. 'That would be fuckin' insane, Mary! Apart from what it'd do to my business, you'd be undermining the very essence of Ludlow. Bell would go spare.'

'For what it's worth, I wouldn't like to do that either,' Merrily said. 'But I'm interested in why you think it would be insane.'

'Really? All right. Come with me, then.'

'Where?'

'Not far.' He stood up and put on his motorbike jacket. Its chains rattled like an alarm, and two retired-looking couples at the next table all turned round at once.

Jon Scole wiped his mouth and beard with the back of a hand. 'You psychic yourself, Mary?'

'No more than anybody.'

'As long as you're receptive, you'll feel it. There's some places with more resonance than others, especially in this town. Not sure why, but it's fact. Physically, it's got a lot to set it apart – built on a kind of promontory, two rivers, a very ancient church... and I mean *very* ancient. And, like, the whole atmosphere here, you can feel it... it's rich and heavy, like it's drenched in some ancient incense, you know what I'm saying?'

'Actually, I do. Especially in the evening.'

'You don't need the evening.'

25

His Element

DOWN PAST TESCO'S, towards the bottom of Corve Street, yew trees overhung a high stone wall and they could see the roof of the chapel.

'Dogs,' Jon Scole said. 'They reckon the dogs know.'

He had to shout over an old yellow furniture van clattering out of town. It had one word diagonally on the side: LACKLAND.

'Dogs?' Merrily said.

'Dogs are supposed to go bonkers this end of the Street. Out of control. Well, I've seen it. Some old dear hauling on the lead: Brutus! Heel! No chance. Very strong atmosphere. Accumulation of psychic energy. So, anyway, this is where she walks.'

'Sorry... who?'

'Who do you think?'

Jon Scole led her through the gateway, where cars were parked next to a circle of youngish yews, gloomily wrestling for the light. The chapel was set back, regular and Victorian-looking like the chapels you found in cemeteries, which was what it appeared to have been.

There was an information board on a lectern. It told you that the chapel had been built partly on the site of a Carmelite friary dating back to 1349, in use until suppressed by Henry VIII in 1539 when its buildings were sold and demolished. And then came the cemetery.

'No, don't read it, Mary, come and see it.'

Jon Scole led her down past the chapel, which was some kind of print workshop now – and that was good, she thought, much better than dereliction, brought a flow of people down here, kept up a flow of energy.

Merrily blinked. Bloody hell, she was thinking like Jane.

But there was an energy in Ludlow, the kind you didn't find in too many ancient towns, and even the rolling roof of Tesco's was urging it in. The town was prosperous, sure, but not in any self-conscious way, and what Bernie Dunmore had said about the buildings being preserved in aspic was misleading. Nothing that she'd seen here was in aspic; it was all still in use, and it buzzed, and it hummed, and it chattered.

Even the graveyard. A path ran down the middle; Jon Scole was strolling along it, but Merrily had stopped. There were cemeteries and there were graveyards, and the thing about cemeteries was that most of them weren't places you'd want to end up.

Jon Scole turned and came back. He was beaming.

'Surprising, eh? When they ran out of room at St Laurence's this was where they came. And then this one got full. There's supposed to be fourteen hundred graves here.'

Very few of them were fully visible any more because someone had taken an inspired decision. The result was that St Leonard's graveyard was vibrantly alive: a tangly, scuffling, mossy-green delirium, busy with birdsong, rich with moisture and slime. Merrily looked around, saw a fat, hollowed-out yew tree and two shiny, rippling domes of ivy that probably used to be headstones. In the summer, the air would be shimmering with butterflies, haunted at night by bats and moths.

'They gave it back to nature,' she said. 'They just… let it go.'

'What you got here, Mary, is part of a kind of secret passageway linking the oldest parts of town – and the two rivers. The Corve down at this end, which is this narrow, private kind of river, and the big one, the Teme, at the other.'

Between the trees, over the bushes and the rooftops, you could see the tower of St Laurence's, as if this graveyard was still intimately linked to it. Which, in a way, it was. Merrily was enchanted. Not in some flimsy, poetic way; there was a real and powerful enchantment happening here.

Maybe it was a combination of the rose-coloured glasses and her own disconnection from the diocese: Jane's pagan forces reaching out for her. Maybe this was just an overgrown graveyard.

'We're going the opposite way from the way she walks,' Jon said, back on the path. 'She comes up from The Weir House, up the steps and into The Linney, which goes from just above the Teme, up to the church and then starts again on the other side of the church and comes down again, and you wind up here. Magic.'

'How often does she... walk?'

'Whenever the mood takes her. No, that's wrong, she probably follows some pattern. Late at night, or in the hour before dawn. Something's got to be turning her on, though, hasn't it?'

'Meaning?'

'Well... you know. There's obviously a lot of places she finds a bit of a turn-on. That's why she came here. Like I say, this is just a very haunted town, and it feels like it, know what I mean?'

'It feels nice.'

'It feels *haunted*, Mary. Everywhere you go. Look at all the stories... you got an old woman in a dressing gown in the churchyard, and heavy footsteps. You got Catherine of Aragon – allegedly – at the Castle Lodge. Summat shivery at The Reader's House. You got haunted shops, a hairdresser's with a poltergeist. And... look over there...'

A view had opened on the left, the kind of view that seemed like it was planned. Anywhere else, there'd have been a viewing point with a telescope that you could feed 10p coins into.

It was the castle, as she'd never seen it before. It was away on the other side of the town but, from here, it appeared to be nestling in lush greenery, the scene uninterrupted by modern buildings or, in fact, any buildings – as if you were viewing it along a wooded valley. As if you were back then, when there was only the castle.

'Jon, it's like this place – this cemetery – is linked with every-where. You turn a corner and...'

'Magic,' Jon Scole said. 'Everything in this town is connected up. Like electric wires. Like a circuit. If you know how, you can plug yourself in.'

'Bell told you that?'

'Just once. And then she shut up, like she were giving too much away. Links through time – all the sacred places inter-linked, and there are special spots where all the... like the eras of time come together. When she walks here, it's like... you know?'

'Like she doesn't walk alone? Or at least she feels...'

'Feels, yeah. Doesn't see nowt, but... I tell you, if I could get that woman into the ghost-walks, as a regular, I'd bloody clean up. As it is, I'm just taking it all in, I feel like I'm tapping into her consciousness.'

Merrily remembered Lol suggesting that inside Belladonna's consciousness was not a safe place to be.

'... Learned a lot about Bell,' Jon was saying. 'I mean, the music, that's only half of it. This is a heavy lady, Mary.' He paused, nodding his head. "Course, she's also halfway out of her fuckin' tree.'

They went and stood under the dark, feathery awning of the yew, and she felt stupid with her glasses on, turning everything the colour of ripening plums.

'Presumably,' she said, 'you've heard about the other things she's supposed to have done. I mean, apart from walk.'

'Naked!' He laughed. 'With a feller. Just over there, it was, apparently, where the ivy's all thick on the ground. You've got to hand it to her, at her age. They must've been scratched to buggery.'

'The Mayor was not amused.'

'Well, what d'you expect? I mean, George Lackland... his generation... he's not exactly a left-wing espouser of liberal values, is he? I mean, she was in rock music. They don't operate according to George's rules. They don't live on the same planet.'

'George lives on Planet Ludlow,' Merrily said. 'Isn't that where Bell wants to be, too?'

'She wants to be part of it, that's true. But like, if she gets off on doing it in places where' – making quote marks in the air with crooked fingers – 'The Veil is Thin… I can connect with that. Sex produces a lot of psychic energy. And if there's this vortex of energy there already, you probably get a top buzz. 'Least, you do if you're Bell. You know what I mean?'

'In a way.'

It was still a graveyard, though. Death-fixated erotomania was how Nigel Saltash might describe it. The yew tree was draped around them, exposing its insides. Ancient yews always looked like they'd been dead and come through it.

'She's built a career around an obsession,' Jon Scole said. 'If you've heard the music you'll know that. She's made a shitload of money, but she's had a couple of brushes with the big D along the way, so she knows what a tightrope life is, even if you're loaded. And she's not getting any younger. So she's not playing any more, and she doesn't care what people think. She wants to know what she's got coming.'

'We all want to know,' Merrily said. 'Even the clergy.'

'Yeah, but you got distractions. You got other things to do. This woman… she's done the lot. Every way you can gratify yourself in this life, she's done it. What's left? Think about it.'

'You sound as if you understand her.'

'I try. I mean, she's here… I'm here… there's potential.'

'But you said she was out of her tree?'

'Halfway out of her tree.'

'How would I get to meet her?'

'You don't meet her. She meets you… if she wants to. You can hang round here all night, and it's like waiting for some rare crea-ture – you might get lucky, you probably won't. When she first came to live in Ludlow, reporters'd show up, full of themselves, and they'd all go back with nowt. Unless she wanted to talk. Which mostly she didn't. Talked to the *Journal* 'cos that were the local paper. Wouldn't even talk to the *Star*, 'cos it circulates outside.'

'And that's why local people protect her?'

'That's one of the reasons. She's eccentric, Mary. This town likes eccentrics.'

'George doesn't. And a few others.'

'No. Well...'

'So if I wanted to meet her?'

'You'd have to be someone she was interested in.'

'Like Robbie Walsh?'

'Let's get back into the light, eh?' Jon Scole said.

They stood inside the chapel gateway, near the information board, their backs to the surrounding wall and Corve Street. A young man came out of the print-shop with two carrier bags, smiled at Merrily.

'Don't believe a word this feller tells you. Most frightening thing you'll ever see in Ludlow is him at closing time.'

'Right...' Jon Scole levelled a finger. 'That order for four hundred Ghostours leaflets? Consider it bloody cancelled!'

He dropped his grin as the guy walked away. Turned to Merrily and shook his head.

'What happened to Robbie, that were the worst thing of all. Great kid. Great to have around, you know? All that knowledge, he was like a wassername, prodigy. You'd see him wandering around, world of his own, and you'd go, All right, Robbie? You OK, mate? Be like he was coming down off something. Blink, blink – where am I?'

'He used to go on the ghost-walk?'

'Towards the end, he were practically a fixture. At first, he'd just tag along – well, I couldn't charge him, could I? 'Sides, people liked him. He used to do half my job – knew everything about every building we came to. I didn't, hadn't been here long enough. Loved telling people about the past. In his element.'

'He was interested in ghosts?'

'Not so much the ghosts as the 'ist'ry. I did the ghosts, he did the 'ist'ry. We were quite a team, all through Easter. See... he could give you a picture. He was like a kid that'd just walked out of the Middle Ages. When he died, I were just fuckin' gutted, Mary.'

Jon recalled the funeral – only right the service should be at St Laurence's; even though he wasn't local, he'd made himself local. Jon had waited to talk to old Mrs Mumford afterwards, telling her how much they'd all thought of Robbie.

'Including Mrs Pepper?'

'What do you think?'

'So how did they meet?'

'On the ghost-walk. Some nights, when it's a bit quiet, she'll just show up. Tag along. Tourists leave her alone; she's a bit forbidding in that cloak. Anyway, one night – this'd be around last Christmas, when I was just getting the shop together – Robbie was there, and I were a bit knackered so I let him do most of it. He knew all the stories, better than me. And he just… little bugger brought it alive, standing there under a lantern on a stick. Especially the medieval stuff. He'd tell you what they were wearing, what the streets were like… the smells, even. Not in an academic way – he were still a young lad, no big words. But it was like the rest of us were in the here and now, and he was walking the same street, but he was in the twelfth century. You had to see it.'

'He sounds remarkable. I hadn't quite realized…'

'I don't wanna build him up too much, Mary, he were just a lad.'

'And Bell…?'

'Riveted, obviously. A young lad who seemed to be seeing things she couldn't?'

'What did you think about that?'

'Me? I just thought he'd read a lot of books.'

'And they became friends – Robbie and Bell?'

'She made sure of that.'

'Guy I spoke to said they seemed like… mother and son.'

'They were mates.' Jon looked irritated. 'Let's not get silly about it.'

'Did you talk to him about her?'

'Once or twice.'

'And how did he relate to her... special interests?'

'You mean was he exposed to Bell's obsession with all things death? I don't know. This copper asked me that. Detective. You know what they're like, trying to make you say things.'

Mumford.

'I mean, what is this, Mary? Is this some scheme of Lackland's to get her out of his hair for good? Stitch her up for assisting Robbie to do himself in? Turn the whole town against her?'

Merrily stared at him. 'What makes you think he did himself in?'

'I dunno.' Jon jammed his hands in the lowest pockets of his leather jacket, rattling chains. 'It just never made a lot of sense to me that he'd just fall off. Kid knew his way around every passage in that castle with his eyes shut. And then that girl – not much doubt about that, is there? She came here to die.'

'Did you ever have any reason to think Robbie was depressed about anything?'

'No, he were full of life when he... I never thought, you know? He said things maybe I should've put together. Like, you'd ask him about his parents, and his face would cloud over. I was thinking maybe divorce, so I stopped asking. Didn't wanna upset him. We just don't know, do we, how to react for the best? What do you think?'

'I think there are some questions that nobody's been asking. And I think everybody's been walking round Belladonna as if she's the Queen.'

'Mary, next to Bell, the Queen's anybody's.' He looked at her, standing a bit too close. 'She could be interested in you. I mean, you know your stuff, don't you? It's just... the priest thing. And an exorcist, even worse. Like Rentokil for ghosts.'

'We're not—'

'I know you're not. I'm telling you how she'd see you.'

'Doesn't mind being in the church, though.'

'That's because it's where it is. It's obvious the church is one of the places. Right at the top of the town, at the centre, where all the lanes and alleyways come out. View from the top of the tower – amazing. You should see that, makes the Hanging Tower look like jumping off a stepladder. You been there yet?'

'Not yet.'

'Blimey, you gotta see that. We could go there now. Ten minutes. You got time?'

Merrily looked at her watch. It was coming up to one p.m. She needed a break to think about all this, and she wanted to speak to Mumford. But more than any of this, she felt the need to break the spell.

'All right, what are you doing around, say, four o'clock?' Jon said. 'Suppose I meet you at the entrance to the car park, near the castle?'

She nodded. She'd have to see it sometime. At least this guy would know the exact spot. Four p.m. would give her time to talk to Mumford and try to see the interior decorator who, according to George Lackland, had had some peculiar requests made of him by Mrs Pepper.

'OK.'

'Ace. Meanwhile – Bell. Let me think about this. I mean, I reckon she'd take to you as a person.' Jon Scole grinned. 'They say she goes both ways.'

'Not with me she doesn't, Jonathan.'

'Just kidding, Mary.'

26

The Mix

THERE WAS THIS feeling of unease now, whenever Merrily thought about Andy Mumford. Wouldn't have been too surprised to spot him back on the prowl here in Ludlow. She felt he was teetering like Jemima Pegler had, and perhaps Robbie Walsh, over a long drop.

But when she rang from the Volvo he was at home.

'How're you?' His voice was still higher than usual; he would hate that – every time he spoke, a reminder of the kid with the chain.

'I'm fine.' She was in the car park at the top of town, close to the castle. The day had dulled, thin grey clouds windshielding the sun like smoked glass. She crumpled up the cellophane wrapping of her lunch, one free-range egg-and-cress sandwich. 'You seen a doctor, Andy?'

'No need. It's better than it was.'

'Doesn't sound it.'

'That's because it hurts more.' Mumford wheezed out a laugh. 'Where you calling from?'

'I'm back in Ludlow.'

'That a fact.'

'I've got a few days off.' She could hardly tell him about the Bishop or George Lackland. 'Vicar with a black eye doesn't look good in the pulpit. And I thought that, with you being persona non grata here, maybe I could… check a few things out?'

'Good of you.'

'So I went to talk to Jonathan Scole.'

'Boy tried to bullshit me.'

'I think it's his way. He does seem to have been fond of Robbie, however. Poor kid had a virtual season ticket on the ghost-walk in return for lecturing the punters on local history.'

'What about the woman?'

'She seems to have milked Robbie, too. If I ever get to see her, I'll let you know.'

'Thank you, Mrs Watkins,' Mumford said. Paused. 'Oh... I had a bit of information, too. From headquarters.'

'You finally spoke to Bliss?'

'No, no. Another person this was, in the Division. Distant relation. Second cousin to a second cousin, kind of thing. Gives me a call now and then, we chats about this and that.'

Family. In this part of the world, no matter how thinly a blood link was stretched, it was there to be rediscovered when necessary.

'Seems Jason Mebus finally turned seventeen,' Mumford said.

'And you missed his party.'

'They had his party below stairs at Hereford, attended by former colleagues of mine. Jason got into a confrontation at the Orchard Gardens last night – pub by the Plascarreg? Two boys finished up seriously hammered in the car park.'

'By Jason?'

'By four of them, but the others were juveniles. Jason's charged with ABH. His first as an adult.'

'He's off the streets, then?'

'That en't gonner happen till he kills somebody. He was bailed. If the presiding magistrate's in a real bad mood, he'll get community service, the others'll have a stern ticking-off. One of the others, by the way, was Chain-boy – Connor Boyd, his name.'

'How do you know it's him?'

'Moron still had the chain.'

'Ah.' She watched a young couple loading babies and groceries into a people-carrier parked against the wall under the castle, where some siege engine might once have stood. 'Andy, does this... relative know what they did to you?'

'Said I had a throat infection. Another one of them's Connor's half-brother, Shane Nicklin, twelve. I reckon he was likely the little angel who came in to see us on his own. Regular at juvenile court. Shot a toddler in the eye with an airgun when he was seven.'

'A good family, then.'

'An example to us all,' Mumford said.

'I'm rather embarrassed about this,' Callum Corey said. 'You shouldn't be putting me in this position.'

He looked about twenty-three and wore a white silk shirt. He stretched his legs out, swivelling sulkily from side to side in his leather chair. On the wall behind his desk were framed photo blow-ups of the restoration jobs Coreys had handled, and it was impressive: baronial interiors, open log fires.

'It's all word-of-mouth in our profession, Mrs Watkins,' Mr Corey said. 'Any gossip of this sort gets out, it can do us immense harm. My father thought he was doing old Lackland a favour – didn't think he was going to blab it all over town.'

'I don't actually think,' Merrily said, 'that confiding it to a priest amounts to blabbing it all over town. Besides, he didn't actually tell me what happened, he just suggested that I might have a word with you.'

'You don't look like a priest to me.'

'What's a priest look like?'

Mr Corey was the new type of ex-public-school painter and decorator, working out of this tasteful Georgian town house in Broad Street, which sloped to the old town gate and then to the river at the Horseshoe Weir where Mrs Mumford had drowned. The office was the size of a small ballroom, with blue-washed walls and four long Georgian windows. Trestle tables displayed leather-bound catalogues and samples of moulding and dressed stone.

'OK.' Merrily stood up. 'I can see I'm putting you in a difficult position. I'll go. Thank you for seeing me, Mr Corey.'

'No, look—' He came half out of his chair. 'Wait… sit down. I just wondered… how the Church came into it. We… we've done some work for the Church.'

'One word from me and all that would be over for good.'

He looked startled for a moment. Merrily smiled.

'Joke, Mr Corey. OK, how do we come into it? Well… there've been incidents in St Laurence's. We don't like to involve the police if we can deal with these things ourselves. And I'd be grateful if this wasn't blabbed all over town either.'

A glass-fronted cast-iron wood-burning stove was burning low, more for effect than heat at this time of year. Callum Corey pulled his chair away from it.

'It wasn't our job, originally. The Weir House was a project by the Raphaels – hit-and-run restorers. Move into a place, do it up, sell it, move on. Except in this case they virtually had to build from the foundations up. One of the old Palmers' Guild houses. Look, please sit down. Would you like something to drink?'

'Just had lunch, thanks.' She sat down across the desk from him. 'I'm afraid I don't know anything about the Palmers' Guild.'

'Name's now been appropriated by Mrs Pepper for a conservation trust she's setting up. I'm afraid I'll believe that when I see it. Originally, they were well-off pilgrims to the Holy Land in the Middle Ages. Brought a palm leaf back to prove it, something like that. That was how it started. Then they became a sort of cooperative movement that employed priests exclusively to pray for the immortal souls of their members. They became immensely wealthy and lasted for several centuries.'

'Just in Ludlow?'

'Began in Ludlow, spread over a wide area. Put huge amounts into the fabric of the church and financed the building of about fifty houses in the town. Including the ruin that the Raphaels renamed The Weir House.'

'Mrs Pepper bought it off these Raphaels?'

'Very quickly, apparently. There were still bits and pieces left to complete – but that's always the case with these quick-bodge merchants. It's all about appearances.'

'So Mrs Pepper hired you to finish it off.'

'Perfect it,' Callum said. 'There's an impressive central room with an immense stone fireplace. One wall had been improperly finished and was miasmic.'

'You mean it was damp?'

'They'd used a gypsum mix on top of the stones but it hadn't worked. What it needed was something more sympathetic.'

'Like lime?'

'Exactly.' He looked surprised that she'd know.

'I live in a four-hundred-year-old vicarage.'

'Ah. We're asked to renovate churches, but rarely touch vicarages and rectories still owned by the Church. They don't seem prepared to spend too much money on dwelling houses.'

'Unlike Mrs Pepper.'

'Mrs Pepper didn't quibble at all about the price. However, she had in mind certain… refinements of her own. Originally, horsehair was often mixed with the slaked lime. Did you know that?'

'I've heard of it.'

'Mrs Pepper had something similar in mind. But she wanted to use… her own hair.'

'I see.'

'I'm not sure you do, actually.' Callum looked down at his unused blotter. 'We do get a few odd requests of this nature sometimes – the craze for feng shui, fuelled by those dreadful TV make-over programmes. Some of the proposals contravene listed-building regulations, but we do what we can to satisfy the customer.'

'So you went along with it.'

'I did the work myself. She said too many people trampling around the place… that would not be acceptable.'

'For reasons of privacy.'

'I thought so, yes. I didn't realize quite... Well, anyway, she presented me with a cardboard box with hair in it. Her own hair is blonde – whether it's dyed or not, I'm not qualified to say. But this hair, um, wasn't. It was darker and clearly of a different... consistency.'

'It was someone else's hair?'

Callum stood up and walked over to one of the long windows which overlooked not Broad Street but a small, flagged court-yard with a tall cedar tree at the bottom.

'That wasn't the impression I had,' he said. 'My impression, by the lack of length and the, er, texture of the hair was that it... hadn't been taken from her head.'

'Oh. And did you go ahead with the job? Did you mix it in?

'Yes, I did.'

'And was she happy with it?'

'Er... very happy. She insisted on helping me. She got the plaster all over her hands. I did suggest she wear gloves, but she... seemed to want it on her skin. She then... at some point... she asked me if I would also like to add something of myself to the wall. As it were. I was quite wary by this time. I don't really like working alone in houses where there's only a woman at home.'

Merrily smiled. 'I always thought you builders were men of the world.'

'I am not a builder. Well, I am, but... This is a small town, and we're a respected company, and my father's a town councillor.'

'You made an excuse and left?'

'I did. Wasn't just that she was old enough to be my mother, she... it wasn't healthy.'

'She lives there on her own?'

'She has a cleaner and a gardener who come in. Seems to have most of her meals in restaurants in the town.'

'That must be costly.'

'Not a problem, it seems, for Mrs Pepper. The house is filled with... "antiques" would perhaps not be the word. There's a sink, for instance, fashioned from what appears to be a stone coffin. They become available sometimes when old churches are converted into houses.'

'So she had a wall plastered with hair... not from her head. Anything else she... wanted you to do?'

'I'm not going to elaborate on what she invited me to add to the mix.'

'Oh dear.'

'Quite,' said Mr Corey.

27

Carrying a Light

IT WAS JUST after three p.m. when Merrily left Corey's, walking, more or less aimlessly, up Broad Street, past de Grey's café and then the clothing shop which Bernie Dunmore had told her had been retail premises since the fourteenth century.

She started imagining Robbie Walsh drifting this way, his self-educated inner vision replacing tarmac with cobbles, delivery vans with wooden carts, coats with cloaks, Levis with leggings. Ending the exercise when, without trying too hard, she was able to turn a man with a charity tin on the steps of the Buttercross into a leper in rags with a peeling face and wretched, burning eyes.

There's some places with more resonance than others, Jon Scole had said. All it would take would be a moment of slippage, a mental stumbling, and she'd be seeing through Mrs Mumford's eyes: dead Robbie shivering in sun-splashed glass.

She hurried away and didn't look into shop windows.

There were times when you needed spiritual advice. Back in the car, she rang Huw Owen at his rectory in the Beacons, and, thank God, he was there.

'How old is she, lass?'

'Late forties, fifty, hard to say exactly; she's wearing well.'

'Been around?'

'In every sense. She seems to have had a fairly nomadic exist-ence, maybe not able to settle anywhere until she found this place.'

'That would figure. Feels she's come home at last. This is the place she should always have been. She has to make up for lost time.'

'I think that's exactly right. She's bought a rebuilt medieval house on an old site. When a wall needs replastering, she gets the builder to mix in some of her own hair.'

'Instead of horsehair.'

'Exactly. Only, this is evidently pubic hair.'

'Nice touch,' Huw said.

'What are we looking at here, then? Sympathetic magic?'

'All magic's sympathetic magic, lass. But this goes back to folk custom. When I were a lad, I remember an owd bloke saying that if you wanted to really make a house your own, you and the missus should make sure you use every room. "Use" being the operative word.'

'That would figure, too, from what I hear.'

'You'd probably also find that she's drawn some of her own blood and mixed it with paint or varnish,' Huw said. 'Or she might use urine or... any other bodily fluids that come to hand.'

Merrily wrinkled her nose. 'So it's about belonging.'

'Or, if she feels the house is haunted – say a presence from the past appears to be the dominant force there – then, by infusing her own essence into the fabric of the place, she's making it clear who's possessing who.'

'You're good, Huw.'

'Ah, you know all this yourself, really, lass. This is just belt and braces.'

'It's what I need right now.' She told him what Bernie Dunmore had suggested about Siân Callaghan-Clarke. 'All rumour and conjecture, of course.'

His voice grew concerned. 'So you're really working privately for bloody Dunmore...'

'Not as such. Just that we haven't told anybody.'

'Serving his agenda, though, not yours. I'd go home if I were you, Merrily. Keep your head down. Not the time for being a maverick. I'm not kidding. There's summat here needs looking at. What's that woman after? Why you?'

'Dunno. I do, however, want to find out how Belladonna ties in – if she does – to the death of Robbie Walsh. And then I'll back off. I've got your support, haven't I? Counts for a lot, Huw. It's kind of strengthening. Can I tell you the rest?'

'There's more?'

'The house is only the beginning. She's operating on a much wider scale. I think this is all about acceptance by the town itself, on all kinds of levels.'

She was already halfway to working this out. It was always fascinating to watch incomers and how they tried to get themselves accepted, grab a stake in the community – like, in Ledwardine, it was always the new people who organized the festivals, usually for the benefit of other newcomers. It drove Jane mad.

'But of course Belladonna's already famous, a bit notorious, and she doesn't want to advertise her presence. Definitely doesn't want to be a tourist attraction.'

'But knows she's a stranger,' Huw said, 'and that's how people regard her – a newcomer... doesn't fit and not entitled to. Has to earn her place.'

'We know she's already given a lot of money for conservation. Saved some land from possibly unsympathetic development.'

'That'll happen win her more friends than enemies – but some enemies.'

'But I think that being accepted by the living people, Huw – that's only a small part of what she wants, because... OK, this is what she does: she walks the streets alone at night, dressed in a long cape, burning candles. Following a specific route, it looks like, through the oldest parts of the town. Some people find it eerie, but they'll accept it without too many questions, because...'

'Poor folk are mental cases, rich folk are merely eccentric.'

'Mmm. And then... here comes the sexual element again.'

She told him about St Leonard's graveyard and what Jon Scole had said. 'But that could be gossip.'

'He could be right, though – fusing her own energies with the energies of the place. In the same way as witches'll use sex at the culmination of a ritual at a sacred site – stone circle or whatever. Who was the partner?'

'No idea.'

'He should be local, for maximum benefit.'

'Or she, apparently.'

'Ah. Interesting. See, this is all very practical, Merrily. Your woman's found the little town she wants to stay in for the rest of her life. If she's carrying a light from her home, all the way around the town and back again, passing through the most ancient and holiest places, on a ritual basis – time and time again – she's taking her spirit into that town, isn't she?'

'And becoming accepted by the spirit of the town? Or spirits…'

'Which spirits?'

'We know she's been milking Jon Scole and anyone else for information about the best-established ghost stories – and there are quite a lot of them here, Victorian, Tudor, medieval… She wants to know who they are, and where they walk.'

'Happen she sees the ghosts as the oldest permanent residents. Gain their acceptance and you're in.'

'There's another thing, too… damn…'

'Take your time. Put the mobile to your other ear for a bit, don't want to fry your brains.'

'No. Quite.' She switched ears and leaned back in the driving seat, eyes closed. 'Ah… I know… the church.'

'It's old and it's big.'

'And it has some famous misericords. On several occasions, Belladonna appears to have left a… tampon or a pad pushed down the side of one of them. This is blood again, isn't it?'

'Even better, this is menstrual blood. The deepest power of womanhood. Fertility on every level. A woman is at her most… fearsome, if you like… when she's menstruating – as most fellers find out, to their cost. In the ancient world, you'd have a lot of ritual centred on menstruation – its connection with the moon.'

'Ah,' Merrily said.

'But you knew that, anyway.'

'You have a great ability, Huw, to make me aware of the significance of what I already might have known.'

'Just be careful,' Huw said. 'Keep looking over your shoulder.'

'Yes.'

There was still ten minutes to spare before Merrily was due to meet Jon Scole at the entrance to the car park. She walked back into Castle Square, where the historic buildings fell away and the timeless, grey-flecked sky opened up.

The castle gateway was guarded by a huge old cannon and a line of recently pollarded trees. There wasn't time to go in now; she crossed the square towards the shops: Woolworths, the Castle Bookshop. She was looking in the bookshop window when worlds collided again.

There, on the fringe of a display of books on local history, was a large-format paperback with a red and white cover and heraldic symbols in each corner. In one of those moments of total awareness of everything around her, she went into the shop.

'Could I... just have a copy of that book in the window: *Everyday Life in the Middle Ages, in Pictures*?'

She heard the bookseller saying that he thought it was the last copy, making a note to reorder some as she pulled out her purse.

Somebody had laid a wreath at the foot of the yew tree where they'd found Jemima Pegler. No name on it, no identifying card. Some of the pink and white flowers were already browning, petals picked off by the wind.

Merrily looked up into the denseness of the yew tree which was said to have grown on the spot where the body of Marion de la Bruyère had come to rest. The tree threw a circle of darkness. It was probably hundreds of years old, its leathery trunk knobbed and warted and suggestive, here and there, of twisted faces. Behind it was the dizzying sheerness of cliff… wall… tower… sky. About a dozen black window spaces had been punched in the tower walls, irregular, like holes in cheese.

'This girl Jemima came out of one of them,' Jon Scole said. 'Didn't look too bad, according to what people say. I'll have to use her, eventually. She'll become part of the myth. You think that's tasteless?'

'It's what you do,' Merrily said.

Walking down from The Linney – very steep, too narrow for cars, old houses on one side built up against the castle walls – he'd told Merrily about his efforts to get some kind of relationship going with Bell Pepper, whose Weir House was below them, hidden in the bristle of pines above the river.

Seeing the look on her face, he'd gone backing off, hands up, tangled blond hair bobbing, chains jangling.

'Whoa! No, not that kind of relationship. When I'm with her, I'm dead careful to make sure we don't accidentally, like, touch. No blue sparks.'

'Blue sparks?'

'Apart from us being not exactly contemporaries, Mary, it would probably ruin any chance of a business arrangement.'

He was probably right to be cautious. It was unlikely, for instance, that Callum Corey would be lured back to The Weir House, no matter how much money was on the table.

'What kind of business arrangement did you have in mind?'

'Dunno, really. But if I can't make a few quid out of her, who can?'

'You selling her albums in the shop?'

'Sore point, Mary. I started selling the albums – *Nightshades*, very moody cover – and then Doug Lackland, George's elder son, he drops in one afternoon for a discreet word.' Jon did the accent. ' "Now, we don't want to underline that she's livin' here, do we, Jonathan?" CDs quietly disappear. Dougie bought the lot. No skin off my nose, but it's not on, is it?'

They'd followed the rising stone wall to the walkway below the castle along which, Jon said, demure Edwardian ladies with parasols had once paraded. As distinct from a volatile Viking in a motorbike jacket and a scruffy little vicar in jeans, a well-worn fleece and tinted glasses.

'See where that shelf of rock projects?' he said now. 'Back of Jemmie's head hit that with some force, so that were a bit messy, you know, but her face wasn't damaged. That's what they say. It's kind of a – what would you say? – an elemental way to go.'

'People say you're dead before you hit the ground,' Merrily said dully. 'Or maybe that's when the parachute doesn't open.' She looked up. 'It doesn't seem far enough for that.'

The clouds, empurpled by Merrily's glasses, were foaming now, with not-quite-rain. She walked up to a jagged crevice in the bottom of the rock face or the castle foundations. It was like the beginnings of a cave, or a recess where a statue should be placed – a natural shrine. Someone had left a small posy of flowers in there: anemones.

'Would've smashed every bone in her body,' Jon Scole said.

'I thought you said—?'

'No, I'm thinking Marion now. Would've been all rock down here then. I 'spect it's worn away a lot in eight centuries. And she most likely came from the top.'

'It's a very violent way to go,' Merrily said. 'A tumult of emotion there. A feeling of betrayal, sure, but she'd also just killed the man she'd loved. Absolute desolation.'

'You talk like Robbie,' Jon said.

'What?'

'Robbie... the way he'd talk you through it. This little stunted kid in a woolly hat under a lantern in the dark. He didn't use big words like "desolation" but he'd tell you about all these enemy soldiers swarming up the rope ladder, swords and knives coming out. The guards and retainers not expecting it, having their throats cut. Stone stairs all slippery with blood. Marion running up ahead of them, wi' blood all over her nightdress and her hands soaked from hacking to death, as you say, the man she loved. And I remember, Robbie said she was sick. He said she had to stop on the stairs to be sick. I mean, that's not in the story, is it?'

'Rings true, though. If you imagine all the adrenalin and the extreme violence. The heavy action going on all around, with the enemy pouring in. Everything happening so fast, and her own frenzied reaction when she worked out what she'd let happen. And then she looks back for a moment, realizes what she's just done to Arnold de Lisle, and her stomach…'

Jon Scole smiled. 'You want a part-time job?'

A twig snapped under Merrily's shoe, and she spun round.

'You're even scaring yourself,' Jon said.

'Was he that vivid about all the ghost stories? Robbie?'

'Fair to say that were probably his best.'

'Because if it wasn't an accident and he killed himself because he couldn't bear to leave his beloved Ludlow, why did he jump off the wrong tower? Why didn't he jump off Marion's tower?'

Jon blew out his lips. 'Got me there. I mean, I remember he used to say we couldn't really be sure of anything, because a lot of the castle were built afterwards – after Marion died, that is, which was back in the reign of Henry II or somewhere around there. So it would've all looked different, then, anyway.'

'But Marion didn't throw herself off the keep. That's a certainty, isn't it?'

'It's a longer drop, though. You can go right to the top. You'd be more sure of a result.' Jon Scole walked over to the ancient yew, fingered its swarthy, resinous skin. 'If this old bugger could talk.' He grinned. 'Maybe it can. A lot of mysticism around yew trees.'

'So I've heard.'

'All about immortality, Mary. Yews go on for ever. Some of them are two thousand years old. They've always got them in churchyards, and sometimes they're older than the church.'

'I don't think that's my kind of immortality,' Merrily said. 'Rooted in one spot, for ever and ever.'

'That would depend on the spot,' the woman said.

It was hard to say how long she'd been standing there, on the edge of the path, her back to the river and the hills and the forestry. She wasn't wearing a cape, just one of those ankle-length Barbour stockman's coats, in dark blue, fastened to the top, the storm-flap half covering her chin.

Merrily thought, *How quiet she looks, how demure, how genteel.*

'Actually, I understood that yew trees did well in church-yards because they thrived on corpses,' the woman said.

28

Tonguing the Yew

IT WAS STRANGE, the fame thing. You told yourself that you would never be overawed by people just because you'd seen them on TV or they were in the Cabinet or the Royal Family. Experience had told you that movie stars and government ministers were often narrow and paranoid, and that power not only corrupted, it reduced.

But it was different with someone who had been famous in the days when you'd been impressed by celebrity and notoriety. There was some part of you that wasn't going to let go of that, and the old shiver went through Merrily.

'Historians say the sacred tree of the Druids was the oak.' That voice of dark green glass. 'But the Druids wouldn't have got it that wrong.'

Merrily said nothing, but found she was nodding, in that instinctive, subservient way she always despised. Still, oaks versus yews wasn't something she had an opinion on, anyway.

'I love and venerate them,' Mrs Pepper said. 'Some protected oaks on my land were apparently removed. No big deal, oaks are all right – solid, dependable, functional, but they haven't got the intellect, or the cunning. Or the true key to survival. Isn't that right, Jonathan?'

'If you say so, ma'am.' Jon Scole bowed his head – he actually did that.

'So my yew – I've got this incredible yew at home – something ensured that it was left well alone when they took out the oaks. Because removing the yew would have been a very bad thing to do, wouldn't it? Even Jonathan knows that.'

Jon Scole did another small bow; if there was an underlying disrespect here, it wasn't immediately obvious. Mrs Pepper came up onto the path, her long coat making a soft, slithery sound around her. She approached the tree.

'In the great yew-tree scheme of things, this one's still pretty young, but it was born out of death.' Talking as if she was addressing a larger group. 'The yew communicates nature's most important message about death within life, life within death.'

She had the rhythm going now: the glistening, seamless voice which used to step down, mid-song, into the spoken word without losing the flow. Merrily tried to bring up all the loony images: the sanitary goods under the misericords, the bodies rolling in the ivy among the graves, the lime mix fortified with pubic hair. Somehow, none of this diminished her.

'I'm going to do the lecture now – short one, don't worry. Here's what happens: after one or two centuries, the heart of the tree begins to die, which is why so many of them are hollow. But the outer layer just goes on growing around the hollow space, and the tree gets wider and thicker. When a branch breaks off, the yew self-heals and puts out new shoots. And they go on like that for sometimes thousands of years.'

'Immortality,' Jon said. 'Awesome.'

The sky was a deep, soft grey now, and Mrs Pepper shone against it. Her plaited hair had the remains of many colours in it, a woven rainbow. She bared her teeth, which were small and mischievously pointed, and her big eyes were a startling turquoise.

'And what's really cunning about the yew is that the death of the heartwood eradicates the rings by which you can tell how old the tree is. So the yew becomes totally fucking ageless… my kind of tree.'

She opened her arms and embraced the yew, and put out her tongue to its warty pigskin trunk, Merrily thinking, *Spare us the theatrics, please…*

… As Belladonna began to lick the bark of the yew tree, a slow, intense, liquid lapping.

'For God's sake!' Merrily yelled. 'It's pois—'

Bell Pepper looked over her shoulder, gaze locked on Merrily's, tongue curling up around her upper lip then slowly retracted between small, pointed teeth.

'Country girl, eh?'

'I just know it's very poisonous,' Merrily said. 'To animals, anyway. It kills cows and horses. Another reason it's said they were planted in churchyards was so that farmers would keep their cattle out.'

'Predates both farming and churchyards, sweetheart – even Jonathan knows that.'

Mrs Pepper bent her head on one side, kissed the tree lavishly, with her mouth open. And then she moved away, smiling, the neck of her coat undone, her throat exposed, turning to Merrily.

'So who are you, darling? You're not the woman?'

'Uh… this is Mary,' Jon Scole said. 'Mary, this is… Bell.'

'Hello,' Merrily said. 'Bell.'

Bell looked cross. 'Jonathan, I'm not sure you heard me. I said, is this the woman?'

Jon Scole seemed worried for a few moments. He looked down at the base of the tree, hacking his trainer into the dust, hands in his pockets nervously flapping his motorbike jacket and making his chains rattle. When he looked up, though, his old smile was returning. He didn't look at Merrily, but he beamed at Bell Pepper.

'Yeah,' he said. 'That's right. This is the woman.'

A face projected onto an already-fraught night by blue emergency beacons… that was just an image. This quiet confrontation on a mild, cloudy afternoon was something else. Especially when the face – this icon of punk-goth perversity – was suddenly behaving entirely in accordance with the legend.

Tonguing the yew, for heaven's sake!

Merrily trying to be dismissive – maybe Belladonna just wasn't getting enough attention these days, maybe that was the answer to all of it – so not picking up, at first, on what Jon Scole was doing.

This is the woman?

'Oh, shit, this is really unfair,' Jon said. 'Mary hasn't the faintest idea what we're talking about. I haven't even told her about any of this yet. We'd just, like, walked over here, and I were— I'm sorry, Mary, I was gonna put it to you later. Like, I know you don't just do this for everybody and money doesn't make any difference, but I thought maybe this once, you know?'

Merrily stayed silent. Jon Scole tossed back his flaxen locks and put his hands together, as if in prayer. His gaze locked on to Merrily's and he raised an eyebrow fractionally.

'Bell's house – just down there.' Tipping a thumb towards the river. 'I was gonna ask you to take a look at it. See if you got anything?'

Now he was looking at her hard, his mouth slightly smiling, his eyes imploring.

'I see,' Merrily said.

'As a psychometrist,' Jon said. 'As, uh, a psychic.'

Mrs Pepper said, 'I'm sorry… Mary? Is it Mary? I must've made a very unfavourable first impression. This boy tends to bring out the worst in me.'

'It's just his way,' Merrily said.

'So I'm going to carry on with my walk,' Bell refastened her coat. 'Let you two work this out.'

She moved off, the way they'd come, up towards The Linney and the centre of the town. Her feet were bare inside skimpy sandals, and it occurred to Merrily that she could well be entirely naked under the stockman's coat.

Or maybe that was just the legend talking.

***

Down the path, now, the castle opening out on their left, as they walked, Jon Scole trampling last year's brambles.

'I'm not gonna apologize for this, Mary. You wanted to get close to her, this is your chance.'

'You set me up,' Merrily said.

'I were thinkin' on me feet. I said I'd help you and I have. I told you about her, the way she is: thinks she senses, but she wants someone to help her know. If I told her you were clergy, you wouldn't get within a mile, and if she knew you were an exorcist... she wants her ghosts exorcizing like she wants a double mastectomy.'

Merrily zipped up her fleece, sank her hands into its pockets, the day swirling around her, out of control.

'She said she gets strong feelings coming off the house,' Jon said. 'I say, why don't you get a medium in? She goes dead sneery – she's like, Oh, I used to go to mediums once, spiritualist churches, they were a joke. Plus, they kept bringing God into it, doing little prayers.'

'Isn't her house a new house, strictly speaking?'

'Built out of the ruins of the old, though. She reckons it was connected with the castle. She's opened up a pathway so she can walk up here, to the yew. See, this is where it begins. Bell's walk. A big circle... up The Linney, through the churchyard, down to St Leonard's graveyard – route marked out by ancient yews... and then back through the town.'

'OK, I'm getting the picture. What did you tell her about me?'

'Well... it wasn't about you to begin with. This goes back to me saying, look, Bell, some mates of mine, they're psychic investigators – which is true, they got all the kit and they've had some good results. Why don't we come in, I say, give your place a full going-over? She says forget it. Because, what it is, she doesn't trust anybody. She thinks they're gonna talk about it, sell the story. And she doesn't trust me because I make money out of it, and she's been ripped off too many times by fakes and phoneys. So I say, OK, I know somebody – a psychic, a psychometrist – who's so red hot she won't do it for money. In fact she won't do it at all unless it's to further her researches, know what I mean? The real thing. Well, she was interested, I could tell straight off she was interested.'

'And do you know a psychometrist?'

'Well… kind of. But I were taking it dead slow. I see her periodically, and I go, bloody hell, I saw that woman and I forgot to flaming mention it. Bugger! Letting her think it's no big deal to me, but avoiding giving her the woman's name.'

'Because this woman doesn't exist, right?'

'Uh… not exactly.' Jon stopped. There was a bench up against the castle wall, near a gateway into the outer ruins. He gestured for Merrily to sit down.

'You really do sail close to the wind, don't you, Jon?'

'What life's all about, Mary, i'n't it? See, there's a friend of mine, lives over in Bewdley, does the same business – ghost-walks. Anyway, I met this girl when I were just setting up, and we had a bit of a thing going and she give me a few tips. Still do each other favours. She was gonna do it, play the psychic for me.'

'But she's not a psychic?'

'Well, we all are a bit, aren't we? I mean, it's easy – there are staples in haunted houses: man in uniform, woman at the window. Baby crying. Cold spots. It's how mediums do it. You mention something – old geezer always wore a muffler, somebody goes, yeah, that's my grandad. Only in a house, they go yeah, I did feel something in that pantry. Piece of piss, Mary.'

'Well, forgive me for being—'

'I'm telling you, you go in there, tell her you can hear a baby crying or something, I guarantee you'll get a result.'

'Jon, have you forgotten what I do normally?'

'God'll protect you, then, won't He? Look, you genuinely know about this stuff, right? What you were giving me earlier about phantasms of the living – that's serious, in-depth knowledge. You could carry it off, no problem. I tell you, she thinks she's getting something out of you, she's a pussycat.'

276

'And what do you want out of this, Jon? What do you want out of her?'

It was a still day; you could hear the weir. Over Wales, the sun was just visible, like a coin pressed into tinfoil.

'What do you think I want?' Jon Scole gripped his knees, leaning forward. 'How much you think it costs these days to have a shop in Ludlow? Keep enough stock to attract people in?'

'I don't know.'

'Me parents left me enough to get a bit of a business going, but costs are always higher than you think they're gonna be, especially here. The ghost-walks don't do badly in the season, but it's peanuts really. And if the Mayor and his family wanna squeeze me out they can do it any time. Could make sure the lease don't get renewed, for a start.'

'He wouldn't do that.'

'He bloody would, Mary. And could I afford to buy anything proper? Not the way property's going in this town.'

'I thought you sold a café to the Little Chef?'

Jon sighed. 'I sold a bit of land with a prefabricated transport caff on it. No comparison with posh high-street business premises in an upmarket place like this.'

'So you're looking for a backer, in other words.'

'Think what she's spent on that house. And buying the land to stop the building? You heard about that? Imagine what that cost. Bought it straight out, no financial juggling required. Imagine.'

'So if she sees you as someone who's done her a few favours…?'

'Who knows? Bit of a tightrope, I'll give you that.' He rubbed his eyes. 'I'm sorry to've hung this on you. I just thought… Well, obviously, I didn't think at all, did I? I just come out with it.'

He looked a bit lost. He was younger than he'd seemed, maybe no more than thirty. The beard was deceptive, as it was no doubt intended to be.

'Look,' he said, 'you go back to your vicarage, have a think, and if I don't hear from you again… well, it's been interesting, hasn't it?'

'There's just one problem here, Jon. Supposing we find out that she did something that could take her away from here? How would that help you?'

'What, to prison?'

'Well, I'm not going to arrest her, I'm just a jobbing priest, but…'

'I'm under no illusions, girl,' Jon said. 'The day she finds it impossible to live in Ludlow, that's the Mayor's birthday. And you wouldn't shed any tears neither if you found Robbie's death was in some way down to Bell. But I reckon whatever you did find out you'd accept it, wouldn't you? You wouldn't try to twist it or move the goalposts. So if it turns out she's, OK, out of her tree, but basically harmless, that's all right, i'n't it?'

'We'll… have to see.'

'I believe in fate, me,' Jon Scole said. 'Whatever's gonna happen is gonna happen.'

Merrily got back into the car and lit a cigarette.

It could hardly be worse, could it? Either she could go along with it, faking ridiculous psychic skills just to gain some kind of access to Bell Pepper (and then what?) or make an ignominious retreat, put the whole issue in front of the Deliverance Panel, let them dismiss it out of hand, accept an official rebuke for not informing them earlier and then wait for the axe to fall.

How the hell had she got into this?

She supposed the paper bag on the passenger seat answered that question. She picked it up and shook out the book: *Everyday Life in the Middle Ages, in Pictures*. What had a boy as clued-up as Robbie Walsh wanted with a picture book anyway?

She laid it on the passenger seat and flicked through it, expecting cartoon-like artist's impressions; in fact, most of the illustrations seemed to be from old engravings, stained glass, carvings on tombs. This made more sense – he would have wanted as authentic an illustration as possible of what life in the Middle Ages had been like. It had obviously been important to him, as he'd walked these streets, to see through medieval eyes.

Why had that been so important? Why had an evidently personable adolescent boy needed to retreat through time? What had made the present so unbearable?

She leafed through the book – the reason she'd bought it, for £7.99 – for where the page had been ripped out. Just one missing page, and the facing one had been about... Trial by Ordeal? Was that it? She turned to the chapter headed 'Medieval Misdeeds and Retribution'.

Page ninety-one had a reproduction of a sombre woodcut, depicting a man hanging from a gibbet, his head bowed over a tightened noose. Several people were gathered around, watching. Some appeared to be smiling.

Merrily stared at it, recalling how the page had been quite carefully removed from Robbie's copy. The reverse, page ninety-two, had a black and white photograph of the reconstruction of a medieval wooden gibbet from some interpretive museum. Immediately, she was hearing Bernie Dunmore telling her how Bell Pepper might have been dealt with in times gone by on Gallows Hill, still preserved as open space in Ludlow.

Unfortunately, I think our old execution site is underneath Plascarreg. Don't you dare make anything of that.

She wasn't about to; it seemed unlikely to be relevant, but it was worth mentioning, and so she called Mumford.

No answer. She rang the Bishop, managed to get him at home. He even seemed relieved to hear her.

'Woke up in the night, deeply troubled about all this, Merrily. Wondering what I'd let you in for. Came out in a sweat – couldn't get a handle on what I was expecting you to resolve. Just some great amorphous wrongness. Ludicrous.'

' "A great amorphous wrongness." I do like talking to an experienced metaphysician.'

'Pack it in and come home. It was stupid of me to even—'

'We can't disappoint Dennis Beckett now, Bernie. Erm... something that keeps coming up: The Palmers' Guild. What's that about?'

'In what context?'

'You remember the Mayor told us Mrs Pepper was setting up a trust to help conserve old buildings in Ludlow? She's apparently named it after The Palmers' Guild, which may have built the original house on the site where she's living.'

'There's a window in the church – I'm not an expert on this, Merrily, but you can't operate in Ludlow without coming across the Guild. Sometimes spelt "Gild" without the "u", in the old way. They were probably the original Ludlow conservationists – kept the church standing, anyway. Started, I think, in the thirteenth century when a great deal of wealth in the town was coming out of the wool industry. Guilds conferred a kind of pseudo-aristocratic social standing on rich businessmen.'

'They invested in property.'

'A couple of hundred properties at one time. Some of the income was used for the benefit of members who had fallen on hard times. It was a cooperative movement.'

'But the religious side of it—'

'Right. The Palmers' window in St Laurence's has eight stained-glass panels depicting what we can only think of as a legend put about to give the Palmers some authenticity. It was said that, in the eleventh century, pilgrims from Ludlow had brought back a ring from St John the Evangelist which they presented to the King of England at the time, Edward the Confessor. That's what the window illustrates. It's probably a fabrication.'

'On which basis the Guild appointed priests, right?'

'To devote their prayers to speeding its deceased members out of purgatory. A medieval conceit, difficult for us to comprehend, but it's clear that this was the main function of the Guild. Started out employing three chaplains, who also served the parish church, but there were as many as eight in the fifteenth century, catering to the whims of four thousand Guild members. A lot of prayer, a lot of Masses.'

'All focused on immortality.'

'They were certainly considerably more concerned about what happens afterwards than our society. Even if they did think God was open to back-handers.'

'I met Mrs Pepper this afternoon.' Merrily tamped out her cigarette in the ashtray. 'Briefly.'

'And did she appear mad?'

'On one level, barking. She was kissing a yew tree.'

'I beg your—'

'Kissing a yew tree. Very sensuously.'

'I don't know how to react to that.'

'The yew is nature's prime symbol of immortality. I'm just trying to find a link here with The Palmers' Guild, who built her house and who evidently had a similar obsession.'

'No more than anyone in those days. And this woman doesn't appear to be particularly well disposed towards Christianity.'

'But she's very much obsessed with place-memories. Ghosts. The way that Ludlow exists in more than one time-frame. It's as if she wants to experience other... I don't know. I don't know if there are hallucinogenic drugs involved here or what. It's fascinating, in a way. My impression was that she was putting on a show today. Partly because she used to be a rock singer at the theatrical end of the business, and outrageous exhibitionism comes naturally... and partly because it's a good smokescreen. People think you're mad, they leave you alone. How people react to your madness tells you whether they... sorry, you still there, Bernie?'

'Merrily, you're not... I don't like to think of you being drawn into anything.'

'Me?'

'I realize you must be feeling terribly insecure at the moment.'

'Insecure,' Merrily said. 'She's evidently looking for some kind of security. Acceptance.'

'But by whom? Not by George Lackland, clearly.'

'By the dead?' Merrily said. 'Do you think?'

29

All the Big Words

MERRILY DIDN'T REMEMBER when Jane had last been this amused – turning off The Coral on the CD player, coming back to the sofa and curling up in the lamplight, with a cushion clutched to her chest like she used to do when she was twelve, small pulses of amusement producing little choking noises in her throat.

'This' – fiendish smile – 'could be the long-delayed beginning, Mum. The start of the new you, in floaty frocks and snaky bangles. And it'll be, like, so cool that you never return to the grim old Church, and the future opens out for you like... like something that opens out. A sunflower. Whatever.'

'And we'll give up the vicarage,' Merrily said, 'and put our names down for a mobile home with wind-chimes, where we have to share a bedroom, and a shower block with the neighbours, and—'

'Hell, no, you'll live with Lol!'

Lol. Merrily looked at the clock. He'd be on stage now, having dealt with his nerves with the help of Moira Cairns, for whom he was opening, the woman who had coerced him back to gigs, who had become a kind of talisman for Lol.

Maybe he should be living with Moira Cairns.

Jane was staring at her, wide-eyed. God, had she actually said that out loud?

'Wow,' Jane said. 'You're actually still paranoid about Moira.'

'Oh, that's rid—'

'Hah!'

'I'm an actual grown-up now, Jane.'

'This is because you've never met her,' Jane said. 'For what it's worth, when she first appeared, I used to be worried about that, too, because she is, admittedly, mesmerically beautiful. But also, for someone who's almost a big star, she's actually relatively OK. She understands things. She once called me a wee pain in the arse.'

'That was penetratingly perceptive of her.'

'Seriously,' Jane said, 'there are things you could learn from Moira. Like how to step back from other people's problems and learn to live? Because, when you think about it, neither you nor Lol's ever had a normal life. Pregnant at nineteen. Widowed with a small and delightfully complex child while you're still in your twenties...'

'I'm sorry, when did I ever say you were delightful?'

'And your only real experience of student life' – Jane wrinkled her nose in distaste – 'is bloody theological college... as a mature student... toting a kid. Like, where were the years of clubbing and getting pissed and waking up in strange beds?'

'Actually that was how it all—'

'What?'

'Forget it.'

'Hmm.' Jane smiled, and then her brow furrowed. 'Listen, there's no penance to be paid, Mum. I mean, OK, yeah, we've finally got Lol into the village. But you're still not getting it right. You're taking a week off the parish to do this private-eye stuff in Ludlow for the Bishop, but you won't take a break to maybe go somewhere special with Lol.'

'You know...' Merrily repositioned herself on the sofa, awkwardly. 'I think I was happier when you were just laughing at the idea of me pretending to be psychic.'

'Yeah, well, that was the wrong attitude. I've decided to take it seriously.' Jane put the cushion behind her on the sofa and sat up straight. 'You need specialist advice, or that woman is going to take you apart. She'll just, like, totally dismantle your façade in about ten minutes.'

'And you can, erm, school me, can you?'

Jane shrugged. 'I've read the books. Spent a few months, if you recall, attempting to worship the moon... when I was young.'

'It was less than two years ago.' Merrily looked into Jane's eyes, surely greyer than they used to be.

'I mean, I'm not claiming to be anything more than some kind of failed neophyte, Mum, but I reckon I could probably save you from total humiliation.'

Merrily considered this.

When exactly had Jane's paganism ceased to be a problem for her?

At first it had seemed like a basic teenage rebellion thing: Jane resenting the Church, seeing poor Lucy Devenish, with her talk of apple-lore and nature spirits, as a kind of guru... and then, after Lucy's death, lying about her age to get into a goddess-worshipping group based at a Hereford health-food shop. In just a couple of years, Jane had encountered pagans and psychics, good and bad, and emerged, at the age of seventeen... oddly clear-headed.

Yes, it was still there in some form, Jane's paganism, but no, it wasn't quite a problem any more.

'All right,' Merrily said. 'Can we go through it?'

Yew trees. Jane appeared to have read entire books about yew trees.

'Making love to one. That's totally... I mean, I can connect with that.'

'Are they poisonous to people? I'm not sure.'

'I wouldn't personally exchange life-fluids with one to find out,' Jane said. 'But I do get the point. She's embracing immortality. Some yew trees could be the oldest living beings on this planet – and that's heavy. The idea of a tree being a repository of ancient wisdom is not so crazy. So if she has an ancient yew near her house, and that's the start of her ritual walk, and then she proceeds to this yew at the castle where Marion fell... Where's the next one? Bound to be one in the churchyard.'

'Several, apparently. I think there's the remains of a yew alley,' Merrily said. 'I asked Jon Scole about that.'

'Cool.' Jane spread Merrily's new street map of Ludlow over the OS map of the wider area. 'And then one in this old cemetery?'

'St Leonard's, yes.'

'So you've probably got an ancient and sacred route... maybe even pre-Christian. Maybe a processional route up and over the holy hill between the two rivers. If you think, way back, before there was a town or a castle there'd just be this hill... a holy hill.'

'How do you know it was holy?'

'Hah!' Jane beamed in satisfaction. 'I looked it up. It's in one of my books upstairs, and I got some more off the Net. This is amazing stuff. The name "Ludlow", right? "Low" usually refers to a tumulus or a burial mound, and sure enough there was one.'

'Where?'

'On top of the hills. What's now the highest point of the town.'

'The church? St Laurence's?'

'There was a tumulus which, until the end of the twelfth century, was right next to the original church. And then they extended the church into the tumulus and found that it contained bodies – bones. Which were alleged at the time to be the remains of three Irish saints, because in those days if anybody found any bones near a church it would be, like, more kudos if they were holy relics. They were probably the bones of Bronze Age chieftains... which is cool.'

'They've gone now, presumably?'

'Doesn't matter. What matters is that the tower – the tallest tower on the border, OK, the Cathedral of the Marches – is rising up directly out of a pagan site, so it's like' – Jane held up a fist – 'one of ours.'

'Congratulations.'

'It's what they did,' Jane said. 'These are geopsychically sensitive sites. If the Church hadn't built on existing places of power, Christianity would probably have vanished by the end of the Middle Ages. So if Belladonna's making a personal connection with the sacred centres of Ludlow, that's the big one.'

'Well, she certainly goes into the church, even if she doesn't go to actual services.'

'There you go. She's opening herself up to the vibrations.'

'Opening herself up, all right.'

'Sorry?'

'Never mind.' Ethel jumped into Merrily's lap and started to wash her paws. 'What exactly is she doing, do you think, Jane? Where's she coming from? We looking at witchcraft, or what?'

'She on her own?'

'There are some young people who seem to have formed some sort of attachment to her. When I first saw her, she was with, I think, four of them – two men, two women, all wearing Edwardian-type gear, slightly funereal.'

'Could be part of a coven. Doesn't seem too likely, though.'

'They just struck me as basic goths.'

'OK, listen…' Jane leaned into the corner of the sofa. 'I've been thinking about this… Could she have any ancestry in the town? Are there any family roots she maybe wants to pick up on? Because that might explain why she was always with Robbie Walsh – he could've been helping research it, couldn't he? That seems to have been the kind of thing he enjoyed.'

'That's actually not a bad theory,' Merrily said.

'Or, if you want to extend it in a more mystical direction, could she have been, like, hypnotically regressed into recalling some past life in Ludlow? For instance – and this makes sense – suppose she believes she's the reincarnation of somebody like, for instance…'

Merrily brought her hands together. 'Marion de la Bruyère!'

'Well…?'

'It's a fascinating thought, flower.'

287

'And it explains the suicide links,' Jane said. 'And it's exactly the kind of bollocks a mad old slapper like Belladonna would go for.'

Afterwards, Lol followed Moira back up the M4 to the Severn Bridge services, where she was spending the night. They sat in the café by the big windows where you could see the sweep of the suspension bridge into Wales and the lights bouncing off the estuary's dark water.

'I've never done that before,' Lol said. 'Never.'

Two verses in, freezing up in the heat of the lights, standing quivering, like the mental patient he was singing about.

'You mean it wasnae deliberate?' Moira raised an eyebrow, cup of hot chocolate held in both hands, like a chalice. 'Even I thought it was part of the act. And when you started laughing like that...'

'Couldn't stop.'

Doubled up, he'd noticed her watching him from the shadows at the side of the stage, in her long, sea-green dress, the strand of white in her hair like the crack of light down a doorway at night. Expecting her to walk on, gently detach the mike and salvage his set.

Not necessary, as it turned out. The audience had started laughing with him, with no idea why. In the lobby afterwards, Moira's merchandising guy had sold over sixty copies of *Alien*. Now he was higher than the Severn Bridge and, every so often, he would shiver at the memory.

'It was a wild moment, but you never looked back,' Moira said. 'You were soaring like a gull. I'm thinking, Jesus, he's become a performer at last – wee Lol. However, just for the record... why?' She'd put down her cup. Her hair was tied up now. She wore a grey woolly sweater and white jeans. 'Go on... just out of interest. For m' personal files...'

'Must've been the song,' Lol admitted. 'It's always that song. It's got... something in it I can't always control.'

' "Heavy Medication Day"?'

'The day I refused to take the pills,' Lol remembered, 'Dr Gascoigne said... and I remember him leaning over me, I was sitting in a high-backed chair in the main day-room, and I'd turned it away from the TV, and he leaned over me and he said in my ear, "Don't go thinking you're ever going to leave here, Mr Robinson. You see that door? One day, when I've been long retired to the south of France, you'll be straining to get your Zimmer frame through it." '

'Jesus. This is a shrink? This is how they talk?'

'Well, it's been said before, but it's true…'

'That if it wasnae for the white coat you'd never know which were the patients, right? I tell you what… by the time you'd finished laughing and you did the whole song again, they were with you for the duration.'

'Um, to change the subject – slightly – I was talking to Tom Storey.'

'Poor Tom,' Moira said. 'Wasnae so rich and famous he'd probably have been under the shrinks years ago.'

Moira had once, way back, been in a band with Tom Storey. It was a very small pond, the British folk-rock scene.

Lol told her how he'd wound up talking to Tom. Moira rolled her eyes.

'Belladonna, eh? The extraordinary Bell. Used to fancy the hell out of Tom, simply because he was rumoured to be, you know…?'

'Sensitive?'

'Amazing the number of women went after him because of that. To guys, a guitar hero. To women, a *psychic* guitar hero. None of them realizing it was the best way to have the poor guy heading for the airport. Bell couldnae figure it at all – she could've had anybody at that time.'

'You knew her?'

'Nobody knew her. We did a couple of the same festivals – you did one, I recall. This'd be before America discovered her. She was older than me and always kind of superior – she's an artist, slumming, and I'm this folk-club kid on the make. And she resented me, probably for the same reason she fancied Tom.'

'Because she'd heard you were…'

'A touch fey, aye. Oh, and she'd made a wee pass at me and got soundly rebuffed. That didnae help.'

'Went both ways?'

'She went a hundred ways, Laurence, although I tend to think the allegations of actual necrophilia were no more than malicious gossip. It was all a major fetish thing. Other bands and singers, it was a phase. Her, it went on when goth stuff was no longer big-money cool, so…'

'So there had to be a cause,' Lol said.

'Always a cause. They're saying even schizophrenia's no' something you're born with. The guy I did know was Eric Bryers, her boyfriend way back. Session bass-player, absolutely besotted with Bell. Do anything for her – coke, smack, acid. If you get ma point. She was gonnae have his child and everything, and it was all cosy-cosy, then she suddenly disappears – this is Eric's version of events – and the next he hears of her she's in LA and a big star, with no mention of a baby.'

'Had it adopted, Tom said. He was furious.'

'Ah, the adoption story, that's one version. What I heard, the baby was stillborn, and she had a big funeral for it, fancy Gothic grave – that would be more in keeping. Last time I saw Eric, he… Aw, he was busking with another guy in Manchester – I had a gig at the Free Trade Hall, and there he was busking. I'm ashamed to say I couldnae face him, so I walked past quick, with ma scarf around ma head, and slipped all the cash I had on me intae his hat. Talked to a guy some time later, said Eric used to follow Bell's gigs around the country, busking near the theatres, and getting arrested and moved on. I think he had a solid habit by then, and nobody was using him.'

'Dead now.'

'Aye. They got him off the smack and he turned to drink and his behaviour became erratic, and one day the poor devil threw himself off the top of a skyscraper block in London.'

'Like Seress.' Lol started to feel a little weird.

'What?'

'Rezso Seress – "Gloomy Sunday"?'

'It's late,' Moira said. 'Start again.'

'There was this song about suicide which, according to the

urban myths, has been leading to people actually topping themselves. By a Hungarian, Rezso Seress. He also died by throwing himself off a building. The Hungarian Suicide Song. Occasionally gets covered by artists feeling a bit daring.'

'Bell?'

'Very faithful version. Exactly like the original, down to the scratches.'

'See, that's just the kind of fuckin' stupid thing that woman would do,' Moira said. 'The way Eric was, I can actually imagine him sitting there playing the damn thing over and over and refilling his glass. I'd like to give her a good slap.'

'You ever see her now?'

'Not in years, she's well off the circuit – doesnae need it; weird kids keep rediscovering her. They also began using her music on commercials a lot – when TV commercials started becoming so diffuse and surreal you weren't sure what they were advertising. Stroke me, poke me, invoke me – however that shit went. Only it would be a car. You staying here tonight?'

'Going home, I think. It's only just over an hour.'

'Home,' Moira said. 'That's such a nice word, isn't it?'

It seemed unlikely he'd be back yet, but around midnight Merrily went to the end of the vicarage drive to see if there was a light on at Lol's.

There wasn't. There were no lights on anywhere in Church Street. It was a warm night, with no moon. She lit a cigarette, looked up at the window of Jane's attic apartment, and there was no light there either. Good. The kid had done enough research for one night.

Kid. It wasn't respectful even to think of her as a kid any more. She was smart and funny and perceptive and increasingly good to have around. And in eighteen months' time she'd almost certainly be leaving home.

Home. Merrily turned her back on the vicarage. It had never really felt like home. Seven bedrooms – how the hell could she live here alone? Maybe one of the other five parishes she'd be invited to take on would have a smaller vicarage. Or maybe, when Jane finished school, it would be time to move on, out of the diocese. Maybe the writing was already on the wall, next to a hazy outline sketch of Siân Callaghan-Clarke in episcopal purple.

The image made her angry and she thought, *Sod it, I'm going to do it – Mary the bloody psychic.*

'You know the way to be really convincing as a psychometrist?' Jane had said as she went up to bed. 'Just wander around and don't say a thing. Don't claim you've had any visions or sensations at all. Say absolutely nothing.'

'What good will that do?'

'Because all phoney psychics come out with a mass of crap, and when you respond to some detail they snatch on it, and that's how it works. If you say nothing she'll think either you don't want to reveal what you've picked up until you're absolutely certain, or you know it would scare the pants off her.'

Made sense. Merrily pinched out her cigarette and went in.

Lol drove across the bridge into Wales and slowly up the border, along the deep, moon-tinted, green-washed Wye Valley into the lights of Monmouth and back into England and up towards...

Home, yes.

It would be overstating it to say that Moira could read you like a book, but she could see all the big words in your life as if they were spelled out in neon on your forehead.

Home... that was one of them. The last time he'd lived in Ledwardine, it had been a refuge, the place he'd hidden rather than lived in. Now... well, now he actually felt he was probably the right person to be in the house of Lucy Devenish.

And Merrily... that would work itself out. It had to.

Because she was the real meaning of home.

He left the Astra on the square, alongside the oak-pillared market hall. Perhaps he should think about renting a garage somewhere. Tonight, they'd sold more copies of his album than they'd sold of Moira's. Well, OK, most of the audience would already have had all Moira's albums, so that was understandable, but sixty copies…

It was twenty to two in the morning. Friday morning, Ledwardine hanging in timeless silence, a bat flittering overhead. Lol stood for a moment on the cobbles, looking across at the vicarage drive – a small, dim light on somewhere in the woody heart of the old house. *There should always*, he thought, *be a light in there.*

Tears came into his eyes and he hurried away.

Remembering, as he often would, the first night he'd met Merrily, when Ethel the cat had been given a kicking by Karl Windling and Lol had wound up carrying her to the vicarage. And Merrily had tended Ethel and, although it had been a very bad night for her in ways that he hadn't yet known about, she'd sat down and lit a cigarette and had said, in a voice full of ironic uncertainty, *Talk to me, Mr Robinson… I'm a priest.*

Lol unlocked the door and stumbled through the darkness towards the parlour, until he remembered he had power.

He had power.

He clicked the switch and the bulb over the foot of the stairs drizzled out its low-wattage light. *Lampshade*, Lol thought. *Lampshade tomorrow.*

A rectangle of white.

Shit.

Before he'd picked the envelope off the mat, he knew what it was.

Somehow he'd forgotten. He really had forgotten. Hadn't thought about it for ages. It belonged to the days of oil lamps and paint-trays, before he had power.

He almost crumpled it up and threw it away. But the night had already darkened. He tore it open at the door and held it under the bulb.

Your a sick man.
How long you been hitting her

30

Victim

NEXT MORNING, AS soon as Jane had left for school, Merrily drove straight to Hereford, letting herself into the gatehouse office with her own key before Sophie had arrived.

Dressed-down again, jeans and fleece, as yesterday, she sat at Sophie's desk and rang Lol on his mobile. Still switched off. She left her second so-how-did-it-go? message of the morning. She knew he was back; she'd seen his car on the square.

Outside it was raining hard, Broad Street speckled with umbrellas. In the dullness of the office, the figure 2 was glowing from the message window on the answering machine.

No glow, however, in the messages.

'Sophie, I think we must talk on the subject of office reorganization – and Mrs Watkins. Call me, please. Thank you.'

Callaghan-Clarke, clipped, concise and ominous. The teacher: see me.

And so barefaced about it, because Mrs Watkins was on holiday. Finding she could hardly get her breath, Merrily was close to phoning back herself. Instead she lit a cigarette, her hands unsteady, fumbling with the Zippo, listening to the second message: Andy Mumford.

'Mrs Watkins, tried to get you before you left. Don't know

whether you listened to the local radio…'

Actually, in the car on the way here, she'd been listening to Lol's album with the volume well up, his breathy vocals on 'Camera Lies' reassuring with their sense of his need: *the camera lies, she might vaporize.* A song he'd written in the tingling dawn of their relationship.

'… *Big dawn raid on the Plascarreg,'* Mumford was saying.

Sophie arrived, turning in the doorway and shaking her umbrella over the stone stairwell. She heard the answering machine, left the umbrella outside and came in to listen.

'Large selection of Class A drugs removed. Three dealers nicked, it looks like. Well… too much of a coincidence, see. Wouldn't surprise me if Mebus and his little mates hadn't grassed up their neighbours with a view to avoiding prosecution. I been trying to get my relative on the phone, without success so far, but I'll keep you informed. Thank you.'

Merrily put the machine on hold and then played the message again. Mumford had not sounded exactly euphoric. But, then, if Jason Mebus was back on the streets without a stain…? And where had Jason found the nerve to grass up his neighbours? Something didn't sound right.

'Long overdue,' Sophie said. 'Half the drugs in Hereford seem to have come through that estate. I had the radio on just before leaving the house, and it's now five arrests. Quantities of heroin and crack-cocaine with a street value of somewhere around three-quarters of a million pounds.'

'That's huge, for Hereford.'

'There'll be large, and possibly liquid, breakfasts in the police canteen, no doubt.' Sophie slipped out of her coat, hung it behind the door.

'There's also a message from Siân Callaghan-Clarke,' Merrily said. 'Wants to talk to you about office reorganization.'

'One can hardly contain one's anticipation,' Sophie said.

'And about me.'

'In which case, I ought to call her back while you're still here. However, you didn't come in to pass on my messages, did you?'

'I'm in a quandary,' Merrily said. 'Need advice from a wise and entirely balanced individual.'

Sophie nodded. It wouldn't be arrogance that stopped her denying these qualities; she just didn't believe in wasting time. She sat down on what was usually Merrily's side of the desk.

'Tell me.'

Merrily had taken it as far as the encounter with Belladonna outside the castle walls – more bizarre the more she thought about it – when the phone rang. She motioned for Sophie to take it.

'Gatehouse,' Sophie said. 'Ah. Good morning, Canon Callaghan-Clarke.'

Merrily pulled her bag across the desk, took out the cigarettes and the Zippo.

The call lasted less than five minutes but seemed longer. Most of Sophie's replies were monosyllabic and negative – *No... not at all... never* – but her minimal facial responses sent out signals of extreme danger. At one point, a corner of her mouth twitched sharply, as though a wasp had landed there.

Finally she said calmly, 'Canon Clarke, I think you'll find that such a conclusion is absolutely and utterly preposterous.'

When she put the phone down, the rain was stopping, and a gauzy sunlight powdered part of the room. When Sophie reached out and clicked on the desk lamp, Merrily sensed this was, as was customary with Siân, going to be worse than she could have imagined.

Sophie straightened the notepad on the desk, took a long breath and let it escape slowly.

'As you've probably guessed, Merrily, that wasn't about office reorganization, it was entirely about you.'

'There's flattering.'

'No,' Sophie said.

'No, I didn't think it would be.'

'To begin with, she said she didn't want to hear any more manufactured stories from me, because she now knew precisely why you'd suddenly felt compelled to take a holiday.'

'She's bluffing. Couldn't possibly know, unless Bernie—'

'Nothing to do with that. Nothing to do with the Bishop or Ludlow or Ms Pepper.' Sophie coughed. 'You appear to have taken a holiday to conceal the fact that you've become a victim of domestic violence.'

Merrily sprang out of her chair.

'I'll make some tea,' Sophie said.

Lol rang.

'How did it go?' Merrily trying to sound bright, the way you did in church on grey Sundays.

'It was really good.' His own tone was small and somehow distant, as though it was floating inside a balloon. 'They... sold over sixty copies of the CD.'

'That's incredible, Lol.'

'Yes, Prof'll be...'

'Mmm. He will. And it was OK? I mean, on stage?'

'In the end. I'll tell you tonight... maybe?'

'Definitely.'

And they went on like that for another minute or so, this thick wedge of the unspoken between them, furtive fingers of sunlight sliding between the rainclouds and across the desk, steam rising as Sophie poured boiling water into the pot.

Merrily put the phone down and stared at it, as if it might be bugged.

'Can't have leaked out through Mumford. And it couldn't have come out of Hereford. I didn't even take off the other glasses to try on the new ones in Chave and Jackson, just held them up to the light. Which leaves only one source.'

'You live in a village.' Sophie carried the teapot to the desk.

'With a shop. Called in the other night for a bottle of wine and some cigarettes and I left my glasses in the car. Never thought about it.'

'But I thought the people there—'

'The Prossers are fine, they'd never... No, it was night-time, you see, and the new girl, Paris, was on the till – that is, new to the shop, not the village. Ledwardine born and bred. She probably told everybody who came in and everybody she met on the way home. I didn't think. I'm so stupid.'

'And how would it get to Canon Clarke?'

'I can guess.' Merrily stood up and took off her glasses in disgust. 'What exactly did she say about Lol?'

'She said that – there's no nice way I can put this – that someone had suggested this was no more than anyone could expect if they became involved with a mental patient with… his history.'

'Who?' Merrily was hot with fury. 'Who – knowing him – would say that?'

'Canon Clarke said how regrettable it was that so many people still had such a primitive attitude towards mental illness.'

'But he—' Merrily hurled her cigarette packet at the desk. 'Lol was never—'

'I know that.'

'And she has no reason to think that either, but she chooses not to correct anyone's impression.' Merrily sat down, hands dangling between her knees, head thrown back. 'What am I going to do about this, Soph?'

'Merrily, most black eyes have quite a simple explanation, connected with tripping up, cupboard doors…'

'No, they don't. Most black eyes are caused by people getting hit. I go around now, telling people I've walked into a lamp-post, what's that going to sound like, at this stage? And I obviously can't exactly open the Plascarreg can of worms, can I? I mean, apart from implicating Mumford, it would seem a bit coincidental after today's news. I'm… I'm stuffed here, Sophie. And the worst thing of all… I've damaged Lol.'

'Do you want to hear the rest?'

'Not particularly.'

'Canon Clarke is wondering, judging by your recent… erratic behaviour—'

'Erratic, how?'

'—If this violence hasn't been a long-term difficulty. Not unknown, in her experience, among the female clergy, who are sometimes rather too assiduous about turning the other cheek.'

'That woman is so full of crap.'

'Husbands who resent the ubiquity of religion in the home, become violently jealous of God. So many cases have come to light, apparently, that there's a special counselling service operating now, within the Church, for just such situations.'

'I know,' Merrily said, 'but this... Sophie, has it occurred to you why she's telling you about it?'

'I assume because it's the quickest way of getting it back to you.'

'Exactly. Why?'

'I don't know. Perhaps... rather fewer people than you fear have been exposed to this nonsense. However, if you start to... overreact and go around looking for people to blame, you're going to spread it over quite a wide circle. Perhaps that's what she wants.'

'You do think she has an agenda, then?'

'We both know she has an agenda, Merrily. I think it's probably no more complicated than a ferocious ambition.'

'You know the Archdeacon's suggesting they hang a bunch of extra parishes on me?'

'Oh. So that's true.'

'Who planted the idea?'

'I suspect we'll never get further than a guess. It's fairly clear that an anti-Deliverance movement is gathering ground within the diocese. I don't know how we're going to fight it, but my feeling is that the best way to frustrate this stupid rumour is for you to continue as normal. Not rise to it.'

'Wearing the glasses or not?'

'Not, I should say. You have absolutely nothing to hide – if necessary, tell people exactly what happened, you don't have to name the estate. Anyway, the swelling's reduced considerably this morning.'

'And Lol. What does he do? What does he tell people?'

'He's the one they won't ask,' Sophie said, 'I'm afraid.'

31

Smoke

'BASTARDS.' GOMER PARRY accepted a glass of cider. 'Thank you, boy. Longer I live, the less number of folks I gives a shit about, and that's a fact. Bloody gossip-mongering bastards.'

Gomer sat on Lol's new sofa. It was coming up to ten a.m. He took off his cap, and his white hair sprayed out in different directions like an old wallpaper-brush. He said he'd been out early, giving the churchyard a bit of a trim, casually chatting to folks as they came through... and it had come filtering out – people interested in talking to Gomer this morning because they knew he was well in with the vicar.

'All sorts of ole wallop. Folks remembering how they seen the vicar creeping out of yere at night, furtive-like. Like her's got some'ing to be ashamed of. Some daft bitch in the shop, her even said the reason Alison Kinnersley cleared out, went off with Bull-Davies, was you was slappin' her around a bit, too.'

Lol shook his head wearily. 'Gomer, that is just—'

'Aye.' Gomer put down his cider glass, got out his ciggy tin. 'I says, listen, you go and ask Alison. You ask bloody Bull-Davies 'isself. Bastards. All this ole wallop. Makes you sick to the gut. One day you're a hero, next it's, Oh we knew what he was all along, that feller. Look, boy, I'm sorry to have to bring this to your door, but I figured you needed to know what was goin' around.'

'I'm grateful.' Lol was standing by the inglenook, the hearth stale with dead ash.

'How'd she actually get it, boy – the bruise – you don't mind me…?'

'Kids. It was on the Plascarreg Estate in Hereford. She was helping Andy Mumford – family thing – and there was a struggle with some kids. Nothing to—'

'Miserable Andy? He's off the streets now, en't he?'

'Retired, but not exactly off the streets. His nephew?'

'Ar… yeard that boy come off the castle was his nephew.' Gomer licked the end of a cigarette paper. 'All goes deep with Mumford, see. Not a happy family. I remember his ole man, Reg Mumford, when he was a copper. Hard bastard – too fond of discipline, you get my meaning. Too handy with his bloody belt was the word. Has an effect, see. Vicar should take more care, you tell her from me.'

'I will.' Lol wondered if even Gomer might have harboured some small suspicion that the rumour might be true and that was why he'd come. In or out of a JCB, Gomer believed in direct action, shovelling away all the rubble until you reached the core of whatever it was.

'Come on then, boy.' Gomer fired up a ciggy. 'Spit it out. The ole plant-hire's been a bit slack lately, see, so I been letting Danny do the lion's share – needs the money more'n me. You and the vicar wants me to hire a loudspeaker van, go up and down the streets shaming these bastards, I got the time.'

'No, no. God. Look… Gomer… I was wondering, is it possible to trace the source of these stories?'

Gomer thought about it. 'Lucy Devenish could do it, only one as ever could just by lookin' in folks' eyes. Lucy was so deep into this village, her'd just go round asking questions and gazin' into people's faces. Folks spreads stuff they reckons is prob'ly lies, see, they'll never quite look you in the eye. Once you finds the one knows it's a lie, you're getting close.'

'So this isn't just gossip?' Lol said.

'No.' The light boiled in Gomer's glasses. 'Not in my view it en't.'

'Orchestrated?'

'That's the word.'

'Why?'

'Some bastard got it in for the vicar? Can't believe that. What's her ever done but her best? Last vicar, old Alf Hayden, he din't give a monkey's, bumbling round the village, how're you, how're you? Did he care? Did he hell. They don't deserve a decent minister, half o' these bastards. What you got there, boy?'

Lol brought the two anonymous notes over, spread them on the sofa next to Gomer. Gomer took off his glasses, cleaned them on his sleeve and then read each note slowly.

'You been to the cops, boy?'

'What's the point? They're not threatening letters.'

'You reckon?'

'Jane's been round checking the parish noticeboard, the adverts in the shop window, trying to compare the writing.'

'Worst thing is, see, the vicar could go in the pulpit on Sunday, denounce the whole thing in public, and folks'd still be shakin' their daft heads, going no smoke without fire, kind of thing.'

'She won't be in the pulpit next Sunday,' Lol said. 'There's another guy booked to take the services.'

'Bugger.' Gomer took out his ciggy tin. 'That en't gonner help, is it? Folks'll think her's gone to one o' them shelters. When'd the last one come?'

'Last night. I had a concert over in Bristol, didn't get back till the early hours.'

'Many folks yere know you was gonner be out that long?'

'Apart from Merrily and Jane, nobody.'

'Chances were it got delivered not long after you went out, then. En't much cover in this street. Likely they was seen.'

'You reckon.'

'Possible.' Gomer chewed the end of his ciggy. 'Quite possible.'

Around mid-morning, Mumford rang. He hadn't quite got his old voice back, but there was a crunch to it that hadn't been there since he'd retired.

'I was right, Mrs Watkins.'

'Sorry… Mebus?'

'Well… he wasn't the grass. Nor Chain-boy, nor Chain-boy's half-brother. It was another boy with them, Niall Collins. He told 'em where the warehouse was – one of the industrial workshops between Plascarreg and the Barn Church. Crack and heroin turnover of twenty grand a week, near enough.'

'Did we meet this Niall the other night?'

'I reckon he was the one shouted there was a car coming, when there wasn't.'

'Yellow fleece? I remember thinking he looked a bit worried about the way it was going.'

'He would be. Thirteen, and no form. First offence, see. Mate of Robbie's, as it happened. Not a big mate, he didn't have any big mates, but this Niall talked to him a bit.'

'As distinct from bullying him.'

'That's about it. This Niall's family – his dad lost his job, house repossessed, and they wound up on the Plascarreg. Dad hates it, the drug culture, the need for five locks on your front door. Fairly decent family, in other words.'

'I expect most people there are.'

'So what happens, the dad talks to one of the uniforms, says he's tried to keep his boy away from the scum but it's an impossible job on that estate. Says there's a lot the boy knows about what goes on, but if they spills the beans they can't very well go back living next to the families of the buggers they helped put away. So the uniform fixes up for Mr Collins to talk to Bliss.'

'Oh good.'

'Aye. Result is, when all the police vehicles turns up on the Plascarreg at dawn today, there's a furniture van behind them. While the raid's on, all the shouting and screaming, the Collinses' flat's being quietly emptied of all their furniture, and off they goes into temporary accommodation off the patch.'

'Got to hand it to Bliss.'

'Except that, letting the Collins boy off with a caution, they had to reduce the charges for the others. No ABH any more for

Mebus. Be down to causing an affray or some feeble rubbish like that.'

'Who told you all this?'

Mumford was silent.

'Just that it helps to know, when I'm talking to Bliss. Wouldn't like to accidentally finger your contact.'

Merrily heard Mumford sniff. 'Karen Dowell, it is.'

'Bliss's new bag-carrier?'

'Second cousin, twice removed – whatever. Blood's still thicker than canteen tea. Keep this very much to yourself, Mrs Watkins.'

'Of course. How are you feeling now, Andy?'

'Hard to say,' Mumford said. 'Bliss gets a handful of collars, he's happy. But that don't bring out the truth about Robbie Walsh, do it?'

'It might. Why don't you ease off for a bit?'

'You called last night,' Mumford said. 'Got you off 1471.'

'Oh…' She told him about the missing page from *Everyday Life in the Middle Ages* and what the Bishop had said about the execution site. 'Probably nothing.'

Mumford grunted, said he'd keep her informed. When she put the phone down, there wasn't even time to tell Sophie about the development before it rang again, and she automatically picked it up.

Sophie reached across. 'Let me—'

'Gatehouse,' Merrily said. If it was Siân, this was as good a time as any.

'Oh, good morning. This is Smith, Sebald and Partners, solicitors, in Ludlow. I have Miss Susannah Pepper for Mrs Watkins.'

Merrily went out to clear her head. Ran through the thinning rain across the Cathedral Green and around the corner to the health-food shop to grab something for lunch for her and Sophie. Came back and spread it all over the two desks – bean pasties and rice crackers with sun-dried tomato dip. Bars of

305

Green and Black's Maya Gold chocolate. She was on holiday; it was a picnic.

'What was she like?' Sophie asked.

'She wasn't like anything. OK, she wasn't like any*body*. Robotic. A machine for processing wills and conveyancing houses. She talked like' – Merrily nodded at the computer – 'you know the voice that comes out of an iMac to alert you to an error?'

She leaned back against the window sill, her black fleece open to the old Radiohead T-shirt that Jane wouldn't be seen dead in any more.

'OK, I'm exaggerating. She was neither friendly nor unfriendly. She simply informed me that she'd had a long and detailed discussion with her future father-in-law... not that she called him that, she referred to him throughout as County Councillor G. H. Lackland— What are you smiling at?'

'Nothing.' Sophie began to brush crumbs from the desk with the side of a hand. 'Go on.'

'The substance of it was that if I – or anyone in my *department* – wanted to elicit any information from her client, Mrs Pepper, all inquiries should be made through her office. In writing.'

'And what did you say?'

'You heard me. I said, "Thank you very much, Miss Pepper." What can you say to someone like that? Could've said that if she wanted to develop her acquaintance with Jesus the Saviour she should make the initial approach through *my* office—'

'You're annoyed.'

'I'm annoyed. I'm very annoyed. Bloody lawyers.'

She was remembering her marriage and the seepage of disillusion. The divorce that would surely have happened if a car crash hadn't made her a widow.

'Who told her about you, do you think?' Sophie said.

'Could have been anybody – Callum Corey? I wasn't trying too hard to be discreet. I could tell she just couldn't wait for me to give her an opening to bring up the subject of harassment and injunctions. "Stay away from The Weir House or..."'

'You studied law, didn't you, Merrily?'

'Till the embryonic Jane delivered the first kick. About a year. I was also married to one who I thought was going to be a crusader for justice but turned out to be a crusader *against* justice. Like most of the greedy bastards.'

'Could they get an injunction to keep you away from this woman?'

'Unlikely. Anyway, they'd be shooting themselves in the foot, bringing it into the public domain.' Merrily stood up, decided that she couldn't face lunch after all. 'Well, they can't do a Mumford on me, accuse me of impersonating a priest.'

'You're going back, then?'

'You're glad?'

'I hate to see you defensive and frustrated. Shouldn't be too difficult. You going home now?'

'I need to talk to Lol. And Jane. I'd hate her to find out about these rumours from anyone else.'

'Quite.'

'But first, I think I'll pop into the Cathedral for a while. Some of the sensations I've been experiencing today could fall under the category of Unholy.'

'As long as you don't let Him talk you out of anything.'

Merrily blinked. 'You're very hawkish today, Sophie.'

'Sometimes I feel the phrase "turning the other cheek" should come with a number of get-out clauses.'

'Mmm.' Merrily nodded, zipping her fleece.

It occurred to her, for the first time, that the level of anger behind Sophie's cashmere calm might well exceed even her own.

She never made it to the Cathedral.

It was unavoidable. Cream suit, beard like it had been ironed on, he was following his smile in long strides across the green.

'Merrily!'

'Nigel.'

'Tiresome meeting with the Dean and the Chairman of the Perpetual Trust.'

Challenging Merrily to explain what she was doing here when she was supposed to be on leave. Stuff it, why should she have to tell him anything?

'And how is your poor aunt?' Saltash said. 'It *is* your aunt, isn't it?'

'Yes,' she said. 'It is.'

'Great pity you haven't been available. I rather thought we might have discussed the difficulties over in Ludlow.'

'I thought we'd drawn a line under that.'

'We should, however, I think, decide where we stand on the issue. In case any of us is... approached.'

'Approached?'

'For assistance. Or advice.'

'I thought you had been. By the police. And the media.'

'Purely as a psychiatrist,' Saltash said.

'Special adviser on mental health to the diocese, as I recall.'

'And, naturally, I cleared it with the Coordinator before making any comment.'

'You mean Siân.'

'It's so important that we're aware of what we're all doing. Effective teamwork, acting in unison, speaking with one voice...' Saltash looked Merrily in the eyes in a way that made it very clear he was looking at her glasses. 'Crucial, wouldn't you say? In such an unstable society.'

32

Media Studies

By the time Merrily heard the school bus rattling onto the square, she'd been home two hours, doing a manic clean-up of the vicarage, not answering the phone. Going over the black-eye rumours situation, deciding how much to tell the kid. Conclusion: everything... almost.

She finishing hoovering the hall, and looked up into the wizened, thorn-tortured face of Jesus Christ in Holman-Hunt's *The Light of the World*, the picture that said, with all its Pre-Raphaelite pedantry, *there are no short cuts.*

Jane first. And then, tonight, there would be Lol: a different approach.

Jane's feeling of responsibility towards Lol sometimes verged, Merrily suspected, on the maternal. It had a long history. It was, unquestionably, Jane who had decided that this relationship needed to happen. Jane who had shielded the sparks from the wind, added twigs to the fire. Jane who, when it was going well, liked to bask in its glow. And, when it wasn't going well, blame her mother.

Merrily touched her eye experimentally. It didn't hurt.

Jane's key turned in the lock.

This would hurt.

'So who was it?' Jane was gazing steadily into her mug of tea as if its surface would ripple and form into a face. 'Who do we have to destroy?'

This was after she'd calmed down. Approaching seven o'clock, and the sun had come out to set and to mellow the kitchen in spite of everything.

'I don't do destruction,' Merrily said. 'I'm a vicar.'

'I'm a pagan. We're less squeamish.'

'Not tonight, huh?' Merrily said.

'It's clear you've got a good idea who in this village is trying to shaft you.'

'Narrowed down the list of suspects, that's all.'

Down to one.

'Names?'

Merrily shook her head. 'Not till I'm sure. I wouldn't like innocent people to die. Eirion picking you up tonight?'

'Eight o'clock. Maybe we'll just go to the Swan.'

'I think not. You're still only seventeen. While I'm not naive enough to think you haven't been going in pubs for the last couple of years, the rule is still *not in this village.*'

'Irene's eighteen.'

'Anyway, the only reason you want to go into the Black Swan is to broadcast exactly what you're going to do when you find out who's been putting it around that Lol hits me.'

'So? Something wrong with that? I mean, *you* won't, will you? Because you're the vicar. You have to take it on the chin.' Jane pushed her tea away. 'And in the eye.'

'Look, when I first heard about it, I reacted just like you. Well, almost. It took Sophie to explain why that could only make things worse.'

'Sophie exists to smooth things over. Sophie's like human cold-cream.'

'Whoever started the rumour wants us to react badly and, in the process, tell everybody who hasn't already heard it. Thus doing their job for them. I think that makes sense.'

'Doing nothing makes sense? Letting people think that Lol's unstable again? You know where they'll take it next, don't you? They'll think back to what happened last Christmas, and, like, where that used to be good – what a hero, saved Alice's life

– they'll be like, yeah, but there was violence involved. OK, he never laid a finger… or did he?'

'Don't let your imagination—'

'Mum, this is a bloody village.'

'Jane, will you just…' Merrily bit down on it. 'What are you planning to do tomorrow?'

'Go round the square, knock on a few doors, hold a kitchen knife to a few people's throats. Dunno, really.'

Merrily thought about this. Contemplated the lesser of two potential evils. It would be unwise to leave Jane alone here, on a Saturday with the village crowded with locals and tourists and the whole day to consume.

'You fancy coming over to Ludlow?'

'Why would I?'

'Meet a mad woman?' Merrily said. 'Make like a pagan?'

She could see the flaring of excitement in Jane's eyes and how subtly it was extinguished.

'Yeah, OK,' Jane said.

Jane decided she didn't want to do the clubs in Hereford tonight. Too expensive, even if Eirion was still living off the loot from his eighteenth birthday, and too loud to talk. And, naturally, she wanted to be home not-too-late and up early, nice and fresh, for the siege of The Weir House.

Belladonna. Oh boy… Couldn't believe Mum was involving her to this extent. This was a major rites-of-passage situation. Not to mention a seminal event in Christian–pagan relations.

Between them, they would really nail this mad bitch to the wall.

So, in the end, she and Eirion ended up doing the old snog-walk through the white lights of Left Bank Village, down to the Wye, which some of the sad planning anoraks at Hereford Council were determined to see as like the Seine, only narrower and with just the one café.

She told Eirion about Operation Belladonna – how she was holding her breath in case Mum changed her mind. After which, it seemed legit to discuss the domestic-violence outrage.

'The trouble is, Mum and Lol, they're both so totally naive.' Jane watched the white lights in the water, like a submerged birthday cake. 'Plus the rock-bottom self-esteem problem. They won't fight.'

'Which means you have to fight on their behalf?' Eirion said. 'I'm sorry, Jane, but we've been through this before, and it doesn't mean that. When you think of all the trouble you've caused in the past by acting first and thinking... well, not thinking at all.'

'Ah, that old Welsh caution... as you cowards like to call it.'

'It's how we survived centuries of English imperialism.'

'Nah.' She searched his broad face, what she could see of it. 'You're too sophisticated to believe that crap.'

'However,' Eirion said, 'from my humble Welsh perspective, I do tend to think that Lol is becoming less easy to damage. You only have to listen to the new music. The very fact that the music is now dealing with some of the bad things that people have done to him... like he's absorbing it in a creative way.'

'However, you're a pretentious git sometimes, Irene.'

'I'm right, though. I think he'll absorb this, too.'

'He's emotionally vulnerable,' Jane said stubbornly.

'Well, so am I.' Eirion going all pathetic. 'And I have to carry the Welsh chip on my shoulder. And do you have sympathy for me?' He slid his stubby Celtic fingers down her waist to the top of her thigh. 'Lighten up, Jane. Your mother's right, you'll only make it worse. That's why she's taking you to Ludlow.'

'Well, I prefer to think she needs an occult consultant with a pagan perspective.'

'And you're fascinated.'

'Not by Belladonna. She was always crap. Now she's crap and passé.'

'She's surely part of your mum's essential history. Doesn't that interest you at all?'

'Goth frocks and fuck-me shoes? I don't think so.'

'I bet your mum looked—'

'Don't go there, Irene.' Jane brandished a menacing finger. 'Just... don't.'

Eirion grinned.

'Besides,' Jane said, 'if I'm generously putting my years of intensive pagan studies at the disposal of the bloody Church of England, even though it doesn't deserve it... Where are we going?'

'Isn't there a nice, quiet bench somewhere along here where we can watch the play of light upon the river?'

'And feel the play of hands inside the bra?'

Eirion moaned softly. Then this shout came from somewhere, like a stone skimming over the water.

'Lewis!'

'Oh no.' Eirion stopped. 'Who's this?'

Two guys were strolling crookedly along the bank from the direction of the bridge.

Jane sighed. This was always a problem. On a Friday night, most of Eirion's sad, rich mates from the Cathedral School seemed to hit Hereford in force. So much for the quiet bench.

They slunk over. One was about Eirion's size, the other taller, kind of droopy and languid-looking, hair flopping over his eyes. They stood there gawping at Jane, total inane tossers clutching long cans of lager.

'Hey, hey,' the tall one said. 'This must be the vicar's daughter.'

'She was only a vicar's daughter...' The other one struck this ridiculous pose, then swayed and stumbled. He steadied himself. 'Der... she was only a vicar's daughter, but she... Shit, I can't think of one, what's the matter with me tonight?'

'You're pissed,' Eirion said. 'Bugger off.'

'I can't be pissed, Lewis, it's not ten o'clock yet.'

'Well, go and get on with it,' Eirion said. 'You've only a couple of hours before it's time to start vomiting in the gutter.'

Neither of them moved.

'So,' the shorter one said, 'you two just sloping off for a shag?'

'Don't let us stop you,' the tall, languid one said. 'We've not had a good laugh all night, have we, Darwin?'

Darwin? Was that his first name? Jane looked at them and mouthed the word at Eirion.

'Well, come on,' Darwin said. 'There's a bush over there. Kit off, girlie, chop, chop.'

A fine rain was in the air, like the mist from an aerosol.

'Oh dear.' Jane looked at the two guys. 'How embarrassing, Eirion. You didn't tell me this was a gay meeting-place...'

'Jane.' Eirion gripped her wrist. 'Don't start.'

'Little bitch,' the tall one said, kind of surprised. He leaned forward, lager slurping out of his can, and one of the floodlights from somewhere splashed on his face, and Jane blinked.

Darwin spread his arms. 'Hang on... hang on... it's coming.'

'That was quick,' Eirion said, 'and I never even saw you slide your hand in your pocket. Come on, Jane, let's...'

'She was only a vicar's daughter,' Darwin said. 'She was only a vicar's daughter, but he pulled out his dick and said... pulpit!'

They were both still laughing, while Eirion was dragging Jane away, along the bank and back up into the crowds and the lights of Left Bank Village, straight through and out into Bridge Street.

'Never,' he said, panting, 'get into a scene like that so close to a river.'

Jane looked behind. Nobody following them. They started to walk up the hill towards King Street which led to the Cathedral. Eirion was saying something; Jane didn't hear over the putter of a kerb-crawling taxi and the sound of her own thoughts. It couldn't be.

It was, though.

'Irene...' Tugging on his hand to stop him.

'What?'

'The taller guy. How come you know him?'

'Because I go to school with him, Jane.'

'He's like... one of the students?'

'Well, he's not the bloody Head, is he?'

'Irene, that's… I mean.' Jane backed into the doorway of a darkened shop. 'Oh God…'

He moved in next to her. 'You all right?'

'What's his actual name?'

'The streak of piss? J.D. Fyneham. He's in my media-studies group.'

'Media studies, huh?' Jane said.

'It's a fairly new thing. There's only a few of us serious about it, the rest are just skiving off.'

'What's he like?'

'Fyneham? Obsessive. Also, reckons he knows it all on account of his dad was a journalist, and he's had tips from all his dad's mates. Refuses to write for the school magazine, because it's so unprofessional.'

'Um… how long's he been writing for *Q* magazine?'

'In his dreams.'

'No, Irene, listen… he's the guy who interviewed Lol.'

Silence.

'What are you saying, Jane…?'

'Irene, I'm not kidding. I saw him with Lol. On the square. Taking his picture. It was definitely him, no question… That… I mean, that's not very likely, is it?'

'J.D. fucking Fyneham?'

'Gave his name as Jack Fine, Lol said.'

Eirion stood on the kerb. The lights here weren't terrific, but his face looked, like, black with rage. Eirion stepped back onto the pavement, turned back towards Bridge Street.

'Right…'

'No!' Jane grabbed his arm. 'Let's… let's think about this…'

As Lol didn't have a table yet, they'd spread the notes out on the kitchen unit, from 'vicerage' to 'your a sick man'.

'Same writing,' Merrily said. 'No question. If it isn't connected, it's a bit of a coincidence.'

She was relieved that, without having left the house all day, Lol seemed to know more about this than she did, thanks to

315

Gomer Parry. You could always count on Gomer – the crucial disc in the spine of the village since Lucy Devenish died. The fact that Gomer had been round, taken the initiative, made her feel a little better.

'Or the writer simply reacts to events,' Lol said. 'An opportunist.'

'Do you have any idea who it might conceivably be?'

Lol shook his head. 'You?'

'Well… yes.'

'You do?'

'Not the notes, but certainly the rumours. It's a bit obvious, but… Siân Callaghan-Clarke knew everything, OK? I can see only one direct route from Ledwardine to Siân, and it goes through Saltash. Therefore it has to go via the surgery. Because, every week, Saltash goes jogging with Kent Asprey.'

'Asprey told him?'

'Breeding ground for germs and gossip, that surgery. Asprey would have been one of the first to know.'

'I don't get it. Does Asprey have anything against either of us?'

'He'd pass it on to Saltash without thinking. A doctor thing.'

'We can take it neither of them wrote these, then,' Lol said.

'Huh? Oh… too legible.'

'Grammar too correct, also.'

They stood there in Lol's kitchen, smiling at one another like fools, making light of it. Yeah, trivial, really, something and nothing.

But even though the power was connected now, the place was full of shadows. It was as if some great cosmic force – to which Merrily refused to put a name – had decided that she and Lol… this unlikely liaison was never going to be allowed to work out.

Unsurprisingly, the confrontation by the river and its aftermath had stripped the night of what passed for romance in Hereford, and Jane got taken home well before midnight.

Eirion – normally well balanced and philosophical to the point where you wanted to shake him – was seriously pissed off. She knew he'd been quietly committed for some time to building a career in the media, and the idea that a guy at school his age already had one… Driving back to Ledwardine, Eirion had conceded that it was just about conceivable that this Fyneham had contributed snippets, maybe even the odd concert review to Q. But an interview? A freaking *interview*?

She hadn't seen him like this before – saying how he was going to crack this wide open, and he wasn't going to wait till Monday, because if this bastard was scamming Lol…

Well, right. Enough shit had happened to Lol, and so J.D. Fyneham was on borrowed time with Jane. too. But she wouldn't get in Eirion's way on this; she'd go to Ludlow tomorrow with Mum, do the dutiful-daughter thing.

It was good to find, when she let herself into the vicarage, that Mum was still at Lol's. She put the kettle on, went up to the apartment, raided her shelves for any books that might mention Ludlow and brought them down to the scullery, where she sat with Ethel and switched on the computer.

J. Watkins, pagan-consultant. She could very much live with that.

However, paganism-wise, apart from the siting of the church, there didn't seem to be much happening in Ludlow itself… although there were more suggestions that the wider area had been significant in the Bronze Age. Over twenty prehistoric burial mounds had been found at Bromfield, a mile or two north of the town – the Bromfield Necropolis. Cool term.

She checked out the church tumulus again, downloading more detail.

The Irish saints whose remains were found inside the mound were identified as Cochel, Fercher and Ona, who had come to live in the area. However, holy relics were much prized in those days…

Et cetera, et cetera…

Mum had come in, was leaning over her shoulder.

'It's OK, I'm quite willing to accept they were more likely to have been the remains of three guys with big beards and horns on their helmets.'

Jane looked up. 'You sound happier.'

'We rationalized the situation.'

'Lol's OK with it?'

'Yeah, Lol's... more OK than I expected.'

Jane smiled and nodded. Best not to tell Mum about J.D. Fyneham until it was confirmed one way or the other. She pointed at the screen, which showed an aerial photo of Ludlow with the church and the castle vying for prominence and the church probably winning, even though the castle had much more ground and the church was crowded by streets on three sides.

'I think we should maybe check out the church, before we see her,' Jane said. 'OK?'

'But before that we should pop into our own church.'

Jane looked over her shoulder. 'Why?'

'I'm not making a big thing of this. I'd just like us to do St Pat's breastplate and the Lord's Prayer... if that's OK?'

'You think we need spiritual protection?'

'There's nothing lost.'

'OK.' Jane shrugged. 'I've never been a chauvinistic pagan. But, like, you really think this achingly sad, faded, 1980s icon is a source of satanic evil?'

'I'll be honest – I don't know. We don't know what she's collected over the years.'

'No gold discs, that's for sure,' Jane said. 'Sorry. Sorry.'

She thought of the last time they'd done something like this, before the Boy Bishop ceremony in Hereford Cathedral, back when Mick Hunter was Bishop and Mum was a novice exorcist. It had followed one of the biggest rows they'd ever had, and it seemed like half a lifetime ago, and it was good to think how much more adult they both were about this kind of thing now.

'Look,' Mum said, 'it's not that I feel particularly insecure about assuming a role which admittedly is in... explicit denial of my Christianity... if that's what you're thinking.'

'Didn't say a thing.'

'OK...' Mum put a hand to her forehead. 'I'm probably lying. Of course I feel insecure. And I really don't know if it's a good thing to have you along or not.'

'I can watch your back,' Jane said. 'You know me.'

Mum rolled her eyes and winced at the pain this evidently caused. The swelling had gone down now, but it was still conspicuously a black eye.

The phone rang. They both stared at it.

'Might be Lol?' Jane said.

They carried on staring at it, because this was late for any kind of call, until the machine cut in. Then there was a man's voice Jane didn't recognize, a Northern kind of voice.

'Mary... if you're still up... Shit... I got a problem here. With Bell. I didn't know who to—'

Mum picked up.

'Jon?'

Jane could hear a sound of apparent relief, then a lot of gabbled talk, Mum listening, the computer screen turning her face mauve.

'What about the police?' Mum said. And then she said, 'Isn't there a cottage hospital?' And then, after about half a minute, she said, 'All right, I'll come over,' and put the phone down and stood there for a moment with her lips set into a tight line.

'What?' Jane said.

Mum let out a breath. 'Jon Scole, the ghost-walk guy. She turned up on his doorstep, about half an hour ago. He's got a flat over his shop, and there's an alleyway and some steps, and she was on her hands and knees...'

'Belladonna?'

'She was doing her... walk, and they were waiting for her, where The Linney goes down towards St Leonards and the river. Dark, narrow, secluded...'

'Who were?'

'Seems to have been girls – women. They were waiting for her, and they started hurling abuse. And then they… they just beat her up.'

'The women did?'

'And she won't have the police brought in, and her step-daughter's away for the weekend, and Jon Scole doesn't know what to do.'

'We're going over there?'

'Looks like I'm going,' Mum said.

'What about me?'

'You get some sleep. I'll be back as soon as I can. And we'll still go back tomorrow.'

'It *is* tomorrow,' Jane said.

And sensed that everything was about to go seriously wrong.

When the phone went again, not five minutes after Mum had left, Jane didn't even have the heart to do the spoof-answering-machine bit.

'Ledwardine Vicarage.'

'Is that Mrs Watkins?'

'She's… not available. This is Jane Watkins.'

'It's Gail Mumford here. Andy Mumford's wife.'

'Oh, yeah, I know.'

'She isn't with my husband again, is she?'

Jane smiled. It was like Mum and Mumford were having some kind of torrid affair.

'I can honestly say she isn't.'

'You haven't heard from him, have you?'

'I…' Jane had picked up some serious strain in this woman's voice. 'No, I'm pretty sure we haven't. He's out somewhere?'

'He's been out all day, I think. I don't know what's the matter with him. When he was with the police, at least you— Look, I don't know how old you are—'

'Old enough,' Jane said. 'Look, Mum's had to go over to Ludlow. I don't think she's expecting to see Andy there, but I'll give her a call, and if…'

Jane noticed Mum's mobile, left behind on the sermon pad. Bugger.

'… If I get to speak to her, and she knows anything, I'll get back to you. Will you be up for a bit?'

'Of course I'll be up.'

'OK. And, of course, if we hear from Andy meanwhile—'

'If you hear from him, you tell him he might not have a wife here when he gets back,' Mrs Mumford said.

33

Lift Shaft into Heaven

MERRILY LEFT THE Volvo outside the health-food shop at the bottom of the row, just up Corve Street from St Leonard's chapel, and walked up to Lodelowe, its small window misted crimson from a lamp burning in the recesses. It made her think of shrines.

The alleyway next to the shop door was unlit and made her think of the Plascarreg Estate, and that made her want not to enter the alley.

The night was mild, almost warm. She peered into the shop window, over the painted plaster models of timber-framed houses, a stack of tourist pamphlets: *Haunted Ludlow*. No movement in there, and – she backed off and looked up towards the centre of town – no movement on the street, either, apart from shifting shadows and the glimmer of street lamps and the waning moon in old windows and the traffic lights near the crest of the hill. Always an eeriness about traffic lights in the dead of night, when there was minimal traffic, as though the lights must be a warning of something else that had always travelled these streets, silent and invisible.

She stumbled over the kerb as a ribbon of female laughter unravelled from somewhere not too close. She thought of women and girls binge-drinking in packs, beating people up. Was this a twenty-first-century phenomenon, or was it happening just the same when this town was young, in the days of

Merrie England, when street violence was part of the merrie system? And therefore the apparent growth of civilization was all illusion – God seeing right through it, looking down with weary cynicism, the oil running low in his lamp of eternal love.

Night thoughts. Merrily stepped back as a light was put on, and all the bricks in the alley came to life.

'Mary?'

'I'm here.'

She stepped into the alley. Jon Scole was standing at the bottom of some steps, under an iron-framed coach lamp, his leather waistcoat undone over a black T-shirt, a bunch of keys hanging from his belt, like a jailer's keys.

'Hey, listen, I'm sorry, Mary, I did try to ring you back.'

'Damn.' Patting the pockets of her fleece. 'Came out without the phone.'

'Anyway,' he said, 'she's gone now.'

'Where?'

'You better come in.' He stepped back for her to go up the stairs, which were concrete, a kind of fire escape.

'Is she hurt?'

'Not much, I don't think. Sick, though.'

'Sick?'

'Go on up.'

Climbing the steep steps, Merrily realized how tired she was. A long day, or was that yesterday?

The door at the top was ajar. It was an old door, patched and stained, the light inside mauve-tinted. She went through, directly into the room over the shop, a room that shouted temporary. Strip lights were hanging crookedly from a bumpy ceiling shouldered by old beams smeared with new plaster. The furniture was second-hand rather than old – the kind of stuff Lackland Modern Furnishings might have sold twenty-five years ago. There was a wide-screen TV and a stereo with silver speaker cabinets, and a flat-screen computer that looked expensive.

The room smelled of curry.

'Bit of a mess,' Jon Scole said. 'Haven't had time to tart it up yet. Can I get you a drink? Red wine? White wine?'

'Jon, it's after midnight, I'm a bit knackered.'

'Sorry.' His flaxen hair was slicked back, and his beard looked damp, as though he'd held his face under a tap to sober himself up. 'I'm not thinking. She does your head in. Look, at least sit down. Cup of coffee, yeah?'

'No, really…' She lowered herself to the edge of a red, uphol-stered chair with wooden arms. 'Just tell me what happened.'

'It's like I said, she comes banging at the shop door. I'd not been in long, been down the pub with some tourists after the ghost-walk. She's like, "They're after me." '

'Who were they?'

'Just girls… women. See, she's safe, more or less, if she stays up the posh end of town. Anywhere else, pushing her luck. She's not popular in some quarters. It's like, rich slag doesn't give a shit for the poor young people she's forcing out.'

'Meaning what?'

'Meaning the land over there, below the castle, that this guy was gonna build on and she bought off him?'

'I thought people were delighted about that.'

'*Some* people were delighted – the neighbours who've got all the old houses near hers, the ones as were faced with losing their view and getting kids on bikes, and lawnmowers and radios and idiots cleaning the fuckin' car on a Sunday morning – they were delighted, the Ludlow bourgeoisie. But, you see, there's a ruling now from the council that if you're building new housing you've got to include a percentage of affordable homes.'

'I get it.'

''Course, this guy Dickins, the feller planning to build down here, he'd agreed to double the low-cost quota. He'd've wormed out of it if he'd got planning permission, but he gets the benefit of the doubt, unlike the bitch who's denied young people their only chance of having an affordable house in a decent part of town. So that's why they went after her, I reckon. Get tanked up and then it's like, Let's wait for the rich bitch. Rage and booze, Mary.'

Jon Scole went and stood by the window. It overlooked Corve Street, a red-brick Georgian dwelling opposite, under a street lamp: the unattainable, unless you'd sold your house in London.

'What did they do to her, Jon?'

'Mucked her up a bit. Mauled her about. She wouldn't go into details.'

'It's a police matter.'

'She don't want the publicity. If I rang the cops, she'd never speak to me again. Anyway— Bloody hell' – he squatted at her feet and looked up into her bruised eye – 'what happened to you?'

'I have a dangerous job,' Merrily said. 'Where's she gone?'

'So that's why you were wearing them sexy shades.'

'How long was she here?'

'Went in the bathroom to clean herself up, and that was when I phoned you. I see you're not wearing a wedding ring.'

'You told her I was coming?'

'She wasn't gonna wait. Just hung on till it had gone quiet and then she was off. About quarter of an hour ago. You got a boyfriend, Mary?'

Merrily didn't move; if she leaned away from him she'd be trapped in the armchair, if she edged forward she'd be touching his knees. He was evidently still a little drunk. It would, on the whole, have made more sense not to come up here.

'What was she wearing?'

'Aye, well…' Jon Scole stood up. 'That couldn't've helped.' The keys clunked at his belt; he seemed to like wearing things that made metallic noises.

Merrily took the opportunity to stand up, too, stepping nearer the door.

'She's got… kind of a nightdress on,' he said. 'Satin. It laces up at the sides. It looked… strange.'

'She was walking through the streets like that?'

'I offered to drive her home. She wouldn't let me. Just as well, I expect I'm a touch over the limit.'

'You could've walked back with her.'

'Mary, nobody's allowed to do that. When she walks at night, she walks alone.'

'Don't you think you should ring the police now?'

'She'd know who it was. I keep telling you, Mary, I don't want to blow it with her. She's like...' He waggled his hands. 'Look, if you wanna make sure she's OK, I know which way she goes.'

'What sort of state was she in?'

'How do you mean?'

'Shocked? Distressed?'

'I don't know...' He went to the window, looked down into the street. 'Angry... electric.'

'In what way?' Merrily moved nearer the door.

'It's like something charges her up. I went to watch her, once. I waited for her in the churchyard, behind a tree – just to watch what she did, you know? I'd waited for bloody ages by the time she showed. I mean showed – faded up, not a sound. Weird. She was like she was in a trance – like her mind was somewhere else, but her body was... wooar... trembling. Vibrating, you know? Like it was aglow. I'm probably exaggerating this a bit, she was just a woman walking in the dark. Anybody like that in these streets is bound to look a bit spooky.'

'You approach her?'

'Break the spell? She'd have had me eyes out. I let her go past, and I went home.'

'What did you think was happening?'

'She was getting off on it.'

'On what?'

'I don't know.' Scole seemed almost angry that he didn't know. 'When she comes banging on the door tonight, she's all over me. Hot and... you know. Burning up. It's why I called you. Anybody could see she were burnin' up...'

Merrily waited by the door. There was a dark green waste bin next to it, with chip paper in it, a curry carton, squashed lager cans.

'I din't trust meself, all right?' He looked down at his trainers. 'Didn't wanna blow it.' He looked up, across at Merrily, punched his palm. 'I cannot believe you're a priest. What's a woman like you doin' bein' a fuckin' priest?'

'Which way did she go, Jon?'

'Dunno. Back towards St Leonard's? Makes no difference, she'll pass through St Laurence's churchyard. Whichever way she goes, it always takes in the churchyard. I'll show you, eh?'

'No, I think it's best if I go on my own, thanks. We don't want her to feel threatened. Not after what happened.'

'You think that's safe, Mary, on your own?'

'It's Ludlow, Jon, not Glasgow.'

'I wouldn't touch you,' Jon Scole said, plaintive.

'I know. I just… maybe I should talk to her on my own. Maybe it's the best chance I'll get.'

'As a psychic?' He laughed.

'Something like that.' She pushed down the door handle and the door sprang against her hand, and she was grateful he hadn't locked them in. 'And, yes,' she said, 'for future reference, I have got a boyfriend.'

'Well, he's a lucky twat,' Jon Scole said bitterly, not moving from the window. 'Hey…'

'What?'

'You wanna watch yourself, Mary. She likes women, too.'

'But not priests, apparently,' Merrily said. 'If it gets difficult, I can always flash the cross.'

There were still a few people around as Merrily walked quickly up through the centre of the town towards the Buttercross: the inevitable sad drunk, the inevitable couple-in-a-shop-doorway and, more curiously, two women with one small boy trotting ahead of them, a good six hours after his bedtime. All the untold stories of night streets.

At the Buttercross, she slipped like a cat into the tightness of Church Street, narrow as a garden path, with its pub and its bijou shops and galleries, most windows dark now. Behind this street – seamed by alleyways, made intimate by moonlight and scary by shadows – was the church of St Laurence with its great tower, the axle through the wheel of the town.

She stood at the main entrance, looking directly up at the Beacon of the Marches, taller by far than the castle keep. The tower, with its lantern windows, seemed to be racing away from her, a lift shaft into heaven, and she thought about the Palmers' Guild, convinced it was pressing the right buttons. Medieval Christianity: two steps up from magic.

The night was soft and close here, the air still sweet with woodsmoke from dying fires in deserted hearths, and the sky was olive green, lightly stroked with orange in the north.

She stood listening for a couple of minutes, almost convinced that if there was anything abusive or violent occurring anywhere in Ludlow she'd be able to hear it, because this was the nerve centre. Never had a cluster of buildings felt more like some kind of living organism, and she wondered if Belladonna, of whom there was no sign at all, was standing somewhere, just like this, letting it heal her.

Or perhaps she'd simply run all the way home.

Merrily walked past the body of the church into what she thought was College Street, old walls closing in – was this the college where the chaplains appointed by the Palmers' Guild had lived? Turning a dark corner, now, and emerging into what could only be The Linney, the narrow lane that followed the castle wall to the river, the backstairs from the country to the heart of the town.

She walked quietly down the centre of the lane, which would be just about wide enough for one car if you were daring enough to risk it. Terraces and stone cottages were wedged either side, most of them unlit, backing onto the darkness of the castle's curtain wall to the left and the edge of the hill to the right, a gap between houses revealing the countryside below salted with tiny lights.

Feeling as if she was balancing on Ludlow's curving spine,

she stopped and listened again. No movement, and no obvious place of concealment in the narrows of The Linney. There was a sign announcing a new restaurant, and someone had stuck a white paper flyer on it that read, *The Lord will tear down the temples of gluttony!*

After the last house, a path to the left... surely the path that burrowed among the castle foundations, the path she'd taken with Jon Scole to the yew tree where Marion fell, where Jemima Pegler fell with the heroin raging through her veins.

Here, the ground softened underfoot and the texture of the night seemed to have altered, the shapes of trees morphing into matt shadows and the woodsmoke aroma becoming the raw stench of damp earth.

And the castle was a hard form, a stronghold again, the land falling invisibly away to the right of the track, through the trees and into darkening fenced fields, sports clubs, and the river and the woodland around The Weir House.

And Merrily knew, then, that it was too quiet.

There should be wildlife-rustlings, foxes prowling, badgers scrabbling, night birds, and... and there wasn't anything.

She stopped.

Sometimes on still evenings, before a church clock chimed somewhere, you would be aware of a pause in the atmosphere itself – a soft, hollowed-out moment, all movement suspended. And then a vibration, like a shiver, as if the air knew what was coming. When you spent days and nights hanging around churches, it became a familiar phenomenon. It seemed like part of the mechanism, and maybe it was – some ancient acoustic collusion between night and clocks.

Usually it was clocks. In a town like Ludlow, on a night like this, it ought to have been clocks.

She reached up and felt for the ridge of the tiny cross under the fleece and the T-shirt, pressing it into the cleft between her breasts, and heard a voice, hollow with pain.

Might have been just an owl inside the castle grounds. Or, a moment later, two distinct species of owl in sequence: the breathless fluting of the woodland tawny overtaken by an ethereal screech – barn owl. That was all, that was—

As she was plunging into pockets for the cigarettes and the Zippo, it started up again, bloating into something swollen and visceral that wasn't like any kind of owl but definitely like a woman.

Then a harsh, white shriek.

'TAKE ME!'

The castle wall was caught by a blade of moonlight.

'TURN ME!'

Merrily stood looking up, frozen. The jagged windows of the Hanging Tower were holes in mouldy cheese,

'TAKE ME, TURN ME... TEACH ME...

'PLOUGH ME, PLY ME, PLEACH ME!'

The words seemed to be crawling up the wall.

'TAKE ME, RAKE ME...'

She knew it, of course. It was from *Nightshades*. It was twenty years old.

When it stopped, the air was alive again, as if the night was frayed and abraded.

And from below the Hanging Tower, the same voice, only different. Soft and breathy, ethereal.

Wee Willie Winkie running through the town
Upstairs, downstairs, in his nightgown
Rapping on the—

A stifled sob. In the distance, Merrily heard a car horn, the furry rumble of an aeroplane. And then there was coughing and the voice came back, husky and earthen and bitter.

'*You lie like carrion...*'

And then rising, fainter and frailer but spiralling up again like pale light.

'... *I'll fly like Marion.*'

Mumford

THE DOOR WAS on a chain, a strip of light sliding out over the concrete landing and her teeth bared at him in the gap.

'Never get the message, do you? You're not wanted yere, you was never wanted. Got nothin' to say to each other. Not at half-past one in the morning, not any time.'

Half-one? Was it really? How time flew when you were plugged in again.

Aye, he'd accept it was a bit late to be calling on even your closest living relative. But he'd seen the lights on, guessing they stayed up half the night and then went to bed till the afternoon: the half-life of the worthless.

'Just wanner talk a while, Angela,' Mumford said calmly. 'En't gonner keep you more'n half an hour. Just some things I need to get sorted out.'

'Well, you can fuck off,' Ange said through those guard-dog teeth, 'and you leave us alone from now on. I don't wanner see your fat face ever again, yeah? Clear enough?'

Mumford nodded. Fair play, he'd started out politely enough, telling her he thought he should inform her it was Mam's funeral on Tuesday and listening, without comment, to the expected response – not even bothering to wipe what had accompanied it from his face. Being imperturbable.

He could smell the spliff from here, knowing that the reason Ange instead of Mathiesson had come to the door was that Mathiesson would be busy flushing it all down the toilet in case Mumford wasn't on his own. Probably a few ounces of blow wasn't the half of it, but when the boys raided the estate they'd likely let this particular flat alone, thinking mabbe this family had suffered enough and Mathiesson was only small-time, anyway. Bliss could be thoughtful, on occasion.

'Well,' Mumford said, like his feelings were hurt, 'if that's how you feel, en't much more I can say.'

Backing off as he spoke, his eyes on the tension in the chain, and when he saw it go slack as she was about to slam the door in his face, he turned his shoulder and met it with the full force of his fifteen and a half stone.

Ange's screech was simultaneous with the splintering of wood as the chain came away, pulling out a wad of cheap Plascarreg door frame, the door flying back and Mumford going in there fast, grabbing her as she spun away, desperate to stop her falling because she was, after all, pregnant.

Holding her arms tight to her side, he manoeuvred her backwards into the living room. She wouldn't give him the satisfaction of making her scream again, but he held on because, if he slackened his grip, she'd have one of his fingers between her teeth before he knew it.

She was her father's daughter, was Angela.

Mumford gave her the heavy-lidded, level stare.

''Fore you says a word, I'll pay for it, all right? I'll leave a hundred on the table when I go. And you can tell that scum he can stop flushing, 'cause I en't remotely interested in what he puts up his nose tonight.'

Ange breathing through her teeth, eyes black with what Mumford took as hate. He went on staring into them, imperturbable.

'All right?' He saw her mouth working on the saliva, and he gave her a little shake. 'No. Now you listen to me... no, listen!'

'Your level now, Mumford, eh?' Mathiesson standing in a doorway, stripped to the waist. 'Pregnant woman?'

'You wanner dispense with the heroics, boy, seeing as we're in your place and it's all your stuff that gets broken?'

Looking at the stuff in here, this was no bad deal he was offering. Sony TV size of a double wardrobe, screening some slasher-horror DVD with the sound down. Had to be ten grand's worth of hardware. A subtle hint here that Ange and Mathiesson were existing on a bit more than the sickness benefit from Mathiesson's famous bad back.

Mumford thought about Robbie Walsh's broken neck and his snapped spine, and a surge of the old volcano went through him, and he caught himself hoping that Mathiesson would try and take him. But Mathiesson didn't move and Mumford turned back to Ange.

'Now,' he said, 'either I holds on to you the whole while, or we all sits down nice and quiet and you answer my questions, in full. On the basis I en't a copper no more and nobody gets nicked, or—'

'We got nothin' to say to each other no more,' Ange said. 'Not that we ever had much.'

'—Or I go down the station at Hereford and have a chat with a few of my old colleagues. Who'll mabbe see to it that you're a single parent, for a while, this time around.'

Ange looked at Mathiesson, and Mumford kept on looking at Ange. She was wearing a red towelling robe, the wide sleeves falling over his hands where they gripped her arms.

'You're hurting me,' Ange admitted.

'Your decision.'

'He's on his own,' Mathiesson said. 'No witnesses.'

Mumford let Ange go and moved away quickly and went to stand next to the Sony. Ange sat down on the big cream sofa, rubbing her arms, then pulling her dressing gown tight across her chest, not looking at him. Mumford turned to Mathiesson.

'You ever work – if that's the word – at the old Aconbury Engineering factory, Lenny? Edge of the Barnchurch?'

'Never heard of it,' Mathiesson said.

'I see. So that's gonner be the level of our conversation, is it?'

'It's closed down.'

'Well, aye, been closed down eighteen months, far as engineering goes. Far as preparation and distribution of crack goes, it was turning a tidy profit until... oh, the day before yesterday?'

'If I was involved, I'd've been arrested, wouldn't I?'

'Well, mabbe it's not over yet, that part,' Mumford said, and Mathiesson's jaw twitched.

Ange snatched the remote from the arm of the sofa and snapped off the TV.

'Thank you,' Mumford said. 'Now I'm gonner come clean, Angela. I'm gonner be dead straight with you. Wasn't the ole lady responsible for what happened to Robbie.'

'Look,' Ange said, 'I was upset that night. What you expect? I was lashing out.'

''Course you were. And you were in shock. But you were lashing out at the wrong person. Only one member of this family's responsible for the boy's death, and it wasn't an ole lady with rising senile dementia.'

'I'm pregnant!' Ange yelled. 'I get tired. I didn't have no time—'

'I mean me, Angela,' Mumford said. 'I was responsible. Me.'

For the first time, Ange shut her mouth.

'I could give you a lot of bloody excuses about pressure of work, but the fact is there wasn't much pressure at work that last week. No point in giving a man cases he en't gonner be able to see through to a result. Truth was, I just didn't wanner hang round with my family, 'cause that looked too much like the future. First time, I didn't pick Robbie up, start of his holidays, and take him over to his gran's. Know why? 'Cause I couldn't face the ole man leering at me – one of us, now, boy, a pensioner. That's why.'

'Ole man never had no tact,' Ange said. 'Anyway, we put Robbie on the train. Lenny took him down the station.'

'Normal way of it, see, Robbie and me, we'd have a chat on the way there. Hard goin' sometimes, mind.'

'Hard goin' for anybody,' Ange said, low-voiced, eyes downcast. 'Unless you was a professor of history.'

'Truth of it was,' Mumford said, 'Mam told me at least three time how the boy couldn't wait to see me. I didn't understand. I thought she was finding me a bit of retirement work. Child-minding.'

Clenched his fists, hearing his mam on the phone.

Robbie, he wants to show you all his favourite places in the town, don't you, Robbie? He's nodding, see. He's always saying, when's Uncle Andy coming?

'I never went. I was angry. Insulted. Scared, too. Scared of the future.'

'Couldn't throw your weight about no more, eh?' Mathiesson said. 'Couldn't kick the shit out of nobody when you was feelin' a bit frustrated. You poor ole fuck.'

'Shut up, Lenny,' Ange said quietly.

'Now I know exactly what he wanted to talk to me about,' Mumford said. 'Question is, did you?'

Ange said nothing.

'I been for a chat with some people tonight, see. Former neighbours of yours. The Collinses.'

'Collinses are as good as dead,' Mathiesson said.

'Not the wisest response, Lenny, you don't mind me saying so.'

'Thought you said this was off the record.'

'It is. But see, there was someone else knew what was happening at the old Aconbury Engineering factory. I'm saying factory – not much more than a workshop, really, a starter-factory. Nice secluded site, though, since they stopped building any more due to nobody wanting to run a business so close to the Plascarreg. Nice quiet site, next to a little pine wood.'

'I don't know what you're on about.'

'Or mabbe there was a funny feeling about the place,' Mumford said. 'Being as it used to be the site of the civic gallows. Or, at least, that's what some folks reckon.'

'You lost me way back.' Mathiesson came into the room, draped himself over the back of the sofa, started playing with Ange's hair.

She shook him off. 'This is Robbie, en't it?'

'What'd he tell you?' Mumford said.

'I never took much notice.' Ange sat up, holding her dressing gown across her throat. She looked cold, though it must've been ninety degrees in the room. 'He... got on your nerves, sometimes, poor little sod. Yeah, I do remember he was real excited – few weeks ago... months maybe, I dunno. Said did I know they used to hang people round the back of the flats. Said he'd worked out where it was.'

'There's still a mound, apparently, on the edge of the pines. It was covered over by trees until they started extending the Barnchurch. That's the most likely site.'

'I didn't take much notice. He was always going on about something – usually it was something in bloody Ludlow, so I never even took it in. I probably only remembered this because it was yere.'

'Told his mate Niall Collins all about it. Niall said, you don't wanner go messing round there, they en't gonner like it. Doubt if Robbie even took it in, what the boy was trying to tell him. All these years he'd hated the Plascarreg because – not just because it was tacky and run-down, I don't reckon he even noticed any of that – but because everything was so new. Now at last here's some real history on his doorstep. Wasn't nothing gonner keep him away.'

'I don't even know where he got that idea from,' Ange said.

'The gallows? Local history venture, Angela. Somebody got a Lottery grant to run a local history project in the South Wye area of town. You probably didn't notice.'

'Yeah, we... something came through the door. Robbie took it.'

'This?' Mumford reached into the inside pocket of his jacket, brought out a printed pamphlet: *South Wye History Project*. 'It was with his stuff. Project starts end of May. They were asking for volunteers to help produce a booklet on the history of the area. According to Niall, Robbie seems to have met one of the archaeologists in charge, who made him copies of old documents, and Robbie started doing his own research. Either he found the old execution site or he didn't, but poking around that workshop with a spade night after night, threatening to bring the whole team down for a dig...'

Ange shut her eyes, began softly pummelling her knees, going, 'Shhhhit, shhhit...' very quietly.

'I don't suppose they'd understand what the boy was after,' Mumford said. 'Mabbe somebody else had a quiet word with him – told him seriously to keep away. Somebody like Jason Mebus. He afraid of people like Jason, Angela?'

'You'd think he would be, wouldn't you?' Ange looked up. What he'd taken for hate just looked like tired black circles around her eyes. 'Truth was, I don't reckon he even noticed them. He just went his own way. Read his books, messed about on his computer and went off on his own.'

'Seems to me,' Mumford said, 'that Robbie's enthusiasm for history and the past and that stuff would prove stronger than any quiet warning to stay away.'

'So bloody innocent, he wouldn't even have known what they was on about.' Ange started to cry. 'I never had time...'

'You know what they done, finally, to make him understand?'

Ange shaking her head, hands over her face. Mumford stopped and turned away. Saw someone walking past the window, not four feet away from where he was standing. No getting away from anybody here. This was what Niall's dad, Mark Collins, had told him; it was like being in a cell block, but without any prison officers to protect you.

As soon as he'd left that house, Mumford had realized that he'd finally blown it. By now, Collins would already have talked to Bliss or somebody less sympathetic about the lone cop who'd come to question young Niall at their temporary home in Malvern.

They'd never asked to see Mumford's ID. Nobody ever had, even when he'd carried a warrant card. Wasted exercise; Bliss had once said Mumford looked like a copper the way a sheep looked like a sheep.

Just hoped he hadn't dropped Karen in it.

'What I think,' he said to his sister, 'is Robbie tried to make them understand how important it was, this discovery he'd made – actual site of a Middle Ages gallows. Showed them a picture of it in this book he had. Somehow, the relevant page got ripped out. Niall remembers Jason Mebus had that page.'

'What page?' Ange looked at him through splayed fingers. 'I don't—'

'Picture of a gallows on it,' Mumford said. 'Or a gibbet. Picture of a feller being hanged. And a detailed picture of a working model.'

And he decided there and then that he wasn't gonner say any more about this aspect of it. Poor bloody Ange. She'd been a crap mother, but it was clear enough now that she hadn't known any of this. Whether Mathiesson had and had chosen to keep quiet about it was something to be considered later. For now… well, there'd be enough shadows over Ange for the rest of her life without the details Mumford had finally got out of Niall Collins – the kid refusing to talk about it until Mumford had applied the kind of emotional pressure that had brought Mark Collins and his wife rushing in and would undoubtedly be relayed to Bliss and probably Annie Howe.

Which was why Mumford couldn't go home until this was finished.

'What I wanted to ask you,' he said, 'was how well known was it that Robbie went to Ludlow during his holidays?'

Ange looked up at Mathiesson, his tattoos gleaming with sweat.

'Don't look at me – I never told nobody. Why would I?'

'It en't far to go, is it?' Mumford said. 'My original thought, see, was they was just bullying him 'cause he was a bit of a swot, didn't fit in. And mabbe they made his life such a bloody misery

340

that he couldn't bear to come back yere and so, last day of his holidays—'

'Stop it!' Ange started rocking from side to side, holding herself and Robbie's unborn sibling. Mathiesson straightening up in shock, suddenly getting the point.

'They wouldn't! Shit, they wouldn't kill him, Mumford, just keep him quiet… wouldn't top him just to keep him out their hair…'

'Mabbe it was an accident, Lenny. Mabbe they just wanted to put the fear of God into him. But, then again, I always said it was only a matter of time with Jason Mebus.'

'The Collins boy told you this?'

'It don't matter where I got it from. But what you got with the likes of Mebus, see – and wossisname, Chain-boy, Connor – is kids who's up here with the excitement of it. Wanner prove themselves as hard men. You been through that phase, surely, Lenny…'

Mathiesson said nothing.

Ange said, 'If you think Lenny had anything to do with it, you're wrong.'

'And I'd like to think I was,' Mumford said, 'for your sake if nothing else.'

'He had every reason to keep Robbie alive.'

'Ange…' Mathiesson gripped her shoulders. 'There's no need. He en't a copper no more. You don't have to—'

'Sit down, Andy,' Ange said, real quiet.

34

Old Stock

WHEN THE SINGING stopped, Merrily was aware that the warm night and the foliage had come alive, but not with foxes or badgers or bats or rats.

Unease made her stop on the edge of the path, looking all around her. Over her shoulder the top of the church tower was visible, its weathercock spiking a cluster of mushroom-coloured night clouds. And somewhere, although the singing had stopped, she could hear voices, rushing through the under-growth like blown leaves. When a giggle crept up behind her, she spun round. Shadows were moving among the bushes, skid-ding feet.

A girl's voice squeaked, 'No, Nez, don't!'

What sounded like a beer can bounced off the castle wall, and somebody shouted after it, 'Mad ole slapper!' and Merrily became aware of a bunch of them at the side of the track, about ten yards away. She felt a glow of very basic fear. But it couldn't be the women who had attacked Bell; these were just kids.

Just kids.

We had some awesome laughs with Robbie.

'What do you want?' Her voice coming out cracked and coarsened by twenty years of smoke. She started to cough, muf-fled it with an arm.

A kid said, 'Whossat?'

'Police,' Merrily said, with determination. 'This path is closed. Now push off, the lot of you, or you'll be banged up for the night.'

'Aw, get lost, you're not the police.'

'Then you'll be able to pretend in the morning that you're not having your breakfast in a cell.' Remembering the mini-Maglite torch she'd stuffed into a pocket of her jeans before leaving the car, she started fumbling under her fleece. 'Now, do you want to go in the van or—'

The little torch was bugger-all use for hitting anybody, but it was very bright. She flashed it at head height, found a girl in a shocking-pink top who looked about thirteen, and the girl squealed and backed off, stumbling.

A boy said, 'You're never protecting that mad ole slapper, are you?'

Then, 'Oh, no!' the girl was wailing. 'My heel's gone! Nez, you bloody wuss, I told you I didn't want to come down here.'

'I'll carry you...'

'Oh, get—'

'What's going on?'

Outrage and a yellow light, probably from one of the cottages in The Linney.

'Shit,' one of them whispered. 'It's my grandad. Sorry, OK? We're off now. We just wanted to see if it was true, all right? We'll leave you to it. Goodnight.'

'Erm... yeah... Goodnight.' Merrily smiled.

She switched off the flashlight, waited until it was quiet again and the light in The Linney had gone out. *We just wanted to see if it was true.* How often did this happen?

She put the torch on again, twisted the neck until there was just a thin beam, directing it at the ground, following it along the track until it found the fat bole of Marion's yew tree. And Bell Pepper sitting under it, in silence now, with something across her knees, her elbows resting on it and her face between her hands, a small light at her feet.

'I don't want protection,' she said.

'You've been getting it, anyway.' Merrily switched off the torch. 'For a long time.'

'Oh.' Bell Pepper turned her head. 'I thought I… it's Mary, isn't it?'

'I'm sorry, I followed you. Didn't like to think of you going back out there after what happened.'

'It was very stupid of Jonathan to phone you.'

'He was worried, too. Can we talk?'

Merrily sat down next to her, between the roots. The space under the yew's dense canopy was lit like an earthen grotto by the candle in the lantern, and she could make out Belladonna's once-famous patrician profile, recalling an album cover where her face had been sprayed with creamy white plaster, eyes calmly closed, like a death mask.

'Children,' Bell said. 'I expect I was some kind of goddess to their parents. Now I'm a mad old slapper.' She gazed out between the trees towards the invisible river. 'When they're spraying your name three feet high on walls, you never imagine that one day you'll be…'

Normal, Merrily thought. *Ordinary*. It was odd – she'd always thought that Lol was the exception in his line of work because he seemed, in spite of everything, so normal. Odd how you could be taken in by the intentional mythologizing of rock musicians.

'Maybe in ten years' time those kids'll think you're a goddess, too,' she said. 'Tastes change rapidly in music. And then they bounce back again.'

'How would you know?'

'I was a fan. I came to one of your gigs once. And my boy-friend's in the business.'

'Business?'

'Music. He plays. Writes songs.'

'You poor cow. Would I have heard of him?'

'I don't know. Lol Robinson? OK if I smoke? Tobacco, that is. I'm feeling a bit…'

'Go ahead. Christ, I remember Lol Robinson. Hazey Jane?

They put him away, didn't they?'

'Psychiatric hospital.' Merrily found the Zippo and the Silk Cut packet, crushed, in her fleece. 'He fell into the system.'

'OK now?'

'He always was.' Merrily held out the cigs to Bell. 'You do nicotine these days?'

'Only vice I've ever given up, Mary.'

Merrily lit up, inhaled and let out the smoke on the back of a sigh. It was not comfortable, sitting in the dirt at the foot of the yew.

'But not, I assure you,' Belladonna said, 'because I didn't want to die. That would be...'

'Positively hypocritical, in your case.'

Bell laughed. 'Am I right in thinking you and Jonathan are...?'

'God, no.'

'That was emphatic.'

'I told you, I have a boyfriend.'

'How quaint. Is he as quaint when he's on tour?'

'He's so quaint that old ladies want to buy him.'

'I see.'

'You?' Merrily lowered the cigarette; the smoke was making her bad eye smart.

'Me, what?' Bell said.

'Jonathan?'

'Makes you think that?'

'I think he's awfully interested in you.'

'Most men are. But some are also frightened, and he, I suspect, is frightened.'

'Jon?'

'Just because he looks like a mad biker with a taste for rape and plunder... Actually, on reflection, most men are scared. And most women hate me. And children peer at me from behind the bushes.'

'Except...' Merrily snatched a shot of nicotine and went for it. 'Except for Robbie Walsh?'

Belladonna looked at her, full face in the shivering candle-light, and Merrily saw that her mouth was slightly twisted, blots of dried blood on her jawline, dirt still scraped across one cheek, a pinkening lump on her forehead above the proud, aquiline nose.

Ludlow is my heaven.

Oh God, something was very wrong here. This woman was not normal. Merrily became aware of the garment that Jon Scole had described as a nightdress. It was probably satin. Shapeless as an operating gown. She glimpsed a ribbon under one of Bell's arms.

Merrily tightened up, gripping her knees.

Bell said slowly, 'Who told you about Robbie and me?'

'Couple of people who saw you with him. Around the castle.'

'I gather some people have been saying he committed suicide. And therefore I must have helped him nurture his depression.'

'Who's saying that?'

'He wasn't depressed. Absolutely not. Robbie Walsh would walk these streets in a state of near-ecstasy. Jonathan'll confirm that. He was happier than any child I ever saw.'

'While he was here.'

'Yes.'

'Because he was here. He had a passion for history.'

'A passion for Ludlow. And your interest in him is…?'

'I have a friend who was his uncle. He feels he… he feels more than a bit responsible.'

'We all feel that.'

'Did Robbie come here with you? To this tree?'

'Oh yes. I think he was very much in love with Marion.' Bell leaned her head back against the tree, stretching her neck. The garment was torn on one shoulder, strands of the white fabric making loops. 'Schoolboy crush. If Robbie was going to have his first crush, it would have to be someone from the Middle Ages, wouldn't it? Only a small part of him was living in the present. You know what I'm saying, don't you?'

347

'I think we've all experienced it.'

Bell let out a small, exasperated hiss. 'I don't know about you. Only what Jonathan's said, and Jonathan's prone to the most awful hyperbole.'

'I think,' Merrily said carefully, remembering Jane's advice, 'that we all have heightened experiences in a town this close to its own history.'

'Yes.'

'And although I never met Robbie Walsh...'

'He'd describe scenes to you... like a sighted person interpreting for the blind. He'd read the names on all the plaques outside the old houses so many times that he knew them all off by heart – by heart, Mary, the town was in his heart. He knew who'd lived in every house, and he'd describe them to me. And he'd come here and he'd describe Marion.'

'Oh? What did she look like?'

'Quite small. Brown hair, brown eyes – passionate, angry eyes. Robbie was an adolescent boy, he wasn't sophisticated, his terminology was simple. He was in love with Marion because she was everything you rarely find any more. She was... all feelings. All strong passion and impulse, in comparison with all the apathetic, jaded kids he had to mix with. Can't you feel her, Mary? Now? Here?'

'I can feel her confusion,' Merrily said, and it was true. 'I can feel her uncontrollable rage. And her despair.'

'This was possibly the time of night she did it... hacked the bastard down and took a dive. Out of the window just above us. No tree here then, just stones. Marion plummeting down with a scream of terminal anguish. Her body bouncing as it lands, breaking, finally coming to rest—'

'Coming to unrest,' Merrily said.

'—Where we're sitting now, blood issuing from her mouth.' A fluid thrill, like oil, under Bell's voice now. 'Oh, you do understand, don't you?'

'I understand Marion. Marion's easy. She was both the betrayed and the betrayer. She'd let the enemy in. She didn't see

348

a way out, except through one of these windows. Jemima Pegler, however... that's much more complex. And so's Robbie Walsh. This friend of mine, he took me to see his mother, Robbie's gran. Because she said she was seeing him around the house and around the town...'

'He asked you to help her, as a psychic.'

'Something like that. She said she was seeing Robbie reflected in mirrors and shop windows. And... in the water.'

'She drowned...'

'I was there that night,' Merrily said. 'And you came down to the river, with a bunch of... goths, it looked like.'

Bell stared at her, her arms in the ragged sleeves lifting what had lain on her knees – a black instrument case, too big for a violin, too small for a guitar.

'And you seemed to know who it would be,' Merrily said. 'Who they'd found in the water.'

'What are you suggesting...? Oh, look, all right... It was one of the band heard it was Robbie's grandmother. Couple of them were in the town, and they heard someone—'

'The band?'

'It's a young band, called Le Fanu, who come here sometimes. They've been influenced by my music and they come down some weekends and we play. They're... my support mechanism, if you like. We hang out and we get a little stoned sometimes and... we're putting an album together. Look, I hear stories that I'm flooding the town with fucking goths, but it's just Le Fanu and their hangers-on.'

'And was... one of them involved in a stabbing incident?'

Something squirmed, some creature, rattling twigs in the undergrowth on the other side of the path. Bell let out a breath.

'Yes, yes... He was a roadie, and he doesn't work for them any more. It was a very minor incident, I...' She hugged the case. '... I don't mind being considered mad – I am mad – but I won't be accused of importing violence, do you understand?'

Her voice was breaking up now and she was trembling.

'You're shivering. You're cold.'

'I like being cold, you must've heard that. Cold as the grave.'

'I didn't mean to—'

'Mary, are you writing a fucking book about me, or something?'

'I'm—' Merrily had to break off, take a breath. The cigarette lay dead between her fingers. Her spine was starting to ache, and her bum had gone numb. If she wasn't careful she was going to come out with the truth. 'I just think some of the things being said about you are probably all wrong. Jon—'

'Jonathan's an idiot. Him and his ghost-walk – irrelevant, an irritant.'

'Maybe you just want to be an enigma,' Merrily said. 'The mad woman of Ludlow who walks in the night and sings her old songs to the moon while sitting under this… age-old symbol of life and death and immortality, wearing… wearing a bloody shroud…'

Bell Pepper started to laugh. 'I really think you're the first to notice.'

Oh God, and she'd been hoping it wasn't. She stared out, past the lantern, at the ominous black forestry across the river, towards the Welsh border.

'I didn't think they made them like that any more. They seem to use paper now, or the body's dressed in ordinary clothes.'

'They *don't* make them like this any more,' Bell said. 'I had a friend, an undertaker. He found them in a stockroom. Six of them. Old stock. Years old, even then. Probably post-Victorian, nineteen-thirties, I don't know.'

'I see.'

'This was the guy who did the arrangements for my baby, if you were wondering.'

'Your baby died…?'

'My baby… had no life outside of me. When they pulled him out, he was dead meat.'

'I'm sorry.'

'No need to be. It works both ways. Ever since – over twenty-five years – a part of me has been where he is.'

'I'm sorry,' Merrily said, 'I'm going to have to stand up, my back's starting to seize up…'

She rose awkwardly and walked out of the penumbra of the yew. She was surprised to see the sky like deep copper foil over the Hanging Tower. It didn't mean dawn, just another mood of an increasingly crazy night.

'Do you want to come home with me, Mary?'

Bell Pepper was at her shoulder, the musical-instrument case at her feet, her hands around its stem.

'I… I've got a daughter at home, I…'

'How old?'

'Seventeen.'

'Hardly a problem, then. You're obviously not as comfortable here as I am. Come back to The Weir House.' Bell touched her arm. Her fingers felt like the wet tips of icicles. 'You want to know, don't you? About Robbie?'

Merrily didn't reply.

'I was entirely shattered when he died.' That dark, translucent voice, the poshest pop star since Marianne Faithfull. 'It was like – for me – some awful kind of retribution.'

Merrily turned to her. 'Why?'

'Because Robbie Walsh was my son,' Bell Pepper said.

35

A Resort for the Dead

THE PHONE WAS ringing. Jane woke up under the duvet on the sofa in the parlour, Ethel on her feet. She was fully dressed, more or less. Padded through to the scullery.

The clock said two-fifteen a.m. She'd unplugged the answering machine, so the phone was still ringing, and she snatched it.

'Mum?'

'Jane…?'

'Lol!'

'What's wrong?' Lol said.

'Wrong?'

'All the lights are on. I'm sorry, I'm becoming the neighbour from hell. Maybe it'll be better when I get a bed. I woke up on the sofa and I felt something wasn't right, and I went to the front door and… all the lights are on in the vicarage. Well, not all the lights, just… more lights than usual. Sorry.'

'She got called out to Ludlow. Belladonna was… assaulted.'

Jane explained. She was wide awake now. Waking up had never been a problem and she thought it was good, in one way, that Lol had noticed the lights. He cared.

Well, of course he cared.

'She left her phone behind. I don't think it was intentional, she was in a hurry. But I'm a bit pissed off, actually. I was supposed to be going with her tomorrow to sort out Belladonna.'

'She was going to expose Belladonna to you?'

'Maybe she senses I've mellowed. Do you want to come over for some hot chocolate or something, Lol? We could sit by the phone together.'

'Not a safe thing to do in this village at the moment, with your mum conspicuously not at home. If we're awake, someone else will be. Then you happen to trip up outside and cut your lip, and I'm back on Victoria Ward, and—'

'Lol!'

'You could give me a discreet call when she comes in. Or do you think I should maybe go over—'

'Certainly not!'

'You're right. That would be... intrusive. Unforgivable. I need to keep my nose out.'

'You don't like Belladonna, do you?' Jane said.

'I don't know her.'

'You don't trust her, then.'

'Well, not from what I've heard, no, but we shouldn't always believe rumours, should we?'

'No. Lol' – Jane sat at the desk, flicked on the anglepoise '– about that. The rumours. Do you have any idea who's been spreading them?'

'Not really. As long as the right people don't believe them, I'm not going to worry.'

'You heard from Q magazine yet? When the piece is going in?'

'Should I have?'

'You could ring them and ask.'

'Why would I do that?'

'Well, I wouldn't like to miss it.'

'Eirion gets it, doesn't he?'

'Yeah. So he does.'

'Is this small talk, Jane?'

'Bit late for that,' Jane said ambiguously.

With no chance of getting back to sleep, Jane made some hot chocolate and took it back to the computer. Put Belladonna into

Google and found, like, six million mentions. Put in Belladonna/ religion and got it down to a couple of thousand. What it seemed to amount to was that this woman had tried everything and rejected most of it, including forms of paganism, mostly eastern.

When she found herself back in the Departure Lounge with Karone the bastard Boatman, Jane typed in: *You still here, Karone? Suggest consult own website and act accordingly*.

She Googled The Weir House, where Belladonna lived. There were three mentions, two negligible, one cursory. Essentially, a new house created authentically on the site of a fourteenth-century ruin, with a connection to the Palmers' Guild. Jane Googled the Guild and came up with this fairly detailed article about a quasi-spiritual organization that had played a major part in making Ludlow what it was today – well preserved and not short of a few quid.

She printed it out and read it twice. It tied in fairly well with what she already knew, from A-level history, about the medieval social system – the need for wealth, status and godliness in equal measures. Like, forget all that rich man/eye of the needle crap; if you had the money you could provide for an afterlife. Jane was reminded of 'Stairway to Heaven', the ancient and interminable Led Zeppelin song that Eirion had in his anorak's collection. Apparently, Tony Blair knew all the chords. Figured, somehow.

She tried Belladonna/Ludlow and hit on a short item from one of these *Heat*-type celeb magazines, which included this little gem:

> *'Do you know how many ghosts there are in this place?' Bell has been saying to friends. 'Dozens. Everywhere is haunted. This town is like a resort for the dead.'*

She printed this out, too, sensing some significance here, and then checked the e-mails. There was one from Eirion, marked *For Jane*.

***

Cariad: If you get this before you go off to play pagans, I couldn't sleep, due to underlying blind rage, so put some checks in, and I'm 99% certain JDF and Q are not any kind of item. I'm now going to find out where he lives so as to plan dawn raid. Well, OK, half-elevenish raid. Will keep you informed.

The e-mail was timed at 1.55 a.m. Chances were he was still vaguely conscious. Jane rang his mobile.

'Yes, I'm very nearly naked,' Eirion said. 'And, sadly, alone. Are you in bed also, your body glistening with oriental oils?'

'You sound pleased with yourself.'

'I've found out where the shit lives. It's one of those Georgian piles behind a ten-foot wall at Breinton, overlooking the city.'

'So you'll be going through Ledwardine to get there.'

'No.'

'Just that the Ludlow trip could be off.'

'Does this mean I don't get to do something potentially rewarding all on my own?'

'You can do what you like after you switch the light out, but maybe you could call for me in the morning. I feel strongly about this, too. Lol's my... whatever you call the bloke your mother's having an unaccountably clandestine relationship with. And he's... he's taken enough shit this week.'

'You told Lol about Fyneham?'

'No. Not a word. I mean, let's find out what the score is first. Like, if it turns out you're wrong and the guy actually is working for Q...'

'Jane, I went through a pile of back copies, looking for the name Jack Fine in all the concert reviews and small stuff, and then every known music website. I put him into every available search engine. If Fyneham's working for Q, I'm going to leave school, get a job on a remote hill farm in Snowdonia and shag sheep.'

'Yeah, OK, we get the point.'

'Call me when you know if you're going or not?'

'I will do that.' Jane noticed a new e-mail for Mum from the Deliverance office. It was highlighted with one of those red exclamation marks, conveying urgency. Sophie, who knew Mum always checked her e-mails before bed.

'If I don't hear from you before ten forty-five,' Eirion said. 'I'll just go straight over there, OK?'

'And, like, will you be armed?' Jane said.

She put the computer to sleep and went to the window. A fox was standing in the dark garden, as though embossed on the wall. Jane didn't move either; foxes were cool. She supposed she ought to grab a couple of hours' sleep. Flushing out Fyneham would be second-best to penetrating Belladonna's lair, but still better than an average Saturday.

And then the phone rang and the fox sloped away towards the orchard and the churchyard.

Mum, this time. 'What on earth are you doing still up? I was going to leave you a message on the machine.'

'Running the switchboard. You left your—'

'Phone. I know. Jane, I'm just… it doesn't look like I'll be back till the morning, OK?'

'Is everything all right?'

'Yes, everything's fine.'

'You sound like you can't talk.'

'Well, there you are, then.'

'Somebody's there?'

'Absolutely.'

'Right.' They'd become good at this over the years. Jane focused on the computer's hypnotic lemon sleep-light as it swelled and faded like a nervous sun. 'Could this be Belladonna? You're with Belladonna, in person?'

'Very intuitive, flower.'

'Is she mad?'

'Bit early to say. Definitely before lunch.'

'I mean, you're not in need of help?'

'No, I don't think so.'

'So where are you exactly? Like, where are you going to sleep? *Are* you going to sleep?'

'Well, just a bit… weary. Been a long day.'

'Wow… you're at The Weir House?'

'Exactly. So get some sleep yourself, all right?'

'Oh, I forgot…' Jane leaned forward and revived the computer. 'There's an e-mail from Sophie, marked urgent. You want me to read it?'

'Quickly, then.'

'OK, one sec…'

Merrily, this came just before I left, from a secretary at Lackland Modern Furnishings. The attachment is a scan of a petition received by the Mayor of Ludlow this afternoon. It was marked for your information (by the Mayor, this is). Hard to say if it's important or merely an attempt by someone to pre-empt your inquiries and perhaps pressure you into unnecessary action, but I thought you should see it.

'I'm opening the attachment, Mum, OK? If it's a virus, you know who to blame. Uh-oh.'

'What?'

'Looks like the fundamentalist loonies are on your back again.'

to the mayor of ludlow, County Councillor G. H. Lackland.

Sir,

A GREAT GODLESSNESS.

It has come to our notice that you have been in discussion with the diocese of hereford with regard to recent tragic events at ludlow castle. we are glad that, as our first citizen and a practising christian, you have shown such

commendable regard for the spiritual and moral health of
the community and trust that you will support our call for
suitable action to remove what many townsfolk regard as the
shadow of darkness and dissolution.

with respect,
(followed by 443 signatures)

'Notice that "shadow of darkness",' Jane said. 'As distinct from a shadow of light. Who wrote this turgid crap?'

'Well, thank you, flower,' Mum said. 'That's made my night.'

'But what do they mean? OK, you can't… I understand. Anyway, if that's the worst thing that happens to you before dawn you'll be OK. But, like, if I was having to sleep in Belladonna's house, I'd make sure my bedroom door was well locked.'

36

The Legend

IT SMELLED OLD: this was what you noticed first. Because the trees around it made everything so dark and close, and there was a night mist down here near the water, there wasn't much to see until you were inside, where the smell met you: the dusty sweetness of woodsmoke and warm stone, like the balm of a small church.

Even when Bell put on the lamps, it remained dim. An entrance hall with a low ceiling. The beams, Merrily noticed, were rough-cut, retaining an element of bark. Two lanterns projected from the swollen, ochre walls – electric, but the bulbs were no bigger than match flames, and so the room was no brighter than it would have been in the Middle Ages, lit by candles or rushlights.

The phone was in a niche in the wall, like an aumbry for the sacrament. But this was evidently for the concealment of an anachronism, and Bell drew the short curtain back across it.

'Your daughter was still up, then?'

Bell Pepper was faintly haloed by the clay-coloured light. She'd brushed her fair hair and washed her face. It looked pale and puffy, like creased linen, and there were shadows under her eyes, but no blood – except down the front of the shroud, like an emblem of war.

'She was waiting for me to call,' Merrily said. 'She'll go to bed now.'

'My son was born dead,' Bell said bluntly. 'He died inside me.'

Some belligerence there. This was a famous-artist thing: you demanded privacy, railed against media intrusion, but it was important that people should realize that your experiences were always more dramatic and significant than theirs.

'I was dreaming a great deal, then.' Bell's voice softening, a hint of the years in California rolling in like surf. 'Lucid dreams in which I was walking the streets of an old, old town, and I had no body. I was light.'

Merrily said nothing. Hormonal. So many chemicals at work during pregnancy.

'And during this really vivid dream, Mary – a dream full of colours and the scent of woodsmoke – during this dream, I was aware of someone beside me, and I was so sure that my baby had died.'

'Yes, I… can understand that.'

'And yet I didn't feel the way you'd expect.' Bell smiled – those crossover teeth, what Lol had called that strange kind of uneven beauty. 'No sorrow, more a kind of… Come and have some wine, Mary.'

'Well, it's a bit—'

But Bell had moved away through a low Gothic doorway, coffin-shaped around her, and Merrily shrugged and followed her into a passage that was low and narrow and unlit, sensing this woman's smile moving ahead of them like a guiding light, something separate.

'It was more like a kind of awe,' Bell said, 'that I was carrying death inside me. That I was containing death. That death had happened inside me. I knew from that moment that I'd always have death with me. And that death is like love… it must be nurtured.'

Turning to face Merrily at the end of the passage. Even in the gloom, Merrily could see that Bell's eyes were alight.

'But, you see, Mary, I was never very good at love.'

Merrily stopped in the passage. Beginning to see everything

now, the whole purpose of this woman's cycle of ritual: the candles burnt in ancient, sacred places, the menstrual blood in the church... the shroud, her magical apparel on a ghost-walk from the yew outside this house, over the spiritual summit of the town, to the yew in the overgrown cemetery of St Leonard's that was humming and rustling with energy.

'Death is eternal life without pain,' Merrily whispered. 'We make our own eternity.'

There was a momentary silence, except for the small sounds of a sleeping fire in the space behind Belladonna, where there were glimmerings of red and orange.

'You *know*,' Bell said, in a kind of awe.

They'd walked from The Linney, down some steps under the castle wall, like descending from the high town into the country.

Once, a sensor had found them and set off an imitation Victorian gas-lamp in the tiered, tree-snuggled garden of a modern bungalow, and Bell Pepper had stopped and turned around, with the musical-instrument case held by her side. Her shroud had a high, ruffled neck and came close to the ground where her feet were in sandals. She seemed, for a moment, to be flickering in time, and that was when Merrily had had the first inkling.

Soon, the buildings were separating out, town houses giving way to farmhouses, brick to stone, walls to high hedges, viridian-grey under the egg-shaped moon. The pavement narrowing, so Bell was walking some way ahead of Merrily, the pale shroud like a waving handkerchief.

There were stone gateposts at The Weir House drive and high, iron gates. But a smaller gate to the side had been unlocked, and Bell had led Merrily into a pathway which took them not to the house but to a yew tree which the path encircled. The yew was the width of one of Gomer Parry's diggers, very softly floodlit from below, green and gold. Like so many in churchyards, it was the remains of a long slow implosion, the great tree serving up its own entrails in a blackened tangle of pipes, like a ruined church organ.

Bell had walked inside.

Not uncommon to find them alive and hollow; there was one at Much Marcle with a seat inside. Merrily had hung back, didn't want to go inside the tree with Belladonna. Emerging a few moments later, Bell had stepped back and bowed to the tree and walked away, with no explanation.

But she hadn't been carrying the instrument case any more, only a long key.

'That was quite a shock.' Bell laughed nervously, a glass of red wine at her lips. 'I thought for a moment— But I suppose Jonathan told you, didn't he? He was here when we rehearsed it. That particular line – we make our own eternity – is on the album, the thing I'm doing with Le Fanu. Which we haven't yet recorded. Jonathan was dropping so many hints I let him in once to listen – special treat. Little bastard, I expect he was making notes.'

'I wouldn't know about that,' Merrily said. 'Jonathan didn't tell me.'

The laugh was snapped off, and then Bell, face glowing in the firelight, said, with uncertainty, 'There is no other way you could—'

'Yes, I'm afraid there is.'

There was what looked like half a small tree on the fire in the great stone hearth. There must have been some draught system under the hearth because Bell had awoken the fire, and they were sitting in its sporadic light in these hopelessly uncomfortable oak chairs, no more than carved wooden boxes with vertical backrests and the fronts blocked in like commodes. Velvet cushions helped a bit, not much. Bell leaned out of hers.

'But of course Jonathan maintains you're the best natural psychic he's ever encountered. I was inclined not to believe him. Jonathan is… how shall I…?'

'Prone to hyperbole.' Carving on the chair's upright spine bit into Merrily's back. She sat up, sinking her hands into the pockets of her fleece. 'Mrs Pepper, I read it on the Internet.'

'I don't know anything about the Internet!' Bell's voice rose erratically. 'Computers suck your energy. You couldn't have!'

'The quote was on a website. Well, more of a chat-room.'

'I don't even know what a fucking chat-room is.'

'It's like a forum. Where people can send messages to each other? In this case, people interested in suicide.'

'What?'

'Where would-be suicides gather to talk it over online. It was quoted in a reply to someone who was planning to take her own life. I couldn't tell you where they got it from, but the Internet moves almost as fast as you can think. Passing thoughts suddenly get shared with thousands of people.'

Merrily looked around into the darkness. They might as well have been sitting outside in front of a brazier. This would be a very atmospheric rehearsal room, but as living space, despite the heavy tapestries on the walls and the sheepskins on the floor, it was too big, too cold, too rudimentary. Too starkly, uncompromisingly medieval.

Bell Pepper was watching her intently over her wine glass. 'Why were you looking at this suicide website?'

'I was trying to help my friend, Robbie's uncle. I wanted to understand Robbie and why he died.'

'You think he committed suicide?'

'His uncle thinks it's possible. What do you think?'

Bell's face went blank. 'I don't know.'

'He seems to have been victimized – bullied – on the estate where he lived. There's evidence that he didn't want to go back. That he took his life to… stay here…'

'No, that's not true.'

'So we looked at his computer and he—'

'No! Listen… I didn't put that stuff there. Yeah, yeah, there's a computer here that Le Fanu use – for the music, they download sounds, sample stuff, I don't know how it works, I don't have to, I'm not an Internet freak like fucking Bowie… and I didn't put those words out, or any of that song… I didn't.'

'I never said you did,' Merrily said. 'And, for what it's worth, there's no evidence that Robbie went near those sites. But, since I've just quoted that line back to you, somebody must have, mustn't they? Did one of the band do it – Le Fanu? Your songs appear to be widely available on the suicide network, did you know that?'

'It's nothing to do with me. Anybody could… Everybody knows what I did.'

'Sorry, I'm getting confused, what are we—?'

'It's in the books. The unauthorized biographies.'

'I've never read them,' Merrily said. 'I just know the music. I just… wore the clothes.'

'When I was fifteen,' Bell said, a tired incantation, 'I tried to kill myself. I took an overdose. I spent quality time on a stomach pump. I was fifteen and I was overweight, bad skin, repressed and horribly shy, and I had a heart defect and I was not allowed to do games and my parents drove me everywhere – even if I went out at night with friends they drove me there and collected me – and I also had a disgusting brace on my twisted teeth, so I tried to kill myself. It's in the books.'

'I'm sorry. I didn't know about that.'

Bell craned her neck forward. 'Darling, it's part of the legend. The next part is when I was seventeen and someone said I could sing and someone else pointed out that if you took the middle out of my dreary name, Isabella Donachie, you had the magic word Belladonna – poisonous, the most resonant name for a singer in those days – and that seemed like some glorious epiphany, and I snatched the brace off my teeth and slept with about a hundred men in six months.'

'Legend?'

Bell sniffed. 'You see, I'd grown up to whispers behind my back: doctors to parents, parents to relatives. Peering through the banisters, ears flapping – children have such sharp ears and an acute understanding of the basics. By the time I was ten, I knew I was going to die before my time.'

'You're still here…'

'And I still have a heart defect, apparently – it wasn't a mistake or anything: they picked up on it again when I was having the baby. I mean, I could still die any time. I just haven't died yet. But death and me...' Bell enclosed one hand with another. 'Close, Mary. Very close, always. And it's been a remarkable relationship.'

'It's certainly produced some remarkable music.'

'All about sailing close to the precipice. When I swallowed the pills, I was convinced just a handful would finish me off – someone already hanging delicately over the great abyss? Didn't happen. When I was twenty-one, I recorded the Hungarian Suicide Song and had all the scratches put into the mix, just like the original. Singing close to the precipice.'

Merrily said hesitantly, 'They say that knowledge and acceptance of death can show you how to live... intensively.'

Bell leaned back in her box. 'That's not quite true. It induces, more than anything, a sense of the temporary. I couldn't settle. Couldn't settle in a place – travelled all over the world or, at least, back and forth across the Atlantic. Couldn't stay with a man, either. Pepper was the best, he was a nice guy – why I kept his name – but I was turning him into a nervous wreck, so he appealed to my better instincts and I let him go. But there was only one constant, and that was my son.'

'Because he was dead?'

'And then I fetched up in Ludlow, visiting Saul's daughter, Susannah, who was now my legal and financial adviser – business manager, I guess – and it was... another epiphany.'

'The town you'd dreamed of when the baby was...'

'Yes. Knew it soon as I got out of the car. Didn't quite believe it at first, so I went away. Had the dream again. Came back, and the pull was even stronger. A town that, like me, was outside of its time. And the child... well, the child wanted to come back.'

'Are we talking about... Robbie?'

'You're getting there.' Bell sighed. 'I must be insane – you could be a reporter.'

Merrily smiled.

'But when you've been courted and worshipped and shafted by thousands of people the world over, you pride yourself on being able to recognize the ones who're going to be of some importance. When I saw you with Jonathan at Marion's yew, I thought, yeah... No, don't say anything, Mary, don't feel flattered, I'll be a burden to you, I always am.'

'Robbie?'

'Is my son. *Is* my son. I wasn't looking for a child, for God's sake. I was probably looking for a man. And then one day you're face to face with your twin soul, and it's a... a bloody little boy.' Bell drank some wine, tears like lenses over her eyes.

'Someone I spoke to,' Merrily said, 'actually said you were like mother and son.'

'We *were* mother and son. Birth parents are merely that – seldom of any consequence, an impedance more often than not. We were part of the same spiritual seed... essence. And we were both connected with this town and realized it. We'd both come home. We saw the town burning with the same golden light. I remember, in my first dream, walking from the castle to the church, stopping and gazing up at the steeple, and it was like a bar of gold, and the sky was red with sunset, and I felt... well, you can imagine how I felt.'

'Euphoric.'

'Oh, well beyond euphoric.'

'Like a near-death experience? Bell, are we talking reincarnation here?'

Bell shook her head. 'I don't believe in that shit.'

'Someone... that is, I wondered if you felt you were connected with Marion de la Bruyère.'

'No, not at all. Marion's an entry point. She's important because most of the ghosts here are nebulous presences, and she's fully formed. We know where she died, and how and why. And she's very much here – like Robbie. So I went to see his grandmother.'

'Mrs Mumford?'

'When he'd gone back to school, last January, I went to see

the old woman. Realized, soon as I started talking to her, that there was no way I could explain the half of it. I said I was impressed with his knowledge and his enthusiasm and wondered if there was some way I could help with his education. It was pretty clear that she wouldn't understand.'

'Would you have expected her to?'

'Probably not. So, in the end, I went to see the mother. I went to this crummy estate in Hereford. And I met the mother. And it became very obvious, very quickly, that this woman and I would be able to find a common… currency.'

'Currency?'

'I'm not speaking metaphorically. Look at this place… it's a shell. I walk through this house like another ghost. I wanted…'

Merrily sat up, hard. 'You wanted to adopt him?'

'My stepdaughter could deal with the formalities. But the essence of it, as far as the mother was concerned, was a large – not to say life-changing – one-off payment.'

'Christ,' Merrily said.

'He didn't know. I wanted to be sure, before I discussed it with him, that nobody would get in the way. It was obvious Phyllis Mumford wouldn't be in any state to look after him for much longer. As for Angela… Angela's eyes positively lit up at the implications.'

'God.'

'And then he died,' Bell said. 'He died like Marion. And everything shifted. The whole axis of the town shifted under me.' She stared at Merrily, and her eyes looked as if they were melting in the firelight. 'It's the endgame now, Mary.'

The fireplace reared over them. Bell was in shadow, but her breathing was loud and uneven, and you could smell the wine.

'This is the endgame,' she said again. 'It's as if we're all part of some great, tragic tapestry across time. And now I'm walking this house and this town like a ghost. Like the ghost…'

'Like the ghost,' Merrily said softly, 'that you'll become?'

37

Like in the Belfry

WHILE JANE WAS in the kitchen, scrambling a basic breakfast together, the phone rang in the scullery.

'Put your mother on, please, Jane.'

'She's not here.'

'Well, get her,' Sophie Hill said.

It was about half-nine. Outside the scullery window, the first blossom was ghosting the apple trees, although the sky was dull. Ethel was sitting on the wall, watching for movements among the graves in the churchyard.

'Not so easy,' Jane said. 'She went over to Ludlow last night, and she's not back yet. And, of course, she forgot her mobile.'

'Oh my God,' Sophie said. It was Saturday, so she was probably calling from home. 'She's there now?'

'What's the matter?'

Sophie drew breath as if she was about to explain something.

'Sophie? Is there something wrong? Something I can tell her if she—?'

'Thank you, Jane,' Sophie said and hung up.

And Jane was worried now because Sophie was worried – conspicuously.

A woman not known for displaying unwarranted emotion.

Lol had been up for a couple of hours when Gomer Parry arrived at the back door.

Gomer had a small boy with him – about ten, fair hair, combat trousers.

'Tell him,' Gomer said.

The small boy looked at Lol, then over the fence into the orchard. Then he tried to run past Gomer into the entry that led back into Church Street.

Gomer caught him. 'Tell him.'

'Get off me, you ole paedophile!'

'We gonner do this the easy way, boy, or the hard way?' Gomer said. 'Either you tells this man what you did or we goes and talks to your dad.' He looked across at Lol, who was standing in the doorway. 'His dad's on the Hereford council – Lib Dem, hangin' on by his fingertips last time. Hate it to get out that his boy was in the poison-pen business. Now tell the man.'

The kid looked at the step Lol was standing on.

'Posted you a letter.'

'I see,' Lol said. 'And did you, er, write the letter?'

'Tell him,' Gomer growled.

'Yeah,' the kid said. 'But I din't make it up. He told me what to write.'

'Who tole you?' Gomer said.

'Bloke.'

'What bloke?'

'I don't know! I keep tellin' you and you don't believe me. He give me a quid both times.'

'How much?'

'Fiver.' The kid looked up at Gomer. The light flared in Gomer's glasses. 'Tenner. To keep quiet.'

'So let's get this clear, boy. Bloke gives you the paper, tells you what to write on it, then he puts it in the envelope, tells you where to take it, right?'

'Yeah. When it's dark.'

'What do he look like, this bloke?'

'I dunno – tall.'

'Local?'

'Uh?'

'You seen him before round yere?'

'No.'

'Was he in a car?'

'Yeah.'

'All right,' Gomer said. 'You see him again, you come and tell me. You know where I live – bungalow down the hill, with the big sheds.'

'Yeah.'

'You tell me quick enough, mabbe I'll give you a tenner. Or mabbe I just won't tell your dad. Now bugger off.'

When the kid had gone, Lol said, 'I don't understand.'

'Paedophile – you yere that? Bloody hell, it don't take the little bastards long, do it?'

'How did you find out about him?'

'Maggie Tomlin – lives across the way. Sits in a wheelchair by the window, listenin' to the radio. Knows everybody. Jasper Ashe, her says, straight off. Thought he was delivering flyers for a car boot or some'ing, but he only delivered the one. Gavin Ashe's boy. Gavin had Rod Powell's ole seat on the council, but the Tory woman run him close last time, see.'

'I don't get it, Gomer.'

'Ar, it's a puzzler,' Gomer conceded. 'Somebody got it in for you and the vicar, but they en't local. But mabbe you're supposed to think they are local.'

'Making me paranoid. Unsettled.'

'Sure to, ennit.'

'Well... thanks, Gomer.'

'Us incomers gotter stick together,' Gomer said.

'Er... yes.' As Lol understood it, Gomer had been born approximately ten miles outside Ledwardine. 'Right.'

'Where's the vicar?'

'Over in Ludlow.'

'Been out all night, looks like.'

'Er...' Lol heard his mobile from inside the house, playing the first few bars of the tune that Jane had keyed in – 'Sunny Days'.

'You better get that, boy, might be her.'

'It might.'

'You wanner keep an eye on that little woman,' Gomer said. 'Some funny folks in Ludlow now, what I yeard.'

The next caller had asked for Mrs Watkins. Jane hadn't recognized the voice, but it was too precise to be, like, Emma from Everest Double-glazing or somebody in Delhi calling on behalf of British Telecom. This voice was also actually quite low and pleasant.

'Would that be... Jane?'

'It would, yes.'

'Jane, this is Siân Callaghan-Clarke. Canon Callaghan-Clarke, from Hereford.'

'Oh, hello.'

Big warning bells, up close and agonizingly loud, like in the belfry on a Sunday morning.

'Jane, I'm awfully sorry to bother you, but it's most important I get hold of your mother before... other people do.'

'Other people?'

'The media, for instance.'

'She's pretty good with the media, actually.'

'Yes, so I understand. Do you know where she might be? Does she routinely tell you where she's going?'

'You mean, like, am I a latchkey kid who gets her own meals?'

Siân Callaghan-Clarke laughed lightly.

'Actually, she normally tells me everything,' Jane said, 'but I'm afraid I got in rather late last night myself – the bus broke down – and I, um, overslept. She's usually up very early, on her hands and knees, scrubbing the church floor, or visiting the sick, and I'm afraid I have to go out again in a minute, so...'

'Hmm.'

'I could leave a note for her.'

'You're sure she hasn't gone to Ludlow, Jane?'

'Ludlow.' Jane paused. 'That's in Shropshire, isn't it?'

'Thank you,' Siân Callaghan-Clarke said. 'You've been very helpful.'

Mistake.

'So something's gone down,' Jane said to Lol. 'And I don't know what it is. And Mum hasn't rung and I can't get hold of her because bloody Belladonna's ex-directory. And Eirion's gonna be here any minute to pick me up.'

'What can I do?'

'Maybe you could come over to the vicarage and just like… stay here? Man the phone and stuff?'

'You think I'm responsible enough?'

'Please, Lol, it really is the best thing you could do right now. Something's happened, and I don't know what it is. I've got the radio on – Hereford and Worcester – and there's nothing. Lol, please…'

In the dream – and she knew all along that it was a dream – Merrily was at a junction of several old streets with gilded buildings on either side. They had timbers like bars of dull gold and small bricks like jewels, and the entrance of each street, as she approached it, was aglow with enticing lights, the air perfumed with applewood smoke. But the further in she went, the darker and closer it all became, the brickwork crumbling, the beams blackening and the perfume gradually corrupted by a rising stench of dampness and rot. And ahead of her – slapping of sandals on dry flagstones – a woman with a musical-instrument case swinging like a censer from one hand.

Scared, Merrily began wading out of the dream. She opened her eyes, and one of them hurt. The light was grey and rationed, sweat congealing on her face like a sour syrup. She pushed the plain cream duvet away, tentatively lowered her bare feet to bare boards.

No splinters on this floor. This was very old wood, worn smooth long before it had been laid here. Could have come from anywhere. Had its own history.

The Weir House. Hundreds of disparate histories mingled here, their vibrations filtered through reclaimed timbers and the stones of demolished barns from miles away and nothing would be—

God, what time is it?

In bra and pants and small pectoral cross, she stumbled across to the only window, a Gothic slit with just one pane, and peered out.

She saw a short track with a metal gate at the end. There was a flat field, a glint of river and, above it all, sprouting out of the wooded bank and a sky that was as cold and hard as marble, something like a ragged and monstrous clump of giant brown mushrooms.

Use the castle room. Bell Pepper opening the door for her but not entering. An engaging smile through twisted teeth. *But if you see Marion, be careful. She's unstable.*

Merrily had not wanted, at that time, to see Marion. She remembered sitting down on the bed, alone, to think and to pray: St Patrick's Breastplate – *Hold me safe from the forces of evil. On each of my dyings shed your light.*

Must have slept, for… She went back to the bed. The rest of her clothes – T-shirt, jeans, fleece – were in a heap beside it, her watch on top. It was nearly eleven-thirty a.m. She'd slept for nearly six hours.

She had to start talking to people – Jane, Lol, Mumford, the Bishop.

Recalling a bathroom somewhere, mercifully modern, she grabbed her clothes into a bundle and unlocked the oak door – yes, it did have a key and she had locked it – and went out into a short passage that was daylight-dim: interior lime-plastered walls of wattle and daub, which was basically clay and cow muck over a framework of branches and twigs. Clay and cow muck and animal fat and whatever other personal ingredients—

Merrily stopped, clutching the bundle to her chest. The woman standing at the end of the passage was not Belladonna.

38

Like *Hello!*

BREINTON WAS ON the western side of Hereford in sloping, wooded countryside that managed to conceal most of the city's lower, more modern buildings, so that from the road outside the Fyneham residence you could see the cathedral apparently poking out of greenery, as if the city centre was a neighbouring village.

Eirion parked his Peugeot half on the grass verge, just out of sight of the solid wooden gates that were like castle gates: all you could see of the house was a brick wall, a chimney and a burglar alarm. Homes up here cost an arm and a leg now.

'Hereford's Beverly Hills,' Jane said sourly. She was seriously uptight, the world full of invisible hostility. If she'd been a hedgehog she'd have been rolled up in a ball, spikes out.

'If that's meant to be an insult, it would escape Fyneham.' Eirion locked the car. 'He's a Beverly Hills kind of person. How do you reckon we get to the front door?'

'You need one of those little battering-ram things the cops have.'

'Jane…' Eirion was looking at her as though she might have been secretly carrying one. 'Don't do anything, right? Leave this to me.'

'You know me, Irene.' Jane put on an icy smile. 'Walking definition of the word discretion. Look – dinky little door in the wall.'

There was a black iron ball-handle; when Eirion turned it, the door opened onto a short gravel drive and this imposing, blindingly white conservatory porch with a Victorian type of bell pull that turned out to be electric and sent Big Ben chimes bonging through the house.

The woman who responded was serious second-wife material: bleached blonde, about thirty-five, and dressed for hovering hopelessly with hi-tech secateurs. She stayed inside, keeping a hand on the door, Eirion treating her to his winning smile.

'Oh, hi. Sorry to just turn up like this, but Jack said if we were ever passing…'

'I'm sorry?'

'This is the right house, isn't it? Jack Fyneham?'

'Jack?' She looked blank for a moment and then she said, 'Oh, you mean Johnno.'

'Actually, we just know him as JD at school.'

'Oh, I see, you're—'

'This for me, Tessa?' J.D. Fyneham appeared in person at her shoulder, wearing a half-smile that faded with gratifying speed into this oh-shit expression when he saw who was outside. Jane smiled at him.

'Why don't you take them up to your rooms, Johnno?' Tessa said. 'I've got this guy coming about the pool, which your dad, of course, conveniently forgot about…'

'Cool.' Eirion beamed. 'JD's told us so much about his rooms.'

In the first hour, nobody rang. Lol went upstairs to Merrily's bedroom and brought down the Washburn he kept there and tuned it and played fingerstyle to Ethel, the way he had when he'd lived in Blackberry Lane and Ethel had been his cat and he'd probably still been half-mental.

Walking across to the vicarage, he'd seen a woman looking at him and then she'd frowned and looked away and Lol had thought, *Jesus, no…* and put his head down and almost run across and into the driveway. Jane, in the doorway with Eirion, waiting to leave, had glared at him with a kind of furious pity.

And now there was a knock on the front door, and he put down the guitar and didn't know whether or not to answer it.

Someone had paid a child twenty quid to write and deliver two anonymous letters, the latest accusing him of beating up his half-secret girlfriend, the parish priest. *No smoke.* Not everyone would believe Gomer Parry. He envisioned a drab lynch mob of Ledwardine villagers clustered around the porch: *What have you done with the vicar?*

He closed his eyes and held his breath. Immediately Lucy Devenish sprang out of the shadows, and he almost reeled back from the draught caused by the admonishing swirl of her poncho: *Sitting there listening to your mournful, wistful records. It's spring! Open your heart to the eternal! Let the world flow into you!*

'Mr Robinson.'

Just one man at the door. Close-cropped red hair and a blue plaid jacket.

'Ah,' Lol said.

'Now, don't think we're targeting you now you're a successful recording artist, but experience has taught us that many of your kind still like to conduct experiments of a chemical nature in order to, shall we say, stimulate the creative juices.'

'So how much do you want, Frannie?' Lol said. 'Couple of grams see you through the graveyard shift?'

Frannie Bliss beamed. 'How are you, Laurence? Can I come in?'

'Well, you can,' Lol said. 'But she's not here.'

'That's a shame.' Bliss stepped inside, followed Lol into the kitchen. 'Hoped I'd catch her. My day off, strictly speaking, but, with having to go over to Leominster to see Gail Mumford, I thought I'd call in.'

'I haven't spoken to Merrily this morning. I'm just here kind of minding the phone.'

'She'll be in Ludlow, then, will she?'

'Why would you say that?'

'You know anything about that peculiar business?'

'What?'

'Let's deal with Merrily and Mumford.' Bliss rubbed his forehead. 'Lol... being straight with each other now can only save a lorra serious pain later. Had a call at home this morning from Karen, my new DC. You won't have met her. Karen's current headache is being second cousin, twice removed, to Mumford, who seems to have forgotten he's no longer permitted to hit people with his truncheon, as it were. Basically, Karen's feeling guilty because, for reasons of Family, she's been doing PNC checks for him and divulging things she shouldn't have.'

'Family,' Lol said. He didn't seem to have one any more, outside of Merrily and Jane.

Bliss sat down at the pine refectory table. 'It's bloody lucky I understand how this area operates. This got passed up to headquarters, Karen'd be ironing her uniform tonight. How much do you know about the Robbie Walsh business?'

'I just live a quiet life, Mr Bliss,' Lol said, 'writing my little songs.'

'But you do have the ear of the Reverend. And other bits, too, it's rumoured. Lol, let me put it this way: Andy Mumford was a fine detective, with a good nose. But once you're out, you're out, and Andy's crossed a line you do not cross.'

Bliss talked about a family on the Plascarreg Estate, name of Collins, who were being looked after by the police after fingering several drug dealers. They had a son, Niall, formerly associated with some youngsters who, it seemed, had not been nice to Robbie Walsh.

'I had Karen looking after them. There was a message for her this morning, to ring the Collinses at their safe-house. Seems they're not too happy about this strange copper who turned up to talk to Niall, in some detail, about Robbie Walsh and things that got done to him. Drugs are one thing, but the Collinses are sincerely hoping their son's not gonna be called to give evidence against his former playmates on this one. For reasons that may become apparent.'

'Have you spoken to Mumford?'

'Laurence… this is the whole point: we can't find Mumford. His wife says he went out yesterday, saying he was finalizing arrangements about his mother's funeral, and didn't come back. He phoned – would you believe? – a neighbour, asking her to convey to Gail that he was OK.'

'Why would he do that?'

'He doesn't like confrontation. And whether he thinks we…' Bliss shrugged helplessly. 'I don't know, Lol. He's not himself. Or maybe he is himself, and he shouldn't be any more, because he's fuckin' retired. Gail is, consequently, frantic. Gail knows how he's been lately and how far he might go.'

'Compulsory retirement's like a jail sentence in reverse, and probably just as stressful,' Lol said. 'He'll have something to prove, if only to himself. Maybe he won't feel able to come home until he's done it.'

'I agree,' Bliss said. 'But it's worse than that. OK… our colleagues in Shropshire had Robbie down as accidental death – no evidence to the contrary, no suicide note, no one else involved they knew of. Mumford seems to have thought there was more to it, and this was getting to him.'

'Because he thought, as a copper, he should have seen it and stopped it.'

'Exactly. And it looks like he could be right. Knowing what we now know – thanks, it seems, to Mumford – there's reason to think the lad was so terrified of going back to the Plascarreg he topped himself.'

'And what is the reason to think that?'

'I can't tell you that.'

'And frankly I don't really want to know,' Lol said. 'But it might help Merrily.'

'You think he's still in contact with her?'

'None of us is in contact with her – she went out without her phone. The thing is… Do you want a cup of tea, Frannie? Glass of cider?'

'No, ta. I want to know what the thing is.'

'I can't tell you that,' Lol said.

Bliss smiled. 'Bastard.'

Lol shrugged.

'All right,' Bliss said. 'You first.'

'She went out with Mumford to the Plascarreg, and she got hurt.'

Bliss half-rose. 'She got hairt?'

'Bruised face. Black eye. Some kids. Mumford found Robbie's computer, and they were seeing what he had on it there – in this garage. These kids evidently thought there might be something on the computer that could incriminate them, so they... smashed it. Mumford got attacked, and Merrily was hurt trying to get some kid off him. Kid was trying to choke him with a chain.'

Bliss leaned back, breathed down his nose. 'And she didn't report this incident to me because...?'

'Because of Mumford.'

'Don't.' Bliss stood up. 'Don't say another word, Laurence. I encounter Mumford, I'm likely to nick the bastard meself. I just urge you, if you talk to Merrily, and she's in contact with him, to tell him to...'

'Give himself up? I mean, what's he actually done?'

'Impersonated a police officer.'

'Impersonated himself, in fact.'

'It's what he *could* do,' Bliss said.

'To whom? I think I need to know, don't I?'

'Yeh,' Bliss said. 'All right, I'll have a glass of cider, please. This looks like being a long day.'

'Holy shit!' Eirion said. 'You bastard.'

Somehow, Jane had expected him to have calmed down since last night, but it was clear that his usual chapel-whipped, Welsh-speaking caution had failed to re-engage. What if going out with her had fatally damaged his equilibrium?

Still, she could see that J.D. Fyneham's home office, occupying the upstairs of what seemed like a whole wing of a very sizeable house, was something to inspire strong feelings – envy, lust, that kind of reaction – in the male of the species.

The room was dotted with pinpoint lights and underlaid with a low hum. It had this blue-mauve ambience, from concealed lighting with daylight-quality bulbs. Most of the stuff in here, Jane was unsure what it actually did. There were three computers – one was an Evesham, and they didn't come cheap – on plush, kidney-shaped workstations, a cluster of printers and scanners and other hi-tech-looking items of hardware which seemed to be connected with… well, desktop publishing, she guessed.

Like, on an industrial scale.

'You could…' Eirion seemed to be having respiratory problems. 'You could produce bloody *Vogue* up here.'

'Pays its way, Lewis, pays its way,' J.D. Fyneham said.

The way he kept calling Eirion 'Lewis', it was like that sneering way that Inspector Morse talked to Sergeant Lewis on the TV. He was wearing a deep purple rugby shirt and black trousers in this kind of snakeskin leather.

'That's all you need to know,' he said. 'Now what do you want? I'm busy.'

'Obviously,' Eirion said bitterly.

'Look, we were a bit pissed last night, all right?'

'It's not about last night,' Eirion said.

Jane had wandered over to a side table stacked with A4-sized glossy magazines. The top one had a picture on the cover of a black and white village that she was sure she ought to recognize. Beside the magazine was a stack of flyers.

'Come away from those!' Fyneham snapped, but Jane had grabbed one.

Do YOU want to make your parish magazine into a genuine going-concern – a professional publication that every parishioner will want to buy?

'Well, well…'

'It's a legitimate business,' Fyneham said sulkily.

'Jane?' Eirion walked over.

'JD seems to be the guy behind Parish Pump, Irene. It offers a service to vicars and parish councils, to turn their parish magazines into, like, *Hello!*'

'Oh, please,' Fyneham said. 'I'm offering to teach them the basic craft of journalism.'

'I don't know anything about this,' Eirion said.

'He probably hasn't hit Wales yet. Mum got the package, but decided people wouldn't want to see pictures of the parish council in the nude and, like, read about the churchwarden's private habits.'

'You may take the piss,' Fyneham said, 'but seven parishes have already signed up for the introductory package.'

'And what does that do for them, exactly?' Eirion said.

'They learn the basics of journalism. How to spot a story, how to write it. I spend a couple of weekends in the parish and sub the first issue for them. Or produce the whole thing, for a fee. It's a shit-hot idea, Lewis, and it's working. If a parish magazine looks halfway decent, local businesses are more inclined to advertise, and they can charge more for display ads. That way they get the new steeple before the rest of the church falls down.'

Jane was forced to concede that it wasn't such a bad concept.

'You do it all yourself?'

'So far, but I expect I'll soon be able to employ some of the guys from the media studies group on a part-time basis. Not that Lewis would be interested...'

'This is all your dad's kit?' Eirion said. 'He produces real glossies – trade stuff, right?'

'Nah, this is just overspill. He's got a proper plant down in town, with a few staff.' Fyneham shrugged. 'We help each other out.'

There was a noticeboard at the end of the long room, with some magazine covers pinned to it: *Microlite Monthly. You and Your DigiCam. The Clinical Therapist. International Readers'- Group Forum. What Hereford Council Can Do for You.*

All crap, really.

'Tell the truth, the old man hates what he does,' Fyneham said. 'He'd rather be a real journalist any day of the week, but real journalists don't have a pad like this with five acres and a pool. It's swings and roundabouts, Lewis. The old man goes on about secure income. If I have this to fall back on, I can go out there and, like, soar.'

Eirion looked faintly contemptuous – but then his family had been loaded since for ever. Jane started to wonder if Fyneham would maybe give her a weekend job. Hadn't earned a penny of her own since the maid thing at Stanner Hall.

But then she remembered why they were here.

'Does your dad own *Q*, then?'

Fyneham stared down at her, eyes narrowing. She noticed a faint sheen on his face, above the weekend stubble that Eirion said some guys in his year started cultivating from about Wednesday.

'We're talking about Lol Robinson,' Eirion said.

'Aw...' Fyneham shuffled out this crooked grin. 'Look, maybe it'll get in, maybe it won't.'

'You're saying you did it on spec?'

'You've never done that? Written a piece for a magazine and just sent it in, see if it gets used?'

'Can't say I have, JD.'

'Scared of rejection, huh? I've had quite a few pieces published – OK, not in *Q* yet, but some of the others.'

'Fanzines?'

'Oh, better than that. Look, somebody tells me about this guy who's just brought an album out and how he used to be halfway famous, way back, and how he used to be a mental patient with a police record. Burns me a CD. Like, I don't personally go for that acoustic shit, but I get onto the Net, dredge up some background and think, yeah, I'll go and interview him.'

'You told him you worked for *Q*,' Eirion said.

'I told him I was a freelance. What's wrong with that?'

'You told him it was definitely going in,' Jane said.

'I told him I couldn't be sure when it would go in. And I couldn't.'

Jane looked at Eirion. He was red-faced and tight-lipped and looking far younger than he had when he was smarming the second wife at the door. It was all turning out to be no big deal; just another wannabe chancing his arm. OK, a wannabe with a head start... well, a head start on Eirion, anyway.

She wished they'd never come now. She wished she was in Ludlow with Mum. She wished they could just get out of here.

'Anyway, it wasn't fair,' she said to Fyneham, more for Eirion's sake than anything. 'Lol Robinson's a really decent guy, with a lot of talent, and you conned him.'

'You won't say that if it makes it into the magazine.' Fyneham knowing he was on top now, his grin turning into a sneer or maybe it had been a sneer all along. 'Anyway, why should you be worried about the guy being conned, when he's beating the shit out of your mother?'

A few seconds later, Jane was hearing Eirion saying, like from a long way away, 'Jane, no...'

But it was like when she'd tried on Mum's new glasses: the whole room had gone red – all the printers and the binders, and the scanners and the copiers and the state-of-the-art flat-screen computers.

Including the big, handsome one that she was holding in her arms, maybe sixteen hundred quid's worth, its cables wrenched out of their sockets and dragging along the carpet as she backed away towards the window.

Fyneham snarling, 'You're insane! You'll be paying for that for the rest of your—'

'It fell off the desk,' Jane said through her teeth. 'Our word against yours. Keep away from me, you scumbag!'

She tripped over an extension cable and had to go down on one knee to prevent the computer slipping out of her arms, and Fyneham let out a screech.

'For Christ's sake, Lewis, do something about this bitch!'

'Out of my hands, JD.'

'And it'll be out of mine,' Jane said, 'if you take one more step.'

'What do you want?'

'I want to know where you got it from.'

'Got what?'

'You know what. You've been trying to bullshit us all along. You think we're like hicks or something, and you're this big-time professional journalist...'

'I don't know what you're—'

'You...' Jane hefting the computer above the level of her chin: further to fall, more damage. 'You do!'

'Put it down!' Fyneham like went into spasm. 'Put it down and we'll talk.'

'We'll talk first.'

'It's not paid for, you stupid bitch!'

'Oh dear.'

'Look,' Fyneham said, 'I was just told what to ask, OK, and he bought me—'

Eirion came over then, and Jane clutched the computer to her chest in case he snatched it. But he just stood between her and Fyneham, who looked close to tears, Eirion just looking puzzled.

'Bought you what?'

Fyneham looked down at his trainers, arms stiffened, fists clenched by his sides.

'The Evesham.'

'Your dad bought you the Evesham?'

'He bought it, and I'm paying him off week by week. My dad... he came up the hard way. He doesn't do anything for nothing.'

'But he got you the Evesham if you asked Lol some questions?'

'He'll kill me.'

'Is that what happened?'

'Lewis, will you please tell that bi— your girlfriend to put it down?'

387

'Could you put it down, Jane?'

Jane stood for a few moments trying to work out what was coming out here, when all she'd wanted to know was who'd told Fyneham this evil crap about Lol giving Mum the black eye.

'Jane?'

She looked into Eirion's worried eyes, and picked up what they were saying: If you drop that thing now, we've lost it...

... Whatever it is.

She carried the big computer across the room to the nearest table to the door and let it down slowly, keeping her hands on the base in case she had to snatch it up again. This was a relief, frankly, but it was Fyneham who nearly sobbed.

'All right, let's go right back to the beginning, JD,' Eirion said.

Bliss said there were some small factories, not much more than workshops, on the edge of the Barnchurch industrial estate. Not the halfway respectable part, where the shops and warehouses were, but at the rough end, where it joined the Plascarreg.

Only one of these had ever been let. A light-engineering plant there had gone bust fairly soon, but a 'small business syndicate' on the Plascarreg had paid the tenants to pretend otherwise and sublet part of their unit for the preparation and distribution of crack cocaine and other commodities.

It was a relatively foolproof arrangement, and nobody had ever disturbed this enterprise until Robbie Walsh discovered that the site to the rear of the workshop was of archaeological importance, being a one-time place of execution.

Such was Robbie's enthusiasm for first-hand knowledge of the past that he was disinclined to take 'Piss off, son, and forget all this exists' as a useful piece of advice. And so particular youngsters on the estate were encouraged to take an interest in Robbie and his leisure pursuits, to the extent of borrowing some of his books.

'What did they do to him?' Lol asked eventually, wanting to get this over with.

'Each of the workshops has a storage shed at the rear,' Bliss said. 'Wood shed, traditional design with exposed cross-beam.'

Bliss stared into his glass of Gomer Parry's cloudy home-made cider, the colour of rust and border clay. Threw down names that Lol had never heard before: Jason Mebus, Connor Boyd, Shane Nicklin.

'The first time they hanged him,' Bliss said, 'they cut him down fairly quickly.'

39

Raw Madness

THE BACKSTAIRS WERE a dim half-spiral, coldly lit by one vertical slit too high to see through. Merrily was half-expecting the kitchen below to have a greasy spit and dead meat hanging from hooks, but it wasn't like that.

'Good morning again,' the woman said.

The kitchen was warm and glazed with light tinted orange and emerald from illuminated glass in Gothic tracery around the tops of two long, thin windows. Pale ash units with olive-tiled work surfaces were built around a double-oven Aga. A rack of oak shelves displayed an apothecary's collection of coloured jars and stoppered bottles.

'Bell asked me to take care of you.' The woman, who hadn't yet introduced herself, had tufted brown hair, wore a white-and-grey-checked suit, no jewellery. 'If not quite, I have to say, in those words.'

Coffee was percolating, and she was making wholemeal toast.

'Have a seat, Mrs Watkins.'

Oh.

Merrily said nothing. A stone trough of red and orange tulips sent up a warm glow from below the twin windows, which opened up views across the fields to where the town rose in steep tiers to the church tower.

'It's rather late for breakfast,' the woman said, 'but I don't suppose you particularly feel like lunch.'

'Tea or coffee would be' – Merrily had noticed that the tulips were in fact growing out of a stone coffin, its interior shaped for a body – 'fine.'

Life directly out of death. Symbolism everywhere.

The woman wrinkled her nose, tapped the coffin with a shoe. 'I'm still trying to persuade her to put that morbid artefact outside. Having already bribed the plumber to say there was no way it was going to work as a kitchen sink.'

No way she'd have it outside, either. Bell must have been cosying up to death since her teens.

'She must be a... challenging person to accommodate,' Merrily said.

'Actually we accommodate each other fairly well. I call in most days, on the way to or from the office, or for lunch. Organize all the maintenance people and the services and the cleaner and the gardener and everyone else she's far too vague to deal with. Do grab yourself a seat.'

There was a round table, with wooden chairs reflecting the design of seventeenth-century Glastonbury church chairs, with stubby X-legs. Merrily slid one out and sat down cautiously.

'I think we spoke on the phone.'

'Briefly.' Susannah Pepper put the tray of coffee and toast in the centre of the table and sat down opposite her and smiled.

Ominous. A friendly, relaxed lawyer was rarely a good omen. 'Where's Bell?'

'I don't know.' Susannah looked Merrily in the eyes. She was about thirty, and she seemed fit and confident and capable. Her skin was softly furry, like a peach's. 'I persuaded her to go out and let me handle things. She's awfully disappointed in you. Feels betrayed.'

Silence. The sun had come out, setting fire to the orange glass in the tracery at the top of the windows, and the tulips in the stone coffin reached up like small goblets waiting to be filled.

'All right,' Merrily said at last. 'I'm going to have to ask, aren't I? How did you know who I was?'

Susannah stood up and went out of the room and came back

with a leather briefcase, extracting a folded newspaper and tossing it on the table.

'This morning's edition.'

Merrily opened the paper and stared down, growing cold with dismay, at two pictures, one of the Hanging Tower, the other of herself, in colour, full face, under the headline:

EXORCIZE OUR CASTLE OF DEATH
Evil ghost must go, say townsfolk

She looked up. 'This is crap.'

'I think you should read it.'

She read it. It was overdramatized and dumbed-down. It was crass. It was full of conjecture. But at the centre of it...

The Mayor of Ludlow, George Lackland, confirmed last night that he had discussed the issue with Hereford exorcist, the Rev. Merrily Watkins.

'It's very much a matter for the Church,' he said. 'Whether you believe in ghosts or not, there's no doubt in my mind that a religious service, or an exorcism, would make many people feel more at peace.

'It's been suggested that these tragic deaths have brought tourists into the town, but to my mind notoriety of this kind is no good for anyone in the long run.'

'OK. It's not crap. Not entirely.'

'Thank you.'

'It's misleading, but it's come from an actual petition sent to George Lackland. Someone obviously sent a copy to the press. But nobody's spoken to me about it. I mean, one reason I'm here is to try and avoid anything drastic or...'

'Laughable,' Susannah said. 'Holy water and incantations. Or am I misrepresenting your occupation?'

'Don't know where this picture came from, either,' Merrily said. 'Looks like an old one... couple of years old, anyway.'

She was outside Ledwardine church, and she was in the full kit. It looked like an official picture from the diocese. She didn't remember it being taken.

And now Bell Pepper had evidently seen it. Bell, who disliked the clergy, had learned that she was not only a minister but a working exorcist, and she wasn't called Mary. Everything was now entirely clear, and the situation couldn't be worse.

'Would you mind if I had a cigarette?'

'Yes, I would,' Susannah said. 'Cigarettes are disgusting. And let's drop the bullshit, shall we? Why are you associating my client with what you've come here to do? Bearing in mind, before you answer, that I've talked to George Lackland.'

'In which case you'll be aware that it was George Lackland who approached us – the diocese.'

'George is an old-fashioned man,' Susannah said. 'He still thinks the Church should have a role in the way this town is run, and he seems to have fallen for the myth that the deaths of two children and one old woman are manifestations of some kind of spiritual malaise.'

'And is he entirely wrong there?'

'He's in danger of becoming a laughing stock.'

'Well...' Now that George had dropped her in it, there seemed little point in dressing this up. 'A lot of people saw Bell with Robbie Walsh in the days before he died. A woman famously obsessed with death. Last night, she told me she'd been taking steps to adopt him, which would explain quite a lot. Can you confirm that?'

'I don't have to confirm anything to you,' Susannah said. 'Your ridiculous role with a failing religion gives you no right, legal or moral, to probe into people's private lives.'

'Up to you, Susannah, but adoption at least offers a plausible explanation for—'

'All right, yes.' Susannah leaned back and opened her jacket. 'It was already in progress. It was to have been a substantial settlement, and the mother was practically biting our hands off. Kept ringing me up, just to make sure we weren't going off the idea.'

'Figures.' Merrily thought of all the things Mumford had said about his sister: the extreme bitterness towards their own mother after the boy died. Big money, maybe life-changing money, had just gone down the pan.

'He'd have moved in here,' Susannah said, 'and gone to school in Ludlow. And his gran – of whom he was fond but who was becoming unfit to look after him – would have seen far more of him than she already did. I don't claim to have fully fathomed out the relationship between Bell and the boy. But they certainly had shared interests which he seems to have been unable to pursue at home.'

'And perhaps she needed an heir? Of sorts. Would that be...?'

'You mean for the New Palmers' Guild Trust?'

'What exactly is that?'

'No big secret. The Trust, into which most of Bell's assets will pass when she dies, will support, in perpetuity, specific historic features of the town.'

Merrily nodded. 'Like the maintenance of the St Leonard's cemetery as a wilderness with corpses?'

'Be assured that I and my successors will administer the Trust entirely according to my client's wishes.'

'And the conservation of certain yew trees? Preservation of public rights of way connecting sacred places? And perhaps keeping particular viewpoints open, in the face of possible future development?'

'The specific details have yet to be sorted out. And you still haven't explained what you're doing here.'

'I'm getting to it,' Merrily said. 'But I'm trying to find out how much you know and how much you understand about Bell's other plans for when she dies.'

'Don't know what you mean.'

'Don't you? I mean, you really don't?'

'Perhaps you should spell it out.'

'I'm wary,' Merrily said. 'I think I'd rather be speaking to her stepdaughter than her lawyer. I mean, what does your father say about all this?'

'Dad? Dad says be kind to her, never exploit her – and keep me the hell out of it.' Susannah's eyes narrowed. 'What do you know about my dad?'

'Music producer… bewitched by Bell's obvious charms… maybe liked unusual music, but couldn't handle the extreme lifestyle which, in her case, went with it.'

'He lives in Sacramento now, has three children, plays golf.'

'Your mother was his first wife?'

'Whom he left for Bell, but that's all well in the past. My mother's second husband, if you want the full nepotism bit, is David Sebald, brother of Peter Sebald, one of the original partners in the firm I'm working for.'

'But you and Bell—'

'Never got on all that well with David's other kids, so I used to spend quite a few weekends with Dad and Bell. Who was so completely out of it most of the time that I sometimes felt, at the age of about fifteen, like her step*mother*. Like I said, we've always accommodated each other. I'm not judgemental.'

'Mmm.' Bringing Smith, Sebald one of their wealthiest private clients would have done Susannah no harm at all with the firm.

'That's to say, where no criminal law or local statutes are infringed, I don't question her behaviour,' Susannah said. 'This town's full of eccentrics.'

'You must be worried about her, though.'

'Put it this way, my private life would have been a whole lot easier if the firm had been based in Birmingham.'

'Because then Bell would have come to visit and gone home the next day. But this being where it is, she doesn't want to leave. Not ever, in fact. Do you know what I'm saying?'

Through the long window, the town glittered on its hill, the sun gilding the pinnacles on the church tower and coating what you could see of the castle walls with crusted honey. No motor vehicles visible. A living dream of Olde Englande.

'That's pretty ridiculous.' Susannah finally looked unnerved.

'You must realize that.'

'If I started dismissing ideas that seemed ridiculous, I wouldn't get very far in this job.'

'Then it's a ridiculous job.'

'It's apparently been estimated,' Merrily said, 'that one in three people has had a paranormal experience, and one in ten has seen a ghost. It all makes perfect sense to Bell.'

'You're saying she's become completely insane?'

'No, I don't think she— OK, it's not good, it's not healthy, it's spiritually… a bit squalid, frankly. But it's not insane. In fact, it's all been worked out very practically.'

'I'm sorry.' Susannah backed away, folding her arms. 'But if there was any truth in what you've just outlined, she'd… in my view, she'd be guaranteed certifiable.'

'Then how do you explain it? How do you explain her nocturnal perambulations?'

'She's a night person. In every sense – her albums are dark and doomy, she likes to mix with goths and weirdos and she's a bloody exhibitionist.'

'An exhibitionist who wants to protect her private life and won't talk to the media, except the local media?'

'That's not so unusual. It's part of the star-mentality. They like to have it both ways.'

'Look,' Merrily said. 'She's led what she calls a temporary kind of life. She says she was diagnosed at an early age with a congenital heart defect and she's lived her whole life with the angel of death standing outside the door, sharpening his scythe. I don't know if that's true or not—'

'I'd like to get her to a heart specialist, but she won't. She has a fear of dying in hospital.'

'Or anywhere but here. She's moved from place to place – she's had the money to do that – and she can't settle anywhere. Until she arrives in the place of her dreams. Literally. All right, whether she *had* been dreaming about Ludlow for years is anybody's guess, but she's convinced herself she had. And she comes here and she connects. It's a town where you can walk from century to century, and it's not been over-cosmeticized. It's as it was. And for Bell the atmosphere everywhere is dense with… eternity.'

'Oh, for heaven's sake, it's pretty and it's a good place to work. I can understand her falling in love with it.'

'For Bell, those streets up there sing. Especially at dead of night, when she's on her own. They sing, she sings…'

'Oh, please—'

'OK, you don't get it, you don't feel the density. That's fine.'

'Well, hey, I'm sorry.' Susannah threw up her arms. 'I'm sorry I'm not a bloody airy-fairy artist, merely a humble solicitor. We just grease the wheels that keep the world turning, and I'm really sorry but we don't have time to drift off into the ether. Unlike poets. And priests, apparently.'

'I'm not saying I can feel it on that level, or anywhere near.'

'She walks around at night in unorthodox clothing and she sings sometimes. Wow.'

'She's feeding herself into the fabric of the town. I realize this is bollocks to you, but to her it's everything and she doesn't know how much time she has left, and when that time's up she wants to…'

'… To be a ghost?'

'To be a ghost *here*. Catherine of Aragon, Prince Arthur, Marion de la Bruyère… Belladonna.'

Susannah snorted and turned away. Saul Pepper's regular daughter, with a solid job and no weird, music-business links.

'Did you bring this paper in here this morning?' Merrily said. 'I mean, you actually showed this to her?'

'It's all over town. Someone would have told her, sooner or later.'

'And what exactly did she say?'

Susannah turned round. 'She became… distressed. She told me you were in the house, upstairs. That she'd invited you into her house, and you were betraying her. I told her to let me handle it. I didn't want her wailing and screaming at you, like one of her albums. I told her I'd get rid of you, make sure you never bothered her again.'

'And how would you have done that? Some kind of injunction?'

'I'd've had you restrained. Gone to a higher authority.'

Merrily put her head on one side. 'God?'

'Don't be stupid. After I spoke to you the other morning, I wasn't satisfied that you'd taken any notice.'

'Damn right.'

'So I spoke to some other people in the Church, and I was referred to your superior, the... Director of Deliverance?'

'What?'

'Canon Clarke? I've got it written down at the office.'

It felt as though the room shook.

'She told me that you'd now virtually resigned from your official position,' Susannah said, 'because of personal problems. She said you were overstressed. She said if I had any more trouble I should contact her immediately.'

'I see.'

'She said we could deal with it between us. I hadn't realized she was a barrister.'

'That must've been a comfort to you.'

'If you want the truth,' Susannah said, 'I had the feeling of some personal friction, and that's why I decided to talk to you myself. And now I'm wishing I hadn't.'

'OK...' Merrily took a breath. 'I want to get something right. Did Bell actually use the word "betrayal"? About me.'

'She said you'd won her trust and entered her fortress by deceit and you'd betrayed her in the worst way possible. She... she lost it for a while. I was glad to get her out of the house.'

'How long ago?'

'Hour or so? Hour and a half?'

'Any idea at all where she's gone?'

Susannah shook her head. 'She just put on her long coat and walked away, and then, a minute or two later, she just, you know, screamed. Just once. She's always been a screamer, hasn't she?'

'You mean you took no notice.'

'I went to the window. There was no sign of her.'

'Well, I think I have to find her, don't I?' Merrily said.

'Don't you ever give up?'

'No, look, tell me if I'm wrong here. Robbie's death – the way it happened, and where it happened – took something out of Bell's life that I don't think she'll ever get back. Now she thinks we're about to try and take something else away. Doesn't she?'

'I just can't believe any of that.' Susannah moved away across the flags, a trickle of sweat gleaming on her forehead. 'It's not rational… even for her.'

'It's *very* rational – for her. And now she thinks the town's turned against her. Did she tell you she was attacked last night? Did you see her face?'

'She said she tripped.' Susannah stood with her back to the window, her mouth half open, her control slipping away fast. 'Tripped, coming down The Linney.'

'But now, worst of all, the town's conspiring with the Church to have Marion exorcized. Marion. And all she represents.'

You'll lie like carrion… I'll fly like Marion.

'Look, that petition's virtually a fake!' Susannah shouted.

'I'm sorry?'

'Most people here couldn't care less about all this nonsense. Yes, there were petition forms in a few shops, but hardly anybody signed. It's George, can't you see that? My bloody soon-to-be father-in-law, God help me. George is behind it.'

'Why would—?'

'Ask him. You go and ask the old bastard.'

On the way back to the road – mid-afternoon, now – Merrily stopped to look back at The Weir House, a shambling timbered and stone farmhouse, born again. Trees on two sides were thickening into spring, and the grass was getting longer, and either she could hear the river or the hissing was in her head.

She walked across to the yew tree, where the paths converged, the hollow yew growing anew around its own exposed entrails, wondering if she'd dreamed last night that there was a door in it, like in a fairy tale – Bell stowing something in there, the mandolin in its case. Was this the same mandolin that had appeared on the cover of *Nightshades*? If so, what was its significance? She couldn't play it, she probably couldn't play any instrument. And anyway…

… There was no door, only a black and gaping hole, as if the tree had been shot with a cannon ball. Merrily paused, glanced over her shoulder and then stepped over the roots and into the tree, the ripe and resinous yew scent all around her.

The door was here. It was in the tree, loose, separated.

She edged it out. It was the real thing, beautifully shaped to fit the elliptical hole in the tree into which a solid frame had been moulded. The door looked like oak and had strong cast-iron hinges, one hanging off.

The key, presumably, was kept hidden somewhere in the tangle of tree. But there was no need for it, because the door had been brutally removed; you could see the marks left by the crowbar or whatever had been used to wrench it off.

Merrily went back into the hole, and kicked something with her trainer. Picked it up and brought it out: a prayer book. No need to look inside to know this was going to be the one that George Lackland said had been taken from St Laurence's.

Someone had forced an entry, and Bell must have discovered it when she left.

She just, you know, screamed. Just once.

Merrily went back in, further this time, pushing up her sleeves. Seemed there was room to fit a couple of people in here at least. Her fingers found something regular and rigid and jutting out at about chest height: a ledge, a shelf. She felt around on top of it and drew back with a shudder – something slick and slippery like fat on bone.

Right. She brought out the Zippo.

The fatty item was a candle. Two of them on the wooden ledge; she lit one and watched the ancient organism becoming a brackish grotto around her, parts of its walls hanging like fragments of a rotting rood-screen, other segments moist and alive like hard flesh.

The candle flame was reflected in several small jars with stoppers, like the ones on the apothecary shelves in the kitchen, only clear. One had what looked like water in it, with some sediment at the bottom. Others contained sandy soil, crumbled dead leaves and what looked like chips of stone. Two bigger jars held coils of hair, yellow and white, and there was a small one with what seemed to be thin wood-shavings, but were probably nail clippings.

No mandolin case.

Just, you know, screamed…

'What are you doing?'

Merrily came out of the tree. Susannah Pepper stood in the grass, her business suit vainly buttoned against the raw madness in the air.

'You knew about this, Susannah?'

'I thought you were going to look for her.'

'Somebody broke into the tree. That would be why she screamed.'

'It cost her a fortune. She had this guy who does wood sculptures up from Herefordshire. She told him she was going to make it into a summer house.'

'Not exactly. Do you know what she kept in there?'

'Private things. That was the point. We weren't supposed to know.'

'Good an excuse as any,' Merrily said. 'I was once married to a lawyer. The thing he used to say that I was most uneasy about was, "You can sleep better if you know when to stop asking questions." There's one thing missing from here.'

'I don't—'

'The mandolin case she put in here last night?'

'I don't know anything about that. I think I've seen it, obviously…'

'She play the mandolin often, Susannah? She play anything?'

'She plays games,' Susannah said.

Mumford

WAITED ON THE spare land round by the old Greyhound Dog pub, and he was wearing the new clothes he'd bought at Millet's – sort of clothes he'd never worn in his life before, jogger's clothes. Felt real strange, too loose. Like he was naked.

Also had on Robbie's baseball cap, the one that was always far too big on the boy, made him look dafter than he'd known. Mabbe there was another reason Mumford was wearing that cap, but he didn't want to think about that.

Thing was, nobody was looking at him. Half his life, folks had seen him coming – *looked like a copper the way a sheep looked like a sheep* – and now, feeling more conspicuous than at any time since his first day in uniform thirty years ago, he was aware of folks passing by and nobody noticing him. And he realized the so-called plain clothes he'd been wearing for work all those years weren't plain clothes at all these days, they were obvious copper's clothes.

Stayed at the Green Dragon last night, biggest hotel in Hereford, therefore the most anonymous. Money no object. Emerging this morning in his jogging kit: dumpy, middle-aged, bastard, casual civilian.

And even Jason Mebus never noticed him.

After he'd come out the pub, round about half-one, Jason had been straight down the chip shop, the Fries Tuck, and he was walking up now, over Greyfriars Bridge, loping along,

403

eating his chips and still making faster progress than the two lines of cars queuing up to get into town. Saturday-afternoon shoppers. It was all queues in Hereford now – more useless chain stores and still no bypass on the schedules. Be gridlocked soon, this city.

Mabbe Jason was meeting somebody in town – a girl or one of his scumbag mates. Mumford let him get close enough to the end of the bridge and then he started jogging.

Smiling at himself. This was what retired bastards did, to stay alive. All looking like Mumford in his tracksuit top and his pale blue trousers with elasticized bottoms, and his trainers.

Nobody else even walking this side of the bridge. He could see the traffic lights up ahead now, the vehicles nose-to-tail. Over the wall on his left was the River Wye where there used to be a restaurant. All this kind of recreation happening across the road now at Left Bank Village, so it was lucky Jason wasn't heading towards town on that side. No chance there; far too crowded.

Thirty yards behind Jason now, and the sound of his trainers was muffled by the growling traffic. Had his baseball cap pulled down over his eyes, looking down at the footpath, and just as well; with fifteen or twenty yards to go, Jason heard him and glanced over his shoulder and then back into his chips – just some sad ole jogger.

What Mumford did next was start smiling. Beaming all over his face. It didn't come easy, never had, but he did it. Dumpy, middle-aged, genial, smiling bastard civilian.

Drawing level with Jason now, puffing a bit and slowing up as the traffic lights turned fortuitously to green, all the drivers' attention fixed on getting through.

And Jason, stuffing a chip in his gob, never seen it coming.

Soon as the boy's hand was back in the chip bag, Mumford's shoulder connected with the muscle near the top of his arm, the bag flying up in the air.

'Oh, sorry, mate! Sorry!'

'You fuckin' clumsy—'

'Let me help you, boy,' Mumford said and, with his back to the traffic, smacked Jason in the mouth, not too hard but hard enough.

The boy was still choking on the chip while Mumford was propelling him down the street to the left and across the car park, back towards the underside of the bridge. Figuring that under the bridge was best. Be nobody about on this side. Nice bit of dereliction, fair bit of cover.

Plenty of time, plenty of river. And he had the bastard who, one way or another, had murdered Robbie Walsh.

40

Heavier Than You Know

'LEDWARDINE VICARAGE,' LOL said.

'Is the vicar there?' Woman's voice, local accent.

Lol said the vicar was out and asked if he could take a message.

He was unhappy. He'd answered two calls so far from parishioners, both of whom seemed to have recognized his voice, neither of whom had wanted to discuss the nature of their business with him. The tones suggesting that they thought the vicar was not out at all but was perhaps upstairs, sobbing into her pillow, aching from dozens of bruises in places where they wouldn't show.

'When will she be back? I mean, can you contact her? Has she got a mobile?'

'No, she hasn't. Not at the moment. I can't contact her, I'm afraid.'

Lol heard a door opening behind him. Jane came into the scullery, looking flushed, followed by Eirion.

'Damn,' the woman said. 'Look, if she comes in, can you get her to ring me. Like, just me, OK? Anybody else answers, don't talk to them. Can you tell her that? My name's Karen Dowell. Tell her I'm Andy Mumford's... something or other, relation. She'll know.'

'Oh. You're calling from police headquarters.'

Pause. 'Who are you, exactly?' Karen Dowell said.

'My name's Lol Robinson. I'm a... friend.'

Jane was making handle-turning motions at him, to wind this up. He tucked the phone between his shoulder and his cheek and raised both hands at her.

'OK,' Karen Dowell said, 'I know who you are. Mr Robinson, have you heard from Andy?'

'No, but I've had Bliss here.'

'I know that. He said he was going to talk to the vicar. They all seem to trust the vicar.'

'He talked to me instead.'

'Where exactly is Mrs Watkins?'

'She's in Ludlow.'

'Damn,' Karen said. 'Listen, can I really trust—'

'Yes, you can.'

'Not a word to Bliss, not to anybody, apart from the vicar and Andy, if he calls.'

'I understand,' Lol said.

'Don't even make notes, you only need the sense of this.'

'OK.'

'I've been doing PNC checks for Andy – police computer, yeah?'

'Right.'

'And following stuff up. I'm good with computers, it's my thing. Checked out a number of people connected with the Plascarreg, which you don't need to know about. The one you do need to know about is Jonathan Swift.'

'The writer?'

'It's a guy in Ludlow who Andy asked me to check a few days ago. He calls himself something else there, but this is the name in which his car's registered. He hasn't got a record, but I'm always suspicious when there's a name change involved, so I made a few calls. We had a previous address for him in Cheshire, near Stockport, so I belled a bloke I was at the police college with, works at Greater Manchester Police. Keeping it off the record. And he put me onto another guy, OK? I'm stressing again that this is unofficial, Mr Robinson, and only for (a)

408

Andy, (b) the vicar, right? My neck's gonner be on the block here.'

'Is this a man called Jonathan Scole?'

'That's correct. His real name's Swift, and the crux of it is his parents were shot dead. Both of them. They... you there, Mr Robinson?'

'Yes.'

'You on your own?'

Lol caught Jane's eye, pointed at the door. 'Yes.'

'All right: Swift's parents ran a transport caff – greasy spoon, yeah? They were shot as they were leaving at closing time, just before midnight. Takings stolen. I remember this one, actually, although no reason you would. Major police hunt, but nobody ever caught. Very efficient. Head shots with a handgun. Well, no shortage of them in the Manchester area these days.'

'Recently?' Lol nodded as Jane shrugged and slipped out, with Eirion.

'Last year. I've got the date somewhere, but that don't matter. Bit of a puzzler, though, because the takings came to just over three hundred. Peanuts, in other words. Two people shot dead at close range, for three hundred? Even in Manchester, you don't get that. It was on *Crimewatch* and they got zilch from the public. It was all very carefully planned, and kids after money for drugs aren't that careful, take my word.'

'And so... what's the significance?'

'Contract killing,' Karen said. 'That's the whisper. That's the unspoken. Not a shred of evidence, mind.'

'The parents were, like, underworld figures?'

'Good God, no, they were respectable people who worked day and night and didn't even have any points on their driving licences. Contract killing en't what it used to be, Mr Robinson. Too many guns about now, and too many evil little buggers who'll do it for a thousand or less.'

'So this guy in Ludlow changed his name... because his parents were murdered?'

'He changed his name, originally, on police advice, because people started pointing the finger. Collected a lot of money, see – sale of a house, sale of a café to a national chain looking for a site. Now, he was personally in the clear – away on a business-studies course. Full alibi. But, as I say, neighbours and friends of Mr and Mrs Swift were whispering about terrible domestic rows. Had a temper on him, see. Not a happy family.'

'Look,' Lol said, feeling his chest going tight, 'can you spell this out? What are we worrying about, in particular? I don't know this guy, but I think Merrily does.'

'Well, Mr Robinson, I don't know, do I? I'm just passing on what I've discovered. It might be something or nothing. But I'd feel real bad if I hadn't passed it on and then something happened. Which is why I'm telling you now rather than wait till Andy shows up. And that's another problem, ennit?'

'If I'm allowed to write your number down,' Lol said, 'I'll call you back if I hear from Andy.'

'That would be very good of you, long as you remember—'

'Don't talk to anyone else, if you're not there.'

'That's exactly right,' Karen said.

Jane didn't even ask who he'd been talking to. She pressed him into a chair in the kitchen, knelt down facing him, gripping the chair arms.

'Lol, listen… just listen, and then answer the questions. When Jack Fine from Q magazine came, what exactly—?'

'Jane, we need to swap over.' Lol pushed himself up, patting his jeans to make sure he had his car keys. 'You need to stay here, and I have to go over to Ludlow.'

'Huh? Mum is OK, isn't she?'

'I'm sure she's fine. Just some things I need to tell her.'

'What things?'

Jane's eyes were concentrated and glittering with so much awareness it was scary. Age of transition: old enough to drive, almost old enough to vote for a new government and get drunk in pubs with the state's blessing. Old enough to have no more adult so-called secrets being whispered behind your back.

But telling her about her mother and a man who the police didn't like because his parents had been shot dead... and about the kids on the Plascarreg who'd shown Robbie Walsh what it was like to be hanged... how could any of this really help?

'You're feeling sidelined, aren't you? Out of it,' Jane said. 'She never thinks about that.'

'She doesn't have time.'

'You make too many excuses for her. Sometimes she needs to put her own relationship first. Yeah, OK, do it. You go, we'll stay. But first, we need to ask you some things.'

'It's called The Weir House, right, and it's down below the castle, near the river?'

'She might not even be there now. Lol—'

'It's a small town, I'll find her.'

'Lol, you can spare, like, ten... OK, five... five minutes? You do want to know who set you up, don't you? The anonymous notes?'

'It was a little kid. I've just—'

'It was a big kid, actually.'

'Lol,' Eirion said, 'she's right, for once. This is heavier than you know. For starters, Jack Fine's not from *Q* magazine, he's this bastard I go to school with, and he was here purely to get information out of you. I don't want to hold you up or anything, but basically Jane recognized him and this morning we went to his dad's house to face him up.'

'His dad publishes magazines,' Jane said. 'He used to be a national-paper journalist, and now he publishes all kinds of trade and, like, professional magazines and junk like that. He also tips off the papers on stories, and the son, J.D. Fyneham – Jack Fine – his personal weekend job is on much the same lines. He's got all this desktop publishing kit, and he does this church-magazine scam, and he's open for commissions and it seems to me he's not fussy where they come from.'

'We got so far with him,' Eirion said, 'and then it became clear there were people he was more intimidated by than, like, Jane.'

'What, you mean he edits the Yardies' international news-letter?' Lol stood up. 'Look, guys, I'm sure this is significant stuff I'll really want to know about... tonight?'

'Just tell us what questions Fyneham asked you,' Eirion said. 'And then you can go, and we'll stop here by the phone.'

'Well, he... he did try to find out about Merrily and me. I suspect he'd heard something, but I headed him off. I said I wasn't in any particular relationship at present.'

'Oh, we know he'd heard something,' Eirion said. 'In fact, any day now you could open the *Sun* and find, like, "Villagers have been shocked by the violent love-affair between their woman vicar and a rock singer with a conviction for a sex offence." Well, more guarded than that, obviously...'

'He's not kidding, Lol,' Jane said, watching his eyes.

'Jane, I didn't tell him anything.'

'Well, somebody did. Either he's been sniffing around the village in his spare time, or somebody's been feeding him sick gossip.'

'All right.' Lol told them about Gomer Parry and the small boy and the ten quid. 'You're actually saying this guy was behind that?'

'We don't know, to be honest,' Jane said. 'We think he's got to be. But who's behind him? What else did he ask you about?'

'He went into the court case and what led up to it and the loony-bin years, all that. He knew about it already, and I just made sure he got it right. Told him it really wasn't much of a story any more.'

'Hmm,' Jane said.

'And the rest was mainly about the music. Was I putting all my bad experiences into songs, like "Heavy Medication Day"? Which was fair enough. He said it sounded like this Dr Gascoigne had done some unpleasant things to me. He was trying to find out what they were. I didn't tell him.'

'Anything else?'

'I don't think so. If I think of anything else, I'll call you on the mobile.'

'Well, leave it switched on,' Jane said.

'OK.' Lol paused in the doorway. 'So Jack Fine really wasn't doing an actual interview for *Q*? Or anything?'

'I'm sorry.'

'OK,' Lol said.

He walked across to the square to collect his Astra, a nobody again. Thinking that it was always harder for a nobody to defend himself, his loved ones, his reputation.

When Lol had gone, Jane switched on the computer, thinking how wise it had been of her to persuade Mum to have an extra phone line installed.

'Where do we start?'

Eirion raised his eyes to the ceiling. Meaning Jane's attic apartment where, last summer, she'd lost her virginity to him – not realizing that, despite all his man-of-the-world crap, he was simultaneously losing his to her. Never quite forgiven him for that.

'Out of the question,' Jane said.

'I didn't say anything.'

'The way you were sitting said it all.' Jane clicked into Internet Explorer. 'What are we looking for? Like, has Lol really told us anything we didn't already know?'

It had become interesting when Fyneham had admitted that the new Evesham computer Jane had been threatening with extinction had been bought for him in return for helping one of his dad's... hard to say if it was a friend or just a client. But the guy had wanted to know about Merrily and Lol, particularly Lol, which was bizarre.

What he'd wanted to know, basically, as Jane had understood it, was like, well... dirt. Anything damaging. Lol and Mum? Someone wanted to damage Lol and Mum?

Just then, unfortunately, Fyneham's dad's Alfa had pulled up outside. Back-up. So Fyneham had become braver. Presumably the old man was as bent as his son. So JD had gone back on his story, claiming he'd been, like, just saying that about this guy, to wind them up.

Eirion pulled out a Parish Pump leaflet he'd picked up from a pile in the office suite. Jane at once snatched it and screwed it up.

'Parish *Pimp*, more like.'

'No!' Eirion grabbed it back, smoothed it out. 'I made some notes on this. Listed all the titles his dad publishes.'

'Does that help us?'

'Might do. *What Hereford Council Can Do for You*? Do we know any bent councillors your mum might have offended?'

'Most councillors wind up bent after a few years. What else is on the list? I forget.'

'*Microlite Monthly*? *DigiCam*!'

'Anorak rags.'

'I was saving the best one. *The Clinical Therapist*.'

'You reckon?'

'Google it,' Eirion said.

The Clinical Therapist. *Biannual digest of new developments in clinical psychiatry aimed primarily at hospital-based psychiatrists and allied practitioners. Est. 1999. Lord Shipston. DClinPsych, MSc.*

'Not many cartoons, then,' Eirion said.

'Lol once told me, in one of his more embittered moments, that the majority of shrinks rise to the top by having nothing at all to do with people but just writing papers for dismal publications like this. I mean, Lord Shipston? How many neurotics has he ever had on the couch? Let's go back and snatch Fyneham when he leaves the house.'

'We're supposed to be minding the phone. We'll just have to sit here and amuse ourselves.'

'Actually, Irene,' Jane said, 'I think I'm probably having a frigid day. Too much exposure to male greed, male dishonesty, immorality, hypocrisy – that kind of stuff.'

'Thanks.'

'Don't you put your bloody Huw Edwards chapel face on, you're no better. You told me you weren't a virgin. You totally spoiled my first experience. All the time I'm thinking, Oh no, I'm going to be such a disappointment compared with all the others.'

'What do you think *I* was feeling?'

'I remember exactly what you were feeling, I just didn't realize you'd never felt one before.'

The phone rang. Jane snatched it.

'She's still not back?'

'No, I'm sorry, Sophie.'

'I see.' Sophie still thought Jane should call her Mrs Hill. Too bad.

'What did you want, exactly?'

'I wanted to talk to her, Jane.'

'Sophie,' Jane said. 'How old will I have to be before you recognize me as someone of mature intelligence and perception?'

'In your case, Jane, although it's possible I may live long enough to change my mind—'

'Yeah, yeah... Look, can I sound you out about something, while you're on? Eirion and me, we've been talking to this guy who was set up to interview Lol, maybe to find stuff out about him and Mum.'

'Who's this?'

'Guy called J.D. Fyneham. His dad's a magazine publisher. Fyneham does this... have you come across this Parish Pump thing, offers to revamp parish magazines?'

'I have, actually,' Sophie said. 'Bryce Orford left some leaflets for me to hand out to—'

'Who's Bryce Orford?'

'The Dean. What's this about, again?'

'Somebody's trying to damage Lol and Mum, that's the bottom line. I mean, you must know that's happening.'

'Yes, I believe it is. I just hope this isn't one of your—'

'This is absolutely on the level, Sophie, I swear on... on the grave of Lucy Devenish. And I think you know something, don't you?'

Jane held her breath, watching Eirion's stony chapel face awaken into human interest.

'All right, tell me everything,' Sophie said.

Jane had relented and, about twenty minutes later, she and Eirion were into some mild petting on the rug by the desk when Sophie called back.

'That was, um, quick.'

'Jane, I'm in the office now, and it's very important that I talk to your mother.'

'Well, Lol's gone over to Ludlow now, and he's got a phone, so we expect to be in contact soon.'

'The best we can hope for, I suppose. Jane, you should know that I'm now treating you as a person of mature intelligence.'

'Right...' Jane had a hand under her top, repositioning her bra. She blushed. 'Thank you.'

'I've had to come into the office after a call from the Bishop. Something's happened, and the Bishop was in a quandary and, in the absence of Merrily, I'm afraid, he was forced to refer it to the Deliverance Panel. Telling me at the same time, of course, in the hope that the information would also reach Merrily.'

'She rang,' Jane remembered. 'The Callaghan-Clarke woman.'

'When?'

'This morning. She thought the media might be after Mum. I forgot. So much was... Do you know what that was about?'

'I think I do, but this is something else that's just developed. Merrily probably knows about it already, which is why she hasn't been in touch. Jane, I can hardly believe it.'

Sophie's tone indicating that she just had to talk to somebody or she'd go crazy.

'What's...?' Jane raised her eyebrows at Eirion, who was on his feet, face full of questions.

'It's the castle again,' Sophie said bleakly. 'Another child.'

PART FOUR

Sam

'If man does survive, does he produce ghosts? I think this could only be assumed if he retained his psyche-field.'

T. C. Lethbridge, Ghost and Divining Rod (1963)

'Rapping on the windows
And crying through the locks...'

Anon.

41

Big Bump

WHEN MERRILY CAME hurrying onto Castle Square, the whole space seemed to be vibrating – *duss, duss, duss* – to the dampened thud of some Saturday busker's bass drum, set up down by the deli.

Duss, duss, duss: the sound of an execution day.

She crossed the square and stood by the tourist office and looked around through the crowd.

Bell... where the hell are you?

The clarity had gone from the sky. Gauzy, mauvish clouds were smothering the sun, and there was no breeze to flutter the red and white pennants hanging between gables like a row of teeth set in bleeding gums.

She'd been down to the bottom of Corve Street to fetch the Volvo, a parking penalty under one of the wipers. Turned the key seven times, and it kept failing to start – another sign of mortality to join the ticking behind the dash, the rattle under the chassis, the grinding on corners. She'd still been shaking the wheel in frustration when she found that it had somehow started, two wheels crashing down from the kerb.

To charge up the battery or whatever, she'd driven through town, down by the side of the castle to the stooping community of Dinham with its twelfth-century chapel dedicated to murdered St Thomas, and then to the hissing River Teme – a vain search for the woman who wanted to fly like Marion. Back in the car park at the top of town, she'd paid for a full day, near enough, and then found a phone box to call Jane... engaged.

Single-lane vehicles were threading around the square, but the main traffic was people, scurrying about like figures in a Brueghel. So many clothes now – T-shirts, sweatshirts, fleeces and hooded tops – reflecting, in their myriad colours, the outerwear of Merrie Englande. And so many people talking to one another – a sense of community you seldom saw anywhere else.

Robbie Walsh would walk these streets in a state of near-ecstasy. *He was happier than any child I ever saw*. She felt she was inside Robbie again, seeing images of how things were, how they worked, the nuts and bolts of medieval life. Looking at now and feeling then, as if, in some mystical way, this might point her towards Bell.

'Mrs Watkins!'

A man was wading through the crowd towards her, a brown overall flapping around his knees like the uniforms of shopkeepers when she was a kid, his eyes glittering under the jutting shelf of his forehead. A prophet from a children's Bible.

Duss, duss, duss.

'Mr Mayor.'

'We told that boy to keep on playing.' The Mayor nodded towards the busker, who also had a guitar and a harmonica, but it was the drumbeat that carried, like plodding boots, across the square. 'Anything to make it seem like a normal Saturday.'

'You haven't seen Bell, have you?'

'I don't go looking for her, Mrs Watkins. Besides—'

'You'll have seen the papers, I suppose.'

'Now, look, there was nothing I could do about that. I've had three radio stations on already this morning – that's why I left the house. And now this. My God, Mrs Watkins, is there no end?'

'About the petition,' Merrily said. 'I think it's time you—'

'Aren't you going in?' He stared down at her.

'In where?'

'You only just got here, or what?'

420

'I… more or less, yes.'

'You mean you don't know about the girl?'

Before Merrily could ask him what he meant, George Lackland had taken her by the elbow and was steering her towards the castle gate. Where, for the first time, she noticed that nobody was going in, which probably accounted for the excess of people on the square. The big gates were open, as if to let vehicles in and out, but the way was blocked by police, two men and a woman, George striding over to address them.

'Where's Steve Britton?'

'Gone back in, Mr Lackland.'

'Only, I got Mrs Watkins here, from the Bishop's office.'

The male cop's expression said, So? Merrily saw that the gift shop, where visitors normally paid their entrance fees, was closed, unattended stands of booklets and postcards, pottery, tapestry, stationery all half-lit.

Again?

'Top-heavy with clergy already, you ask me,' the police-woman muttered. But George Lackland wasn't listening.

'Can we come in or not?'

The policeman thought about it, maybe remembering George's top-table seat on the West Mercia Police Committee, but then he shook his head.

'Can't, sir. Sorry. Can you wait for the sergeant?'

Merrily followed George Lackland back towards the big cannon and the pollarded trees outside the walls.

Again…?

'They got scaffolding up, see,' George said. 'On the inside of the Hanging Tower – idea being they're going to bar them windows, stop this happening once and for all.' His accent was broadening under stress. 'Fellers doing the work, they gets here 'bout half-nine, so obviously nobody could get up while they was there. Girl – teenager – must've known that, too, waits till they breaks for lunch, and then she's up the scaffolding like a monkey and well up on the ledge before anybody spots her.'

The square seemed to tilt like a giant board game.

'And she…' Merrily looked up. This close to the curtain wall, the only tower visible was the Keep, from which Robbie Walsh had fallen. 'The girl's still up there?'

'Far's I know, aye. They blocked off the footpath, back of the castle. Somebody told me she'd warned 'em if they brought the fire brigade with a ladder, she'd… well, she'd go off.'

'She's threatening to jump?'

'Oh aye. Oh, bloody hell, yes.'

'They know who she is?'

'I don't. They got this psychiatrist there now, reckons he's got it all worked out. Reckons she'll come down if they keeps it low-key. Police got all the visitors out, and there's an ambulance standing by.'

'This psychiatrist…'

'I dunno who he is, but what I reckon is, you should be in there.' George sank his hands into the pockets of his slacks, looking at the ground. 'It was me rang Bernard, see… I wanted him to come over. But he wouldn't.'

That was no surprise. Bishops didn't do hands-on. Certainly not in a situation this public, this critical. And who, apart from George and a handful of cranks, would think it was anything at all to do with the Church?

She looked at the crowded square with a new awareness, saw that most of the shoppers and the tourists knew exactly what was going on but were putting on an act of responsible British disinterest, not glancing at the castle walls at least until they were past the police. And the animated sense of community… that was simply locals and tourists united in veiled voyeurism.

The local kids were less circumspect, small gangs of them gathering, a boy of about eight dancing around the police-woman on the gate.

'Kelly, how will we know if she jumps, Kelly?'

'You'll hear a big bump – now go away.'

Same laconic policewoman who'd dealt with Bell after Phyllis Mumford drowned. The boy looked mildly shocked for a moment, then let out a cackle of laughter.

'Kids,' Merrily said. 'All heart.'

And thought, *Bell?*

Realizing then that she'd been aware, for some moments, of a familiar BMW sports car parked near the Castle Bookshop. She could see a notice in its window, guessed it would say Doctor on Call.

Well, of course. And she was in no position to say anything. While claiming she was on leave, she'd gone behind Saltash's back and, worse, Callaghan-Clarke's, and had had a meeting with George Lackland to discuss the possibility of an exorcism-of-place – must be true, it was in the papers, with a nice big incriminating picture. Merrily Watkins, Deliverance Consultant, had lied from the beginning.

And she couldn't, in her own defence, mention Bernie Dunmore's role in the deception because, after she fell, Bernie was likely to be the principal target. All she could do now to save him from an ignominious exit – and the diocese from the possibility of a disastrous successor – was to resign quietly. Take on the extra parishes and disappear.

Just around the corner at the end of the block, an elderly man in a hat and a woman in a pink Puffa jacket were standing outside the Assembly Rooms, a placard made of corrugated cardboard stretched between them, its message scrappily written in thick fibre-tip.

THE INNOCENTS ARE DYING. ONLY THE POWER OF GOD CAN STOP THIS NOW.

'Friends of yours, Mr Mayor?'

'I know them.'

'Mmm.'

'What you saying, Mrs Watkins?'

'Why did you want Bernie here, Mr Mayor?'

'You know why. Because, whatever he says, he believes there's something evil here.' George looked over Merrily's head, across the town. 'He's seen it, after all.'

Merrily watched a fire engine rumbling onto the square, no speed, no lights, no warbler. The emergency services apparently did not take their instructions from a disturbed teenager.

And here was the Mayor of Ludlow, still publicly hanging all this on an 800-year-old ghost rather than a living woman in a period shroud – an increasingly pitiable woman who, for some reason, he regarded as his Nemesis. Why?

'If you're a real friend of the Bishop's, George,' Merrily said, 'you won't mention that ten-quid bet ever again.'

Another policeman was approaching the castle gateway from the inside.

'Ah, here's Sergeant Britton,' George said. 'Let's see if we can get you in there.'

But she was uncertain. This was no time for a confrontation with Saltash.

And was it really a young girl up there, or…?

Do something, Lucy Devenish had told him. How many times had Lucy said that?

Lol drove due north, up the Welsh border, under an unsure sky in which clouds would gather and then fall away like discarded underwear. Spring was an unbalanced time, made him nervous. He didn't really know what to do, apart from act as some kind of messenger boy. All he was doing as he drove was thinking about Andy Mumford, without whom none of this – not least that perfidious eye-injury – would ever have happened.

Thinking about Mumford – not something that enough people seemed to have done over the years. What had this glum, anonymous man stirred up?

'Miserable Andy' was what Gomer Parry called him because he rarely smiled, never seemed to be particularly enjoying his work. Gomer must be twenty years older and still riding his JCB like he was part of some heavy-metal rodeo, but Gomer was self-employed and could retire if and when he wanted to, while Mumford had been forced into it and, like Dylan Thomas had advised, he wasn't going gentle. Retirement: maybe this was the most savage rite of passage.

Which made Lol think about himself and the received wisdom that said that if you hadn't made it in the music business by the time you reached thirty it wasn't going to happen, ever. So it probably wasn't going to happen. Was that worse than being like Belladonna, an international cult-figure at twenty and now some eerie *Sunset Boulevard* ghost?

As he was approaching the lights in the centre of Leominster, Lol's phone broke ironically into the first bars of 'Sunny Days', the nearest he'd ever come to an actual hit. He pulled off the road into the forecourt of the petrol station on the corner, eased up against some second-hand cars, all of them at least ten years younger than the Astra.

Jane said, 'You'd better pull over, Lol, what I have to tell you could cause an accident.'

'One moment.' He switched off the engine. 'OK.'

'Right,' Jane said. 'First off…'

First off, she told him, he'd be well advised to start looking for Mum in the general area of Ludlow Castle, where a girl was threatening suicide. Yes, another one, and it was no use asking who or why because this was all Sophie had known, therefore it was all Jane knew.

'Christ,' Lol said.

'OK, the second thing. You sure you're off the road?'

'Get on with it, Jane.'

'I'd like to claim total credit for this, but it was Sophie. I didn't think even Mum meant that much to Sophie – well, not in comparison with the cathedral. Just shows, doesn't it? So, like, Sophie talked to the Dean.'

'The Dean.'

'At the cathedral? The steely-eyed number-cruncher in charge of the cathedral? It's pretty clear Sophie's got some serious dirt on the Dean that she's been, like, saving up, and now it's really come good. I mean, circumstantial evidence more than anything else, but the Dean is the missing component that connects everybody.'

'I don't understand,' Lol said. 'What are we talking about?

This is about Mumford? Belladonna?'

The line seemed to fracture.

'... And we checked it on the Net and it's a bit of a gob-smacker.'

'Start again, Jane,' Lol said.

'Can't be done,' Steve Britton said. 'Sorry. Can't allow it. Tense as hell in there, George. That girl goes out the hole, there'll be an inquest on all of us.'

'The hole?' George said.

'Well... window. Jagged hole in the wall. She's up on this deep window ledge, and they can't reach her. She made us take away the scaffolding – leaned back, half out the window, said if we didn't take it away she'd... you know. Don't look that big a drop from below, but when you're up there...'

Steve Britton was probably in his forties, nearly as tall as George, with a scrubbed face and invisible eyebrows. He nodded at Merrily, across the castle gate.

'Friend of Andy Mumford's, right?'

'You seen him lately, Mr Britton?'

He laughed. 'I'm glad to say, no. Poor old boy.'

'Who's in with the girl?'

'Inspector Gee and Dr Saltash. I think you know him, too. My superior suggested he go in, seeing he was around. Also the woman minister. Canon...'

'Callaghan-Clarke.'

'That's it. Seems they been studying the situation,' Steve Britton said. 'It's not an easy one. It's not normal, this, is it?'

'Do you think you could tell them I'm here... and I might just be able to help?'

Steve Britton coughed. 'Like I say, a bit difficult in there just at the moment, Mrs Watkins. Perhaps if you could come back later?'

'I see.' Seemed clear he'd been told that if she turned up she definitely wasn't to be allowed in. She could imagine Saltash briefing Steve Britton, in confidence. *Not for me to try to influ-*

ence you, Sergeant, but a woman with a stress problem in a situation this volatile... would that be wise?

'Inspector Gee's also very much the right person for this,' Steve Britton said. 'You'll remember Sandy Gee, George – DC here, four, five years ago? Went back into uniform to take charge of family liaison in Shrewsbury. Plump person. Three kids, now. Needs somebody a bit mumsy, I reckon. Seems very young, this girl.'

'So it is a girl?' Merrily said. 'I mean, you've seen her yourself?'

'Who'd you think it was?' Steve Britton eyed her, curious.

'Do you know her name yet?'

Steve Britton pursed his lips.

George Lackland snorted. 'God's sake, Stephen, how long you known me, boy?' He turned to Merrily. 'People help each other in a small town. It's how things get done. How good connections get made.'

The Mayor turned back to Steve Britton and gave him a long, considering stare, as if their future relationship and all it might promise was on the line here.

'Samantha Cornwell,' Steve said. 'And it wasn't me told you.'

'Goes without saying, Stephen. Local?'

'Ledbury. Like the other one.'

Merrily blinked. 'That means she knew Jemmie Pegler?'

Steve Britton looked uneasy; he'd already said too much.

'Thank you, boy,' George said. 'It won't be forgotten.'

Merrily followed the Mayor back onto the square, everything reshaping.

She'd assembled a scenario in which Bell, betrayed, had fled to Marion's tower, all ghosts together, but it was wrong. Now the scene in her head was a corner table at the café in a mews across the car park from Hereford Police HQ. On the table, a computer printout, e-mail format:

if i emptied every packet and every bottle in there and swallowed the lot. well just be sick as a dog most likely. how

sad is that, sam. im not going out sad. im not. when i go
theyll fucking know ive gone.

Samantha Cornwell. Sam?

Over by the tourist office, she saw the eight-year-old boy who was waiting for the big bump. He was staying very close now to a woman pushing a pram, presumably his mother, and he was no longer laughing. Often the way with children, the bravado melting in the suddenly frightening heat of reality. The police-woman, Kelly, had known her psychology: just about the last thing this kid wanted to hear was a big bump that would resound in his room at bedtime.

Merrily, too, but what the hell could she do?

The sun bulged like a damaged eye behind purplish cloud. The couple known to George Lackland had shifted their card-board placard closer to the castle wall.

ONLY THE POWER OF GOD CAN STOP THIS NOW.

Tell that to Nigel Saltash.

Duss, duss, duss.

Mumford

JUST THE ONCE, after denying everything with his usual contempt and arrogance and bravado, Jason Mebus tried to leg it.

Choosing his moment perfectly, when Mumford – and it could happen to anybody, there was nothing you could do – let go this unstoppable sneeze.

Bringing his knee up into Mumford's crotch, not quite getting it right but enough to break free. Would have been well away, too, up the river bank, through the grounds of the derelict restaurant under the pines, if he hadn't stopped for the parting gesture, like he always did on the CCTV pictures.

Vicious sneer and a rigid finger up at the camera.

With what he thought was a safe distance between them, he turned round and did it at Mumford, who was on his knees in the dirt.

Mumford did nothing – made a point, in fact, of showing no pain and looking unimpressed, like he'd merely bent to pick up a coin. Which was when Jason started screaming that if he'd had his way, they'd have finished hanging Robbie Walsh. Finished off the job by the time the Collins kid had started crying and run out of the shed and gone to fetch his dipshit dad.

As it was, they'd cut the little gayboy down and they were out of there. Which was a shame, all the trouble they'd gone to, to fix it up like a suicide, even ripping the hanging page out of the history book so it could be left by the body, and then putting the book back in Walsh's school bag.

Jason telling him all this just in case Mumford thought he was dealing with an amateur. How it would've gone down as suicide, no problem 'cause everybody knew Walshie was having a bad time on the Plascarreg. But enough people would know what had really happened to make it crystal clear that there were certain individuals on this estate that you did not fuck with.

'Now that's a lie, ennit, Jason?' Mumford said, back on his feet, strolling nonchalantly towards the vermin. 'No way, see, that you'd leave a body in a shed next to a crack factory.'

'Nah, that was gonner be over, anyway,' Jason said. 'Couldn't trust that unit no more. He might've told somebody. Might even've told you, dad.'

Jason backing off the whole time, along the edge of the water. Knowing he was safe, with his long legs, from this overweight old bastard. Telling Mumford that if his fat face was ever seen on the Plascarreg again it was gonner get sliced off.

Bringing his hand down like a guillotine.

'Sliced off like a side of bacon, dad.'

And it was as he was saying these actual words, making the gesture, that he backed into an empty petrol can with one of his heels and turned round too quickly and lost his footing and nearly went in the river.

Thank you, boy.

Mumford – brain inflamed with the images of Robbie's suffering that Jason had so lovingly invoked, and moving pretty near as fast as when he was a promising athlete in his teens and early twenties – went to rescue the boy, at the same time taking him down with a sharp little knuckle-punch to the throat.

Jason retching pitifully, but all Mumford could hear was him saying, with his casual, hard-boy confidence, *We was only his very best mates, dad. We had some awesome laughs with Robbie.*

The last laugh being at the top of the Keep, at Ludlow Castle.

All added up. They wouldn't have known about the

significance, to Robbie, of the Hanging Tower. The Keep, with steps all the way to the top, was so much easier. What was also useful was that, instead of landing on the public footpath outside, for all to see, the body would drop privately into what they called the Outer Bailey, all locked up for the night.

Jason or, more likely, two of them – Jason and Chain-boy, say – would've hidden out somewhere in the castle with Robbie till the place was closed and then taken him up there, thrown him off, quietly vacated the premises, with all the time in the world. No, they weren't amateurs, these boys.

So why hadn't Robbie told anybody about the hanging?

Or had he? Could be Robbie had told Mathiesson. Mumford could hear the toe-rag laughing. Gotter be a man... stand up to 'em. Telling himself that Robbie had exaggerated the story. Not telling Angela anything.

Mumford drew back his foot as Jason tried to get up. Pity it was only a trainer.

Still, Jason was cowering away, his eyes alive with fear. Or mabbe it was the look on Mumford's face that did that – Mumford listening to his poor drowned mother.

And Robbie, he wants to show you all his favourite places in the town, don't you, Robbie? He's nodding, see. He's always saying, when's Uncle Andy coming?

Uncle Andy, who could easily have gone that very morning to the house opposite Tesco's and had a long and meaningful chat with Robbie, probably ending with a full statement and Robbie not having time to go to the castle that afternoon and therefore still being alive.

Had this not been the same Uncle Andy who just couldn't face the thought of his old man formally welcoming him to the wonderful world of retirement.

Another time, another place, Andy was going to weep.

And he wasn't stupid. Knew that what he was doing now was no substitute, was unlikely to make him feel any better.

But at least Uncle Andy was finally here for Robbie Walsh and all the other Robbie Walshes who would be hanged, cut, beaten by this scum who had every reason to think the useless, bureaucratic, CPS-constricted police service was never gonner touch him.

Mumford looked down at him.

'This river, Jason, the Wye. When I was a boy, much younger than you, folks used to say the River Wye demanded a sacrifice every year. Used to say the mothers was always scared to let their kids go anywhere near the water till somebody somewhere had been pulled out dead. You yeard that one?'

Jason said nothing. There was drool all over his mouth, and his eyes were wet. His famous jacket, with all the zips, had split under an arm.

'Some very old man was considered best,' Mumford said. 'Or a drunk. Or a tramp.'

Jason snuffled and rolled away from the water's edge.

'Or anybody that wouldn't be missed,' Mumford said, thinking how primitive and tribal this had been for the 1950s.

'But we was told we better be good kiddies else *we* might be the ones wouldn't be missed.'

A few minutes later, as he began a more formal interrogation of the suspect, the possibility that this would not end with Jason's death and disposal in the River Wye had dwindled to a minuscule point of light at the end of a very long tunnel already fogged with a suffocating rage against a world that had no further use for the imperturbable Detective Sergeant Mumford.

42

Like Heat

SHE LOOKED SO lonely when he found her, this small figure hunched up in the fleece with the torn pocket. She'd been trying to get it over to a policewoman on the castle gate that the girl in the castle was linked with the last one, Jemima Pegler, and the policewoman had looked at her like she was just another voyeur determined to get in on the action.

'Thank you,' the policewoman said coldly. 'They know.'

That was it, a blank snub: you are irrelevant to this, you're as useless as the people with the power-of-God placard. You are wasting my valuable time.

Go.

Nobody else wanted to talk to her. She said she'd been looking for Belladonna, but there was no sign of her either.

This was Merrily Watkins: any responsibility going spare, she'd accept it.

Lol virtually dragged her into the Assembly Rooms. There was a café upstairs, with big windows from which you could see the edge of the square, and they sat close together like sad young lovers, watching the light beginning to fade, although it was still two hours to sunset.

'You shouldn't have come all this way.'

'You shouldn't have forgotten your mobile,' Lol said. 'Who poisoned the local cops against you? Saltash?'

He was watching her eat, guessing this was the first time today. She was forking up salad in a desultory way as though, if he turned away, she might empty her plate into a pot plant.

'And where is Saltash?'

'In the castle. Dispensing psychological wisdom.'

She'd explained about Jemima's e-mails to the girl called Sam and told him a lot about Belladonna, as if she had to justify her continued presence here even to him.

When Merrily was starting to seem less fraught, Lol ordered some more tea and told her about Jonathan Scole and the killing of the Ghostours man's parents.

She pushed her plate to one side, staring at him. Bombshell.

'He said they'd died in their car. I was thinking, road accident...'

'Don't know where the car comes in. Unless they were shot getting into it after leaving the café.'

'The police think Jon Scole killed his own parents?'

'Couldn't have done it himself – he had an alibi,' Lol said. 'But the proceeds of the robbery were so meagre, the shooting so professional, that the cops were thinking cut-price contract killing. He just seems to have been the only one likely to profit from having them dead.'

'What about...' She scrabbled around. 'I dunno, protection. Maybe they refused to pay protection money. Or a rival café-owner with a grudge?'

'Sure, or they were dealing drugs under the counter. But you'd expect the police up there to have checked all those angles, wouldn't you? Do you like this Scole?'

'He's...' Merrily was looking around – for ashtrays, he guessed, to see if it was OK to smoke in here; apparently not. 'He's driven. A lot of energy, enthusiasm. Yes, he's likeable. Someone who could have both his parents killed? A monster? No.'

Lol said perhaps Scole had been forced to leave the area to escape the damaging gossip. Understandable, in that case, that he'd changed his name. Understandable, too, that he'd simply say that his parents had died rather than have to go into it all with strangers, over and over again.

'I just thought you should know,' Lol said, aware that, for Merrily, more knowledge was more responsibility.

But the main responsibility tonight was his.

He finished his tea. 'What was the name of that other guy?'

'What other guy?'

'The guy who came to you with Saltash and the woman.' Lol stood up. 'Maybe I can get us into the castle.'

Merrily was disturbed. Yes, it felt so much better with Lol here, it always did, but there was something he wasn't telling her. He had this almost startled air, like someone reanimated after a long time in hibernation, this sense of purpose coming off him like heat – a guy who normally felt safer in the shadows and who wasn't, as far as she knew, familiar with this town.

She stood with her back to the castle wall, out of sight while Lol talked softly to the policewoman, Kelly. A big sign said: CASTLE CLOSED. Almost all the shops were shut by now, and the crowds had thinned and the busker had gone.

And cautious, low-key Lol was chatting up a policewoman in a futile bid to get inside the castle. It was not like him.

'I don't get this with you guys,' Kelly said to Lol. 'I don't see it.'

'Trust me,' Lol said.

'I don't trust anybody outside my own family, and I wouldn't trust *them* with any money,' Kelly said. 'Stay there.'

A man was walking quickly up to the top of Mill Street, something swinging by his side that reminded Merrily, at first, of Bell's mandolin case, and then she saw it was a TV camera. Had to happen at some stage.

Lol came back to stand with Merrily. The day's spring heat was spent, and he held one of her cold hands between both of his, as George Lackland strode up from the direction of Woolworths. George without his overall: dark grey suit, tie, watch-chain, a newspaper under his arm. Mr Mayor. She saw the reporter, with a short boom-mike attached to the camera, homing in on him: Amanda Patel, of *BBC Midlands Today*.

'That woman knows me.' She pulled Lol behind the big cannon, as the cameraman positioned George with his back to the castle gate.

'Rolling,' the cameraman said to Amanda, and then George was telling her he didn't know who the girl in there was, and it was beyond devastating that this should happen again.

'We're all praying they can talk her down. There are people in the church now, praying.'

'Mr Lackland,' Amanda said, a small audience, mainly kids, forming behind her, 'you were reported this morning to be calling for an exorcism here. And now this happens. Do you see a connection?'

'Not in so many words,' George said. 'You know me, Amanda, we've had many a drink together in the Feathers, and you know I only act on what I believe the majority of people here would want me to—'

'I'm sorry, George,' Amanda said. 'Could we start again, without the personal stuff; this is likely to go network.' She turned to the cameraman. 'Can you wipe that, Neil?'

George had clearly done this before, many times, knew how to kill a question he didn't want to answer. Amanda was repositioning them for a second take when Merrily heard the voice of the policewoman, Kelly, from the other side of the castle gate.

'Where's he gone? Mr Longbeach!'

Lol hugged Merrily quickly and went to the gate.

'All right, you can go in, Mr Longbeach,' Kelly said. 'Across the green, over the bridge, through the gate at the big tower. Sergeant Britton will be there. Don't talk to anyone but Sergeant Britton, you understand?'

'Thank you,' Lol said.

The sun was hanging like a tarnished penny over distant Mid-Wales hills as they opened the castle gate for Lol, a diminutive figure in his Gomer Parry Plant Hire sweatshirt.

Merrily stared: what was he doing?

His interview over, George spotted Merrily and came across. They were almost alone on the square now, except for police, press people and the couple with the Power of God placard, who had been away and come back. The cameraman was trying to shoot the placard, instructing them not to look into the camera.

'Come and have a coffee, Mrs Watkins,' George said.

'Just had some tea, thanks. I'm fine.'

'You're wasting your time, they're not gonner let you in.'

'No.' She knew how pathetic she must be looking. 'George…'

'You want to come back to the house, talk to Nancy?'

'George, what happened between you and Bell?'

She was watching his face and saw it flinch. Saw his whole frame rock, the way a telegraph pole sometimes seemed to when hit by a sudden gust. But George recovered quickly.

'Mrs Watkins, I think I told you and Bernard that I have as little as possible to do with the woman.'

'Yes, but why?'

'Because she's not my type of person.'

'All right. The petition, then.' She leaned against the great cannon. 'Why did you feel the need to manufacture that petition? What do you care about exorcizing Marion de la Bruyère? Reflecting public demand? Bollocks, George. There virtually isn't any.'

'Not the most seemly language from a lady of the cloth.'

'Why don't you let those poor people take their placard home? They'd much rather be watching *Casualty*.'

'Not very well disposed towards you, are they?' the Mayor said. 'Those folks in the castle.'

'You're changing the subject.'

'Woman with white hair and a dog collar? Doesn't seem to like you at all.'

'Nice try, George.' She looked across at the TV team, on the corner of Mill Street. 'Could be a long night for Amanda. I wonder if she'd like another interview, expressing serious doubts that anyone's interested in disposing of Marion. As

437

such. Only that someone might be hoping someone else might be damaged in the… in the slipstream of an exorcism. Or is cleansing a better word? A general cleansing. The removal of something dirty. Which wouldn't necessarily be my word, but might be yours, Mr Mayor.'

George adjusted his watch-chain. 'Leave this alone, Mrs Watkins. You're on your own here. Even Bernard's keeping his head down. Besides, you're not even wearing your clerical uniform.' He looked across at Amanda. 'She wouldn't—'

'Amanda knows me. I'm like you, done this before. Learned how to use the media to put the cat among the pigeons. And sometimes to take the cat away before it does any damage. Not that I normally go in for that. I just… don't seem to have much to lose tonight.'

'I can't talk about it.' George backed away. 'Not to a woman.'

'Oh, you can,' Merrily said softly. 'I'm very non-judgemental. And awfully discreet.'

'Please…'

'And it's not as if you were the first. Just the first citizen.'

The Inner Bailey was more impressive and better preserved than you would have expected from outside. A serious bit of building: walls and towers, archways and openings. Defensive holes expanded into stone window frames, entrances exposing stone stairways spiralling into the dark.

And it was quite dark in here; the retreating sun, already cloaked in aspiring rain clouds, had slipped away behind the outer walls, and Lol was feeling the chill of second thoughts.

'Just that they weren't expecting you,' Sergeant Britton told him.

'No. Sorry about the casual…' Lol tugged at his Gomer Parry sweatshirt. 'I just had the message from the Bishop's office, and I thought, better not waste any time.'

'Not to worry – they said you were slightly unconventional, sir.'

In the centre of the inner space was a squat round tower with a Norman arch and a mullioned window but no roof. A group of people had assembled outside it, mainly uniformed police and paramedics. Lol kept his distance.

'How's the girl?'

'Sitting tight. Nearly four hours now. Dr Saltash is convinced she has absolutely no intention of doing it, just wants an audience.' Steve Britton sniffed. 'Wouldn't bet on it, meself. She'll be quite rational one minute, accepting a pack of sandwiches, can of Coke... and then she's back up into the window space, all hunched up. And you know that all she's gotter do is lean gently back and it's all over.'

'Salt— Nigel's talking to her himself?'

'Sandy Gee, our family liaison officer – she's doing most of the talking, sometimes the Canon, when the girl starts on about being possessed. Dr Saltash is watching and making observations, offering advice. He says he'll come out and talk to you in a few minutes, if you just hang on here. There's really not that much space in there, and they don't want her to feel crowded or threatened.'

'When you say possessed? Things were a bit rushed. The Bishop's office didn't have time to explain much on the phone.'

'They watch too much TV, sir. Too many DVDs. And what was in the morning papers didn't help, obviously. All I know is she apparently turned up this morning, hung around for a couple of hours, found nothing was happening and got herself in a state. Then she sees the scaffolding in the tower, and up she goes. First she's come to kill herself, then she's waiting for the exorcism. Confused.'

'Have they... done anything? Any kind of...'

'Mumbo-jumbo? Sorry, sir, forgetting who I'm talking to. Long day. No, Dr Saltash advises against it, and I think he's probably right. In my experience, you need to calm people like this down, not overexcite them.'

'Sarge!' The policewoman, Kelly, appeared by the gatehouse, holding up a mobile phone. 'DI Bliss, Hereford. They've found the parents. They were shopping in Worcester.'

'OK,' Steve Britton said. 'Better have a word. Excuse me, Mr Longbeach.'

And so Lol was on his own when Saltash came out of the castle.

Never seen him before, but there could be no mistake. Something in the walk, something in the cursory inspection of the police and paramedics gathered by the sawn-off round tower.

Sometimes, Lol wondered if there really was some trait, some aspect of demeanour, that united psychiatrists or if it was simply something that he projected on men once he knew that this was what they did. And they *were* men, nearly all of them. Maybe most women didn't have the arrogance for it. Maybe they wouldn't be able to sleep so easily.

Saltash wore a cream-coloured cotton suit. His tie was loosened. His face was narrow and evenly tanned, lined rather than wrinkled, and his grey beard was barbered to the length of his grey hair. He stood on the short, tufted grass, where shadows converged, looking around for a man whom Merrily had said was plump and friendly and conspicuously camp. He didn't move, expecting the man to approach him.

Lol wandered over. 'Dr Saltash?'

Saltash stared through him. 'I'm looking for Martin Longbeach. Is he here?'

'I think you're looking for me.'

'I don't think so,' Saltash said. 'Because you don't appear to be Martin Longbeach.'

'And you don't appear to be Lord Shipston,' Lol said, aware of so many years tumbling into this moment. 'But I think you know him.'

43

Nobody but God

THE PALMERS' WINDOW told its tale in reds and blues and gold.

Merrily made out a ship bound for the Holy Land, a stylized ship like a floating horn, with people far too big to fit into it. She saw King Edward the Confessor and St John the Evangelist, whose chapel was dominated by this window. The mystical ring passing between St John and the King, via the Palmers, all dressed in blue.

Mostly myth and wishful thinking. The Saxon King Edward had predated the first of the Ludlow Palmers by about two centuries.

The Chapel of St John, the original Palmers' chapel, was to the left of the high altar in St Laurence's, a dark three-aisle palace of a church, not far short of a cathedral. George Lackland stood at the entrance to the chapel, his back to a narrow door set in stone. Looking down, Merrily saw she was standing on an inscribed tombstone.

'Guild wardens buried under here,' George said.

He and Merrily were alone in the church, George having obtained the keys from the verger on his way out. Who could anyone trust with the keys more than George, former church-warden and a merchant of quality who, in the Middle Ages, would surely have been a prominent Palmer himself?

Not that the Lacklands had been in Ludlow in the Middle Ages; they hadn't left East Anglia until the eighteenth century.

But George, with his tiered face and his slow-burn eyes, looked like part of the story, part of the myth.

It would have been enough for Bell.

'One weekend – a Saturday – we were all here... in the church.' His voice was dry and ashy. 'Nancy and Susannah and Stephen and me. And her.'

Merrily recalled George's description of Bell on that day or a similar one: dressed decently and conservatively. Her Edwardian summer dress, her blonde hair neatly styled. Quite girlish, rather attractive.

A day in the rosy dawn of Bell's love affair with Ludlow. Tripping and gliding around the Buttercross, her smiling face upturned to the sun.

'Like a buttercup,' George said now, his voice laden with a damp sorrow. 'And then she wanted to go to the top of the tower.' He turned to the narrow door behind him. 'This is the way, behind here, see.'

'Famous viewpoint,' Merrily said, 'I'd guess.'

'Spectacular. See for miles. But it's a long old haul – couple of hundred steps, and it seems like more. Bell said would someone like to go up with her? Nancy said, no, thanks, once was enough, and her legs ached for days afterwards. Susannah wasn't particularly interested either, so I said – because, I suppose, I didn't want her to think I was an old man – I said, Aye, I'll go. I'll go up with you.'

George turned his back on the door. He said the steps were very narrow and twisty, so it was necessary to go up in single file. There was a rope that you could hold on to, to help pull yourself up.

Bell went first. *You can catch me if I fall, George,* she said.

'She didn't fall. She was very light on her feet.'

'Oh yes.' Merrily recalled the stage act – split black skirts, bare feet.

'I tried to leave a bit of space between us, see, but when you're on a tight spiral the person in front's apt to disappear around a bend. You know what I mean?'

'Mmm.' Vicars knew about church spirals.

'So, three or four times, Bell would come to a sudden stop on a bend, and I'd go bumping up against her. Which was embarrassing for me, but she'd just laugh. That laugh that she has, far back in her throat.'

George wouldn't look at Merrily while he was talking. His gaze was raised to the Palmers' window, as if he was wishing he could sail away to the Holy Land or anywhere. Merrily felt that the closer George's story took them to the top of the tower, the more it was plummeting to the bottom of his own deepest well.

He'd refused to tell her about this in the street, insisted on coming into the church, knowing it was about to close for the night, as if it was part of his penance to unload it all before God and a woman young enough to be his daughter, who also happened to be an ordained priest.

George in purgatory.

'Anyway,' he said, 'when we finally emerged at the top, Bell starts dancing around, with her arms thrown out. Well… there's not much room up there – big sort of pyramid coming out the middle with the weathercock sticking out the top.'

Such a proud cock, Bell had said and giggled outrageously, the sleeves of her dress rippling up her arms.

George's half-shadowed face was blushing a deeper red than King Edward's footstool in the Palmers' window as he described how he'd turned away from the woman and gone to look out at the view to the west, doing a bit of a commentary.

Over there in the west, behind those hills, that's towards Knighton, see, which is in Radnorshire – and that's Wales. Not many folks know that Ludlow, although it's in England, used to be the main administrative centre for Wales – the military capital.'

When he'd stopped talking, there had been no sound from behind him, no rustling of her papery frock. When he turned, she was nowhere in sight. Ludlow was spread out far below them, like a model village, and his heart had lurched and he'd shouted, in alarm, *Bell!*

And heard her laughing again, a dry, brittle, chattering sound. Looking down in horror to see her coiled on the stones at his feet, those arms and hands weaving in and out of his legs like white serpents.

'Serpents,' George spat.

There was an inviting-looking gift shop at the foot of the vast nave, with cards and all the books and pamphlets about Ludlow and its church. Merrily went to stand there while George stood in the nearest aisle, with his feet together and his head hanging down, like a victim of self-crucifixion.

Of course, it went without saying that he'd never behaved like that in his life before, not even when he was a young man, before he'd been married to Nancy.

Well, no.

George was... the epitome of Old Ludlow... An honourable man. Conservative in every conceivable sense of the word.

'And on the church.' A bony hand tightening on a pew end. 'Of all places, on the tower itself, where...'

Where nobody could see them but God.

As if they were putting on a show for Him.

'On the Monday,' George said. 'I formally handed in my resignation as senior churchwarden. Said I was not able to perform the duties as assiduously as was necessary, due to my impending mayoral year. And this, I'm afraid, is the first time I've been in here since, apart from services. And even then I feel dirty... soiled. Every Sunday, soiled, a disgrace.'

'I'm the first person you've told?'

'Other than in my prayers.'

Merrily didn't know what to say. It wasn't exactly a huge surprise. There had to have been something. She wondered if Susannah had actually known, from Bell, or if she'd just suspected.

'George,' she said. 'Bell... well, she's a bit of an expert at this sort of thing. Knows how to...'

'There can be no excuse!' George's knuckles shone like

marbles. 'If I hadn't already been mayor-elect I'd have turned that down as well.'

'But surely you realize it was...'

But how could he? How much could he possibly have known or even surmised about Bell's behaviour?

Not for her to explain to him the probable truth about why Belladonna had seduced him... here...

... That the tower was the spindle in the centre of the wheel of Ludlow and he was its human equivalent. Bell gathering in all her magic, her charisma, and spraying it out in what Jon Scole had called blue sparks. Spraying her sparks all over poor George Lackland, first citizen.

Sympathetic magic, Huw Owen had said. *All magic's sympathetic magic.*

'George...' Merrily moved away from the table of books. 'Erm... it was... just the once, wasn't it?'

George sprang away from the pew. 'Good God, Mrs Watkins, what do you take me for?'

'A bloke, George.' She smiled. 'You're just a bloke.'

And, for all his local-government guile, a very naive bloke, even for his generation. He hadn't seen it coming: the innocent Edwardian dress, the childlike glee at being in his town. And then his sudden exposure, on the top of his world, to this scented siren from another planet.

And what else was there besides the guilt and the shame at betraying his wife, his church, his status and his town? Had he also fallen – hopelessly, disgracefully, unforgivably – just a little in love with Mrs Pepper?

Or maybe more than a little. Oh God, yes.

I don't go looking for her, Mrs Watkins.

'You can't bear to be near her, can you, George?' she said gently.

George walked out of the aisle, his back to the high altar.

A whisper: 'Can't bear to see her.' It seemed to spiral like smoke to the timbered ceiling.

The prostitutes in this town... they knows their place. And you will agree that place is not, for instance, St Leonard's graveyard.

Could be that nothing of that nature had ever occurred in St Leonard's graveyard. George, perhaps, had been expanding Bell's myth for his own reasons. And always living in fear of it coming out.

'You want her to leave.'

'I need her to leave,' he said. 'She...'

Was still possessing him, like a dark spirit.

And his town as well. Did he know that?

George and Bell fighting for possession of the essence of Ludlow.

'Let's go,' he said.

'Yes, we better had.' Maybe Lol would be waiting.

He stepped back for her to go past. She wanted to do something vaguely priestly, if it was only patting him on the shoulder, but that would make him freeze up. So she just walked out.

As he stepped down after locking the church, an elderly man was walking up from the direction of the old college, with a German shepherd on a lead, the narrow street a valley of shadows around him.

'Can't hardly credit it, can you, George?'

George spun round. 'Oh... Tom.'

'Half of them's touched, you ask me. Youngsters. Drugs, most likely. You ask me, this girl in the castle's on drugs. That's what they're saying about the other one.'

'Yes,' George said. 'I... I've heard that, too. Do you know Mrs Watkins, from the diocese? This is Mr Tom Pritchard. Has the hardware shop just down from us.'

'Got broke into couple of months ago,' Tom said severely, to Merrily. 'Drugs again, I reckon. I hears a noise now, I don't think twice, I sends this young feller in first.' He patted the dog. 'Suppose I'll get sued if one of 'em gets bit, but I reckon I'll risk it. Gotter protect yourself, ennit?' He looked up at the Mayor. 'Town's not what it was, George. Our shop's opened every morning, bar Sundays and Christmas, since the War, come snow, flood, flu, you name it. That boy gets drunk of a night, shop's shut all day.'

'What's that, Tom?' George pocketed the bunch of church keys.

'Scole. Calls himself a shopkeeper. Makes you laugh.'

'I'm sorry?' Merrily said. 'Jon Scole's shop's not been opened all day?'

'They got too much money, these days, that's the thing.' Tom tugged on the lead. 'Come on, Tyson.'

'They're… always called Tyson, aren't they?' Merrily said, as Tom disappeared into the alley to the Buttercross.

Her gaze met George's.

'We better take a look,' George said.

44

Lab Rat

STANDING WITH HIS back to the sandstone, he might have been a Norman baron, his beard like fine chain mail around his face. A baron addressing a serf. Barons, Lol imagined, would seldom actually look at serfs.

And then, when the name of Lord Shipston came out, Saltash did look at him. Really looked at him, for all of a second: at the little round glasses, the too-long hair, the sweatshirt from some minor rural service industry.

Enough for Saltash to avert his eyes, having dismissed him, Lol guessed. Having chosen to forget that Lord Shipston had ever been mentioned, because the one-second inspection had told him that this couldn't be a contest.

'I don't think I know you at all, do I?' Saltash said.

The Inner Bailey, enclosed in stone, was more extensive than a prison exercise yard but, with police on the gate, just as secure. And it reminded Lol of the psychiatric hospital, although that had been Victorian. But Victorian Gothic, and so just as dominating as the castle, with one tower at least as high as the Keep.

'I'm Lol Robinson,' Lol said.

In the hospital, daring to be a person had always been the most difficult part. Remembering you were a person, not just a file, a subject for assessment and monitoring, a lab rat for the multinational pharmaceutical industry.

'No,' Saltash said, smiling, starting to walk away across the great courtyard, throwing out 'Sorry' in his slipstream.

And if he reached the gatehouse, where two police officers stood, there would be no second chance.

'All right.' Lol moved in front of him. 'If you want to take the scenic route, let's talk about Gascoigne.'

Saltash expelled a hiss of exasperation.

'Look, my friend, you probably know that there's a young girl in there, threatening to take her own life. I don't have time to talk to you or anyone, about anything. If you want to make an appointment to see me, that might be arranged.'

Only one PC on the gate now, but he was watching them. Vital to keep Saltash down here. If they reached the gate-house and the police, Saltash would have him thrown out, or maybe even…

… Detained.

Don't go thinking you're ever going to leave here, Mr Robinson. You see that door? One day, when I've been long retired to the south of France, you'll be straining to get your Zimmer frame through it.

But Gascoigne had not retired to the south of France.

'Didn't know…' Something throbbed in Lol's gut, and he started talking, too fast, to quell it. 'Didn't know, until today, that he'd gone to the Department of Health. And the House of Lords, now… a health spokesman. Bloody hell.'

'Lord Shipston,' Saltash said, 'is a fine psychiatrist and a former pupil of mine. Now, I don't know how you—'

'And a good friend?'

'A very good friend, which is why I don't propose to discuss him any further with a stranger. Excuse me.'

Saltash pushed Lol. But he'd been half-expecting it and moved in front again.

'Only, I'm not a stranger.'

'If you don't—'

'Not to him, anyway. Used to see each other every day, once.'

'Ah. I see.' Saltash smiled. His mouth smiled. 'A patient.'

'Makes you think that? Might have been a psychiatric nurse. Could have been a porter.'

'You could not have been anything other than a patient. Are you in what some people still like to call the care of the community now?'

'No, I'm one of the few people lucky enough to leave Dr Gascoigne's ward almost as sane as when I went in.'

Saltash's mouth kept smiling but his eyes frowned. Off balance. Lol remembering what he'd learned about facial signals in his period assisting the Hereford therapist, Dick Lyden. *You're in. Keep going.*

'And I was like... so impressed with my treatment that I wrote this song – it's what I do; bit sad really, but we can't all... Anyway, it's about this guy who's dispensing unnecessary medication like he has shares in the industry, which he probably has, and I... didn't bother to change the name in the song. Not imagining that Gascoigne would ever hear it or I'd ever record it. It was just' – Lol grinned – 'therapy. And then suddenly, there it was on the CD, without me really thinking of the implications. But you knew about that, anyway.'

Saltash didn't react. A woman came out of the castle, carrying a tray with mugs on it, as if there was nothing going on in there except minor conservation work.

'I mean, it was bound to get back. It's had a few reviews, and of course the reviews tend to mention the singer's history, and a couple referred to that song specifically because it's the only explicit loony-bin song on the album. Maybe it's been followed up on the Net, I don't know. Maybe another of Gascoigne's ex-patients picked up on it. Maybe several. Things spread so much faster these days, don't they? Who was it played you the song, Saltash? Gascoigne himself? Or maybe you just heard about it from young Fyneham.'

'If you actually think...' Saltash's smile went into an incredulous slant as he shook his head. 'If you think that a man in Lord Shipston's position has time to even listen to some piffling pop record, you're not exactly supporting your assertion of sanity, Mr—'

'Robinson. It's the name on the album.'

'Well, get out of my way, now, please, Mr Robinson, I've listened to enough of this drivel.'

'Anyway, some friends of mine… they had a long chat with the Fynehams. The Fynehams, of Breinton? Who produce a magazine in which it appears that you have a stake, along with its founder, Lord Shipston?'

Saltash sighed. 'You're on such thin ice, my friend.'

'I'll be honest,' Lol said. 'I don't quite know what you're doing, but then I'm not sure you do either. But I strongly suspect Gascoigne, as a public figure now, would feel a lot happier if my recording career ended here and neither Merrily nor I retained any kind of respect or credibility…'

'This is—'

'A start. A complete loss of respect in the eyes of the community would be a start, wouldn't it? Just in case it ever got out.'

'Do you—?'

'And I'm guessing – because this is not the kind of smear campaign that Gascoigne, or even you, would want to be involved in – that you helped finance Jack's little business venture and left the details to him. Sadly, he's nowhere near as clever as he thinks he is.'

'And neither are you,' Saltash said.

'No? I think I've become a fairly harsh judge of my own limitations.'

Saltash looked at him again. His eyes were like stone, but not this stone, not sandstone, colder than that.

'Mr Robinson, do you know how easy it would be for me to have you removed to a… place of safety? I mean removed now. This evening. We have most of the people for the preliminaries we need close at hand. And I can tell them whatever I consider to be pertinent.'

Memory jolt. Gascoigne, who must have been quite young then – no more than late thirties – murmuring, *In here, I can say what I like about you, never forget that, Laurence, and everyone here listens to me and acts accordingly, and no one will listen to you.*

And Gascoigne had said many things, and written them too, and had them duplicated, passed them into the heart of the system: reports, assessments. If Gascoigne hadn't moved on first, Lol sometimes wondered if he might still be there, on Victoria Ward, on extra medication.

'I could tell them, for instance,' Saltash said, 'about your personal grudge, amounting to dangerous obsession, against people in my profession. And I can tell them about your absurd – but clinically quite explicable – suspicion that I had seduced your lady friend...'

Lol stepped back. 'I'm sorry? What did you just say?'

'... Your very attractive lady friend, already under immense strain after being appointed to a post for which she was quite clearly emotionally unsuitable. As a result of which I and my colleague, a senior cleric, had been unofficially assigned to try and advise her and perhaps restrain her from the kind of erratic behaviour that—'

'You really are psychotic, aren't you?' Lol said.

The policeman by the gatehouse looked up.

Saltash smiled. 'Oh, no, Mr Robinson. I'm not the one who, consumed by jealousy and a sense of inadequacy, attacked my girlfriend, causing at least one serious facial injury. For which, with regard to her social position, she will no doubt have attempted to concoct a plausible explanation, but, of course, it fools nobody in her parish, certainly not my good friend Dr Asprey. Do you think that policeman's about to come over?'

No need to go back into town, George Lackland said, there was a quicker way to Jonathan's place. He led Merrily through the churchyard, down a path with yew trees either side, six of them, through a garden with the small stones of the cremated, flowers everywhere, and the ancient Reader's House opposite.

An entry led down to an inn yard where horse-drawn coaches must once have been unloaded. It was enclosed by black and white brick and timbered buildings, given a mauve cast by the evening sky.

'The Bull Hotel.' George strode across the courtyard and then they were on Corve Street, close to Lackland Modern Furnishings and Tom Pritchard's hardware shop, so much a part of the town that she hadn't noticed it before, only its swinging sign, like a pub sign, with a painting of a shire-horse on it.

'Oldest-established ironmonger's in Ludlow. Eighteenth century, maybe earlier. And a farrier's before that, same site.' George stopped. 'What's going on, Mrs Watkins? I been straight with you. Told you the truth, before God.'

'George, I don't know. Most of it's in Bell's head. She's feeling persecuted… betrayed.'

'By who?'

'You… the women who may or may not have assaulted her in the streets last night…'

'In the streets? When did—?'

'I don't know if that even happened. Forget it. And by me. I spent some time with her under… under false pretences. Then she sees that nice picture of me in the paper, and now I'm the enemy. And the person who introduced me to her – therefore the real traitor – is Jon Scole. There's a hollow yew she's had a door put into, with a lock, where she keeps items of importance to her, and it was broken into last night and something was stolen.'

'She thinks that's Scole?'

'Even I'm beginning to think it's Scole.'

And, oh God, it was true. Who else would have followed them last night?

His own song started playing in his head:

Tuesdays on Victoria Ward,
We always hated Tuesdays.

Reminding him how that song, those opening lines, had conquered his concert-block at the Courtyard in Hereford, because of the suppressed rage behind them… the spontaneous reaction of the audience making it suddenly all right.

Someone's got to pay
Now Dr Gascoigne's on his way
And it's another
Heavy medication day…

The police constable who'd been walking across to them had stopped and had begun talking into a radio or a mobile phone. Lol looked at Saltash, with the round tower behind him in the middle of the Inner Bailey, with its Norman arched doorway. The tower was roofless, hollow, a shell.

'It's not enough, is it?' Lol said. 'It wouldn't hold water. There's no way you can touch me, you arrogant bastard.'

The sky was low and tight and red-veined, and he was aware of his own voice, crisp and contained, like in a recording studio with acoustic panels.

'And Gascoigne – he's not worried about that song, because, even with the very remote possibility that the album got into the outer reaches of the charts, the song doesn't really say anything apart from describing his fondness for handing out pills. It's what's *not* in the song that he's worried about. And I really wasn't going to do anything about that – not my place. Especially with him out of hands-on psychiatry… which, considering some of the places his hands went, is no bad thing—'

'Constable!' Saltash shouted. 'Excuse me, Constable!'

The policeman was still talking. He looked up, lifted a hand to Saltash.

'So I suppose, normally, I'd just have left it at that,' Lol said, 'glad that at least the poor sods who'd been sectioned were no longer exposed to his attentions. Especially the women. Like Helen Weeks.'

'Because I don't have time to deal with you now, Mr Robinson,' Saltash said softly, 'I might simply tell the police you're a journalist who's talked his way in by assuming a false identity.'

'I used to wander around the hospital as much as I could,' Lol said, 'watching ordinary people – people who worked there. Just to stay familiar with normal behaviour, the outside world. Helen Weeks was schizophrenic, so nobody ever believed what she said. She was very pretty and heard voices, and sometimes what the voices were telling her to do, she needed to be protected from that. So, yes' – in case he was wondering – 'I did see Gascoigne giving her a special consultation that wasn't exactly my idea of protection. I climbed on a chair to look over the horrible frosted glass of his office and through the clear glass over the top.'

'You sad little man,' Saltash said.

And Lol finally hated him enough to start lying.

'Well, Nigel, I don't think that's how they'll see it at the Three Counties News Service. You know them? News agency in Gloucester, serving national papers – the *Sun... Mirror... News of the World*? The thing about the Three Counties, it's all about money to them. If one paper turns it down, they'll try another and then another, until everybody knows. Or, a story like this, they'll maybe just send it all round.'

'Not if I obtain an injunction to prevent you—'

'You're too late. A friend of mine has a long e-mail that we put together, detailing the full story, including a phone number for Helen Weeks and her sister who looks after her and two former porters we contacted who knew of other cases. If this friend doesn't hear from me by ten tonight, the e-mail goes to the Three Counties.'

Lol looked into Saltash's eyes and felt a surprising calm in his spine, like a soft shiver.

'Try me, Nigel. Have me thrown out. Attempt to have me detained. Sectioned. Oh, and you're in the e-mail, too, of course, in an attachment – transcript of a recorded conversation with Jack Fyneham. I think he's – God forbid – your godson, isn't he?'

'Is there a problem, Dr Saltash?' the policeman said.

'And the Dean of Hereford,' Lol said to Saltash. 'He's quoted too. Quite extensively.'

Saltash's smile was like glass. 'Everything's fine now, officer, thank you.'

'Always knew there was something not quite right about this boy,' George said, low-voiced, when they were in the alley at the side of the shop. 'Someone that age just turns up in town, goes round the estate agents inquiring about flats to rent, cheap, and then he takes a shop at the kind of rent would turn me pale.'

'How do you know that?' Merrily asked, but he was walking up the steps with the wrought-iron lamp at the top and didn't answer. She thought, Masons, or perhaps some Old Ludlow traders' network that was even more mutually supportive and exchanged intelligence on outsiders.

George took the steps two at a time, and she had a picture of him not going up the steps of the church tower that overheated afternoon, but coming down, very fast, and collapsing against the wall at the bottom, blinded by shame and some forbidden, guilt-gilded exultation that he didn't, to this day, dare acknowledge.

'Jonathan!' Banging the door with a knobbly fist. 'We'd like a word, boy. Councillor Lackland and Mrs Watkins.'

No answer.

'Try the door, George.'

Recalling how it had sprung open when she'd flipped the handle from inside, and how glad she'd been because Jonathan had been coming on to her, in the wake of his apparent rejection of Bell's advances. *She's all over me. Hot and... you know. Anybody could see she were burnin' up...*

'It's open!' George went in. 'Jonathan? It's Councillor Lackland!'

She heard him tramping around, a door opening inside. A muffled 'Jonathan?' A silence. By the time she was halfway up the stairs, he was out again.

'Let's go,' he said hoarsely.

'George?'

He gripped the iron rail and then breathed in sharply and let go of the rail as though it were white-hot. He drove her down the steps, waving both arms as if he was herding ewes.

'Go down.'

Her first thought was that he must have walked into something of a sexual nature, but then, when he began to step carefully down himself, keeping close to the wall, away from the rail, she saw the blood on the hand that had touched it.

There was a bulge like a knuckle in the Mayor's forehead, and it was pulsing.

'Some things a woman shouldn't see,' he said.

45

Marion

'Look, Siân,' Saltash said. 'Martin's here.'

They were in a high but roofless space, some one-time great hall, with the remains of huge fireplaces, one above the other, time-blurred stone heads projecting from the walls along with the weeds. The sergeant, Steve Britton was there, too, as Siân Callaghan-Clarke's pewter-eyed gaze flicked across to Lol and then back to Saltash, where she must have caught a warning look.

'Hello, Martin,' she said, finally.

A woman with presence and authority, Lol thought, but not comfortable here, in her dark grey business suit over the clerical shirt and collar. Not at home in ruins.

'Look.' Saltash jangled keys or something in a trouser pocket. 'I'm afraid I shall have to leave you for a short while. I need to make some phone calls.'

This time Siân didn't need a signal; she followed him out. Saltash's calls would be to Lord Shipston, the Fynehams, his friend the Dean. Plans to make, defences to erect. Only the jittery keys expressing nerves.

'I don't think the Canon's happy with this,' Steve Britton said.

'No.' Lol saw two lightless, narrow openings; one of them had to be the way in to the Hanging Tower.

'Mr Longbeach, let me be frank with you.' Steve Britton's hands moved as though he was hefting invisible weights.

'There's a very disturbed little girl in there, and we don't want it to get dark on her. We don't want to have to bring lights in, make a circus of it. So what I'd like to know – are you the bloke who does this stuff? I mean, I don't know what you do, and I'm pretty damn sure that kid in there doesn't, either. You know what I'm saying? If you haven't got the full bell, book and candle with you, just…'

'Fake it?'

'Fake something.'

'We don't need to fake it,' Lol said. 'There's someone—'

'Not liking this, Steve.' A plump woman in an orange fleece with a reindeer motif had come through one of the dark doorways. Black Country accent. 'I thought we were getting somewhere, now she's gone back into herself. Getting just a bit spooky again, if I must use that word.'

'This is Mr Martin Longbeach, Sandy,' Britton said. 'Another, er, colleague of our friends out there. This is Inspector Sandy Gee, from our family liaison unit.'

Sandy Gee narrowed her eyes at Lol. 'I've seen you somewhere before, haven't I? Never forget a face, Martin. It'll come to me. Meanwhile, I hope you're prepared to do something. Thought we were getting somewhere, but I'm getting a teensy bit anxious. I think the doctor was right about her being delusional, but if we have to go along with a delusion to save her life, let's do that, eh?'

Lol nodded at the opening from which Inspector Gee had emerged. 'She's on her own?'

'Hell, no. Female paramed's in with her. More than two people, she feels threatened, moves further into the window space. We're trying to keep her talking because once or twice she's nearly fallen asleep. Now you'd think that would mean we could nip up and snatch her, but she's so very close to the opening it could just as easily mean she'd rock backwards and… gone.'

Sandy Gee shuddered. She was about Lol's age, had frizzy hair, dyed a deep red, and earrings like joined-up multicoloured paper clips. Family liaison: was this the halfway point between policing and social work?

'What I'd like to do,' he said, 'is bring in someone—'

'To be quite honest, Martin, for the reasons I've just outlined, we really don't want the world and his wife in there.'

'One person...' He hesitated. 'Merrily Watkins?'

Sandy and Steve swapped glances. Sandy said, 'Dr Saltash and the Canon—'

'Have changed their minds about her,' Lol said. 'They're probably discussing it now.'

Sandy Gee sucked in her small mouth, thought about it.

'All right, go and find her, Steve.' She turned to Lol. 'Both of them were very firmly of the opinion that any kind of ceremonial would only fortify the fantasy that Sam's constructed. Dr Saltash insisted that the only sensible strategy would be to gradually make her aware of the reality of her situation.'

'And the fantasy is...?'

'She seems to think that a number of... I don't know, spirits? Dead people want her to join them. That's over-simplifying it. It's a lot to do with guilt at what she thinks she's done, which Dr Saltash tried to tackle. But, in the end, she feels crowded by... influences she can't get rid of.' Sandy glanced over at the entrance to the tower. 'We've managed to find the parents now, and we're bringing them across, although she insists she doesn't want to see them, but we'll argue about that later. You know she was Jemima Pegler's best friend?'

Lol nodded. 'I know about the e-mails.'

'Do you know about the boyfriend situation?'

Lol shook his head. Sandy took his arm and guided him up to the main way out. A police van was parked in the Inner Bailey now, near the separate round tower.

'Jemmie Pegler, the only friend she had was Sam. But then she stole Sam's boyfriend, Harry, so that was the end of that. Sam says Jemmie was letting him have sex with her, which Sam wouldn't. This obviously gave Jemmie a feeling of power – short-lived when she heard what the other boys were saying.

461

Jemmie was fat, you see, like me and, when you're a fatty at school, life is hell, your self-esteem's rock-bottom and you absolutely know you'll never find a boyfriend because you're so disgusting. If anybody ever got round to compiling statistics on this, I'm pretty sure they'd find that well over half the teenage pregnancies are fat girls. We don't want to be chubby and mumsy, Martin, we want to be lithe and slinky and do parties, but in the end we go for what we think we can get.'

'Sam and Jemmie had a falling out?'

'Sam didn't like her any more at all because Jemmie, even before she pinched Sam's boyfriend, had been going well off the rails for a long time. I think Sam was getting frightened of her at this stage. Big girls, when they cease to be jolly and philosophical, can be very dark and threatening. Doing drugs doesn't help. Nothing heavy at that stage, in Jemmie's case – Es and whizz, a bit of blow, but she was moving up, you know? Also hitching rides with stupid little younger boys who'd nicked cars – very ominous. Taking risks. Doesn't care what happens to her – maybe hoping something *will* happen to her. Jemmie was coming apart, no question about that.'

'Didn't having a boyfriend…?'

'Oh well, that didn't last, did it? Thinks she's finally got something steady with Sam's ex-boyfriend… Hoo! Terrific! I'm a real woman! And then, having had his evil way, this lovely Harry dumps her like an old sofa. So Jemmie is now very depressed indeed, because she's lost the feller, and she's also lost her very best friend, the only real friend she's had. So then she's desperately trying to get back with Sam, bombarding her with pitiful, wheedling e-mails, the way these kids do. They were at different schools, you see?'

'Jemmie was manic-depressive?'

'That was certainly what Dr Saltash thought. Now Sam… the thing with her, she's a very soft-hearted girl, basically. She's quite pretty, but not too pretty, and perhaps a bit short on confidence – this is my opinion, you understand, from talking to her and listening to what she's got to say. I'd guess that Sam was friends with Jemmie very much out of pity, in the early days. Because Sam doesn't yet have the confidence to make her own way, she's drawn to the underdogs – well, it's nice to be needed, isn't it? But at the end of the day she's a little girl, she's not a saint, and she's really not going to forgive Jemmie that easily – if at all – for the business over the boy. And I think she was very glad, actually, to be free of Jemmie. Only to find herself, I'm afraid, with another underdog on her hands.'

Sandy Gee folded her arms, bulky in the fleece, and looked at Lol.

'Guess,' she said.

Lol shook his head. Behind the clouds, the sun was setting and the stones were full of detail and texture.

'Robbie Walsh,' Sandy said. 'There's a turn-up, eh?'

In the drabness and dereliction of the Hanging Tower, the first window, the one you could easily reach, was barred.

Or partly. The two bars didn't reach to the top of the window, so it would be possible for anyone determined enough to climb up and squeeze over them.

This window offered a view of the River Teme and the pine woods where The Weir House, apparently, was hidden. Inside the tower, the window was on the ground floor, but outside there was a very long drop to the path at the bottom of the rocks into which the foundations were sunk.

Was this how Jemmie Pegler had gone?

Above it – it would have been one storey up if the floors and ceilings hadn't all gone, leaving the tower as a hollow funnel – was another window, the second of four. A window that would have been inaccessible but for the scaffolding.

'They were going to make it safe,' Sandy murmured. 'Ironic, isn't it?'

The skeleton of galvanized metal tubing ended about three feet under the window, two planks along the top, a brown mug on the end of one. A wooden ladder extended to the top of the scaffolding; a second one had evidently been pushed away and lay at an angle against the wall.

The girl was huddled like a squirrel in the deep recess around the second window, about fifteen feet above the floor. A small girl in a pink hoodie and jeans, short brown hair and the glint of a ring at the end of an eyebrow. The window space almost directly behind her was about four feet high and two or three feet wide, and all you could see through it was the darkening sky.

'You want another coffee, Sam?' Sandy called up.

Sam didn't reply.

'How about a hot chocolate? You must be getting cold up there.'

'No, thank you,' Sam said. They thought she was fourteen or fifteen, but she sounded younger.

'She must be needing to go to the loo by now,' Sandy whispered to Lol. Then she called back up to the ledge, 'Sam, if you want to go to the loo, we can organize something.'

'No, thank you.'

Lol said tentatively, 'I'm... Martin.'

Sam didn't acknowledge him. He wished Steve Britton would get back here, with Merrily.

Sandy whispered in his ear, 'Try again, eh?'

Lol said, 'About Robbie... it really wasn't your fault. I can explain why. Can I do that?'

There was silence. Sandy Gee looked at Lol, showed him fingers crossed on both hands. A bird fluttered at the top of the tower.

'You just keep telling me lies.' This small, lost voice from the stone ledge.

Sandy said, 'This is not a wind-up, Sam. He knows stuff I didn't know.'

Before they came in, she'd told Lol what Sam had said earlier, when she'd been more talkative. It seemed her mother had come to spend a week in Ludlow before Christmas to look after Sam's Auntie Kate, who'd broken a leg, and she'd brought Sam with her, as Sam was very miserable at the time, having just found out about Jemmie and Harry.

At first, Sam had been really bored in Ludlow: didn't know anybody, nothing to do. The turning point was the Friday night her mother had taken her on the ghost-walk this guy ran – which Sam expected would be totally crap, but it had turned out to be kind of fun and scary, too, because she basically believed in ghosts and all that stuff.

And there was this boy there, about Sam's age, and he'd said if she was interested there were some things he could show her, maybe call for her the next day, and she said yeah, OK. So the next day they went to Gallows Bank, where people used to be hanged, and then this Robbie took her to the castle, where she was quite impressed by him being able to get in for nothing.

Anyway, they'd spent most of the week together. They came here quite a few times, to the Hanging Tower, and Robbie told her about Marion's ghost being seen, and they'd stood here and listened for the breathing noise, but they hadn't heard anything.

They were just, like, mates – that was how Sam had seen it. She didn't want another boyfriend so soon after Harry. But it seemed Robbie was more serious about it than Sam was. When she'd gone home, Robbie had kept writing and e-mailing and sending her stuff about Ludlow, and she was interested, but not *that* interested.

'Sam?' Sandy Gee said.

No reply. Sam had half-turned so she was looking out of the window space. From below, Lol could hear ragged singing: a hymn, 'Oh God Our Help in Ages Past'.

'Oh no,' Sandy muttered. 'It's this bloody religious group. We blocked off the path at both ends specifically to avoid this kind of thing. They must be on some footpath coming up from the river or somewhere. Damn, damn, damn.'

'Tell them to go away, or I'll jump,' Sam suddenly shouted. 'Tell them!' She stood up and leaned out over the drop. 'Shut up! Shut up! Shut up!'

'We'll get a message to them,' Sandy said. 'All right?'

What else could she say? From less than twelve feet away from them, Sam was holding all the cards. When the kid turned to face them, she was in tears.

This was pitiful. An obvious cry for help. People rarely kill themselves as self-punishment, Dick Lyden, the psychotherapist, had once told Lol. They kill themselves because life isn't worth living any more. That's it, basically. Nothing subtle.

But what had begun as a cry for help had often ended in tragedy, Dick had emphasized. A cry for help wasn't that easy to stage-manage, and they often lost control.

Suddenly, Lol was remembering something that Merrily had told him the night after Mumford's mother had died.

About a letter that Robbie Walsh had written to a ghost.

'Sam,' he said, 'were you Marion?'

Sandy Gee looked at him in some alarm, like he was suggesting reincarnation. The hymn outside had become 'Rock of Ages'.

'Did Robbie call you Marion?' Lol said. 'Did he write to you, e-mails and stuff… sent to you as Marion?'

Sam moved away from the window, leaning over the scaffolding.

'She's frightened.'

'Who?'

'Marion,' Sam said.

Sandy leaned in, whispered, 'This is what's been happening. Be careful.'

Sam looked down at Lol. It was getting quite dark in here now. Her face was white.

'Tell me about Robbie and Marion,' Lol said.

Sam sat on the ledge, under the window.

'We met up one Saturday. After Christmas.'

'You and Robbie?'

'He just wanted to come here again. Walk round the town and stuff and then come here. I mean, I liked him, but I couldn't… I felt…'

'Did he call you Marion then? While you were with him?'

'Went home.'

'You were feeling... bit suffocated?'

'And then he kept sending me all this stuff from the Net. Pictures that took ages to download. It got... 'Cos this was when she was...'

'Who was? Jemmie?'

Sam sniffed. 'Giving me all this grief. How she was going to take an overdose. How she was going to dope herself up and jump in the river. Rings up at night and texting and stuff. I had to switch my phone off, said I'd lost it. And like every time I switched on the computer there'd be like nineteen e-mails and a pile of attachments and stuff.'

'From Robbie?'

'Yeah.' Sam started to cry again. Steve Britton ducked under a low doorway and came in and straightened up, shaking his head – Sandy Gee waving at him to keep quiet.

'And he's, like, making plans for the Easter holidays,' Sam said. 'How I can get there on the train and what we'll do, and she's like, Oh, I'm really depressed, you're the only friend I've ever had, and why don't we go away together?'

'That must've been... difficult.'

'Up all night some nights, on the computer. Dear Sam. Dear Marion. It just...'

'You didn't tell anybody?'

'Nnn. I was really tired this night, and I sent Robbie one back, and I'm like, please stop sending me stuff, OK, and no I can't come to Ludlow at Easter 'cos we're going to France, and like... I could've been nicer about it, you know?'

'But you were overtired, right?' Sandy said.

'Read it back next day, and I thought, like, what've I done? So I e-mailed him back and I said I was really, really sorry and how I'd been really tired and I had a headache. But he never replied.'

'When was this?' Lol asked.

The kid's face was moon-pale. 'Two weeks before he died.'

'There was no connection,' Lol said. 'You've got to understand that.'

'He killed himself!' Sam breathed in, like a hollow shudder. 'They said it was an accident, but I knew it wasn't. He kept writing to me that he could feel her… me… her… with him. He used to come here at weekends, and he said he could… And I was really like—'

'Sam…' Lol moved to the foot of the scaffolding, held on to the bars so she could see his hands, know he wasn't trying anything. 'What happened after he died?'

She was a long time in replying. Somebody, thank God, had managed to stop the choir. Through the ground-floor window, half-barred, you could see the river, silver and black.

'Couldn't sleep,' Sam said. 'I had these nightmares. There was this one where I switched on the computer and there were all these e-mails and they all said, Dear Marion, and I'd be like scrolling up and scrolling up, and they'd just like go on for ever. Dear Marion, dear Marion, dear—'

She made a noise like a yawn that pitched up into a kind of squeak of distress.

'Let me get you some hot chocolate,' Sandy said.

'Noooo!'

'All right… it's OK.'

'What happened then?' Lol said.

It was clear that Steve Britton hadn't found Merrily. Where was she? This was becoming—

'Told my friend,' Sam said. 'At school. Her name's Bex. I thought she was my friend. I told her – like in confidence, you know? – and she's like, Wow, this Marion's ghost's taken him. And she went and told these other kids, and then everybody's like, Oh, you killed Robbie Walsh, you killed Robbie Walsh. You're like a witch, or something.'

Sandy Gee sighed.

'So I'm getting all this grief at school and I don't want to go, and I'm faking being ill and stuff, and I'm getting into rows at home, 'cos my mum and dad, they think I'm going to be like a brain surgeon or something.'

Lol glanced at Sandy: *We've managed to find the parents now… insists she doesn't want to see them.*

'And then I saw Jemmie Pegler in Ledbury, and she's telling me how she's found all these suicide websites about how to kill yourself with a plastic bag and stuff. Copied one of them over.'

'She copied the suicide site to you?'

'And like I was sure she'd heard about me and Robbie Walsh and she was just being cruel – 'cos she was like that, you know? And I was like really angry, and I just started sending her all this stuff Robbie had sent me, about Marion and the Hanging Tower and I'm like, why don't you like try this instead of a poxy plastic bag, and…'

'Take it easy, Sam,' Sandy said. 'This is very important, what you're telling us.'

'So she starts phoning me at home on the main phone, and I keep pretending I'm not there, and then somebody tells me at school, like do you know Jemmie's got a syringe and she's shooting up, and I thought, like, she'd just told them to tell me that so I'd feel sorry for her again. And then she e-mails and says will you come to Ludlow with me and we'll throw ourselves off the tower – like together – and become free of our bodies.'

'What did she mean?'

'I don't know. It was all this stuff she'd had off the Net – like somebody got hold of the Robbie story and they've twisted it all around. And I couldn't take any more, and it was late at night, and I sent back, yeah, yeah, we'll go tomorrow.'

'Oh God,' Sandy murmured.

'And she bloody did. She went. She came here, and I didn't, and she threw herself—'

Sam let out a wail of despair and spun herself back at the window space, Sandy Gee shouting, 'Sam!' but grabbing Lol's arm as he made a move towards the scaffolding.

He could hear Sam vomiting out of the death-fall window, and then she slumped back down, squatting under the window with her head in her hands.

Sandy hissed, 'Now, will you do something?'

'No Merrily?'

'No sign at all. They're still looking. You'll have to do something.'

'Sandy, listen—'

'No, you listen to me…' Sandy pulled him through a doorway he hadn't noticed, into a chamber the size of a lavatory, steps going up, sealed off with masonry. 'There was an incident earlier on when we nearly lost her. When she thought Jemmie Pegler was hovering on the other side of the window… as if she'd come rising up again from where she'd fallen – that even spooked me, I can tell you. And it's what she's been seeing in dreams, Martin, night after night, and now she's afraid to go to sleep and she's keeping herself awake all night. Look at her – she's overtired, overwrought. We'll have to bring lamps in soon, or she'll use the darkness to… Twice she's started talking to somebody who isn't there.'

'What did Nigel Saltash say about that?'

'He talked about hallucinations and psychological projections. He said there are— Look, it doesn't matter what he—'

'Drugs he could give her to sort it out?'

'Yeah, more or less. We sometimes assume if someone's a highly qualified psychiatrist they're also experienced in counselling, and if he'd talked to me the patronizing way he talked to her I'd have jumped two hours ago. I'm not trying to discredit what he does, all I'm saying is, if she's hallucinating Jemmie Pegler and her fat-girl talk, leave our bodies behind—'

'Jemmie was clearly a dominant, parasitical presence,' Lol said. 'From whichever side of the fence you want to see it, that doesn't necessarily go away with death.'

'You'd know better than me. But this morning it's in the papers about the exorcism and, like Steve keeps saying, she's seen the films. She's convinced she's haunted.'

'Convinced herself she deserves to be haunted.'

'Exactly. By Jemmie and by Robbie Walsh and by the very thought of this place. So she's caught a train and she's here, and she's in the famous Hanging Tower, saying, why aren't they doing it? So don't you tell me to wait any longer, Martin, because it's going dark and when it's dark there's even less reality, isn't there? And I'm afraid you're the only priest we've got.'

46

Gridiron

MERRILY DIDN'T KNOW what she'd expected, and she'd walked into the doorway of Jon's flat before she could change her mind, and the smell – the mixture of smells – came out at her, so dense it was like a smearing of dirty colours on her face.

Oh God, God, God...

What she saw... she had nothing to compare it with. You could live in the countryside for years but contrive never to enter an abattoir.

'Don't go in,' George Lackland whispered. 'Please don't go in.'

'No.'

She stood in the doorway. No need at all to go in. Stood in the doorway for... how many seconds, minutes? George's echo-chamber breathing behind her. And no breathing, no movement at all, inside. Only silence full of stench, as if the atmosphere itself had congealed around it – something so terminally extreme that it had to be environmentally contained.

Oh God, God, God.

What made it worse was that Jonathan – it was Jonathan, wasn't it? Keep looking, be certain, be absolutely certain – appeared to be naked. No clothing to soak up the blood and obscure the wounds. Only the paper, scattered like toilet tissue in a public lavatory when the drains were blocked.

'I can't use the phone in there,' George said.

'No. No, we mustn't touch anything.'

She saw that the papers were newspaper and magazine cuttings and also photocopies of news cuttings and printouts from websites, and there were scores of them... Hundreds, in fact. Most of them about music.

All of them about Belladonna: pictures of her and words about her. Belladonna's high-grain, monochrome face soaking up the lifeblood of Jonathan Scole who had been Jonathan Swift and was now...

She must have sobbed – it was what happened to your breath in moments of immeasurable stress. Felt George's hands gripping her shoulders.

She said, 'Not in my worst...'

The papers had been torn and slashed. Like Jonathan, who was curled on his side, foetal, except for the angle of his head where his throat had been pierced, his face flung back and opened up like a blood orange. A face of multiple expressions, now, like double exposures, like a portrait by Francis Bacon.

Torn-up news cuttings had been scattered over his lower body, glued to it by the blood where Jonathan had been cut and stabbed and slashed, and cut and stabbed and slashed, over and over and—

With the full acceptance that if she was any kind of a real priest she should be saying a prayer for the eternal peace of the savagely, senselessly slain, Merrily stood back and kicked the door shut.

With a wheeze like an explosion of breath, it sprang back, and there was Jonathan again, the wafting of air lifting a piece of newsprint from one of his eyes as if he'd blinked at the repeated intrusion, and Merrily slammed a foot flat against the door and pushed it hard away from her. Keeping the foot clamped there, on the stained panelling, as if she was holding back a tide of blood, until the door clicked. And then she stood at the top of the steps, with George a few steps below her, and just took in air.

'Whoever did this...' George looking up at her, the

knuckle-bump in his forehead gleaming like a big pearl, 'must look like… like a bloody butcher. How can she be walking the streets?'

'In a long coat.' She followed him down the steps.

At the bottom they just stood there, and George said, 'Are you all right?'

'Well, no,' she said. 'Not exactly.'

'Come to my house.'

Merrily sagged. Her lighter fell from the torn pocket of her fleece and bounced on the cobbles.

'I made a terrible mistake, George.' She bent to pick up the lighter, but denied herself a cigarette. 'The worst mistake I've ever made, and, by God, I've made some.'

'Mrs Watkins—'

'I have a qualified, not to say eminent, psychiatrist I'm supposed to work with. And, because I didn't like him much, I kept him completely in the dark about most of this.'

'Mrs Watkins, we all kept people out of this. I wanted Bernard to see to it, as a friend, and Bernard passed it on to you. It was all in confidence. I wanted to keep the lid on – that's the top and bottom of it.'

'And I resisted' – putting a hand to the top of her chest to try and stop herself panting – 'every inclination to think this woman was clinically insane.'

Even as she'd stood clamping the door shut with her foot, she'd been resisting it. Thinking, could this have been someone else? Some enemy from back home in the north? Someone who'd been trying to find him? If his parents' murder had been contracted…

Oh, sure. And plastered him with Belladonna cuttings. There was no story-book twist here; it was as messy and unfathomable as any open-and-shut killing. The level of rage that could have driven a woman to this was beyond all comprehension, but wasn't that always the case? Dear God.

'We'll go to my house,' George said, as though he was helping a child to cross the road. 'Phone the police from there. Come on.'

They came out of the alley into Corve Street, into George Lackland's town. Plenty of people still around in the powdery dusk, Tesco's still open. A tourist coach waiting at the lights.

Over the gravelly sound of the coach engine came the church clock chiming eight. Instinctively, Merrily glanced up to the tower and glimpsed movement at the top: a figure in Palmers' Guild blue moving across from one corner pinnacle to another. Or the distinctive blue of a stockman's coat.

They had reached the first narrow window of Lackland Modern Furnishings.

'George,' she said, casual as she could manage. 'Do you think *you* could report it?'

'I was going to.'

'I mean without mentioning me. Not yet. Please? I need some time.'

He stared down at her. 'You're feeling ill.'

'No, I'm—'

'What's the matter?'

'Do you think I could borrow the keys to the church? I have to… work something out.'

As if she meant she needed to pray. She hoped he would understand that. And anyway, he'd know the truth of it soon enough.

Everybody would.

Lol leaned against the wall outside and knew why Merrily smoked.

He felt faintly sick. He wanted to be on the other side of these walls, looking for her. She would not just have walked off. She would wait. She was good at waiting. He needed her, and the girl needed her, needed someone who could…

… legitimately intercede.

The movements of police and paramedics around the Inner Bailey were becoming shadowed. The Keep, now the gatehouse, was a charcoal monolith.

'I hope you know what you've done, Mr Robinson.'

He didn't know how long the woman had been standing by his side.

'Where's Saltash?'

'He's gone.' She didn't look at him. 'I don't think he'll be coming back tonight. He suggested I might be wise to leave also. Let Mrs Watkins' – the name was expelled like prune stones – 'take over.'

'You've seen her?'

'No. I thought she might already be here. Or perhaps she's with the television people. Doing what she does so well.'

Lol looked at her austere profile. The clouds that had suffocated the sun were relaxing into evening, admitting a wafery moon. Her hair was curling up from the collar of her jacket.

'What is it with you, Ms…' Couldn't remember her damn name.

'Siân will do. What's up with me, as I think you already know, is that my and Merrily's attitudes to the practice of Christianity in a secular age are… incompatible. Never made much of a secret of that. Putting it simplistically, I think there's no room for superstition in what we do, while she appears to nurture it.'

'In which case – sorry to be so naive – why would you want to be connected with Deliverance? What's your agenda?'

Siân looked across the enclosure, dark as a stagnant pond now, towards the Keep with its drooping flag. She sighed.

'It begins to look,' she said, 'as if the agenda was Mrs Watkins herself. Doesn't it? The ubiquitous, self-effacing, photogenic Merrily Watkins.'

'Had her picture in the paper too often? Well…' Lol shrugged. 'That was always going to happen. She hates it. But if you do what she does and… and you look like she looks, then you're going to get your picture in the papers.'

'Who wasn't here when we – the women of Hereford – were battling for the priesthood. Wasn't out there with her placard. Wasn't part of the movement. And was then presented with this outdated but inherently sexy role by a rogue bishop, subsequently discredited. Managing to emerge after his inevitable departure smelling of lavender and honeysuckle. And continuing, for heaven's sake, to get away with it.'

'Not always. And not undamaged.'

'And all of it built on superstition.' Siân finally turned towards Lol. 'Do you know what really got to me? How, when she restored evensong in Ledwardine Church – evensong with a fashionably esoteric tweak – it became an immediate talking point because some local woman had apparently been cured of a life-threatening condition.'

'Which she probably hadn't had in the first place. Misdiagnosis, or the medical records got mixed up.'

'Doesn't matter. It was still all over the Internet, apparently, that the mystical vicar of Ledwardine had healing powers. And the following week it was reported – not in the *Church Times*, thank God, one of the other rags – that her congregation had doubled.'

'Trebled, I think. But she squashed the rumours and it slumped again. So everyone's happy. Except I expect you were really pissed off that she hadn't run with it, gone the way of all the other messianic cranks.'

'Always one step ahead,' Siân said.

'You make it sound political. She doesn't think like that. She offended you just by being there.'

'Yes,' Siân said. 'I suppose she did.'

'So when you were approached by the Dean, whose good friend Saltash had decided he should make his skills available to the Church—'

'No. The approach came from Nigel himself.'

'What did he tell you just now?'

'He didn't have to tell me anything. He'd walked out on a disturbed child. That was enough. Whatever Merrily may think of me, I'm still a Christian. Of sorts.' She looked down at her hands, crossed on her abdomen. 'So I've come back. And I don't quite know what to do about this, Mr Robinson.'

'You're asking me? A recovering psychiatric patient? An abuser of women?'

Siân was silent.

'They can't find Merrily,' Lol said. 'And they think my name's Longbeach and I'm qualified to dispel spirits. They're now telling the girl that I'll do it.'

'Do what, exactly?'

'I was thinking about an exorcism of place. Seems appropriate. Doesn't target anything in particular. Lightens things. Takes away the tension and produces a feeling of calm. Psychology rather than superstition. Also it's the only one I've ever watched.'

Siân looked into the pool of darkness in front of them. 'Is that what Merrily would do?'

Lol shrugged.

'I couldn't,' Siân said.

Lol didn't say anything.

'I'm not sure I'd know where to start.'

'If you were planning to reform it, you must have done some research with the Deliverance handbook.'

'It appalled me. It's fundamentally medieval.'

'This is a medieval town. We're in a medieval castle.'

'I don't carry a copy, anyway.'

'As I understand it,' Lol said, 'it's only a set of guidelines, that book.'

'One can hardly make it up.'

'You don't have to make it all up.'

'Yes, I do realize that elements such as the Lord's Prayer are mainstays of all Deliverance... ritual.'

'Ritual,' Lol said. 'I quite like you when you talk dirty.'

Siân said, 'I want to say... that I wouldn't insult either of you with an apology, but sometimes one's own gullibility results in the most... indefensible behaviour.'

'You can get holy water from the church or somewhere,' Lol said. 'I was with Merrily at a hop-kiln in the Frome Valley, where something unpleasant had happened. A lot of the routine stayed with me. Good memory for verse and things. Something you develop in my line of work, otherwise you're liable to dry up in the middle of a gig.'

'Of course,' Siân said. 'What's your first name? I did know…'

'Lol. Laurence. Like the poor guy they named the church after. Someone once told me what happened to him, but it's slipped my mind.'

'He was roasted on a gridiron over a slow fire.'

'Yes, now I remember,' Lol said.

Tinted by the last of an invisible sun, clouds hung like a sandbank over the round tower that sat in the Inner Bailey like a great turreted cake.

'For God's sake,' Siân said, 'let's not either of us be bloody stupid. Just have one last attempt to find Merrily.'

Leaving the church's main door unlocked, Merrily entered through the huge stone porch and found the lights, the acoustics of the great church giving out a sigh as she went in. Entering a church alone at night was disturbing some secret alchemical process and, increasingly, she'd thought that Jane was probably right about this being at least partly connected with the site itself.

Partly a pagan thing, but it was all mixed up in those days.

She knelt in front of the altar in the chapel of St John the Evangelist, took off her fleece to expose the pectoral cross and prayed for the wisdom to see this through, to drop the curtain before the final act in an insane tragedy.

Prayed that a very cursory knowledge of forensic pathology acquired over two extraordinary years had not led her to the wrong conclusion about the death of Jonathan Scole.

Prayed for the courage to go up the tower and face the mad woman of Ludlow.

She had to. No one else would know how to approach it. If the police went up – as, surely, before long, the police would – it would all be horrifyingly over before the first of them put a boot on the parapet.

How long had Belladonna been here? Had she been behind that door when Merrily came in with George Lackland? Had she listened to George's account of events leading up to their fevered coupling under the weathercock?

Merrily pulled on her fleece, opened the tower door into total darkness.

Obviously, there would be lights here – most likely bulkhead lights at intervals all the way to the top. But if she switched them on she'd be advertising herself.

Not good.

Only one solution. She padded into the nave, came back flicking her Zippo to light a tea-lantern from the gift shop and found she was no longer alone.

'What are you doing?' Lol said.

47

Point of Transition

THE CLUSTER OF candles on a small tray on the floor lit up her face like some Renaissance Madonna's over a glowing crib.

She was sitting with her back to the wall directly below one of the corner stone pinnacles, its conical, notched prong sharp against the last amber in the west.

The pole bearing the weathercock sprouted from the apex of a leaded pyramid that occupied most of this small platform in the sky, a duckboarded walkway around it. It felt isolated, scary if you didn't like heights, which Lol didn't, but the gathering of candlelight against the glistening backcloth of new night made it weirdly intimate.

'Who the fuck are you?' Belladonna said.

She was wearing a long blue stockman's coat, hanging open over something light-coloured.

Two hundreds steps did something unprecedented to the backs of your calves. Lol set the lantern down on the deck and sat down behind it, the two of them facing one another across the width of the tower.

'If you wanted to be alone,' he said, 'you shouldn't have gone walking around the battlements with your candles when everyone knows the church is closed.'

'I'm not alone.'

'You... been up here long?'

'Stopped counting the chimes a while ago. Came in with the tourists, decided not to leave. I asked you a question.'

'Lol. Lol Robinson,' Lol said.

'Oh,' she said. 'I see.'

'We almost met once, at a festival. You wouldn't remember. It wasn't Glastonbury or anything...'

'I'm not in the mood for reminiscence,' Bell said. 'Go away.'

The half-dozen stubby candles on the tray had probably been taken from the votive table in the church. In their glow, her face looked moist and quietly radiant. She hadn't changed much, really. The lines seemed to have added movement, vibrancy. Lol felt an electric curiosity and the need to exercise it, as if the Saltash episode had freed him up for this. *Do something.*

Whatever she'd done, he didn't want her to be insane.

'You shouldn't be alone,' he said. 'Not now.'

'I'm not alone, I told you that.'

'But they can't talk to you.'

'I can talk to them.'

'They don't listen,' Lol said. 'They don't care.'

Merrily had said, *She'll be in a bad way. There's only one reason she's gone up there. If the police go up to try and bring her down, she won't even wait for them to reach the top. Can you get that over to them?*

'Is she with you?' Bell said. 'Your girlfriend.'

'No. She's in the castle.'

'Has she done it yet?'

Did she mean Sam? He didn't reply.

'It's a gesture,' Bell said. 'A meaningless gesture. She's wasting her time. What's here's too powerful.'

He realized that she must mean the exorcism. Maybe she didn't know about Sam.

He saw that each of the stone pinnacles was tipped with a tiny cross. 'But this is the centre of it, isn't it?' he said. 'This is the soul of the town. The point of...'

'Transition.'

'I'm not sure what you mean by that. Would it... would you

482

mind if I stood up? I think I can feel a bit of a cramp coming on.'

'As long as you don't come near me,' Belladonna said.

'Sure.'

Tell them to keep right away from her, Merrily had said. *She might still have the knife.*

This was after he'd reminded her that he couldn't stand heights. She'd been worried about walking away from this. He'd told her he'd stay in the church and try and explain to the police if they showed up. Holding one another for a few seconds and then she'd walked away, kept looking back.

There was, of course, no reason the police would think Bell or anyone was up here, now the tray of candles was in the shadow of the walls.

Lol looked over the battlements once before turning away. Lights were coming on all around the church. When he turned his head, it was like a Catherine wheel, dizzying. He caught a thin, sharp smell from somewhere.

'One hundred and thirty-five feet,' Bell said. 'I watched the police cars converging on Jonathan's shop. Did you find him?'

'Merrily and the Mayor. After the ironmonger told them his shop hadn't been open all day.'

'Garrulous old fool.'

'She... what can I say about this?'

'Rage gives you unlimited strength,' Bell said.

He guessed she'd raised her voice to deal with the tremor, but it was there.

'What had he done to you?'

'I don't have to answer your questions.'

'No.' He looked over the town to where arrows of pale pink were enfolded in a cloud bank over Clee Hill in the east. 'I was talking to a couple of people about you. Tom Storey?'

'How is he?'

'Still working. Still a bit scary.'

Bell laughed. 'He was always scared of me.' She turned to look up at Lol. 'Why aren't you? What do you want?'

'I'm just scared of what you might do. That is what you meant by the point of transition, isn't it?'

She didn't reply. He felt the hours she'd been up here had been spent coming down from something, some wild and terrifying trip she couldn't quite believe she'd made.

'You knew about Scole's parents, I suppose. How they died?'

A pause, then she sighed.

'You mean his adoptive parents? Or his parents?'

He stared at her. She was watching a distant plane, barely audible, crossing a clear patch of night sky like a firefly.

'Jonathan's father was a man called Eric Bryers,' she said.

Lol gripped one of the battlements.

'Bloody junkie tracked him down,' Bell said. 'Vindictive little smackhead bastard.'

'But...'

He watched the plane disappear into cloud, emerge the other side. There were two versions of this story. Moira Cairns had told him the baby had died. It was Tom who'd maintained she'd given up the child for adoption on learning she had a recording contract.

But Tom was neurotic – his version had been the least likely.

'Scole was your son?'

'Eric tracked him down a couple of years ago, not long before he died.' Bell pulled her coat across her knees and gazed into the mesh of candlelight. 'The revelation rather altered Jonathan's view of himself. Or, I suppose, he would have said it confirmed what he'd always felt. His adoptive parents were working the clock round in their seedy little greasy spoon and just wanted a son who'd take over the business – perhaps buy another greasy spoon – so they could retire to Morecambe or some other windswept purgatory. Sent him to college to learn business studies. All desperately short of glamour. He hated it. Thought he'd been born for better.'

'Especially when he found out who his mother was, I imagine,' Lol said. 'And what his mother had... denied him.'

'Oh yes, he hated me. And presumably Eric filled him up with bile before he... did what he did.'

'Jumped from a high building.'

'You ever work with Eric, Lol?'

'Never.'

'I saw him last when he came back to play bass on my determinedly faithful version of "Gloomy Sunday". I was told he carried a copy with him everywhere, like a form of temptation.' Bell laughed, far back in her throat. 'Like a secret agent with a poison capsule. But, of course, that's the sort of person Eric was. Jonathan wouldn't have known that.'

'Not a lot to discover on the Internet about Eric, I suppose. Not like you. That would've been a serious voyage of discovery.'

Cuttings everywhere, Merrily had said, face twisting at the images in her head. Papers, fanzines, website printouts... scattered over his body like some kind of sick confetti.

'Oh yes,' Bell said. 'He'd compiled quite a dossier on the woman who'd deprived him of a life in various mansions... the California coast... the company of rock stars... unlimited lines of coke, strings of delicious girlfriends. Leaving him with a dreary business-studies course and a future serving burgers to fucking truck drivers.'

'And then he followed you here...'

'He'd attempted, indirectly, to contact me before he came here. An approach was made, through some agency, to my solicitor from someone claiming to be my son. I told her it was a try-on because my son was dead. Anyway, I refused to meet him. What was the point? I gave birth to him, that was all.'

'And gave him away for a career.'

'Lol...' For the first time her face registered pain. 'I gave him away because I didn't expect to see him grow up. The one certainty in my life had always been premature death. What he didn't know was that I'd made financial provision for him. My will's always included a substantial bequest to my surviving son.'

'It wasn't money he wanted, though, was it? He had money. Like you said, he just wanted to be part of your life.'

'Well, I didn't want *him*. Certainly not after meeting him. He was crass, he was—'

'Probably the greatest living authority on you. He got to the heart of all your obsessions. Putting himself in a situation where your paths were bound to cross. Buying into the ghost-walk.'

'No! No, he—' There was a small breeze like a puff of breath. Bell looked up, smiled faintly. 'Here's someone...'

Lol blinked.

'Listen,' Bell said, 'he never told me who he was and I... even when I suspected, I said nothing. There was no future in it. Every time I saw him I saw Eric. Besides, I hardly wanted a murderer—'

'You really think he was?' Hadn't seemed like a murderer to Merrily. Not even a murderer by proxy. *He's... driven. A lot of energy, a lot of enthusiasm... likeable.* 'Rather than just a victim of rumours?'

'He was...' Bell came to her feet and teetered forward as though she was on stage, a little stoned and about to grasp a mike stand. 'He was a despicable murderer. He destroyed the most important thing in my life.'

Lol didn't move. Bell's voice dropped to a hiss.

'That boy wouldn't fall off the Keep. He knew every stone of that castle. He was as sure-footed as a goat. And the suicide theory – that he was afraid to go back to the bullies in Hereford – that's shit, too. His mother must have told him about our arrangement. His mistake was to tell Jonathan.'

Bell plunged her hands into the pockets of her long coat and wafted it tightly across her, turning away and making the candle flames shiver as if the tower itself was shaking.

Lol thought of what he'd learned from Merrily and what he'd read. It made sense: Jonathan Scole watching Bell form an increasingly intimate relationship with the history boy – whom he had introduced to her, whom he'd made a part of his ghost-walk just to get close to the mother who'd rejected him. Rejected him twice, and now…

… Now the final insult: the adoption of a son.

Lol thought about Andy Mumford and his Plascarreg theories. If this was true, then Mumford was sailing dangerously close to the wrong wind.

'Bell…'

She turned towards him, strands of white-gold hair across one cheek.

'When exactly did you come to this conclusion?' Lol asked.

'I don't know. Been staring me in the face for… It came to a head last night. I fell. I was walking… in the churchyard, among the yews, and I fell. Hit my head on a root. I was half stunned and suddenly bitterly angry. Everything was falling apart, on this night of all— I decided on impulse to go to his flat and confront him and… and he was drunk. I told him I'd been attacked in the street. He thought… the crass bastard thought I wanted to sleep with him – so like his miserable father. He said he was going to phone your… Mary. So I walked out.'

'And then Merrily came.'

'Found me singing under the castle. It's the only way I stay sane on nights like this. Singing to Marion. Singing "Wee Willie Winkie" to… Anyway, he must have followed us back. He saw me put the… the mandolin case in the yew tree. And then he came back with a crowbar or something and he forced his way in and he took it.'

She bent down and moved the tray of candles to one side. Not much left of some of them now, flames shrinking down into half an inch of hollowing wax. And Lol saw that the tray had not been on the floor itself but on a small black musical-instrument case, which she lifted now and cradled in her arms.

The mandolin case.

She took it to the battlements. It was almost dark now.

'You'll have to go soon,' Bell said. 'I can't let the candles burn away.'

'Bell… it makes no sense.'

'It's all the sense there's ever been,' she said. 'I've always had what I regarded as a temporary life. All I'm looking for in death is a kind of permanence.'

She was on her feet, the heavy coat hanging open to reveal a long, cream-coloured dress, soiled now with large, conspicuous stains, their colours indeterminate in the candlelight. Standing close to the wall and hugging the mandolin case to her breast, she began singing, in a tremulous little-girl voice.

Wee Willie Winkie
Running through the town
Upstairs, downstairs in his nightgown
Rapping at the windows
Crying through the lock
Are all the children in their beds?
It's past eight o'clock.

Sandy Gee was up against the wall of the fat round tower in the Inner Bailey. She had a rubber-covered torch, kept nervously testing its beam on the stonework, having sent one of the uniforms off with a plastic Pepsi bottle, to find a tap.

'And salt,' Merrily said.

'Salt?'

'Holy water involves salt.'

'Maybe we should hold it in one of the bloody restaurants,' Sandy Gee said.

'I wish we could hold it in there.' Merrily nodded at the round tower. 'Plenty of room, and apparently it used to be the medieval chapel of St Mary Magdalene. Not an option, however.'

'It certainly isn't. We need to do it now, in that dirty little tower.'

'Erm, a warning,' Merrily said. 'The aim of this is to bring release and create calm. But we don't know what we're dealing with. And if there's any kind of… if you want to call it energy…

in there, and the kid's in a position where she's very close to a long drop…'

Sandy shone the torch beam into her face. 'I hope to God you're not suggesting this might actually have the reverse effect? Longbeach said you knew what you were doing.'

Siân Callaghan-Clarke cleared her throat. 'Inspector, I think what my colleague is saying is that this is not an exact science.'

'Or a science at all,' Merrily said. 'Perhaps, under cover of the service, you or one of your officers should move closer so that, in the event of any unexpected reaction…'

'You often get unexpected reactions?'

'There is no expected reaction,' Siân said. 'It's about faith.'

'Christ,' Sandy said.

48

Running Through the Town

Sam said, 'Was that you in the paper?'

'It's a lousy picture, isn't it?'

Merrily was standing in the beam of Sandy's torch. All she could see of the girl was a silhouette against the opening in the wall. It was cold and damp in here, colder than outside, a rank and clingy cold.

'Why aren't you wearing... you know?'

'I—'

'Sam, it's like the police,' Siân said. 'Inspector Gee isn't in uniform either. Inspector Gee and Mrs Watkins... When you reach their level, you don't have to wear the uniform.'

Merrily glanced at Siân, stone-faced on the fringe of the torch beam.

Wow.

'How do I...?' Sam inched back, towards the window. 'How do I know it's not a scam? Why you doing it now?'

'It's taken a lot of preparation,' Merrily said. 'We don't take it lightly. We've had holy water and things to prepare. And I have to walk all around the area, sealing off points of access. We don't want to let bad things seep through.'

There was silence – and then Sam said, 'I'm the bad thing.'

'Who told you that?'

'She won't let me sleep,' Sam said.

'Who are we talking about, Sam?'

Siân whispered to Merrily, 'Give me a moment?'

'OK. Two minutes, Sam? Some final things to organize.'

Around the corner, in the one-time great hall, Siân said, 'I don't know if what Nigel managed to elicit from her might help?'

'Anything might help. I don't see this as a cosmetic exercise any more.'

'In which case… Nigel, I think, also became aware that we might be dealing with something unexpected, to which counselling might not provide a complete solution.'

'He admitted that?'

'I said, I think he became aware of it.'

'Ah. Go on.'

'The Pegler girl was a bully. It's hardly unknown for someone who is herself subject to emotional bullying to find someone else on whom she can inflict stress. Pegler was taunted by her peers – boys, mostly, I would guess – for being overweight and unattractive. She initially sought solace with Samantha – a slightly younger and somewhat malleable neighbour. But Jemima was a very angry, rather vindictive person, and soon began to control Samantha, making her do things she would not normally have considered at all appropriate behaviour – like experiments with pills and shoplifting. And then, seeing how far she could push it, Jemima lured away Samantha's boyfriend, with sexual favours, thus enhancing her own power and her superiority.'

'And then Sam meets Robbie, and, although she might not particularly fancy him, he certainly represents a more innocent, less pressured world. It's literally a holiday.'

'But *is* it less pressured?' Siân said.

'Robbie's fallen in love, maybe for the first time – at least the first time with someone who's not been dead for centuries. And he wants Sam to share his world. Even calling her Marion. That's pressure.'

'Our feeling was that Samantha was finding it disquieting to be associated with Marion, the ghost of a young woman who died in a situation of appalling violence. She's not particularly interested in medieval history – certainly not even close to Robbie's level of obsession – and when he kept appealing to her to come back to Ludlow, to spend weekends with him, visiting historic remains she... eventually rebuffed him. And then, unfortunately, he died, and she – already feeling horribly guilty – was unwise enough to share her anguish and became the target for personal taunts by her peers at school. And then... all this came to the notice of Jemima Pegler. Did you see the pictures of her?'

'I saw some party pictures.'

'Not those. Nigel had a school photo, in which she's glowering and looks... almost demonic. You know that famous Myra Hindley photograph, with powerfully hypnotic eyes? I would guess that's the side of Pegler to which Samantha was exposed. The tactic is that, after stealing the boy, Harry, she professes shame and self-hatred, to wheedle her way back into Samantha's life. Once she's there, however, she's worse than ever. We thought that, at one stage, Sam was on the verge of admitting that the girl had been physically assaulting her. She was certainly a violent person, subject to mood swings and severe depression – of which her parents, by the way, were aware. And, in fact...' Siân moved away into the darkness, 'she had been receiving medical attention.'

'She was seeing a psychiatrist?'

'For a time, Nigel discovered, she'd been prescribed medication – Seroxat, we understand.'

'Where have I heard of that?'

'You probably read about it in the papers.'

'Serotonin?'

'Increasing serotonin in the brain as an antiodote to depression. Seroxat was given to thousands of children in the UK. It then began to be linked with suicide and self-harm in some of them.'

'I'm with you.'

'Nigel's initial, somewhat superficial suggestion that Jemima Pegler's suicide was a form of escape from the mundane...'

'Was bollocks, basically.'

'Was a premature reaction because he simply wanted to be involved. When he found out more, it became clear that Jemima's suicide – as the very circumstances, with an overdose of heroin, suggest – was an act of terminal aggression. And it does seem to have been related to this legend of the woman, Marion – who herself committed an act of extreme violence and then killed herself. Exploiting Samantha's vulnerability to taunts in the wake of Robbie's death, Jemima sends her distressing material from a suicide website. Samantha, a little unbalanced by now, sends Jemima in return the Internet material she's received from Robbie relating to Marion – to which Jemima reacts by suggesting that they "leave behind their bodies", or some such... I'm probably not putting this very well.'

'You're putting it brilliantly,' Merrily said. 'What we're looking at, if we go along with it, is Jemmie first attempting to lure Sam into what might be a suicide pact. Maybe bringing along enough heroin for them both, and then, when Sam doesn't turn up...'

'We can't know what was going through her head. All that matters now is what's in Samantha's head.'

'Which is Jemmie, superimposed over Marion. Sam believes Jemmie is still out there and demanding Sam fulfils her side of the bargain. She's taken up residence in Sam's subconscious, she appears in dreams... I think we're looking at a severe case of bullying from beyond the grave. How did Nigel propose to deal with it?'

'In the short term,' Siân said, 'my guess is he had absolutely no idea.'

'Now we can talk,' Bell said. 'Now I feel safe.'

Just looking at her turned Lol's stomach cold.

She was sitting up on the wall between two raised battlements. She'd slipped off her shoes, the way she used to do on stage, and she was rubbing her bare heels against the stone through the hem of her long dress.

She'd casually leaned the mandolin case against the wall and then… he couldn't believe how lightly she'd swung herself up there. Couldn't believe how anyone who wasn't a seasoned steeplejack could sit where she was sitting, with her back to that drop.

All she had to do was tip herself gently back – a hundred and thirty-five feet to the street.

Unless some jagged stonework broke her fall and her spine.

'They let me hold him,' Bell said, 'in the hospital. Private hospital – my father paid. I had a room.'

'The… dead one.'

'I'd asked for a guitar, to take my mind off what was to come, but I found I couldn't handle one over my huge pregnant belly, so somebody brought me a mandolin. I couldn't play it properly, but I could fumble out simple tunes, and when they brought him in I laid him there and played to him: "Wee Willie Winkie".'

'When did you know there were going to be two of them?'

He had to keep her talking now.

'I became aware of a death having taken place inside me.' Pulling the mandolin case up onto her knees. 'Turned out that one baby was strangled, I think, by the cord – I didn't ask too many questions, wasn't about to become a student of obstetrics. I know they were non-identical, or apparently they might both have died. I didn't want to see the survivor, he was going to be someone else's. But this one… he'd died inside me. I'd absorbed his spirit, you see.'

'Yes.'

'Of course you see. You're a sensitive soul, I've always known that from your songs. So, yes, I played to him. He lay dead on the bed, and I played to him and told him that one day we'd go to Wee Willie Winkie's town.'

'I'm not sure I understand that reference,' Lol said.

Bell leaned forward. 'When I was a baby, I had a book of nursery rhymes, and each one had a full-page coloured picture, and the one I loved the most was of Wee Willie Winkie gliding through an old, old town with tall chimneys and houses of warm brick and timbered gables, and lights shining in mullioned windows. I would look at it for hours, entranced. It was where I wanted to be. Often, I'd dream of floating through that town. It was this town. Soon as I got out of the car, that magical connection was made with my earliest memory… I think I wept with happiness.'

'You kept the baby's body,' Lol said. 'How was that possible?'

'When I was a little older,' Bell said, as if she hadn't heard the question, 'and I began to realize there was something wrong with me and it was quite serious, I said to my mother, What happens when you die? And she said, You go to heaven. And I said, What's heaven like? And she said, Heaven's like the most beautiful place you've ever seen. So there you are…'

She lifted the mandolin case and folded her coat over her dress and began to swing backwards and forwards in the air, with the case across her knees, and all Lol could hope for was that somebody down there would see her and…

And what?

'I got to know the undertaker. We had a big, phoney funeral. The undertaker was a fan – a Nico fan, actually. Do you remember Nico? She was with the Velvet Underground.'

'Gothic… Teutonic. Played the harmonium.'

'Deliciously doomy. That's how it happens, you know. You move on from nursery rhymes to *Grimm's Fairy Tales*… and they have the same kind of pictures: ancient, moonlit towns with spiky churches and towers and cobbled streets. Only it grows darker. And all the children who love the Wee Willy Winkie picture rather than the Jack and Jill picture with the green fields and the big sun, they're the ones who become goths. They're the ones who grow to love death.'

'Willie Winkie had a candle in a lantern.'

'And his nightgown was like a shroud. You're right, of course. Willie Winkie was death… a ghostly presence. I recorded the song once.'

'I remember. This heavy, bombastic, thunder-and-lightning rock and suddenly it all stops, and there are these little, light footsteps, and…'

'Wee Willie Winkie, running through the town…' Bell giggled, her face upturned. And then she frowned. 'Some soulless philistine in the *NME* wrote that it was sexual. A song about a sexual predator. They spit on innocence.'

'The undertaker…'

'It's not really illegal. Some health regulations might have been infringed, that's all. He squared it with some guy at the crem, and they burned a coffin with a doll inside. And the baby was embalmed and sealed in the mandolin case, and I kept him in yew trees. Nobody could understand why I'd buy particular houses – ugly houses in unsuitable locations – but there was always an ancient yew tree with a hollow big enough for a mandolin case, and I'd seal him there and know his spirit was being kept alive. He'd have been buried here, though. I thought we'd both found a home.'

'Robbie had his spirit… is that what you're saying?'

'It seemed so right. If I died, it didn't matter any more. The spirit would go on. And he'd keep seeing me. Just like he saw the others. Robbie Walsh saw life in four dimensions. The thought of Robbie Walsh seeing *me*, growing up to administer the trust, with the money to conserve the environment in which we both…'

'This heart condition,' Lol said.

'I don't know. Haven't seen a doctor in years. I don't want to know.'

'Why did you take the baby with you? On your walk through the town. Last night. You don't normally do that, do you?'

Bell smiled. 'It was his birthday.'

'Yesterday?'

'Today. The early hours. Caesarean. They wanted to do it in the daytime, I said no, this is a night baby. Cost extra.'

She looked down. The cluster of candles was about a foot below her feet.

'Bell,' Lol said. 'Should I move the candles?'

She laughed at him. Then she was serious. 'I don't want you to see this, Lol. You are sensitive. You'll never forget it. Please go down. Go down now.'

'No.'

'It'll be very quick, I promise you.'

'Bell—'

'The Beacon of the Marches – did you know they called it that?'

'I... possibly.'

'I'm going to make it a beacon again. Bright light and no pain. When it kicks in I'll smile and I'll wave... and flip over. Like a fireball. And become, in that one climactic moment, a brilliant part of history.' Her voice softened. 'And fly like Marion.'

'You can't.'

'There's nothing left now, but this.'

When he moved towards her, she put up both hands.

'You wouldn't make it, Lol. Can't you smell it?'

'Bell—'

'The bottom of my dress is soaked in lighter fuel,' Belladonna said.

49

An Intimate Eternity

MERRILY SAID, 'LORD, you gave your Church authority to act in your name. We ask you therefore to visit tonight what we visit and bless whatever we bless... and grant that all power of evil may be put to flight and the Angel of Peace enter in. Defend from harm all who enter and leave this door... doorway. And give us protection in our coming in and our going out.'

People had come in and people had gone out, using the two narrow openings. There was so little room in here. Sandy Gee, hands together as if concentrating on prayer, had moved next to the scaffolding, within just a few feet of Sam. One of the paramedics was a Christian and he'd joined them, and so had Steve Britton, holding up a hurricane lamp.

No harsh light, if possible, Merrily had said. No criss-crossing beams.

Quiet light.

The kid had her eyes wide open, her back to the window. She was calm, and looked a little shell-shocked and vacant. She'd refused to have her parents in, said she'd tried to tell them about it and had been accused of making it all up to get out of school.

It would be necessary to talk to the parents afterwards – preferably with Sandy Gee present, because people were suspicious of religion and you could easily be accused of indoctrination and mind-bending. If Sam needed personal attention... this was usually a long-term process, with repeated sessions.

'In the faith of Christ Jesus, we claim this place for God – Father, Son and Holy Spirit.'

A minor exorcism of place was not enough. Merrily looked around for Siân, but she must have stepped out of the tower. It was already crowded in here. And perhaps she was still doubtful about this: exorcism would never be Siân's thing.

Her gaze met Sandy Gee's and Sandy's was saying hurry it up.

Heightened pressure now, Sandy getting some hassle from CID. Before they began in here, she'd said the DCI was on his way from Shrewsbury in connection with… something else? Did Merrily just happen to know anything about something else? Well… yes, she did. Had they spoken to Lol?

Lol?

Martin Longbeach, Merrily had said. At the church.

And the word had gone out.

'Amen,' Merrily said, and the people in the tower repeated it; not much echo, as if the voices had been sucked out like smoke.

Merrily prayed for help. Praying for a foothold on this. Where should it be directed? *What* needed to be brought to peace? Ideally there should be a Requiem for Jemmie Pegler, but without the cooperation of her family this was not an option. Anyway, no time.

Robbie?

Robbie was not, somehow, quite part of this. And Robbie had fallen from the Keep. He still, in some way, stood for an innocence.

It left Marion.

Marion who had made a mistake and accepted the consequences. Marion who so many people – Robbie and Bell and Jemmie Pegler – had moulded to match their own requirements.

Poor Marion.

'Erm… Thank you. I'd like everybody to leave now.'

Sandy Gee's eyes flashed urgently in the light of the hurricane lamp.

'I'd like to work with Sam.'

Sandy's stare told her that she'd better know what she was doing.

She didn't.

When they'd all left, Steve leaving behind, at her request, his hurricane lamp, she said, 'OK if I come up there with you, Sam?'

Lol stood up. He could see, lit up like a distant doll's house, the complex chessboard façade of the Feathers, the main street a chain of lights, the whole town like a jeweller's counter.

He'd have to deal with his own fear, make a rush at her. It was unlikely he'd get close enough even to reach for her before she let the inflammable dress brush the candlelight. But what else could he do?

What else?

'Bell...'

'Yes.'

'Do you really think Marion flies?'

'If you're going to throw your girlfriend's dogma at me—'

'No... No, it's not, but... we've all heard endless accounts of what a ghost looks like, what a ghost sounds like, what a ghost does, but we don't – and nor does anyone – know what a ghost feels.'

'And what do *you* think they feel?'

'I doubt they feel anything, they just exist. Transient, two-dimensional, in flickering shades of grey... Just existing, in little cold pockets of nothing.'

'Beautiful.'

'It's not immortality.'

'Existence without pain.'

'But without any prospect of happiness.'

'I sometimes think our highest aspiration is the avoidance of pain.'

'That's deeply sad,' Lol said, 'coming from an artist.'

And, saying that, he realized that being an artist was the

explanation of most of it. It was not spiritual, not about transcendence... only a projection of a grand design, developed over many years from a single lurid image in a picture book. She'd found a place on which to impose her vision of a multidimensional heaven. An old-fashioned concept album in a beautiful gatefold sleeve.

Not madness, but it was a fine distinction.

Something else occurred to him then, something far more prosaic. If it was the dead baby's birthday, it was also Jon Scole's. No wonder the poor sod had got drunk.

'Bell... how did Jonathan die?'

He was thinking of Merrily's vague suspicion about the blood. How there had not been enough of it.

'You're a creator,' he said. 'You're not a killer. You couldn't kill. Could you?'

Because it was clear she didn't see her own death as an act of self-destruction; it was a great display, a rush of ferocious light that would launch her spirit into an intimate form of eternity.

She'd gone still, with her head on one side, like a Halloween mannequin someone had wedged between the battlements as a joke.

Lol said, 'Did he kill himself? Did he take an overdose or something? Did he prise open the mandolin case, on his birthday, and see where all your maternal love had been going?'

She tilted suddenly, and he thought she was going over, unlit, and he ran at the wall.

'No!' Throwing her hands out, then slapping them back down when the case began to slip, tugging it into her lap.

He stopped.

'He... must have gone on drinking, taken his clothes off and gone to bed, and then... I don't know... Maybe he got up to make a phone call...'

'How do you know that?'

'Because there was a message on my machine this morning. It was full of bile. So drunk he could hardly speak. It was like, "You fucking old bitch... you gave away a baby and kept..."'

Lol could hear voices in the streets and alleys below, guessed that Bell finally had an audience. Without one, there would be no point.

' "… Kept something…" ' She began to play with the clasp on the mandolin case, flicking it up and down with her fingers. ' "… Something looks like a Kentucky fried chicken." '

'He was dead when you found him, right? Come on, Bell, everybody's going to know after the post-mortem.'

She let the clasp snap back. Her sigh was irritable.

'Maybe he went on drinking and choked on his own vomit. I don't know. I was just so angry at him. He'd killed Robbie and he'd got away with it… for what? Such a sordid, ignominious… such a *little* death… He wouldn't… even he wouldn't have wanted that. I… I went into his hovel of a kitchen and I found a knife in a drawer.'

Lol imagined the resulting scene like a concept-art tableau: Tracey Emin meeting Damien Hirst in their own perfect purgatory.

Bell said, 'It's how I imagined Arnold de Lisle dying. Naked. Cut to pieces. Jonathan, if he was nothing else, at least he looked like a warrior. Like Eric. All they ever had was their looks.'

'Arnold de Lisle, huh?' Lol was suddenly furious at her. 'Except that with Arnold there'd have been masses of blood. When someone's already dead, nothing pumping, you can cut through arteries and just get a dribble.'

'I didn't know. Or if I did, I didn't think.'

'So that was pretty sordid, too, really. And you know something else? With your luck, you could throw yourself off this roof and… and land on the porch or something and just wind up a paraplegic.'

'We'll see,' Bell said. She straightened up with a kind of magisterial calm and flicked up the catch and opened the mandolin case, releasing a very strong smell of what could only be more lighter fuel.

'The other difference with Arnold,' Lol said in desperation, 'was that at least he had some love first.'

Bell smiled sadly, with those lovely crooked teeth, a glint of moving light in her eyes as she came down, with the open coffin, to the candles.

Side by side, looking out of the window space towards the river and just a few lights, Merrily and Sam prayed together for Marion de la Bruyère, Merrily murmuring snatches from the Requiem Eucharist.

'We've come to remember, before God, our sister Marion...'

Robbie Walsh had probably chosen well. Marion might well have resembled Sam physically even if, in a border fortress full of tense, wary men, she'd have grown up faster and probably harder.

You promised eternal life to those who believe:
Remember your servant Marion,
as we also remember her.
Bring all who rest in Christ
Into the fullness of your Kingdom
where sins have been forgiven
and death is no more...

And then busking it.

'God, we pray for the release of Marion's spirit from the deluded and the misguided and those who would use her to further their own... agendas. We pray that Marion may...'

It was very cold now, in the Hanging Tower. Sam crept close to Merrily; she was shaking. Her face was in shadow but the tiny ring glittered at the edge of an eyebrow.

'... Fly,' Merrily said.

Quite prepared to become aware of long, slow breathing in the tower, or even what Bernie Dunmore had described as more like an absence of smile. A smile so cold, so bleak, so devoid of hope... only this perpetual, bitter... terminality.

Unprepared for a long and hollow scream from somewhere else.

50

Dead Person Watching

COMING UP TO sunset, Lol's living room was like the inside of a terracotta plant-pot. Even Jane didn't like it any more.

'Who gave you this number?' Lol said into his mobile.

'That doesn't matter.'

'I'll have to change it now.'

'Don't bother,' Lord Shipston said. 'I doubt you'll be hearing from me again. I just wanted to say, do you really want to start all this?'

'Well,' Lol said, 'the album's already out.'

'I don't care about the album. If I'm ever asked, I think I shall accuse you of, shall we say, political satire. Anything beyond that, we'll see each other in court. And I'll win because I can afford the best.'

'You're threatening me again,' Lol said. 'Nothing changes.'

'I'm just pointing out to you the problems of a long and costly libel action.'

'It's nothing to do with courts, Gavin,' Lol said. 'In the end, mud just sticks.'

It went on like that for a while. Lol considered the options but, with guys like this, compromise was not one of them.

'The situation is that I'm quite happy for you to remain with all the other iffy bastards in the House of Lords,' he said eventually. 'I'd just be worried if I'd heard you'd gone back to having direct responsibility for psychiatric patients.'

'That isn't likely to happen,' Shipston said.

'In that case, as long as neither Merrily nor I have any further problems with Saltash or Fyneham or anybody else who may have been unknowingly dragged into it, you won't hear from me again. Or from Helen Weeks.'

'Is that blackmail, Mr Robinson?'

'Is that paranoia?' Lol said, and Shipston cut the call, Lol just hoping he didn't go so far as to check out poor Helen Weeks and find out that she'd died in one of those notorious train crashes on the outskirts of London some years ago. She'd been going back to hospital at the time, accompanied by her sister.

Some people never had any luck.

The sun was setting behind the stubby-pillared market hall as Lol crossed the cobbles to the vicarage. Sunday evening and the street was full of people, but very few of them coming from the church where, in the absence of Ledwardine's own vicar, the Rev. Dennis Beckett was conducting evensong.

Lol didn't recognize most of these people or their posh four-by-fours.

It's all changing, Laurence, Lucy Devenish murmured at his shoulder, frowning down her nose, which had been a little like Belladonna's, except not so… well, not so attractive, not that Lucy would care.

The new type of incomer, Lol reflected. In the days, not so long ago, when property in Herefordshire and Shropshire and mid-Wales was still relatively cheap, you'd get the pioneer type, the urban romantics with rural dreams who wanted a small-holding, their own veg garden, a few sheep and chickens. Now the Border had become the new Cotswolds and it was the wealthy people who were moving in, and they were not satisfied with a low-key existence, side by side with the farmers and the old village families.

They wanted to possess.

There were two more modest cars in the vicarage drive, and he thought he recognized both of them.

'We're not here, Laurence,' Frannie Bliss said. 'Neither of us.'

'Ghosts?' Lol pulled out a chair next to Merrily's at the refectory table. 'Everybody's a ghost.'

Mumford looked up from his tea, his eyes muddy.

'Andy here didn't want to come to HQ,' Bliss explained. 'And I didn't want to be seen with him, either – Annie Howe's much too close to that prick from Shrewsbury.'

Lol didn't understand, and couldn't see any reason why he might need to.

'Jane's out with Eirion.' Merrily poured him some tea. 'I think they're celebrating something. So I thought it would be a good time to, you know…'

'Complicate my life,' Bliss said.

'It might be rubbish, Frannie. Bell might be absolutely right in her belief that Jon Scole killed Robbie. Maybe, but *I* just don't want it to be him. I don't think he had his adoptive parents killed, either. The people you liked, you don't want them to have been the bad guys. Whereas the people you *don't* like…'

Merrily looked at Mumford, who, for his part, had wanted it to be this Jason Mebus. Mumford didn't even look up. He was wearing a suit and tie, and didn't look retired. He looked safe again. Retired people, Lol had decided, were the new delinquents. Lol had heard that, following a phone call from Gomer Parry, Mumford might soon be head-hunted by Jumbo Humphries, Welsh Border garage-owner, feed dealer and private investigator. It would keep Mumford off the streets.

'You must be awful glad you didn't kill the twat, Andy,' Bliss said.

Mumford grunted. 'Was never on the cards.'

Bliss smiled, looked at Lol and Merrily, and lifted his eyebrows.

Merrily said, 'I'm probably just being stupid.'

'Look,' Bliss said. 'It's pretty clear that nobody thought Robbie was an accident, and suicide looks increasingly unlikely. So if there has to be a third suspect, fair enough, I'm always happy to get another lawyer out of the system.'

'I just lay awake thinking about it, and then I woke up thinking about it.' Merrily shook out a cigarette. 'I thought that, well, if Jon Scole wasn't bothered about all the money going to Robbie, here was somebody who definitely was.'

'Go on, then. Spell it out.'

'Well... her childhood was disrupted after her father dumped her mother for Bell. She was virtually expected to be Bell's nursemaid whenever she spent any time with them. And, after her father went off to America, it was her real mother who got her the job with Smith, Sebald. And then she gets saddled with Bell again.'

'She could've said no, Merrily.'

'With Bell in the same town, and her father saying please look after her? OK, on the one hand a good client, but it must have been hell constantly covering things up, wondering what the firm's good name was going to be dragged into next. And then there's her future father-in-law, who... well, a lot of unexplained alienation there that must already be putting a strain on her relationship with Stephen Lackland.'

'And then,' Bliss said, 'the mad woman announces that she's adopting the son of – pardon me, Andy – this grasping bint from the Plascarreg, and making arrangements to ensure *he* and the new Palmers' Guild get the bulk of her considerable estate. Do we know if Susannah Pepper attempted to talk Belladonna out of it?'

Merrily shook her head. 'Dunno, but – something else that occurred to me – if Bell died, Susannah would've been left as Robbie's guardian. Not the way anyone would want to start their married life.'

'*Could* she die?'

'That's her lifetime's ambition, Frannie. Anyway, you could never prove it about the lawyer. I just wanted to unload it. Sorry.'

'No, no... I'll pass it on, discreetly. No doubt the lads in Ludlow will be observing them together when Bell appears in court to face charges of wilful damage to a stiff, or whatever we cobble together. Charge might, of course, get thrown out – who knows?' Bliss finished his tea. 'So you've placed her in the custody of Huw Owen. Interesting.'

For both of them, Lol thought.

It had been Merrily's idea to ask Huw Owen to take care of Bell. They'd told her last night that The Weir House was already surrounded by the media, and they'd brought her back here to the vicarage. It was safe enough for her – and safe *from* her, Lol had thought – in that it wasn't Ludlow.

Although at one stage she'd become disorientated and appeared to think that it was a country-house hotel, Bell had slept for perhaps the first time in over twenty-four hours. By the time she was awake this morning, around eleven, Huw was already here, looking like the stand-in keyboard player from some acid-rock band that had never made it into the 1970s. Bell had acted strange and subdued and seemed in some way hollow, as though some part of her *had* indeed rolled like a fireball from the church tower, and was already haunting the back streets of Ludlow.

Well, Huw knew all the spiritual retreats and the sanctuaries that could turn people around. Plus he had a murky kind of charisma. And he liked strange women.

They hadn't consulted Susannah Pepper.

Just after dawn, Lol had awoken suddenly in Merrily's bed – well, it had been late when they'd got back here, and there was Belladonna to see to – convinced for a knife-edge moment that he was still up there on that tower and that the remaining two candles *hadn't* inexplicably gone out when Bell had lowered herself over them.

It seemed like a bad joke now…

No, it didn't. It still didn't seem like any kind of joke. Maybe it had been the sudden disturbance of the air that had done it, or maybe the fact that the flames, already burning very low, had been *deprived* of air, Bell's dress acting like a big snuffer. Or maybe…

Maybe it had been an act of God. They had, after all, been votive candles.

You believed what you needed to believe.

All Lol wished was that he hadn't accidentally glanced into the open mandolin case.

Even though it was early May now, it was still sufficiently cool to justify a fire in the vicarage drawing room, and they sat on the sofa and did things together that you weren't supposed to do over the age of seventeen, especially if you were a minister of God and this was a Sunday.

Exploring one another, maybe, wondering if they were intact.

'I still feel happier here, I'm afraid,' Merrily said. 'I know this is really stupid, but at your place I always feel Lucy's watching.'

'Giving us a slow handclap.'

No, Lucy had a certain decorum.

'All right – big question,' Merrily said. 'Seriously, do you think Lucy *could* be seeing us in her house, processing the information and responding to it, intellectually or emotionally? A dead person watching. Can someone be earthbound in a benevolent way?'

'What do you want me to say?'

'I don't know. I don't know what this has taught me, if anything, about the nature of ghosts.'

'Why did Siân suddenly scream when you were there in the Hanging Tower with Sam?' Lol said. 'And was this the same moment that the candles on the church tower went out?'

'Wouldn't say a word, you know,' Merrily said. 'Not to me, anyway.'

'Siân?'

'White as a sheet. Said she'd felt faint and gone out for some air. Perhaps thinking – commendably, I suppose – that her own inherent scepticism might damage what we were trying to do. And she walked across the Inner Bailey to the gatehouse.'

'The Keep? Where Robbie fell.'

'And Marion, probably. The Hanging Tower wasn't built in Marion's time, but the Keep definitely was. Maybe, the evening he died, Robbie had taken someone to the top of the Keep to explain to that someone his theory that *this* was actually where it happened.'

'What do you think Siân saw?'

'Or felt? Whatever, she was terrified. I suppose it's so much worse for someone who despises… superstition. Maybe she saw whatever remains of Marion. Whatever it was the Bishop once saw. *Not* terribly benevolent, that. Anyway, Siân wants to resign from her self-appointed role of Deliverance Coordinator.' Merrily leaned back into a corner of the sofa. 'I asked her to stay on. Amazed myself.'

'I liked her,' Lol said.

'You like everybody who isn't a psychiatrist.'

'Ah,' Lol said, 'about that…'

He told her about the call from the ennobled Gavin Gascoigne.

'Bloody hell,' Merrily said. 'Governments scare me more than spooks.'

'They think they're protecting themselves for the well-being of the nation.'

'*Is* Saltash going to back off?'

'He'll do whatever Gascoigne wants. When you think about it, what he did – this kid Fyneham and everything – that was incredibly stupid. People like Saltash and Gascoigne, they're treated like gods for years, gods who can see into the minds of men. And then they retire.' *And become delinquents*, Lol was thinking. 'Anyway, Saltash is my problem. Unfortunately inflicted on you.'

'*Our* problem. A problem shared…'

'What about Sam? You'll go and see her?'

'With Sandy Gee, tomorrow for a start. Pastoral care. Sam's not out of it yet. She started talking about the e-mails Robbie sent her about the bad time he was having on the Plascarreg. All the things she should have done. And then there's Jemmie…

maybe it'll need a Requiem for Jemmie. A dark presence there. Needs attention.'

There was also the question of what to do about the contents of the mandolin case. So much to sort out yet. Nothing ever finished.

Jane and Eirion were planning a raid on the Internet suicide sites tonight – well, safer with two of them, Merrily said. She suspected that Belladonna's ubiquity on death sites and in chat-rooms had been in some way down to Jonathan Scole. Karen Dowell's first dissection of his hard disk had shown that he'd been posting messages on the Net purporting to be from someone very close to Belladonna. Someone calling himself *Revenant*.

Death is eternal life without pain.

Know that we must make our own eternity.

How much of that would Scole have understood at the time? Had he adopted that name, Scole, because it was the name of a village in East Anglia where experiments had famously been carried out into the existence of spirits? Something else they'd never know. Scole had been his mother's son, Merrily said – layered.

'And what about Robbie Walsh?' Lol said. 'Does he get a Requiem?'

'I'll see what Andy thinks about it.'

'Some tension there? Mumford?'

'Mmm, Bliss... I really think Bliss thought Andy might've killed Jason Mebus.'

'Do retired policemen in Hereford routinely kill suspects they couldn't nail?'

'Mumford took him down by the river,' Merrily said. 'Near the old Campions Restaurant? Mebus kept insisting he hadn't, you know, gone to Ludlow to find Robbie. But Mebus is such a smart-arse. Hardened villain already, at Jane's age. Mumford said he didn't believe him. Admitted he completely lost it, had Mebus on the edge of the water. He told Bliss he thought Mebus must've hit him with a stone or something and got away.'

'Mebus did get away?'

'Not for long, however. He and Chain-boy nicked a car last night and turned it over on the A49. Chain-boy has head injuries, Mebus broke his collar bone and fractured two ribs.'

'Karma,' Lol said.

'Don't go there.'

Lol heard a car door slam and then Jane outside, laughing. Jane had a laugh like a firework going off.

'So what did Mumford say to you at the door, after Bliss had left?'

Lol remembered seeing them together by the print of *The Light of the World*. Mumford looking uncomfortable, mumbling something quickly and then leaving without turning back. Merrily standing on the mat, exchanging thoughtful looks with Jesus.

'He said something about… about the face he'd seen reflected in the Wye, when he was forcing Mebus's head down towards the water.'

'Not Mebus?'

'No,' Merrily said. 'Not Mebus.'

Closing Credits

WELL, IT'S ALL there, if you want to check it out... Marion de la Bruyère, the Hanging Tower, the yew tree, the Palmers' Guild, the Hungarian Suicide Song.

Visit Ludlow. You won't regret it.

Detailed history of the town and its church can be found in the many books and leaflets by the tireless David Lloyd. His *The Concise History of Ludlow* (Merlin Unwin Books) is a good place to start. On the subject of the Guild (or Gild) I also consulted Michael Faraday's *Ludlow 1085–1660: A Social, Economic and Political History* (Phillimore) and, on the castle, the sumptuous *Ludlow Castle, Its History and Buildings*, edited by Ron Shoesmith and Andy Johnson and published by the excellent Logaston Press. Peter Underwood's *A Gazetteer of British Ghosts* (Pan, 1973) details relatively recent Marion experiences.

The Ludlow ghost-walks are now devised and led by Stuart Liggins and Leon Bracelin, who has far deeper roots in the world of psychic studies than the unfortunate Jonathan Scole and showed me a few... openings.

Vince Bufton of the *South Shropshire Journal* was very helpful with crucial details, as were Sally Boyce, Mike Kreciala and Alun Lenny. Also Stanton Stephens and Mike Lloyd of the Castle Bookshop and my CWA colleagues Bernard Knight (forensics) and Rebecca Tope (post-mortem *couture*). Nicky

Carey and Lindy Reed, of Nevill Hall Hospital, Abergavenny, made the obstetrics work. Thanks also to Paul Devereux (Earth mysteries) and Merrily's other spiritual consultant, Peter Brooks. The Powis Estate, owners of Ludlow Castle (where children, it's worth emphasizing, must be accompanied by an adult), inadvertently supplied an interesting plot strand by refusing to help and suggesting that I change the location. Thank you, guys.

Thanks, finally, to the cool-headed but sensitive and encouraging editorial team of, in order of appearance, Peter Lavery, John Jarrold and Nick Austin.

As usual, however, before they saw any of it, *The Smile of a Ghost* was exhaustively edited, psychoanalysed, reoriented, sharpened and finally rescued from the abyss, over many weeks, by my wonderful wife, Carol, without whom...